La Dolce VETO

BY CAITLIN ALICE GILBERT

Arndell

LA DOLCE VETO

Published by Arndell, an imprint of Keeperton in 2026
1527 New Hampshire Ave. NW
Washington, D.C. 20036

10 9 8 7 6 5 4 3 2 1

ISBN: 978-1-923232-31-0 Paperback
978-1-923232-32-7 Ebook

Library of Congress Control Number: 2025943781

Printed in the United States of America

Formatted by Six Red Marbles
Cover Design by Bailey McGinn

Sydney | Washington D.C. | London
www.keeperton.com/arndell

Prologue

"A WOMAN'S BODILY AUTONOMY IS NOT WHAT'S UP FOR debate here," Congressman Finch says, the edges of his fingers greasy from the hamburger he just devoured during the lunch break. There's still flecks of salt in his dusty mustache. It's like he saw a picture of Tom Selleck in the '90s, decided he could pull off the same look, then kept it up with a pair of children's safety scissors ever since. "It's the principle of office talk. The message we send to young boys everywhere that their entire lives could be derailed by one flimsily tossed-out sentence."

Members of his party nod in agreement and I want to vomit. We're six hours into congressional hearings about sexual harassment at government agencies. Several, notably male, heads of these agencies have been emphatically testifying that the behavior both they and their, also male, subordinates conducted is protected by free speech and also at the same time didn't happen, and if it *did* happen, it was passing comments with no ill intention behind them. The female employees who testified yesterday feel a lot differently, obviously, and I personally am going to scream if these old men don't shut up about how ranking the most and least fuckable in the office is merely boys being boys.

"Congresswoman Rhodes," the speaker says, and I perk up. "You have the floor. Five minutes."

"Mr. Donaldson," I say, turning toward the head of the Federal Reserve who's currently trying to clear his name. "You said the actions of both yourself and your male colleagues were greatly exaggerated. Is that correct?"

He nods. He's slimy looking, with a head of hair that's almost completely hardened by gel. "That's correct, Congresswoman."

"Thank you," I say. "And are you prepared to say the testimonies of your female colleagues yesterday are greatly exaggerated?"

"Yes," he says, certainly keeping it short and sweet as advised by his attorney.

"Thank you, and one such colleague, Rayna Spear, are you familiar with her?" I ask, even though I already know the answer. Everyone in America knows Rayna Spear. It was her whistleblowing that forced Congress to launch this investigation in the first place.

"Yes," Mr. Donaldson says. "Though Ms. Spear was not a direct report of mine."

"Ms. Spear testified that she was fired after reporting the repeated sexual harassment she endured from her peers and her supervisor."

Mr. Donaldson swallows so hard I see his Adam's apple bobbing up and down from my seat several yards away from him. "I am aware that she testified to that effect, yes."

"Ms. Spear said her supervisor told her aggressors that she reported them and as a result she faced retaliation that was even worse than the original harassment, including crude comments, gestures, and notes left at her desk."

Mr. Donaldson doesn't say anything in response. He looks to his lawyer then back at me. "I'm sorry, Congresswoman, did you have a question?"

"My question is, are you prepared to testify today, under oath, that Ms. Spear lied about these claims?"

"Now hang on—" Congressman Finch interjects, violating like six House rules in the process. "I see what you're doing, Ms. Rhodes."

"Mr. Finch." The speaker cuts him off. "This is Ms. Rhodes's time."

"No, I'm sick of this," he says.

"Mr. Finch—" The speaker tries again.

"I'm sick of this little girl always trying to goad good men into saying something that will make them look indefensible," he says. I merely sit back and watch as he self-destructs.

"Mr. Finch, this is not your time," the speaker reminds him.

"I've known Mr. Donaldson for years and I know him to be a good man," Finch says, his face now red, though it's hard to see past the mustache. "I will not allow Ms. Rhodes to sully his good name for the sake of one woman's comfort at work."

"And what about my comfort at work?" I ask, because after all, it is still my time.

"Oh, you're so uncomfortable as the most famous member of Congress? Is that what it is?" Finch says. "I'm not going to let some 25-year-old kid yell at me—"

"I'm 33 but thank you," I interject.

He scoffs. "The cover of *Vogue* wasn't enough; you have to burn everyone else while you rise to the top?"

"Mr. Finch, that's enough," the speaker says, his tone punishing but nonthreatening, like a sitcom principal.

"It was *Rolling Stone,* actually," I say. And I looked fucking great on that cover. "You're probably confused because I was at the Met Gala, which is sponsored by *Vogue.*"

"You're an insufferable bitch," Mr. Finch says, and the Congress floor and the gallery above gasp in response.

"Mr. Finch, that's enough," the speaker says again, firmly. "Ms. Rhodes, you have four minutes remaining."

"Are you done?" I ask Mr. Finch, who says nothing, now embarrassed by his own outburst because he made the speaker speak louder than his inside voice. "I have a point of order before we continue," I say.

"Go ahead," the speaker says.

"I'd like Mr. Finch's words to be taken down," I say, turning my body to him and remembering to keep my voice calm and even but strong and effective. It's always a balance for a woman in power. "You don't have to like me, Mr. Finch, but I do expect a semblance of respect while we are both here representing the people of the United States."

Mr. Finch glares at me, saying nothing. After a moment, he looks down at his lap. "It's not necessary. I move to strike my words from the record."

"And I'd like an apology," I say, which is not in the congressional rule book, and I might be pushing my luck with our very orderly speaker, but I kind of just want to see if Finch will do it. I look to Marisol, Congresswoman Reyes, and she's suppressing a smile. At 34, Marisol is the only other person on the committee born after the invention of the internet. And my congressional bestie. She gives me an emphatic fist pump which earns the eye rolls of several of our colleagues.

"Excuse me?" he says.

"Excuse me?" I say. "Excuse you. Do you understand where we are? We are in a hearing for systemic sexual harassment in the very government we serve, and you are here openly harassing one of your female colleagues." I look around the room to make sure people are still with me; everyone is leaning forward in their seats to see what happens next, even Mr. Donaldson, so I think I'm good. "By interrupting my time, you showed that you have no respect for me, no respect for these proceedings, and no respect for the women of this country. I am asking for an apology before we move on."

Finch looks to the speaker, but he does nothing. He waits another moment, like maybe I'll take it back and run away like a scared little girl. That's what men in these situations are hoping for, right? That us girls remember our place and choose to flee positions with agency and return to our rightful place in the home. If they make a powerful position uncomfortable for us, it'll be our choice to leave it and they can skirt all blame. Not today. Not on my watch. "An apology," I say again.

Finch audibly sighs into the microphone. "I apologize."

"Good," I say. I turn my attention back to the hearing. "Now, Mr. Donaldson—"

"That was great today," Kate, my campaign manager, says as she escorts me out of the Capitol. "The team's already working on splicing up the clips from the proceedings into a campaign ad. We aren't worried about the female vote, obviously, but this will get the granola men who are passionate about virtue-signaling their support of women's rights."

"An important subset of my district," I say, with zero irony. I represent one of the bougiest quadrants of Los Angeles: West Hollywood, Hollywood, Los Feliz, Silver Lake—I have to court the Sweetgreen vote. "We're all set for the event tomorrow?" I ask. We're only a few weeks out from the election, and despite the fact that the media is obsessed with me, I'm not as comfortably ahead in the polls as I'd like to be.

Kate nods. "Get ready to kiss some babies. We're slightly behind on the stage mom vote." Kate cracks a smile. This time she is joking.

We get into a car right outside the Capitol and go directly to a small, private airport in Virginia. I used to fly commercial back and forth from DC to Los Angeles, but the security risk became too great. My private security detail says I get at least one credible death threat a day. It used to terrify me, but now I find being constantly surrounded by people whose sole job is to keep me safe comforting. We board the jet, which technically belongs to Congressman Jennings, whose family owns half of LA and lets me hitch rides back and forth with him. He's staying behind in DC this break, though, so my team and I get the plane to ourselves.

I change into my sweats once we're onboard and curl up in one of the lush chairs, reading through the latest campaign data. We're almost ready to land at Burbank Airport when I see one of my advisors, Mark, whisper something to Kate that makes concern splash across her face. It's brief, because Kate has a great poker face, but it's enough that my stomach drops. Kate makes her way over to me and sits down next to me. "Izzy," she says. "Levi wants to meet with you when we land."

My heart clenches and for a second I wonder if I'll die from acute stress at 33. "What?" is all I can say. I haven't seen Levi in months. Not in person anyway. Why did he go through my campaign instead of reaching out to me directly?

"He wants to meet you at your office," Kate says. "Tonight."

"Tonight?" I look out the window. It's completely pitch black except for a few bundles of lights from the LA outskirts. It was well after 7 p.m. when we left DC and it's a long flight. I was looking forward to going right to bed when I got home, not meeting Levi.

"Are you ok with this?" Kate asks.

"Yes," I say. "Yes, of course."

We pull up to my district office 45 minutes later. The one advantage of the late hour is there's no traffic, unusual for this part of Los Angeles. Other than a few drunk people wandering into the dive bar on the bottom floor of the building, the block is quiet.

There are still a few campaign staffers working in the office when we make it up the janky elevator. It's an old industrial building in East Hollywood, a conscious parallel to the superstar status I've acquired since I beat out my incumbent in the primary. He was gracious when I won two years ago. He said he'd done all he could do, and it was time for someone younger with more energy to take the reins.

Kate whispers to the staffers and they clear out, so the office is completely empty. "Do you want me to stay?" she asks.

I shake my head. "I'm good, but thank you." She smiles quickly then bows out. I check my face in my phone camera. My makeup from this morning has mostly rubbed off, but I don't look too exhausted. I dot a little concealer under my eyes and run the mascara wand through my eyelashes. Richard, my head of security, catches me fixing my hair and applying a new layer of lip gloss. *"Don't judge me, Richard,"* is what I want to say, but that's not really our dynamic. He nods in my direction then posts himself outside the door, leaving the office for me and soon, Levi. My heart races at the thought of seeing him.

The elevator dings and through the frosted glass I see two heads bob out. One stays outside with Richard while the other reaches for the door. When he swings it open, the unmistakable smell of Tom Ford and two extra-dry martinis wafts through with him.

It takes every bit of energy left in my cells after this extremely long day to not get immediately turned on by the sight of him. He's more polished than before, sharp in custom Armani and shiny shoes that click across the cement floors. When his ocean-blue eyes meet mine, I shiver. Even after everything, his energy alone makes a river of want swell in my gut. "Hi," I say.

Levi nods, forcing out a smile that doesn't reach his eyes. "Hi."

He walks over to me, and I take a step back instinctively. I haven't talked to him like this, on a personal level, in months. There's so much I want to say but so much I know I shouldn't say, it's hard to know where to begin. "I don't know where to start," I say.

Levi looks at me, surprised. "Pardon?" he asks. Genuinely confused.

"I mean, I feel like there's so much we have to say to each other," I say.

Levi's eyebrows twitch and I realize we are not on the same page. We are not on the same page at all. He didn't come here to make peace or to hash things out. He didn't come here for me. "Why are you here?" I ask.

Levi sighs. "Look, this isn't easy. None of this has been easy—" He fishes his phone out of his front pocket. "This is coming out tomorrow," he says, showing me his phone screen, but my eyes struggle to focus. "Your team will probably hear from the press for comment imminently, but I thought I owed you the courtesy of letting you know personally first."

My eyes try to fix on the screen but it's like my brain is protecting me from processing what I am seeing. It's texts. It's our texts. Or more specifically, *my* texts. To him. Plastered into an article about my texts to him. An exclusive. In the fucking *Times*. I force myself to take a breath. "What in the actual fuck?" I exhale.

"I didn't leak them," he says. "But we were made aware of them tonight. And I'm not stopping them from coming out."

I'm going to vomit. Or have a heart attack. Or disintegrate into dust and blow out the window and into the night. "What the fuck," I repeat.

"It's just politics, Isabella," he says, employing my full government name. His insistence on never calling me by my preferred nickname Izzy was charming, suave even, at first, but right now the sound of all four syllables makes me gag. He cocks his head at me, his aggressively beautiful eyes attempting to lock onto mine. "It's not personal."

I dodge to avoid eye contact like he's launching a missile directly at my face. "Not personal?" I ask, gesturing wildly around my head because I'm pretty sure steam is coming out of my ears, and I want it to dissipate before it sets off the fire sprinklers. The last thing I need right now is for my office to be flooded with water that's been sitting in hot, leaded pipes for who knows how many years. "How is this not personal? You're leaking my texts, our texts."

"Like I said," he says, so calmly it adds even more fuel to the rage fire burning in my chest, "I didn't leak them. No one on my team leaked them, it was completely unrelated to my camp—"

"Ugh!" I yell, pushing a stack of *Re-Elect Rhodes* bumper stickers off the table next to me so dramatically, they rain down to the floor in a flurry of red, white, and blue. "Please at least do me the dignity of not repeating that insipid lie." I sit back on the desk behind me and roll up the sleeves of my UCLA sweatshirt. The roar of a fire engine speeding down Hollywood Boulevard is the only sound in the room as Levi is silent.

He toys with his cuff links—tiny gold American flags that cost more than my car—while he, presumably, waits for me to calm down. He's frustratingly handsome in a suit. It was when we were community organizers that I fell for him, in sweaty T-shirts with his unkempt hair splaying out wildly under his royal blue Dodgers hat, but damn it if I don't notice how good he looks all cleaned up. *Presidential* even. I gag again. "I just don't understand why you had to do this to—"

"I did not release the texts!" he interrupts, his forehead creasing as he raises his hands in surrender.

"I don't mean the texts," I say, standing back up and taking a step toward him. This is the first time we've been alone since he announced his candidacy and my body is, as it turns out, apolitical and still craves being close to him. "I mean running in my district. I mean running against me." I take another step closer. He's only a couple of inches taller than me. I forgot about that. On the TV ads when he's listing all the reasons he'd be a better congressperson for California's 45th district than me, on his billboards that line the route from home to my office, on his social media ads that clog my feed when I'm trying to unwind from a long congressional session, he looms so much larger. "Why did you have to run against *me?*"

Levi doesn't answer at first. I watch as his eyes scan over me, and I can't decide if he's feeling the same residual longing under his skin as I am or if he's sizing me up like prey, weighing the best way to go in for the kill as if I'm not already dead in the water. Part of me wants to kiss him just to see what he'd do. Tomorrow there'd probably be 24-hour coverage on how I'm a sexual predator, but at least my pathetic texts would be out of the news. "I don't understand when you decided to hate me." I shift my eyes into his, widening them and willing my tear ducts to create a watery sheen across their surface. The puppy dog eyes. No man, even a congressional candidate with Oval Office aspirations, is immune to the freaking puppy dog eyes.

"Isabella—" Levi starts. He sighs heavily. "I don't hate you." He reaches toward me, resting his hand on the side of my arm. I stiffen my body in response, as much as it wants to melt. I don't want him to feel the muscle memory his touch evokes. He quickly moves his hand away. "Sorry. I—" He tries again, another sigh huffing out of him. "You of all people should understand why this isn't about you. It's about *them*. It's about everyone."

Unfortunately, I know him and his ideals so well that I know exactly what he means despite the broadness of his statement. There was a time where our shared ideals set my heart on fire. We both wanted nothing more than to leave the world better than we found it. To end the suffering of our neighbors. To focus on the collective good. To actually make good on the promise of liberty and justice for *all*. For everyone.

The irony of trampling over me on this grand pursuit toward liberating the huddled masses was lost on him, apparently.

"But why did you have to take my district? Why did you have to go after me?" I ask. This might be the last time I ever speak to Levi, so I might as well stop beating around the bush and ask the question that's been percolating in my brain ever since he announced his intention to run for my seat in January. The election's less than a month away. And thanks to Levi, I'm probably going to lose.

He rubs his lips together, as if he's struggling to come up with an answer, when I know the truth is he's weighing how best to devastate me one final time. I'm not going to like the answer, but let it finally sever the last thin tie that binds the passionate, earnest, loving

Levi of our past to the Hugo Boss ad standing in front of me now. He takes a step closer. "The committee who encouraged me to run noticed some"—he searches for the right words—"vulnerabilities in your candidacy. I wanted to wait another term, I wanted to seek out other solutions. I didn't want to do this, Isabella, I didn't want to run against you, but they made it seem like it was now or never. You know how much I want this."

"Yes," I say. "I do. But you also know how much I wanted this. There was a time when we shared all the same visions for the future, and you were willing to dispel all of that in favor of beating me." I think to his platform, the way it cedes power to the wealthier, to the least burdened members of our—*my* district—instead of supporting those most vulnerable to the perils of a harsh world. The small margin that separated our views wasn't enough for him to pull ahead in the polls, so that's when he turned to attacking me personally.

First it was *Red Carpet Rhodes*, an allusion to the fame that found me when I was elected even though I didn't specifically seek it out, and now it's the texts. It doesn't matter that it's a clear violation of privacy, that they were likely "obtained" illegally—now everyone will see me as the one thing they always feared I was in the back of their head—a woman. A woman who, in spite of her ability to circumvent the conventional curse of housewifery and motherhood, is in fact a human being with bones and blood and, most unpalatably, a desire for sex.

Levi loosens his tie slightly, enough for me to see the beads of sweat forming on his neck. Good. This should be hard for him. "It's not personal," he tries again.

I look at the article on his phone again, the gray bubbles of my shame staring back at me with the soon-to-be-infamous screenshots of my late-night texts. *Sometimes I think of your body on mine and I want to quit Washington and just run away with you; it's been too long since I've touched you; I need you.* Horniness has brought down political leaders before; I just never thought late-night martini-fueled messages sent to my bicoastal situationship would be the death of my dream. I keep scrolling. *I can't wait until things are less chaotic here and we can just be. I love you so much.* I hold back a sudden, strong desire to vomit, cringing at my delusional past self. "This is personal," I say. "This is using what we had against me."

"And what did we have, Isabella?" Levi asks. "Because from what I remember, we couldn't have this"—he points between the two of us—"because of all of this," he says, gesturing around my office.

I stare at him. No, glare. I glare at him. He knows how badly I wanted *us*. We'd danced around each other for years. It wasn't until the night I told him I was running for Congress that he tearfully told me how proud he was of me, that he was waiting for me, that he knew it would be a bad time for us to start something, but that he loved me and as soon as it was right for me, we could be together.

We then spent our first night together working out years of tension and the subsequent time since has been reduced to late-night sexting. I knew the repercussions if I was using my time between congressional sessions for secret trysts with my specifically not-boyfriend and the world found out and besides, he was *waiting* for me. For him to twist our past to convenience whatever narrative he's pushing in his head isn't just a gut-punch, it's offensive. It's enraging.

My stomach tightens as I realize the reason we couldn't be together wasn't self-sacrifice on his part, it was that he couldn't be with someone who was doing better than he was. We'd always had the same dream, the only difference between us now was that mine had come true—and he is willing to do whatever it takes for our circumstances to flip. He weighed his own desires against whatever regard he held for me and ultimately decided his own dream was worth destroying mine. He didn't love me, that much was clear, but he also didn't think I was worthy of the office I'd worked so hard to get, and that is the real knife in the back.

"Brutus," I mumble under my breath. "Fucking Brutus," I say louder, because fuck it, I want him to hear me. "There were better ways to tell me you didn't want to be with me." My phone dings with a news alert—I glance at it and see my name in the headline. By morning, my leaked texts will be at the top of everyone's feeds. Tweeters, Threaders, Instagrammers, TikTokers, and everyone with news outlet push notifications will know that Congresswoman Isabella

Rhodes was sending thirsty texts to her opposition mere days before he decided to run against her. They won't explicitly outline that it was a cause-and-effect situation, but the timeline will heavily imply that he came to the conclusion I was using time that should be spent thinking about my constituents to text my crush.

Levi Cross had no choice but to step in and save them. It doesn't help that his messages back to me were so banal. *Keep focused on the good fight, Isabella,* he'd replied to my drunken desperation. From the bubbles on the screen, it looks like he cared more about my job than I did.

By tomorrow, my supporters will be embarrassed for me, and my enemies will be vindicated. Levi will use his campaign event at the local IATSE chapter to denounce the leak publicly. He will say his campaign is taking all steps possible to find the source and a few days later, some mid-level staffer will come forward. The sacrificial lamb will assure everyone he acted alone and leave Levi looking like the hero of the story, the victim of all the unpleasantness of running a campaign.

And then the focus will be back on me. As long as the texts are out there, they're fair game. Levi will say we were good friends, but he rejected my romantic advances—as is clear in the texts—and he thinks Congresswoman Rhodes is focused on all the wrong things, *I mean, clearly,* he'll joke. I've always kept it civil toward him because people in our community knew we had been friendly. I didn't want to sound petty or at all emotionally affected by my bestie running against me, so I have always insisted we have a mutual respect for one another, and that our goals were the same. It's almost too perfect, really, how easily my words can be twisted into an endorsement now. If any of my supporters have trepidation about jumping ship from Team Rhodes to Team Cross, they have my own glowing recommendation of Levi to turn to.

In other words, I am toast. I am done. My dream has been murdered right in front of me, and I did nothing to stop it from happening. My carefully curated image, down the drain. No one will see the hours upon hours I dedicated to the job every day, they'll see the three minutes I spent texting. It won't matter that I spent every waking hour of my 20s working toward this goal while my friends were starting relationships, marriages, families. I'll look like a fool in love who cared more about getting a boyfriend than getting the job done. I'll look like a giggly teenage girl gunning for prom queen, not a competent elected official. I will look weak.

"For what it's worth, Isabella," Levi says, lowering his voice so it's all sultry and ragged—the last remnants of rasp from his cigarette-smoking days making him sound gravelly and Clooney-esque. It really, really, deeply annoys me how my heart swells in response. Levi presses a hand to the side of my head and despite my better judgment, I lean into it. "I thought you made a great congressperson." I let my eyes land on his and he smiles haphazardly, testing the waters for some kind of truce.

I push his hand away. "But you think you can be a better one."

Three weeks later Levi Cross defeats me in the general election.

My campaign hosts a victory party at the Hollywood Roosevelt Hotel and I throw up in a bathroom allegedly haunted by the ghost of Marilyn Monroe. The poetry of that is not lost on me even as I vomit up the last of the spicy tuna crispy rice I stress-ate over the last four hours since the polls closed. I make a speech conceding the race 45 minutes later.

"All I know is that the best person to represent this district is the person its people chose," I say, but it's bullshit. I'm better for this job than Levi Cross. I care more. I have stronger policy. In the two years since I was first elected, I've accomplished a lot of what I promised, but now all anyone was going to remember me for is this.

The media has a field day with my loss. The pundits parse over what went wrong in excruciating detail. The keyboard warriors on social media twist the knife by making jokes that turn into viral memes. Every corner of the internet is plastered with my failure. None of my colleagues want to meet with me, so despite my desire to drown myself in work for whatever time I have left, I mostly spend my last days in DC binge-watching *Real Housewives* alone.

I finish my term in a daze, and by January, my dream is officially dead.

Chapter One

THE PLANE CLUNKS ONTO THE RUNWAY AND I'M SHAKEN out of my medicated slumber. I look out the window and the outside looks so similar to the dead-grass, industrial-building surroundings of LAX that for a minute I wonder if we were re-routed back to our origin. It's only when I notice my right leg is asleep that I realize we have been up in the air for the flight's full 12 hours, and the sleeping pill I took before take-off worked. I turn on my phone and connect to the airport Wi-Fi out of habit, texting my parents that I made it here safely even though it's the middle of the night in Los Angeles and they're so irritated with me, I doubt they're up late with worry.

I don't blame them. Living with me since the end of my term has been like living with an elder who keeps to her bedchambers, asking for food to be sent up and only periodically coerced out of the house for a few minutes of sunshine. It didn't make sense to keep my LA apartment when I was first elected, so I moved back in with them. I was always working when I was home anyway, and I could barely afford my DC apartment as it was. With the private security, the flights back and forth, my wardrobe that was always meticulously critiqued, there was barely enough of my congressional salary left over to afford food, and I didn't have generational wealth to fall back on like many of my colleagues. But when I moved the last of my stuff out of my minimalist Georgetown studio, the only refuge for the once-great Isabella Rhodes was her mommy and daddy's house, and that's where I've been hiding myself ever since.

Until now.

My tiny attic bedroom in Beachwood Canyon wasn't far enough away from my failure; I had to put an ocean between me and my shame.

"*Benvenuti a Roma,*" the cheery flight attendant says to me as I deplane, and I mutter back some semblance of a "*grazie.*" I haven't been to Italy in over a decade—not since a study abroad program in college. It was the social media flashback post from my friend Emma in the program that led to the first spontaneous decision in my entire life. The sensory memory of the dreamy, sunlight-soaked Umbrian town of La Musa came flooding back. Gelato in the afternoon, late nights drinking wine and eating, long walks at dusk, taking in the clifftop views of endless rolling hills of vineyards—a true worry-free existence. A few clicks later, I had a plane ticket and a room in a villa booked.

The university suspended the study abroad program years ago due to budget cuts, so the town that used to increase its population by a couple dozen college students every summer would instead be filled with aging Italians who, from what I remember, were far removed from American culture. Therefore, completely ignorant to the existence of a certain United States congresswoman—well, *former* United States congresswoman, once named the future of her party, the rising star of politics, the one to watch, who was now, instead of meeting with the budgetary committee, scraping the bottom of her backpack for a loose almond because she slept through breakfast service.

The name Isabella Rhodes will be meaningless to them. Thank god. I am free to be the woman who lost everything, staring listlessly off into the scenic countryside, willing the powers of the Tuscan sun or whatever to heal all I've lost. I'll eat amazing pasta, I'll drink great wine, I'll befriend a wise older local, I'll have a torrid, no-strings affair with a hot local, and before long, all my previous troubles will fade into the background. Now that I'm in Italy, I'll never worry about what happened to me in America ever again. I'll learn the power of distance, of time healing all wounds, of a slower paced life that my culture rejects but I will soon find suits me much better. My perspective on life will change and therefore I will change. I'll wear great outfits.

Congresswoman Rhodes, who once dreamed of building a better America in which all people can thrive, is dead, and now I'm just Izzy in Italy. Screw making the world a better place. It's Levi's problem now.

The drug-induced sleep haze wears off as I chug a piping-hot espresso in the café car on the dusty train from Rome to La Musa. The countryside whips by for close to two hours before I finally see it: a medieval town perched atop a cliff in the middle of rolling green hills of vineyards upon vineyards. The giant *duomo* cathedral with its intersecting arches stands out in the middle of the village, keeping watch. Butterflies swarm in my stomach as the train lurches to a stop at the La Musa station, the first pleasant feeling I can recall in months. I drag my bags off the train in just enough time before it lunges forward, carrying its passengers to more popular destinations like Perugia, Siena, or Florence.

A rickety cable car takes me the rest of the way, up the side of the cliff with the views of the countryside becoming more spectacular as the hills bask in the golden light of the midafternoon sun. I was too young to fully appreciate it when I was 19. Everything was new and exciting then. New experiences were as much of a guarantee as the sun setting and rising every day. My whole future was ahead of me. My dream was my purpose. Now, I know what monotony looks like. I know the grief that comes once the dreaming part is over and reality takes hold.

As I struggle with dragging my four-wheeled suitcase across the cobblestone piazza from the cable car stop at the top of the cliff and to the villa-lined streets that lead to the center of town, I try to find the instructions to my new home. A blank white screen stares back at me when I open my email app. No data, no Wi-Fi. Damn it. I negotiated it all with the woman advertising a big room in her glorious-looking medieval home on Airbnb. I had launched into hyper-fixation mode so swiftly once the idea to relocate here came to me that it seemed like fate when I saw her post. The rent was cheap, and she seemed eager to find a renter. *No one moves here anymore,* she'd said, excited to find someone to take the room.

Looking around now, I see what she meant. While the town looks roughly the same as when I was last here, there's an eeriness in the air as I trudge forward. It feels emptier, sadder than I remember. Shops are closed, no people mill about the winding street. It's colder than I thought for an early April day too, and I wonder if I packed enough of the right clothes. A frigid breeze cuts through, sending a chill down my spine—maybe this wasn't fate, maybe it was just a bad decision. I've never been spontaneous before; I don't know why I thought I could start now.

I try to remember where exactly the house is located. I know it was near the center of town, looked yellowish from her photos, was big—every building in La Musa looks different but also that same shade of historic, beautiful, grand. It had a name though, Villa Farentino. I think. A woman, holding a jacket closed with one hand and a bag of groceries in another, approaches as I round the street closer toward the Piazza Duomo in the heart of La Musa. I figure if I can get there, I can knock on doors until I find the right one. "Mi scusi," I say, and the woman turns toward me, alarmed by the presence of a tall, blond American with a giant suitcase rolling toward her. *"Parla inglese?"* I ask. She shakes her head no. I planned on using my phone to translate in such situations, but again, no data, no Wi-Fi, damn it. I try to scrape together any remnants of the Italian I haven't used in over a decade. *"Dov'è Villa Farentino?"* She smiles, points ahead and answers back in rapid Italian. I catch zero words of what she says but she nods at me and sort of gestures at her groceries in hand to communicate she's not going to help me further. "*Grazie*," I say, though I do not feel thankful.

I keep walking, the wheels of my suitcase clacking harder as the sound of them struggling against the cobblestones echoes down the hill. I reach the clock tower, the second highest structure next to the *duomo* in town, and stare at its big arms pointing out the time at the top. It's nearly 4 p.m. and I haven't eaten since the dinner service last night, or this morning, or whatever time that was in relation to the time it is now. My stomach growls, suddenly activated by the realization of its deprival. Once I find this place and drop my bags off, I'll venture back out and find something to eat. All of the food is good in La Musa, and I was aware of that when I was 19, but now I have money, a more sophisticated palate, and less fear of carbs. That's one good thing about your whole life going to shit: You learn that of all your enemies in the world, pasta is not one of them.

I see another person walking toward me on the other side of the street and I excitedly wave at him, hoping he'll be more helpful than the last lady, but he does not acknowledge me. *"Signore!"* I call out. He looks up at me briefly but does not slow down or cross the street. I pull my suitcase, even less malleable when trying to drag it sideways across the cobblestone, and quickly intercept his path so he has to face me.

When I reach him and he finally looks up at me for longer than a second, I'm surprised to find he's about my age, maybe a little older. He's dressed in a way that suggests he does his shopping outside of the lone boutique in town, with a fitted blue button-down and gray trousers. His hair is slightly unkempt, like he's been running his fingers through it all day in distress, a notable flaw in his otherwise perfectly put-together appearance. And he's handsome. Actually, he's hot. Even through his shirt I can tell his arms are toned, his sleek physique rounded out with strong shoulders and a sharp jawline. If I weren't standing close enough to see the pores in the smooth olive skin that surrounds his piercing hazel eyes, I'd be convinced he was one of Michelangelo's statues. They're a dime a dozen around here anyway.

"*Parla inglese?*" I ask. He nods. Helpful. "Oh, thank god. I'm looking for Villa Farentino. Do you know where that is?" Instead of answering, his thick eyebrows arch in the middle of his face as he glares at me. No, not glares, glowers. He's glowering at me. "*Mi dispiace, non parlo italiano.* I don't speak it very well anyway," I say, trying to show that I'm not some ignorant tourist who came to Italia expecting everyone to speak English. I expected, at the very least, for my phone to translate for me. "Do you understand?" I ask, because he's still glowering.

"I understand perfectly what you are saying," he answers back in crystal-clear English, the slightest hint of an English accent behind his Italian one. "What I don't understand is why you are saying it."

I do not know what he means by this, but I try again. "I am staying at Villa Farentino. The directions on how to get there are in an email, but my data plan doesn't cover international travel, so I have no way of accessing it. If you could just point me in the general direction, that would be great."

His eyes narrow as he sizes me up. Someone this hot scanning my body would be flattering in another circumstance, but it's more like he's a security guard doing his best without a metal detector. "That's not possible," he says. "Villa Farentino does not rent to strange American women on a soul-searching tour or whatever you're doing here."

I laugh because even though he's insulting me, he's got me pegged. Plus, it's much cleverer than I was expecting from this stranger who so far hasn't cracked anything that so much as resembles a smile. "Well, I guess this forlorn American knows something about your town that you don't. The woman of the house, Anita, is renting it to me herself."

His face lights up with surprise. "You spoke to Anita?" I nod. He sighs, running his hand through his hair in distress. I smile to myself to know I pegged him correctly too. "Fine then, follow me. We'll get this sorted." He starts walking back in the direction he came from and after a moment of confusion, I realize I'm meant to follow him, my wheels even noisier as I speed up to catch him.

"She never listens to what I say," he mumbles, not slowing down while I am audibly struggling to maneuver through the central part of La Musa, narrow streets full of restaurants, shops, bars, and cafés—it's empty though and everything's closed. It seems the tough economic times have affected La Musa even more than I realized, and worst of all, I have no idea where I'm going to fill my increasingly agitated stomach. The man continues ranting, and while it's in English, I doubt he's really speaking to me. "I said I would take care of things. I said not to worry and what does she do? Decides to let a random American lady stay in our home. I mean, she could be anyone. She could be a murderer, a thief. No sane person would come to La Musa on vacation in this day and age."

"Oh, I'm definitely not sane," I interject. He turns around to look at me, like he's surprised I could hear his thoughts and he didn't realize he was speaking out loud. "But I'm not here on vacation," I say. "I like, live here now."

He glowers again. "What do you mean, you live here now?"

"So… live, um, *vivo in Italia*… now."

He shakes his head, still looking at me like I am enemy number one. "I understand you—"

"Izzy."

He rolls his eyes, annoyed even at my name. "I understand you, Izzy, what I don't understand is why you would move to La Musa and why you would move into my family's home."

The jet lag makes my brain slower, but I put the pieces together. "Anita is your mother." The man nods. "We're going to be roomies?"

He sighs heavily and continues walking, turning down a small street that leads out of the main part of town and toward the east end of the cliff. Based on the pictures, the house is massive, but I say a quick prayer that my room is on the complete opposite side from Anita's son, lest he try to drive me insane to the point where I choose to leave before the end of my booked dates—three months, as I figure that gives me enough time to settle and find a place of my own—and I'll be charged the full amount, the last of my savings, and be effectively homeless. The internet would have a field day if they ever found out.

He stops in front of a massive wrought-iron gate, but the metal bars aren't enough to obstruct the view of the massive estate behind them. It is yellow, that detail I remembered correctly, and it's three stories, each window framed in a blue molding, a vine traipsing up the front of the house from the palatial oak front door to the red tile roof. If this man wants me to go, he's going to have to work hard, because I am never leaving.

He opens the gate and nods toward the front door. "Come on," he says. "My mother's inside. We can get this all sorted."

I follow him through the great oak door into the foyer. It's just as grand inside and yet, homey and warm. The walls are painted a light blue, illuminated by the midafternoon sun as it drips through the copious amounts of windows, creating a second sky. The foyer leads to a marble staircase and the wall behind is crowded with family photos. I spot the man, presumably, as a child with an older sister and his two parents. "Does your whole family live here?" I ask.

"Just my mother and me. My sister isn't far, in Siena, and my father's been gone for six months." He looks at one of the family photos over my shoulder. He's probably 17 or 18, flanked by his mother and father on either side, his sister in a white dress.

"Oh, I'm sorry."

"No." He chuckles. "He isn't dead. Just… gone." He whistles and points his head toward the back of the house. "*Mamma*'s in the kitchen."

The kitchen's less grand than the rest of the house but still charming. An Italian rustic theme that would make a Nancy Meyers aesthete weep. A petite woman I'd guess to be about my mother's age stands over the sink, scrubbing a large casserole dish.

"Benito," she starts, that must be his name, then says something in Italian I can't make out. She turns to see me standing in her kitchen and raises her tone, shouting more words that are beyond the scope of my mostly transactional abilities.

Benito shouts more Italian back at her, they both shout, competing to see who can raise their voice and gesticulate the most until Benito finally raises his hands in defeat and then switches to English. "She's here. Are you happy? You won."

Anita stares him down then brushes her brown bob out of her eyes as she turns to me and puts on a cheery grin. "Isabella!" she says, walking toward me and taking my hand. "*Piacere.* I am so happy you'll be staying with us." Her voice drips in a caramelly Italian accent, much unlike the rigid way in which her son speaks.

"I'm so happy to be here," I say.

"I'm sorry my son was so rude in not greeting you properly," she says, sending another scolding look toward Benito. "Benito will show you to your room, and please let us know if you need anything at all while you are here." She then mutters some vaguely threatening-sounding Italian back at Benito, who cowers like a dog caught eating something it shouldn't in response.

"Where's the closest restaurant?" I ask. "I think I'm going to pass out if I don't eat within the next 10 minutes, and I'm sure Benito here doesn't want to carry me down the cliff to the hospital."

Benito stares at me with that now trademark disdain. "It's Sunday."

I don't follow.

He tries again. "It's Sunday."

I shake my head. He rolls his eyes. "Everything's closed. Well, Osteria Da Mario opens at dinner, but that's..." he checks his watch, "... three hours away."

My stomach churns in protest. I rack the last functioning parts of my brain and remember that in Italy, almost everything closes on Sundays, especially in a small town like this. "Oh, that's fine," I say. "I think I have an almond somewhere in my backpack."

Anita waves her hands. "Nonsense. I have leftovers from Sunday lunch that would feed a small army." She opens the fridge and digs around, producing tray after tray of food, naming each as she does. "Spaghetti alla carbonara, linguine alle vingole, *cinghiale*..."

I look to Benito with confusion. "Wild boar," he says.

"This all looks amazing," I start. "Thank you so much. Um... but I'm a vegetarian." The word *vegetarian* seems as unfamiliar to Anita as whatever Italian she'd spoken had been to me.

She puts all the trays back into the refrigerator and produces another. "Penne with tomato sauce."

"*Perfetto,*" I reply.

"Benito, serve our guest," Anita demands.

"Oh, it's ok, I can get it—" I go for the tray, but Anita pulls it away from me, glaring at Benito. He walks toward a cupboard and takes out a bowl. He opens a drawer for a spoon and dumps a few scoopfuls of pasta into the bowl.

Anita watches approvingly. "My son. He spends a decade in London and now has all the manners of a plague-ridden rat."

"*Mamma,*" Benito replies, "London is not like La Musa, it has progressed since the 1500s."

Anita rolls her eyes. "See how he speaks to me? The boy I raised knew how to respect his elders." Benito ignores her and heats the bowl in the microwave. He takes a slab of Parmesan and starts grating it methodically. Anita continues, "I hope you treat Sutton with more respect than you do me."

My interest piques. "Sutton?"

Benito blushes. Anita answers, "His girlfriend. She lives in London. Can you imagine? Staying in London while your lover returns to the beautiful place of his birth?"

"Girlfriend, huh?" I say, teasingly, realizing too late that I probably shouldn't mock the love life of a person who knows where I sleep. He shoots me a glare.

Anita laughs jovially. "Believe it or not, he finds the time for a lover between being angry and feeling sad."

"*Mamma!*" Benito shouts, "Do not say 'lover.'"

Anita shares a look with me like we're already in cahoots. I like her, I decide. The jury's still out on the son. The microwave beeps and Benito takes the piping-hot pasta out and slathers it in cheese. It smells so amazing, I have to hold back tears.

"Please, sit," Anita says, gesturing toward a stool at the edge of the kitchen island. Benito places the bowl and a fork in front of me as I oblige, and I immediately dig in. I don't know if it's the near-death hunger talking, but it's the best bowl of pasta I've ever had.

"Anita," I say, between bites, "this is amazing."

She grins. "Welcome to La Musa, Isabella. May every moment here be just as delicious."

Chapter Two

I SETTLE INTO MY ROOM, IMMEDIATELY TESTING THE functionality of my over-10-year-old outlet converters to charge my phone and laptop. Though I'm questioning now why I even brought the latter. It gives me anxiety to be too far away from it, a remnant of my dead career. Maybe my first act of freedom can be to chuck it over the edge of the cliff and let it crash into the hillside below. A chill runs down my spine and I sort of reassuringly tap its outer shell. I would never.

The room is exactly like the photos Anita posted online but bigger in person. It's mostly absent of furniture save a twin-sized bed and small armoire, and the yellow wallpaper, which matches the exterior of the house, is peeling in the corners. There are two framed paintings above the bed; one is of La Musa, the other of the house itself. I don't get the sense this room was ever a permanent residence for anyone, but rather a sparsely used guest room. It's located on the second floor at the end of a long hall lined with heavy oak doors, all closed tightly.

I take my toiletry bag out of my suitcase and cross the hall to the bathroom to set up. The door is shut, and when I swing it open, Benito is standing on the other side washing his hands in one of the double sinks. I yelp.

"Jesus," I say. "You scared me."

"Do you normally walk into a washroom without knocking?" he asks, his expression as stoic as ever, like he isn't surprised I could be so rude.

"I didn't know anyone else was up here," I say. "Anita said the master was on the third floor. I assumed—"

"Old house. No en-suite, marble-countered, spa-tub, rain-shower bathroom for every bedroom like I'm sure you're used to," he says, turning off the faucet and drying his hands.

"Actually, my childhood home only had one and a half bathrooms," I say. It wasn't until my DC apartment that I even had my own bathroom for the first time. "They were both beach themed."

"Why are Americans so obsessed with beach-themed toilets?" Benito asks, though more out loud as a hypothetical and not meant for me to answer.

I glance around the hallway. The sun is starting to set and it's shining brightly through the west-facing window. "So, we're sharing?" I ask. "That was not on the Airbnb listing."

"If you find the accommodations unsuitable, you can leave," Benito says all too quickly. "How did you even get such a long-term visa with no job?"

"I know a guy," I say, because Ralph at the State Department kind of has a thing for me. Benito rolls his eyes. "The accommodations are fine. I've never had a sibling, so I'll get to see what it's like."

He scowls. "You're an only child?" His tone makes it sound like it's a personality flaw and not the result of having parents who waited until their early 40s to have children.

"Which one's your room?" I ask, pointing at the row of doors.

Benito stares at me for a moment then points to the door next to mine.

I laugh. "This is so great. We can stay up late and gossip together." Benito sighs and leaves the bathroom. I put my bag of toiletries down on the counter and follow him. "We can play truth or dare and make prank calls." He's fully ignoring me. "Oh wait, what should I do if I want to bring a guy home? Put a sock on the doorknob?"

He turns back to face me. "Is that a euphemism?"

"No," I say, blushing a little bit. "It's a thing. Like, roommates put socks on the door to let the others know they have someone over—" The first smile I've seen from Benito cracks across his face. "Oh, you know what I'm talking about."

He nods. "I don't think you'll need a sock. There are no single men in La Musa other than Alfredo, who runs the meat market, but he's pushing 90."

"He sounds hot," I say. Benito rubs his lips together, suppressing another grin. "Don't worry. I'll leave you alone," I say seriously. "You'll barely know I'm here."

"I doubt that," Benito says.

"No, seriously, I'm low maintenance," I lie, but I'm trying. I want to be breezy and carefree. I will be breezy and carefree. "If I have any questions or concerns, I will take them to your mother."

"I suppose as the mayor of La Musa, I should say you should bring them to me, but that's fine," he says.

I look at him for a moment. "You're the mayor?"

Benito sighs, tapping on the edge of his door. "Yes. I am newly elected."

The air leaves my lungs at the mere mention of the e-word. Even Benito, who has all the charm of a doorknob sock, can win an election. "Oh," is all I can get out.

He watches me for a moment like he's waiting for me to barb him for his job, but I am temporarily paralyzed. And nauseous. "I'll leave you to get settled, then," he says, opening the door of his room and quickly shutting himself inside.

I unpack while listening to a podcast about *Real Housewives* so my brain doesn't have room to wander. I'm settled and connected to the snail's pace Wi-Fi by 8 p.m. I could venture out, I suppose, but to where? Everything is closed, and even then, I'm too jet-lagged to fight my way through a conversation with my spotty Italian, but I'm also too wired to wind down for the night. I look at my e-reader that holds the digital stack of books I downloaded before the flight. When was the last time I even read something for fun?

My phone lights up with a FaceTime call from Marisol.

"Hello?"

"Bitch," Marisol starts, as she is wont to do, "you are *not* pulling a Diane Lane and going all *Under the Tuscan Sun* on me."

I collapse face-first onto the bed, using a pillow to prop up my head and leaning the phone against the headboard. "Well… technically I'm in Umbria."

"You are not actually in Italy." She's blurry on the screen and I can't tell if it's my internet or her chaotic need to constantly be on the move.

"Mari, sit down, you're making me nauseous," I reply when I see her stirring something in the background.

"Fine." She obliges, sitting at her kitchen table, the orange-and-pink desert sunrise visible in the window behind her. Marisol represents Arizona's Second Congressional District in Tucson. We met on day one of new House member orientation. Marisol, with her undercut hairstyle, nose ring, and tattoos, marched up to me in my pale pink suit and beachy blond waves and proclaimed we'd be the least palatable new members to our older, establishment colleagues, so we ought to be allies. She was right. "What are you doing in Italy?" she asks. "Last I heard you were 'refocusing your efforts on changing politics at a local level.'"

That was the company line with the press when I left DC. Fortunately, Marisol knows it's bullshit. "Wearing sundresses and comically large hats," I say. "Learning how to make pasta from scratch, seeing the sites with a hot tour guide, erasing all remnants of The Hopeful Person Formerly Known as Isabella Rhodes."

"You're not like—" Marisol leans into the phone and lowers her voice. "Offing yourself, right?"

"Jesus, Mari, no!" I sigh. "I'm going to change. I'm going to be different. My whole life was about the dream, and now the dream is dead. I'm over all the bullshit we put up with and completely disenfranchised with the myth of meritocracy. The myth of *democracy*."

"Hey now, be careful what you say. I'm a United States congressperson and I could put you on a list."

"Please exile me. It'd be the best thing that's ever happened to me."

Marisol smiles—she's one of those people who is stoic and expressionless 99% of the time, so it feels like a gift to get even the slightest of chuckles out of her. "Sounds like you don't need the help. By the way, I met lover boy yesterday. He's the absolute worst."

My stomach churns at the mention of Levi. *Levi*. I wonder what he's doing right now. Did he keep any of my staff? Did he rearrange the furniture in my office? Is he watering the snake plant my predecessor gifted me that I left behind as a gesture of goodwill I now regret? "How did he look?"

"Hot," Marisol admits. "But not in a good way," she adds quickly. "Evil hot. Like a young Stalin, you know?"

I laugh, relieving some of the tension that's built up in my shoulders. "I don't think it's ethical to compare your congressional colleague to Stalin."

"My hate for Levi Cross supersedes decorum," she says. "You know that, Izzy. I'm ride or die."

"He hasn't even sent so much as a text," I say, my voice quiet. "I thought we were friends. At the very least, I thought we were good friends. I thought that maybe even behind all of this, we would still be friends. It's just hurtful on so many tiers, you know? I miss him as a friend."

Marisol eyes me for a moment then moves the camera from one hand to the other. "Izzy, that's fucking dumb."

I put my face down into my pillow. "I know," I say, lifting my head back up. "I thought I was too smart to be blinded by love. I hate that I'm one of those girls whose whole life goes up in flames because she fell for the wrong person. That wasn't supposed to happen to me. This wasn't supposed to be my life."

Marisol has heard this all before, so she doesn't say anything but nods sympathetically.

"So, Italy. What are we doing in Italy?" Marisol asks.

"I told you. Wine, pasta, pizza, perching myself pensively on sun-drenched windowsills."

"No, I mean why are you in Italy? And for how long?" She's back on her feet now, sensing the serious moment has passed, and she's unable to sit still for longer than a moment.

"Forever, I guess. I don't know, I just had to go, so I left," I say.

Marisol looks at me, her forehead creasing. "Wait, so you were serious in your email? You've moved to Italy. Like, actually moved? Do you even have a job?"

"I have savings. And when that runs out, I'll get a job at a flower shop or something." There's a clang of something on Marisol's end and she disappears. "Marisol?"

She pops back onscreen. "Sorry, making empanadas to prove to Jenny's parents that I am not a workaholic." Her wife's parents have changed parties since their daughter's marriage, but Mari still feels the need to continuously earn their approval. "Ok, so you moved to Italy. What do you hope to accomplish there?" Her face refocuses on my screen, and I know I have her full attention again.

"Marisol. Literally nothing. I want to be nothing and no one and impact no lives and make absolutely no mark on the world."

Marisol moves out of frame again. There's another clang and I can't tell if it came from Marisol's shock at my statement or her lack of culinary prowess. "Look, Izzy, you know I don't think anyone should feel like they need to serve the greater good ever if they don't want to, but this is contrary to everything I know to be true about you."

I sigh. "What do you mean?"

"Everything you've done your whole life has been because you believe you're destined to leave your mark, to change the world." I see a struggle with the oven, but Marisol continues, "You don't seriously expect me to believe all of that has gone away because you lost one election? Because of one setback?"

"I've had plenty of setbacks. I got a B in AP Chem. Totally ruined my weighted GPA. I almost didn't get into UCLA."

Marisol exhales, exasperated.

I clarify, "I don't know, Mari, this is what it's all been for, this is what all my work has been leading to." The familiar tingle of disappointment from when the election results started to roll in that night in November creeps back to the edges of my limbs. "I failed."

"You did," Marisol affirms. "But that doesn't mean you give up forever."

Her words sound right, but I can't wrap my head around any reasonable path forward that would make them true. "I don't know. I'm just done, Mari. I'm done." I hear a beeping noise in the background. "Is that your smoke detector?"

Marisol's head whips around. "Shit. I have to go."

"Order takeout next time!" I shout. The screen goes black as she hangs up.

It's quiet again. It's *so* quiet. I'm used to falling asleep to city noise. At my parents' canyon home there was always the whir of a helicopter, the boom of fireworks at the Hollywood Bowl, the howl of a nearby coyote, and in DC it was the distant whoop of sirens, drunk college students, my upstairs neighbor working on his beats. Here, it's almost disturbingly quiet. The beginning of a horror movie quiet. Maybe that's what I walked into here. An old house, an ancient town, a grumpy owner—I freak myself out enough to turn the lock on my bedroom door to make sure no one can get in.

There's no TV in the room, so I open my laptop, thank god I didn't throw it out the window, and navigate to my recently most-visited website, allowing the drone of rich middle-aged women arguing about bedrooms on a girls' trip to drown out my thoughts.

Chapter Three

I WAKE THE NEXT MORNING TO THE SUN DRIPPING INTO my room through the slats of my blinds. I fling the window open and breathe in the crisp, cool morning air. I did not sleep well. It was 2 a.m. when I finally gave up on feeling tired and took half of a sleeping pill. My doctor prescribed them to me a year ago, when the constant stimulation from my congressional responsibilities, media appearances, online vitriol, and randomly becoming a celebrity left me feeling permanently wired. I was lucky if I got four hours at night, and if I had time for more, my brain couldn't calm itself down enough to completely shut off. I wouldn't have worried much, my cognitive function never faltered, but my body was starting to shut down. I threw up so often, my team was whispering to each other, wondering if I was pregnant. I always had a dull, persistent headache throbbing at the back of my skull. My muscles ached. I needed rest.

Now all I have ahead of me is rest. It will be good for me. I will feel better.

The house is quiet once I'm dressed and venture downstairs. I guess Benito is at work, assuming Mayor of La Musa is an actual job and not just a vanity title. I walk outside. The wind whips against my face as I close the wrought-iron gate behind me. There's a fog settled over the hillside below and as a result, it looks like the town is floating above a cloud. I take a breath in. Air, fresh air. This is good for me.

I follow the cobblestone street to the center of town. My destination is Caffè del Duomo, the coffee shop that was my favorite study spot when I was a student here. I'm not surprised to find that it hasn't changed at all: a tiny space with stools crammed around a few high-top tables, and the same surly-looking barista behind the counter. I think his name is Giovanni or Giuseppe or one of those Gi-names. There's a spattering of tables on the patio outside that fill up as the day goes on, but for now there's not another person in sight.

That is, except for Giovanni or Giuseppe, who doesn't seem thrilled to have a customer. He looks up when I enter but then goes back to fiddling with the cash register, using the end of his wrinkled gray T-shirt to clean its buttons. I stand at the counter and wait for him to perk up, but several moments go by without any movement.

"Hi—uh, *buongiorno*," I say. Giovanni/Giuseppe doesn't budge. "*Buongiorno*," I decide to take a stab, "Giovanni."

This gets his attention. He glares at me. Oh no. "*Mi chiamo* Giuseppe."

"Damn it. That was my second guess."

He glares at me more. I realize he's expecting me to order. "*Vorrei un cappuccino, per favore,*" can I please have a cappuccino, I ask, "and do you by any chance have oat milk?" I'm too tired to try to translate and I don't think oat milk was a thing the last time I spoke Italian. "*Mi dispiace,*" I apologize. "*Parla inglese?*"

Giuseppe doesn't reply and starts working on my cappuccino without another word.

"*Grazie,*" I say, once he sets the finished drink in front of me. "*Quanto costa?*" I ask, taking out my wallet to pay. Even pre-caffeine, my Italian is thankfully much sharper than yesterday.

Giuseppe waves his hand and goes back to his button-polishing project. "For you, nothing. No oat milk." I think I see the slightest of smiles briefly cross his lips.

Alright, Izzy, I think to myself. *You are doing it. You are in Italy.* I take my cappuccino to one of the tables outside that overlook the Piazza del Duomo, the church's giant frescos shimmering in the morning sun. A few people mill about. A flock of sparrows descends into the piazza, squawking at each other for a few moments before flying away.

I take out my e-reader and scroll through the books I pre-downloaded. They're all nonfiction, the heady, intellectual dram I consumed in the before-times: a biography of Madeleine Albright, the untold story of female combat nurses during World War II, a book about Grover Cleveland's sister who served as his first lady because he was unmarried. I wonder who would do the job if an unmarried woman became president? I don't have any siblings. Would my first lady be my mom? Kate? My childhood bestie, Priya?

I put my Kindle back into my bag. There's no need to escape to other worlds. I *have* escaped to another world. A mother with her two children walks by. The clock tower chimes, signaling the top of the hour. Giuseppe sweeps the floor inside. It's so quiet outside—which is nice, and I love it.

A well-dressed older woman walks by me, her heels clacking against the cobblestone. A man enters the café, orders a shot of espresso, drinks it quickly, then leaves. A hawk circles above the town then flies away.

I can relax here. I can do anything here. But Jesus Christ, what the hell am I supposed to do, and how do I relax?

I finish my cappuccino and walk back to the house.

My stomach growls as I walk inside and smell something delicious. My body's all out of whack, but it's nearly lunchtime. I follow the scent into the kitchen, where a person I've never seen before is standing over the stove, watching a simmering pot. He's a portly man with hair thinning at the top of his head and a sheen of sweat visible all over his body.

"Hello?" I say.

"*Buongiorno!*" he says with a genuine ear-to-ear smile. He walks over to me. "You must be Isabella from California." He shakes my hand.

"Yes, that's me. I go by Izzy."

He walks back to the pot and stirs whatever's inside. "I am taking my daughters to California next year. My younger one, Antonia, has always wanted to meet Elsa from *Frozen*." He presses a palm to his forehead. "She kill me for saying that. She's supposed to be too old and too cool to care about *Frozen* now, but I hear 'Let It Go' coming out of her headphones." He laughs. "And my older one is too cool for everything, but I want to send her down the big water ride. Feel fear, you know?" He laughs heartily. "No, no, I am kidding. They are both good girls. I am a lucky man."

I think I see him start to tear up. I interject, "I'm sure they are. And you are…?"

He laughs uproariously. "I go on and on about Antonia and Beatrice and I don't even say my own name! I am so sorry, Izzy from California. I am Vincenzo. Vincenzo from La Musa."

"Very nice to meet you."

"I work here… I… how do you say, watch the house?" He shakes his head. "I'm sorry, my English is not so good."

"Your English is excellent," I say. "Do you cook for Anita and Benito?"

Vincenzo looks at the pot and laughs again. "Oh no. No, no. I see how you thought that, Izzy from California. No, I watch the sauce for tonight's dinner for Signora Anita. She gives me orders, I listen. That is my job here. And that is my job at home with my wife." He laughs heartily again. "Oh, Benito, hello."

I turn and see Benito walking into the kitchen. "Hi," he says, barely nodding in my direction. "I see you two have met."

"We have," Vincenzo says. "And with Izzy here, I might get my English up to the level of you, my posh British boy."

Benito looks up slowly. I laugh. "No, please, if I'm going to be here, I need to learn Italian. Don't speak English on my account."

"Nonsense," says Vincenzo, "I want to sound as crystal clear as Kristoff by the time I am in America."

"Kristoff?" I ask.

"From *Frozen*!"

"Oh, right. Well, in that case, I'm happy to speak English with you as long as you throw an Italian phrase or two my way every now and then."

Vincenzo lights up. "It would be my pleasure."

Benito clears his throat. "Well, I'm glad that's settled, then."

I look at Vincenzo and we share a smile. "Izzy, here's an Italian phrase: *È un peperino* describes someone who has a sunny disposition and is full of life."

I look over at Benito, then back to Vincenzo. "Oh, I love it, so like… *Benito, è un peperoncino?*" I ask.

Benito rolls his eyes. Vincenzo laughs. "A+ on your first lesson, Izzy from California."

We share a smile and I decide I love him. Benito sighs and opens the refrigerator, scanning its contents. "Since I have you both here," I say. "I wanted to go into town for lunch, but I have no idea where to go."

When I was last here, I was a broke college student saving money for my postgrad dreams, so I exclusively survived off three-euro bottles of wine and jars of Nutella. This time will be different.

"Oh, Izzy," Vincenzo says. "How exciting for you to try all of the food of La Musa for the first time. Every place more delicious than the last. Don't you agree, my boy?"

Benito closes the refrigerator and nods, but it's clear he'd rather be anywhere else. "Sure, of course."

Vincenzo claps his hands together. "You should take Izzy to Trattoria La Buca."

"I'm only on a quick break from work—"

"Oh no, that's really ok—" Benito and I both answer quickly.

"Come on, Benito. Don't let our American friend fend for herself on her first day in Italy."

I look to Benito and can tell he's calculating which one of the sixty different excuses that popped into his head to deploy. I interject, "It's really fine. I like eating alone."

"You cannot eat alone," Vincenzo says. "I eat lunch with my wife. Every day for 20 years…" I think he's tearing up again, but he stops himself. "Benito, you must take Izzy." When neither of us move an inch, Vincenzo waves his hands and goes back to stirring. "Never mind, then. When I tell your mother about this, I'm sure she'll understand."

Benito takes in a long inhale. "Fine. Izzy, let's go."

Trattoria La Buca is a family-owned eatery with peeling wallpaper and cracks in the exterior wall, but like much of La Musa, age can't be a determination of quality. We sit at a small bistro table tucked into a corner. It's dark and cozy inside despite the bright afternoon sun. If I weren't with Benito, who's lukewarm on me so far, I'd think this was a romantic setting.

"So, what's good here?" I ask, knowing I'll have to be in the driver's seat if I want any semblance of conversation.

Benito scans the menu. "I don't know."

"Haven't you been here?"

Benito shrugs. "You saw how at home my mother is in the kitchen, we didn't eat out much." A waiter comes by, and Benito orders a bottle of house red without consultation. He turns to me. "Do you drink?" I cackle so loudly that the only other people in the restaurant, seated a few tables away, glare at me. "I'll take that as a yes," he says.

"Oh yeah. When I was…" I freeze for a moment, lest a slip of the tongue allude to my former life. "At my last job, it was a survival tactic."

"When you were in the U.S. Congress?"

My heart drops. "Wha—? You know?" I feel the sweat start to slick on my palms. No wonder Benito immediately hated me. He knows.

"I recognized you when I met you yesterday." Benito says it so casually, it's like I quit my job at H&R Block after a storied 20-year tenure.

"So you know about…" I trail off. Benito raises his eyebrows. "Oh god." He knows about the texts. He knows about the media frenzy that followed, my shaming in the public square, the scarlet *A* on my chest. "Why didn't you say anything?"

The waiter comes back, and Benito waits to respond until she's poured each of us a glass of wine and left. "I figured you didn't want to talk about it."

He's right about that. "Then why bring it up now?"

"I'm dying to know if the thing about the treasure map on the back of the Declaration of Independence is real," Benito deadpans.

I roll my eyes, avenging the many times he's done the same to me. "I wouldn't know, they don't let you touch it."

Benito looks down at the menu again. "I didn't plan on saying anything, but I felt weird knowing and not telling you."

I try to wrap my head around the fact that my safe hamlet where nobody knows me or my past is not so safe anymore. "Does everyone here know who I am?"

"I'm the mayor, not a telepath."

I sigh.

Benito lowers his voice. "I doubt it. I only know because I worked as an advisor to a lord in the House of Commons and it was my job to keep tabs on the U.S. and our 'special relationship.'"

"Our *what?*"

"Special relationship," he says again.

"You love to say things again instead of explaining, don't you?"

"I wasn't sure if it was my accent, I know Americans struggle to understand dialects outside their own."

He tries again, putting on an American accent. "The special relationship between the U.S. and the U.K."

I laugh, because he sounds like a Southern belle, and while it's a spot-on impression, it doesn't suit him. "Oh! *That* special relationship!" I respond, mockingly. "That was a pretty good accent."

"I went to boarding schools my whole life and they were stuffed with Americans. My best mate in year 10 was an oil billionaire's son from Dallas. He spoke exactly like Owen Wilson."

Despite his standoffish demeanor, I can't quite picture Benito getting along with trust fund kids. I knew them well from a lifetime in Los Angeles, but it's hard to picture Benito skiing the Swiss Alps or schmoozing on a beach in St. Barts. "I thought I heard a little bit of *You, Me and Dupree* in there."

Benito cocks his head. "Really? Of all his roles?"

The waiter returns and asks for our order. I haven't looked at the menu at all. I plan to eat my way through every restaurant in La Musa, but it's overwhelming.

Benito motions for me to put my menu down. "*Io gradirei i ravioli, invece la signora prenderà le linguini al tartufo.*" The waiter nods and walks away. He turns to me. "I ordered you the truffle pasta. Truffles are an Umbrian specialty. Don't worry, no meat."

"Thank you," I say, momentarily touched that he remembered my dietary restrictions.

"I wouldn't want you to ask to speak to the manager when you find meat in your *carbonara*."

I exhale. "My Italian might not be fluent, but I do know there's meat in *carbonara*." I refill the wine glass to numb the pain of knowing we have a long lunch ahead of us. "How long did you live in London?" I ask, hoping to steer the conversation into a neutral zone.

Benito takes a sip of his wine. "A while. I went to university in Cambridge and then I stayed."

"You went to Cambridge?"

He nods.

"Wow. So, you're smart."

"No, I'm a legacy." He says it quickly, like it's a reflex. "My father and his father and his father's father..."

The father who is gone but not dead. "Oh. I mean, I'm sure you got in on your own too." I smirk. "Old institutions never play into nepotism."

He looks at me pointedly. "I think it's much more impressive to get into one such institution on your own merit rather than familiar connections."

Are we talking about my congressional past again? If so, he's teetering on the edge of a compliment, and that's not really our dynamic. "So, boarding school, Cambridge, London... you'd only be in La Musa for holidays and summers growing up, then?"

"I didn't realize this was a hearing, Congresswoman," he says, raising his hands in surrender. "I yield my time."

"That's not how that works." I roll my eyes again. "I'm asking questions, trying to get to know you, that's typically how a conversation goes. Do they not teach you that at Cambridge?"

Benito shakes his head. "No, the core curriculum is focused on maintaining the monarchy and how to charm oligarchs."

A sort of half laugh comes out of me, but I remind myself the most monstrous narcissists I worked with previously were also good at using charm and wit to disarm their opponent. Just because Benito's kind of funny, and kind of pretty, doesn't mean I have to like him. "With such stunning manners, it's no wonder they chased you out of the country and you ended up in your hometown, where you spent…?" I trail off, waiting for him to answer my original question.

"Holidays, yes, sometimes. Sometimes we'd travel. Summers the same or at my father's family home in Lake Como."

It seems like a charmed life to me, but the way Benito speaks about it makes it sound like the summer my parents sent me to that horrible, bedbug-infested camp in Big Bear. "How long have you been back?"

"Six months."

My eyebrows shoot up in surprise. It changes the image I've had of him thus far. I thought he was the golden child of La Musa. The quarterback who stuck around after high school graduation to run his father's mechanic shop, or whatever the Italian equivalent of that is. "That's it?"

"That's it."

"Why'd you come back?"

He looks up at me and we lock eyes. There's an intensity behind his that I haven't noticed before. It's like he's scanning my soul, trying to figure out if I'm worth a real conversation. "I came back because I had to," he says, perhaps deciding I don't deserve the real explanation.

The waiter returns with our food, and the intoxicating aroma wafting off the plate in front of me distracts from whatever judgment lurks behind Benito's gaze. I dive into the pasta. The earthy, hearty flavor of the truffle is complemented with the freshness of lemon and olive oil. It's creamy, it's rich but not too rich, decadent but not overwhelming.

After a moment of quiet reveling in the flavors, Benito dots his mouth with his napkin. "Izzy, how long are you actually going to keep this up?"

"This conversation? At least until the wine is finished," I say.

Benito stares blankly at me. "That's not what I meant." He twirls a noodle with his fork. "I meant how long are you going to pretend you're actually moving to La Musa."

I take a sip of wine calmly, measured. "I did move to La Musa," I say.

He stares at me like he's waiting for me to retract. "Come on."

"Where to?" I say, taking another slow, luxurious sip of wine.

"The future of her party, Congresswoman—" I flinch. Benito raises his hand in surrender. "It's not like Italy is some progressive haven. If anything, moving here is the antithesis of your life's work." He calculates something in his brain. "Unless—is that why you're here?"

I weigh how to best respond. It's not lost on me that Italy has its own set of issues politically, its own battles people like me, the old me, are fighting, but it makes me sound like a fraud if I admit that right now, in this moment, I don't really care. "I'm not trying to fight the thread of resurging fascism in Europe, no," I say.

"Then what is it?" he asks again.

"Nothing."

Benito huffs. "You don't actually expect me to believe you're doing a whole *Eat, Pray, Love* thing."

"Believe what you want."

"An *Under the Tuscan Sun,*" he says.

"Great film." Another sip of wine. Unbothered, unfazed.

"*Roman Holiday,*" he says. "*Letters to Juliet, Room with a View,* need I go on?"

I shrug. "You're naming films. I don't know what this has to do with me."

Benito leans in, suddenly energized. "You aren't actually playing the white woman who leaves everything behind, hoping the answer to all her problems is simply *Italy.*"

My breath stutters. He more or less nailed it, but I uphold a stoic exterior. "I studied abroad in this town. Did you know about that? I needed somewhere to go, and this is a place I could… go. Somewhere familiar but also the complete opposite of the life I was living."

Benito's eyes narrow, studying me. He leans back in his chair and crosses his arms. "You won't last more than a month."

"I will," I say. "I booked three months in the room in your house."

"You won't make it," he says. "Maybe you won't go home, but you'll never stay in La Musa."

I hear it for the first time. An edge to his voice when he says *La Musa*. He hates it here. He's the freaking mayor and he hates it here. "La Musa is beautiful," I say.

"It's decrepit," he replies. He lowers his voice, "Maybe when you were here 20 years ago—"

I almost spit out my wine. "It was closer to ten."

"La Musa used to be the shining gem of Umbria, but it's fallen. Look around. No one comes here anymore. The population is aging. La Musa is on life support. In another 10 years, it'll be nothing."

"Then why are you here?" I ask again.

"Because I—" he starts.

"Because you had to be. Right," I say.

He relaxes a bit, takes a deep breath, and sits up straight. "I don't mean to be so harsh. It has its charm, but I'm realistic. Trust me. By the end of your three months, you'll be hightailing it out of here, if not sooner."

I shake my head. "You see a lack of commerce, I see community. You see nothing for miles, I see natural beauty all around us. You see ruins where I see a preservation of everything and everyone that's come before us."

"I didn't say any of those things." Benito shakes his head.

"Am I wrong?" I ask.

He runs his hand through his hair. "I refuse to believe my prison is your paradise."

I laugh because it's all just so, so dramatic. "I guess we'll see who's right in three months."

The edge of Benito's mouth twitches upward. "I guess we will."

Chapter Four

BY THE NEXT DAY, I AM SITUATED ENOUGH TO WANT TO go out and explore. While I was doing my essentials shopping, La Musa was more alive than it first seemed. The bread baker at the *panetteria* sold me three loaves of ciabatta for three euro. I offered one to Anita as a thank you for feeding me with her leftovers, which she waved off. "You are always welcome to eat whatever's in the house, Izzy," she said, but my congressional sensibilities don't allow me to accept generosity without giving something in return.

I bought six bottles of the locally made Umbrian *Rosso* from the wine shop and stashed them in the cupboard Anita set aside for me. The Farentinos are well stocked on linens, but I bought my own laundry detergent and soap, or at least what I could best guess was soap based on context clues. I updated my data plan this afternoon so I can use my translation app more reliably. By nightfall, I am sufficiently set up as a person who actually lives here, and yet completely restless at the idea of sitting in my bedroom for the third night in a row.

Bar Musa was the local hangout spot when I was a student, so I put on my one sort-of-sexy black dress and head out. It's short and low cut and I immediately regret not wearing a jacket. It's not like there's a wealth of single men in La Musa. As Vincenzo pointed out to me this morning, there's hardly anyone in La Musa who's old enough to drive but too young for laugh lines, but I'll take a silver fox widower if there's one available. It's been way too long since I've been touched, and my skin still burns from the memory of where Levi put his hands. I need a reset. I need new sensory memories. I need to get my yayas out, as Marisol would say. In Washington I was too careful; I knew a secret tryst could be the downfall of my entire career—how ironic that waiting for Levi had the exact same result. A sex scandal with barely any sex. It's all totally unfair.

So, I'm in my short dress with as much cleavage as my B-cups can reasonably give. My "California bronde" hair blow-dried straight for once instead of tied back in my signature power bun. I wear black flats because I know better than to risk the near-fatal combination of heels, cobblestone, and alcohol. It's been so long since I've been to a bar. I used to drink with the other freshmen members at a dingy dive bar in Capitol Hill, but once that became impossible, my social life basically disappeared.

Bar Musa's tucked into a corner in the same piazza as the *duomo*. It's a cozy spot with only half a dozen tables inside but a patio that overflows when it's nice out with locals and tourists alike.

Or at least, it used to be full of tourists.

With the picture Benito painted of the town, I expect it to be empty. I'm surprised when I walk inside to find it mostly full. I scan the room and see mostly couples huddled around the small tables, drinking wine and catching up. No single, hot, one-night-stand-worthy men yet, but it's early.

I go to the bar and order a martini extra dry. The bartender nods through my shaky Italian and repeats the order back in English, to which I humiliatingly nod. Once I have my drink, I settle into a chair at the end of the bar. Back when I had anonymity, I used to love going to bars by myself. There was a bird-themed local haunt near my parents' house in Beachwood with red vinyl booths and a long wooden bar. I'd sit there and eavesdrop on the conversations between washed-up celebrity has-beens, weirdo Hollywood locals, and performers from the comedy theater next door. Now, I can barely make out a *brindiamo* from a *grazie*. Maybe coming here alone was a bad idea. I wonder what Benito's doing tonight—but he's not exactly good company.

"Izzy?" The sound of my name sends a chill down my spine. I turn to see where it's coming from, expecting to find an American tourist who waywardly made their way to La Musa and is about to out my location to the world. Instead, I see Vincenzo holding hands with a stunning woman. She's wearing a slip dress, with her dark, shiny hair in perfect curls past her shoulders.

Vincenzo waves. "Izzy! That *is* you!" He walks over and hugs me, the contact catching me off guard and nearly toppling me off the barstool. The woman with him barely reacts, which gives me the sense she knows this is something Vincenzo does all of the time.

"Hi," I say to her, "I'm Izzy."

Vincenzo facepalms. "Oh my goodness. I am so sorry. I did not introduce." He drapes his arm around the woman. "This is my wife, Valeria."

I stick my hand out, but Valeria quickly dismisses it, instead pulling me into a chic air-kiss on each cheek. "Izzy," she says, "it is so wonderful to meet you. Vincenzo speaks so highly of you."

I smile at her. I have talked to Vincenzo maybe three times, but it's kind of her to say that. "Lovely to meet you," I say. "And likewise. Vincenzo speaks of you and your girls constantly."

Valeria rolls her eyes. "I am surprised to hear that. They are horrible teenagers."

"They are staying with friends tonight," Vincenzo says. "When the cat's away the mice will play." He winks at me. "That's the saying, right?"

"That's right," I say, not really sure if it applies here, but I'm touched that he's making an effort. I turn to Valeria. "Vincenzo's taught me a few Italian phrases."

"Ah," Valeria says, turning to her husband with genuine admiration. "Then you'll be fluent in Italian in no time. In idioms, at least."

Vincenzo beams with pride. "Valeria studied English at the university in Roma. She's taught me everything I know."

He looks on the verge of tears again, so I gesture toward the bartender. "Can I buy you both a drink?"

We trade the barstools for a table in the corner of the bar and split a bottle of wine Vincenzo recommends. It's a Sangiovese from Montepulciano in nearby Tuscany, dry but robust. Valeria tells me she inherited the wine shop in town and has been running it for the past decade after her father retired. "What made you decide to work for the Farentinos?" I ask Vincenzo.

He shrugs. "My father used to manage their estate before me, so it is how it always was to be." It seems to be par for the course in La Musa. Maybe you leave town for university and your early adulthood, but everyone always comes back when it's time to take over the family business.

There's a quaintness to it that makes me ache with jealousy. My parents were environmental lawyers. While their work inspired my affinity for community organizing and public service, I would've dressed as an off-brand cartoon character on the Walk of Fame before I went to law school and followed in their footsteps.

"What made you want to move to La Musa, Izzy?" Valeria asks.

I debate how much to tell them and settle on an abbreviated version of the truth. "I studied here in college—my university used to have a program here. Do you know it?"

Valeria nods enthusiastically. "Yes, yes. Of course. We all remember the days when dozens of American college students would fill the streets of La Musa in the summer."

"They were like centaurs," Vincenzo says. "Half man, half beast." Valeria gives him a stern look. "Though I'm sure our Izzy was not like that," he says.

I laugh. "No, I understand how a bunch of college students let loose in a town where we could suddenly drink legally would be annoying." I take a sip of wine. "I really was here to study, though." Truthfully, I knew how good foreign programs would look on my transcript, how good international experience would look to future voters. Everything I did in college, and everything since, had been to support my dream.

"So you've come back now, what, five years later?" Valeria says with a wink. I love her.

"Give or take," I say. I take another sip. "My life back in the States"—I'm a person who says "the States" now—"was… complicated. I just remember everything here being so delightfully uncomplicated. Not to say it's easy or free from drama, but the pace of life is much slower, in a good way. I need that."

Valeria and Vincenzo smile at each other. "Well, *brindiamo* to that," Valeria says, raising her glass.

I'm significantly drunk by the time Vincenzo opens our third bottle. The door to the bar swings open and I do a double take at the man who walks inside. He's young, probably mid–late 20s, way outside the normal age range of La Musa residents as has been reported to me. He's handsome. Wildly handsome. His face is innocent looking with wide eyes and a round jaw, but there's a vitality to his swagger as he walks through the bar. I feel my cheeks redden and press one of my cool hands to my face. Valeria tracks my eyes to the man and back. "Do you have a boyfriend, Izzy?" she asks.

I blush even harder. "No," I say. "No, not at all."

She smiles and shares a knowing look with Vincenzo, elbowing him in the gut and nodding toward the handsome stranger. Vincenzo takes the hint and raises his hand in the air. "Giacomo, my boy," he says. The man turns and lights up when he sees Vincenzo. He walks over to our table.

He and Vincenzo exchange a quick conversation in Italian before Vincenzo points to me. "This is my new friend, Izzy from California." He places a hand on my shoulder. "Izzy, this is Giac."

Giac smiles at me and it lights up his whole face. His teeth are shiny, and his smile is without flaw. The kind of perfect that in Los Angeles means they've spent an exorbitant amount of money on veneers, but for Giac it's just his natural aura. He's not tall, probably only an inch or two taller than me, but his shoulders are broad and strong. The kind you can cling to when the moment calls for it. Shoulders that make you feel safe. I'm too drunk for this, because I immediately picture myself kissing him. "Hi," I sputter.

"Giac is a teacher. Beatrice is his student," Valeria says.

"One of my best students," Giac says.

I'm still tongue-tied by his handsomeness to find actual words, so I simply nod. Vincenzo gestures to the chair next to me. "Please, join us."

The bartender walks up to us and hands Giac a shot of yellow liquid, limoncello. "I wish I could," Giac says, his voice melodic, like a song that you hear for the first time and know you'll be playing on repeat for the next month. "But I am on the late train back to Perugia." He turns to me. "I live in Perugia but work here." He sips on the limoncello. "I was having dinner with my aunt." Vincenzo and Valeria groan sympathetically. I'll ask later what the deal with the aunt is. Giac finishes the rest of his shot. "I'm sorry to leave so soon. Izzy, it was lovely to meet you."

I nod. "Mmm," is all I can get out.

He smiles at me again and I think I notice a hint of interest in his eyes. I'm not the best at knowing when someone is flirting with me, but the way he looks at me makes something in my stomach spin. "I hope to see you around?"

I nod again. He leaves. Vincenzo sits back down and we're all quiet for a moment. I still feel flushed. It's pathetic, really, how easily a man smiling in my direction leaves me flustered. "Izzy, you are a tomato," Vincenzo says. Valeria playfully hits him on the arm.

I fan myself. "It's hot in here."

"Something is hot in here indeed," Valeria says, raising her eyebrows at me.

I top off my wine glass. "Do you know if Giac is, like…" I twist a lock of hair around my index finger, "… I don't know, single?"

Valeria nods knowingly and leans in conspiratorially, like she was waiting for me to ask. "Since he doesn't live here, I don't know all the details, but what I do know is that he did not bring a date to the end-of-term school banquet." At my blank expression, she clarifies, "*Everyone* brings a date to the end-of-term banquet."

I take another sip of wine, smiling, stopping myself from immediately fantasizing about Giac.

After a moment Vincenzo hits his hands on the table. "Giac, my love. You meant Giac is hot in here. I get it now! You are so clever, *amore mio*."

When I get home I collapse onto my bed, my head spinning from the alcohol. I open my computer to watch more *Housewives,* but it erupts with a FaceTime call from my mom. I hesitantly click accept. Both my parents appear onscreen, scrunched together on a patio sofa, the rugged terrain of their Beachwood Canyon backyard visible behind them. "Izzy? Izzy, can you see us?" my mom says, moving her face closer to the screen as if that would help.

"Yes, Mom. I can see you. How's it going?" I ask, knowing the point is moot because they're calling for a wellness check. I don't blame them for being concerned, considering how rarely I left my dark childhood bedroom in the months before I fled the country.

My mom sits back and turns to my dad. They're coordinating in acid-wash button-downs. It's early afternoon in Los Angeles, but they've probably already had a full day, hiking and gardening. "We're fine. How are you? How's Italy? Do you have everything you need?"

"Yeah, as it turns out, I've had everything I need inside me all along."

I hear a sigh. "Izzy…"

"I'm good. Italy is good. I updated my data plan and bought soap, everything is fine," I say. My mom asks if I have a plan for work, for my next step, for the future, and I shake my head.

"Why not, Iz?" my dad chimes in. "You need to keep yourself busy. You're not an idler. You aren't the type of person to sit around for more than a vacation's worth of time. You need to be needed by something bigger."

In the before-time, I would have agreed with him, but there's no good way to tell the people who made you that nowadays you'd rather lurk in the shadows of the very edges of your existence, like an otherwise well-adjusted Phantom of the Opera. "I have a purpose. I'm adjusting to Italy and I'm making friends. My friend Vincenzo is teaching me Italian. *In bocca al lupo* means good luck."

My mother lights up. "Vincenzo?" She takes on an unnecessary and incorrect Italian accent to repeat his name. "Is he cute? Single?"

"He's at least 45 and happily married. I love his wife too," I reply, wondering if I should tell her about Giac, but what would I say? I briefly met the one handsome young man in town and got so hot and bothered that I could barely speak to him?

My mother sighs dramatically. "Izzy, you *would* move to the one town in Italy with no eligible men—"

"Colleen," my dad cuts her off. "She doesn't need us to pressure her about getting married."

"I wasn't pressuring her—" my mother replies.

"I know," says Dad. "But we said we'd focus on getting her back to her normal self and then we'd ask around for a setup."

This is all news to me. "What do you mean, back to my normal self? And you are *not* setting me up with anyone. I'm an adult. I get to make my own choices."

They share another look. As an only child, I'm used to playing two-on-one with my parents, but they've usually veered more on the side of supportive than manipulative. "You've been easy to raise, Iz," my dad says. "We're overdue for a parenting challenge." He says it with a laugh, but it feels like a jab to the chest. They haven't outright said they're disappointed in me, but I know they are. I knew it as soon as my dad patted me on the back after my concession speech and said, *"Two years to figure out how to beat him, Iz,"* even though I had already decided I was never running for public office again.

"No one is setting me up," I repeat, "and I'm fine. You don't need to worry about me."

They share another look, still unconvinced. They'd never been prouder of me than on my swearing-in day. I kept a framed picture on my desk of their beaming faces standing behind me that day. It used to center me on hard days, to know that if all else failed, I had them. My mother kept the same photo tacked to the refrigerator with a K.C.R.W. magnet. They were supportive when I lost, but I knew it was as hard on them as it was on me. I couldn't look at that picture afterward. I'd given it to Kate and asked her to make sure I never saw it again. When I got home, it wasn't on the fridge anymore either.

"Look," I say. "It's late here. I should go to bed. It'll take a good night's sleep if I have to figure out the rest of my life come tomorrow."

My father sighs. "We're not saying you need to have it all figured out, Iz, but you can't aspire to nothing now that your first dream is over."

I consider. All of my life had been for this one thing and look how that turned out? "I don't need another dream," I say. "I need to aspire to nothing."

"Well," he says, "*in bocca al lupo* with that."

We hang up and I try to go back to my housewives. My buzz has significantly worn off, and I need to hear a woman screaming at another woman or I'm going to have a panic attack. My phone dings with a text.

Marisol: don't look at the news.

I sigh. Now I *have* to look at the news.

Me: why would you say that. Now I'm curious.
Marisol: don't!!!!

I open the news app on my phone and don't see anything out of the ordinary: The world is terrible, the wars are worse, the famines are unresolved. It seems more or less a run-of-the-mill news day in the U.S. I scroll to the celebrity gossip. A lifetime in Hollywood means I don't really care about famous people, but one of my housewives is pregnant and I know *People* has the exclusive on their name reveal. Sue me, I'm curious if it's going to be a Rio or a Cruz.

My heart drops when I see the headline. *Congressman Levi Cross Steps Out with Actress Olivia White.* There are pictures of the two of them. Levi in a crisp oxford shirt and slacks, Olivia in a tiny dress, pumps, and Levi's suit jacket draped over her shoulders. They're holding hands, ducking out of the lights of the camera flashes and yet smiling, glowing. I resist the urge to run to the bathroom and hurl.

It's probably a P.R. relationship. It's not unheard of in either world. An arrangement made by their respective teams for more press and elevated star power, but *still*. What do they even talk about? Olivia was in a teen drama up until last year, she can't be older than 26. Levi's pushing 40 and grew up on a farm outside of Bakersfield. He knows more about different types of soil than television. He judged me for even watching shows like the one Olivia was on. He always wanted to talk about books, symphonies, poetry. He didn't touch any piece of culture that wasn't considered highbrow. I used to think that made him an intellectual, brilliant, but now I think it was more that he was pompous and pretentious.

I hope Olivia learns this soon and dumps him. Or maybe she finds it sexy, and they'll get married, their wedding an exclusive in *Vogue*. Her dress will be a Vera Wang original. Vera did my inauguration ball dress. Fucking traitor.

Levi, who didn't think it was wise for me to be in a relationship during my freshmen term, is now in one publicly. He told me it was better for me to focus on the work, that it wouldn't be right for the voters or for me to try to start something new in the midst of all the fuss. Levi, who was wary of the level of attention I was getting, who told me he was worried it would distract from what I set out to do, is now dating a freaking starlet. And the worst part is, no pundit, internet troll, or fellow congressperson will wonder if he can balance his high-profile relationship and the job. It will only make him more known, more popular, and better liked.

I was no stranger to the media, but I know if it had been the other way around, I would have been ridiculed and my motives would have been questioned.

My phone dings again.

Marisol: You looked, didn't you?
Me: I looked. Wtf adjkflsjfksldfn

The three bubbles appear immediately as Marisol writes out a response.

Marisol: You have more Instagram followers than her <3

I wish that were enough to make me feel better. I shut my laptop, take a sleeping pill, and crawl under the covers.

Chapter Five

"I'M GOING TO HAVE SEX WITH GIAC," I SAY TO MARISOL on the phone a few days later. I have spoken to Giac exactly three times including our introduction at the bar, but I need the distraction. Yesterday, I saw him as I was tonguing two scoops of gelato stracciatella in a cone. He said "*Gelato?*" and I, through a mouthful of vanilla bean and chocolate chips, replied, "*Sì.*"

"No, you're not," Marisol says. It's 2 a.m. in DC but Marisol is wide awake, not yet settled in for her nightly three to four hours of sleep.

"I am," I say. "I need a passionate affair that makes me realize love is the only thing that really matters."

"I don't think you can go into it hoping to force that lesson," Marisol says. I hear the faint drone of cable news in the background. I do my best to tune it out. She continues, "Besides, love is *not* the only thing that matters. Humans can survive without love, we can't survive without clean water, affordable food, and shelter. Those are the things that really matter."

I lean back on my bed, putting my phone on speaker and resting it next to me because the action of holding it to my ear is too much effort. "Can you turn off the politicking for like, one second."

"No," Marisol says with a little laugh. "Sorry, Giac. You're going to have sex with Giac."

"Yes," I say. "Thank you."

"I'm 100% supportive of you banging as much as possible now that you're not in Congress," she says.

"Right?" I say. "And Giac is perfect. He's the only young, single person around, but even in spite of that. He doesn't actually live in La Musa, so if it goes horribly wrong, it's relatively easy to avoid him."

"Always a good reason to sleep with someone," Marisol says, and I'm honestly not sure if she means that or if it's her dry sense of humor and she's mocking me.

"He's hot, I'm attracted to him, I need to get laid, and he's hot." I sit up, my energy suddenly renewed with fresh purpose. "I'm going to fuck Giac."

There's a knock on my door. "Is that you or me?" Marisol asks.

"Me," I respond. "Hold on." I walk over to the door with my phone still in my hand and open it. Benito is standing on the other side. I pray he didn't hear any of our conversation. "Benito?"

"Who's Benito?" Marisol asks.

I quickly press the phone into my shoulder to muffle the sound of her voice. "What's up?" I ask.

Benito shuffles from one foot to the other. "It's Sunday."

I stare at him, waiting for more. "Thank you for the reminder."

He shakes his head. "My mother wants me to invite you to family lunch. It's a whole ordeal every Sunday. My sister's taken the train down from Siena. You are under no obligation if you do not want to—"

"I'd love to come," I say. "I mean, I've been daydreaming about your mom's pasta all week, so I'm happy to indulge in round two."

"Great." Benito nods.

"Noon?" I ask.

Benito nods again. "Noon. Out back." He smiles briefly, flashing a quick wave before walking off.

I put the phone back up to my ear. "Sorry, I'm back." I brace for Marisol's response.

"You failed to mention a Benito."

"He's the mayor," I say, lowering my voice. "And he's horrible, so it wasn't worth bringing up."

Marisol goes quiet for a moment, and I hear typing then clicking in the background. She gasps. "Wait, he's hot."

"How did you find him that fast?"

"Don't ask stupid questions," she says. "What's his deal?"

"He has a girlfriend," I say.

"No, I mean, why is he in your house?" I can hear the smile in Marisol's voice.

"He lives here," I say. "This is his mom's house."

I can hear Marisol calculating in her head. "Interesting," is all she says.

"Not really," I say, before she can imply there's reason to be happy there's a hot man living in the bedroom next door. Not that I think Benito's hot. I mean, I do, but not that it particularly matters. "Ok, I have to go. Try to get some sleep."

Marisol laughs. "You know I won't."

It's warm and humid as I walk back to the house from Valeria's wine shop. It's thankfully open on Sundays, because even though the Farentino home is technically my home, I don't want to show up to lunch empty-handed. My yellow sundress keeps sticking to the back of my thighs, which is unfortunate because I don't have a free hand with a bottle of wine in one and a bouquet of flowers that I picked up at the farmers market on the way home in the other.

I tuck the bottle of wine under my arm when I reach the large oak door and quickly adjust my dress before walking inside. A beautiful, warm-looking young woman I don't recognize opens the door before I can. I purport her to be Benito's sister. "Hi—*Buongiorno,*" I say.

She smiles and of course has one of those smiles that lights up her whole face. "*Buongiorno!* You must be Izzy?" Her voice is dripping in that same caramelly accent as Anita, and I realize she looks a lot like Benito, especially when the sun hits her hazel eyes.

"Hi, yes, and are you—?"

"Benito's sister, Lucia."

"*Piacere,*" I say.

"It's so nice to finally meet you. My brother speaks highly of you."

I look around. Did I accidentally walk into an alternate universe? "He does?"

She widens the door and gestures for me to enter. "Everyone's out back." I walk through the door and am immediately hit with the intoxicating aromas of Anita's cooking. Garlic, basil, onion, pepper. My stomach growls.

Lucia leads me through the front of the house, past the staircase with the photos, through a formal dining room and a grand living room, and another hallway with multiple doors, a part of the house I've respectfully avoided, until we're finally in another living room with floor-to-ceiling glass doors that are flung open to flow seamlessly into the backyard.

Lucia reaches out her arms. "Let me take that," she says, gesturing toward the wine and the bouquet.

I hand her both. "Please make sure your mom knows they're from me. We haven't seen much of each other this week, and I want her to know I appreciate her hospitality and her letting me stay in her home."

Lucia laughs breezily. "Please, you are doing her a favor. She loves having guests." She winks at me. "Benito!" She yells something in Italian at him and he quickly jumps into action, walking over to me with a bottle of wine and an empty glass. Lucia pats him on the head like an obedient golden retriever before disappearing inside, leaving me and Benito alone.

"Your sister is lovely," I say.

Benito hands me the glass, now full of wine. "She's demanding."

"And you bend to her every will. I didn't think you were someone to follow another's orders."

Benito scoffs, "When I was a boy it was either that or psychological torture, so I am conditioned."

"Pavlov's little brother," I say.

Benito grabs a glass off a nearby table and pours wine for himself. "More like the Stanford Prison Experiment. No one's a bigger perpetrator of forceful power and manipulation than an older sister."

I nod. "Remind me to thank my parents for only having one."

There's an awkward silence. I take in the splendor of the yard. There's a swing hanging off a tree, a patio with antique furniture, a sparkling swimming pool, a giant table where I assume we'll be eating, and a spectacular view of the countryside.

The French doors to the kitchen swing open and Anita emerges carrying a large platter of pasta. "If only I had two strong children to help me serve," she says. Benito dutifully walks over to her and takes the platter from her hands. Lucia and Benito take turns disappearing inside and returning with more food: whole branzino, fresh greens, homemade gnocchi, caprese with fresh *mozzarella di bufala*.

I wonder if we're expecting more people, but when I remember the trays of leftovers in Anita's fridge last week, I realize this is par for the course. I dig in when instructed and am once again knocked over by the perfection of Anita's cooking. I wash down an especially generous helping of pesto gnocchi with a glass of crisp Umbrian white wine.

"Benito and Lucia, you have no idea how lucky you are to have grown up with a world-class chef for a mother," I say. "My mother was a great mom, but her culinary expertise started and ended with a takeout menu."

Lucia grins. "Lucky indeed. Though Benito, not so much. Was the food this good at St. George's?"

Benito shakes his head. "Hardly."

"You can blame your father for that," Anita says. "I was perfectly content to have both of you educated here." It's the first time I've heard Anita mention the father who is not dead but gone.

Lucia and Benito share a look. Lucia reaches for the bottle of wine at the center of the table and refills her glass. "So, Izzy," she says, changing the subject. "Have you explored much of Italy since you've been here?"

"Not really," I say. "I've been focused on getting settled. I haven't really thought of where else I'd go."

"You must," Lucia says. "It's a beautiful country, and La Musa is perfectly central for exploring. Two hours to Rome, two hours to Florence."

"You sound like one of your tourism brochures, Lucia," Benito grunts.

Anita leans in toward me. "Lucia and her husband run a guided tour company out of Siena."

"Siena, the Ohio of Tuscany," Benito quips.

Lucia waves off Benito, dismissing him. "Don't listen to him. He's barely been anywhere in Italy except the airports."

"I've been to Siena," I say. "I loved it."

"Thank you, Izzy," Lucia says, passing me the bottle of wine.

"I was actually thinking about going to Rome this weekend," I say. It was half an idea, really, because I was watching a *Housewives* cast trip to Rome last night. "I've been once but only for a few hours, and it was such a blur."

"That's a wonderful idea!" Lucia says. "Roma offers so much. History, culture, fabulous food—"

Benito scoffs. "Lucia, she said she is going, you do not have to sell her on it."

"And maybe I should be selling you," she says, flicking her wrist at Benito. "When was the last time you were anywhere in Italy besides La Musa or Milano with *papà?*"

Benito looks down at his plate. "I think *Mamma* took us to the Uffizi in Florence the summer I was 16."

"Seriously?" I ask.

Lucia gasps and claps her hands together. "I have the best idea. You two should go to Roma together."

I glance at Benito, who's glaring at Lucia. "Oh that's—" I shake my head.

Benito rolls his eyes. "No."

"Why not?" Lucia says. "I'll take care of all the arrangements." She gets out her phone. "It's perfect, really. Neither of you have done it the right way, and I know how to do it the right way."

My eyes flit to Benito, his hazel eyes sparkling in the sunlight as they glare at Lucia. He rolls his sleeves up to his elbows, revealing his strong forearms. I dart my eyes back to my plate. Stupid Marisol reminding me of his objective attractiveness. "That's so kind of you, Lucia, but I know Benito's busy. I can go alone."

"Benito!" Anita bellows. "You would let this poor girl who speaks no Italian travel to Rome all by herself? That is not the boy I raised." She wields a disgusted look in his direction.

"Izzy is a strong, independent woman," Benito says, and my heart skips a beat. Why is he always threading compliments in between his general disdain for me? "She does not need me to accompany her."

"I really don't," I say, though Anita brings up a good point. Rome is a tourist-friendly city, but still, my phone translator app hasn't proved to be as reliable as I'd hoped.

"Nonsense," Anita says. "You will go, Benito."

Lucia smiles, pleased with herself. Benito fixes his stare downward at his plate of pasta, effortfully twirling a long noodle to avoid commenting further on the matter.

"Can't wait," I say.

After lunch, I offer to clean up and Anita orders Benito to help me. We wash dishes side by side at the large farm sink, the only sound the running water and the scratch of the sponge across the porcelain plates. "You really don't have to come with me," I say, breaking the silence. "I won't rat you out to your mom."

Benito pauses scrubbing for a moment as though he's considering it. "She'll know," he says. "Trust me."

We both go back to scrubbing. I cannot imagine spending an entire weekend in Rome with Benito. I used to fantasize about weekend getaways with Levi when I was in office. We could stay at an Airbnb with sweeping views of the Chesapeake Bay or take the train up to New York City. If I was in LA, we could drive up to Santa Barbara and stay at the cottagecore resort that sits right on the coast in Montecito. We never went, obviously.

"You're thinking too hard," Benito says, snapping me out of my daydream.

"Huh?" I panic for a second—can he hear my thoughts?

"I can tell by the look on your face. You look like you're studying for an exam."

I try to brush it off. "I'm fine. It's just been a week."

"What, did you move to a new continent or something?"

I roll my eyes, but his tone is less teasing, more playfully sarcastic—it teeters closer to friendly than we've acted thus far. I put the plate I'm washing on the drying rack and dab my soapy hands with a towel. I glance out the window for a moment, the view of the countryside so picture-perfect it looks like a painting. I never liked spending time with other people's families, but it's surprisingly easy with the Farentinos. Still, I don't feel at ease. My brain churns but with no discernible train of thought. Is it possible to feel like you're in the exact right place and completely lost at the same time?

"Is something wrong?" Benito asks. I glance up at him, instantly brought back to earth when his eyes meet mine. He clears his throat. "I mean, with your accommodations, the house?"

"No, not at all," I say. He continues to stare, concern filling his eyes, disarming me. A strange feeling settles in my stomach, but it's pleasant. Like I've finally pulled myself up onto dry land when I've been fighting like hell not to drown. "I think I'm realizing that I haven't processed it all."

The sun starts to dip in through the big window on the other side of the kitchen counter. Benito's eyes are honey colored in the light. Like a cool, refreshing glass of white wine. I feel the sudden urge to jump in and swim in them. His eyes narrow, cutting off that dangerous train of thought. "You mean moving here or—?"

"All of it," I respond, actively trying not to think about Benito's eyes. "I'm completely separated from any perception I had of myself prior to what happened."

Benito tilts his head sideways. "You must have other interests—"

"Not really," I reply, because it's true. "Every single thing I did up until I was elected to Congress was to take a step toward getting elected to Congress. Everything. Even coming here as a 19-year-old."

"Your parents, did they pressure you...?"

I pick up another plate and start mindlessly scrubbing. "What's with the sudden interest in my life?"

Benito smiles. "I'm asking questions, trying to get to know you, it's how a conversation works."

I hesitate for a moment but continue, "They knew I was capable of a lot, but it was me. It was all me. I wanted to change the world. I wanted to settle for nothing short of changing the world."

"Well, you were the one to save us, Izzy." He leans toward me. "You fucked it all up."

I can't help but let out a laugh. "I tried," I say, throwing my hands up in surrender, soap bubbles flinging off my fingers as I do.

"I know what you mean, though," he says. "All I ever wanted as a kid was to go to London or to New York or Paris. My parents loved the quiet, small-town life, but I never wanted it for myself, and now..." He trails off.

I feel a twinge of empathy for Benito. Maybe we're more alike than I realized. "And now you're back."

"Now I'm back," he repeats.

"We're both losers," I say. "Is that how we ended up here?"

Benito laughs. "No, you're the loser. You're here because you failed and ran out of options. I'm the sad sack who chose to come back even though he swore he never would."

My heart sinks. I'm a failure. Even Benito sees me that way. The once-great Isabella Rhodes flown in from California to stand as a monument to how quickly greatness can crumble.

He must notice my change in demeanor, because he delicately takes the plate I was washing out of my hands and dries it with a rooster-print towel. "Sorry, I don't mean failure. I know it's more complicated than that."

"It's really not," I say back quickly. "Why do you hate La Musa so much?"

"I don't hate it," Benito says. I cock my head at him, unconvinced. Benito takes a deep breath. "I don't *hate* it. La Musa is my home. I love it. I want more for it. That's part of what I'm going to do here."

"Maybe you're too close to it and you can't see. It's beautiful here, and with the right exposure, more people could appreciate it," I say.

"And maybe it's too special to you that you can't see it clearly either," he says. "You came back because you had such a wonderful study abroad experience, right?" He asks. I nod. Benito continues, "And that's not nothing, but it's not a sustainable tourism business model. La Musa needs to change, it needs to evolve."

I think of the aged buildings like the one we're in right now. Other than light maintenance and upgraded technology, everything is more or less the way it's always been. "So, what, you want to add in a Whole Foods and an Apple Store?"

Benito shakes his head. "No, of course not, but look at cities like London. The old exists alongside the new. People say they want to travel and have new experiences and see new things, but ultimately, they want to stay inside their comfort zone as much as possible. With modern touches, La Musa could become a real destination, known for more than just old buildings and pasta."

I consider. With modern touches, wouldn't La Musa be like every other homogenous, globalized small town in the world? "Do we really need to reshape a historical medieval hilltop fortress into a shrine to chain hotels and big box stores?" I ask.

"I don't want that," Benito says. "But less and less people want to live and work in small towns like this. We have very little economy, very little business. If we want to survive, we have to change."

"No," I say, a reflex to the rising storm in my stomach. We were having such a nice conversation, but of course he had to ruin it with talk of *revitalization*.

Benito laughs, amused. "No?"

"No," I repeat. "Don't do that. I came here because it's nothing like the world I'm used to. There are so many other people who'd want to do the same if they knew it existed."

"So you're saying La Musa shouldn't change because you, Izzy Rhodes, don't want it to?" he asks.

I nod. "Yes," I say. "Literally that."

He laughs, shaking his head. "I think I'll keep to my original plan, but thank you for your input."

He puts the last of the plates onto the drying rack and pats his hands against a dry towel, leaving the kitchen once he's done. I can't let him turn La Musa into a cheesy tourist stop with branded photo ops disguised as art installations. But at the same time, it's really none of my business. The public service part of my life is over. It's not my problem to fix.

Chapter Six

BY SATURDAY, MY BRAIN IS BRIMMING WITH IDEAS ON how to make La Musa more popular with tourists. I could reach out to my contact at Condé Nast and convince them to feature La Musa as one of the top travel destinations for next year, same with *The New York Times*. My campaign used Los Angeles-based influencers to help get out the vote in my district and beyond; I could reach out to a handful of them, though I doubt La Musa has the budget to pay for branded content. Maybe I could post about it to my own Instagram—no, that's not what I'm here to do. I don't want people to know where I am. I want to maintain my anonymity.

That's why I'm wearing a scarf around my head and giant sunglasses for my and Benito's Roman holiday.

On the way to the train station, I stop in Caffè del Duomo for a cappuccino. Inside, I see Giac standing at the counter, ordering from Giuseppe. "*Buongiorno,* Giac," I say, grinning probably too hard.

He stares back at me, squinting his eyes. I take off my sunglasses. "It's me, Izzy."

He laughs. "Ah, yes. Izzy. I did not recognize you. How are you?"

It's my turn to order, and Giuseppe stares at me. "*Un cappuccino, per favore,*" I say. I turn back to Giac. "I'm doing well. I'm actually headed to Rome."

"No way!" Giac says. "I love Roma." He breezily offers euros to Giuseppe to pay for both of our drinks without even acknowledging the gesture. "I studied archeology and classics at university. I used to spend hours at the Forum. I still go on digs in the summers."

"That's so cool," I say. "I wish I had you as a tour guide."

Giuseppe sets our matching cappuccinos in front of us. "*Prego,*" he says.

"*Grazie,* Giuseppe," I say.

"You know," Giac says, gesturing toward an outdoor table for us to sit at, "I was about to head back to Perugia, but I don't have other plans today. I could come with you if you'd like."

"Really?" I ask. My heart rate picks up. An entire day with Giac. I picture myself clutching on to him on the back of a Vespa as he veers through the crowded city streets, the edges of my scarf blowing effortlessly in the wind. "That would be amazing."

Giac follows me to the train station where I'm set to meet Benito for the 9 a.m. train to Rome. Lucia booked us rooms in the Centro Storico area, so I've packed a change of clothes and a few other essentials into a small duffel we'll drop at the hotel before we head out to tour. I give Giac the rundown on our itinerary and he excitedly scans it as we wait on the platform.

"Are you really wearing that?" I hear a voice ask. I turn and see Benito walking toward us. "You look like Audrey Hepburn."

He's carrying his own small duffel, dressed in a blue linen button-down and well-tailored khakis. "Since when has that ever been an insult?" I ask. Benito smirks but his face drops when he sees Giac standing next to me. "Oh," I say. "Benito, this is Giac. Giac, Benito."

"The mayor, yes," Giac says, shaking Benito's hand. "I've heard much about you."

"Giac teaches at the school in town," I say.

"Ah," is all Benito mutters back. Polite.

"Giac offered to be our tour guide. He knows a lot about Roman history and architecture." There's a brag in my voice, and I make a mental note to play it cooler.

"Wonderful," Benito says, though his tone sounds sarcastic. He turns to Giac. "Great to have you join us."

Giac smiles back at him genuinely. "Looking forward to it."

The train pulls into the station, and we find seats onboard. I sit on one side of a four-seat row while Giac and Benito face me on the opposite. Giac, perfectly content, looks out the window while Benito fidgets with his shirt cuffs.

"Izzy, what made you want to come to Umbria?" Giac asks. "La Musa doesn't have many American tourists."

I flit my eyes over at Benito. "So I've heard." I repeat the same romantic speech about study abroad, about wanting a slower pace of life, needing somewhere safe and quiet to start over. Giac nods, accepting my answer, but Benito snorts. "What?" I ask.

Benito scans my face like he's waiting for me to flinch. "That's what you're going with?"

"That's the truth," I say, giving him a pointed stare.

"Typical politician," Benito says. "Reframing the truth to fit your narrative."

My heart twists like I've just been stabbed. I glare at him again. Giac looks back and forth between the two of us. "You're a politician?"

I continue glaring at Benito. This was not his story to tell. How dare he out me to Giac? "I assumed he knew because you two are suddenly such great friends," Benito says.

Giac looks back and forth between the two of us, not really overly invested in the answer to the question, more curious about the sudden tension. "I... used to be a politician," I say. "But I'm not anymore." Benito lets out a half laugh. "What?" I snap, my tone curt.

"No, no, nothing." Benito raises his hands. "Clearly you've changed."

I roll my eyes at him. "Say it."

"Say what?" Benito asks.

"Whatever it is you want to say, out with it."

Benito adjusts in his seat. "Nothing. I would just advise against getting too attached to Izzy, Giac."

I heave in a breath. "What is *that* supposed to mean?"

Benito turns to Giac. "Izzy here is under the impression she's moved to La Musa indefinitely, but I've bet her that she won't last more than three months."

"Ah, I see," Giac says. "You do not think an American could ever permanently make such a small hamlet their home?"

"I do not," Benito says.

"Well, you're wrong," I scoff. "Giac, if you want to hang out four months from now, I am free," I say, my eyes still fixed on Benito, willing them to burn lasers into his skull.

"Ok," Giac says. If he feels awkward about the brewing tension, he doesn't show it. "Great."

When we get to Rome, I'm once again taken aback by the breathtaking splendor of the ancient city unfolding right in front of my 21st-century eyes. The Colosseum sits in the middle of an intersection as casually as Staples Center nestles itself into the center of Downtown Los Angeles. The domed top of the Vatican as commonplace as a post office. Famous monuments on every corner like they are as everyday and regular as drugstores.

Giac leads us through the Roman Forum for our first stop, reveling in the details of what happened in what place and which famous emperor did what horrible thing in front of what is now a pile of rocks. He's cute when he's excited about a pile of rocks.

Somewhere between the Temple of Romulus and the Basilica of Maxentius, Benito pulls on my arm. The heat of his touch sends an electric buzz down my spine that catches me off guard. "Izzy, wait," he says.

I turn to face him while Giac reads a placard. "What?" I look down at his hand, still on my arm, and he quickly moves it away.

He inhales sharply and shakes his head. "I feel badly about how our conversation went earlier."

I scoff. I didn't know he had the ability to feel anything other than high and mighty. "You mean where you outed my past to my new friend and told him I wouldn't be staying?"

Benito nods. "Yes."

I wait for him to apologize but no other words follow. "Ok, you feel bad that you were mean to me. That's great. The mayor has empathy. I'll be sure to note that in the next election."

He leans back a little bit from the blow of my comment. "I don't want animosity between us."

"Why do you care how I feel about you?" I fire back.

"I don't know," he says quickly, like it's a surprise to him too. Benito readjusts his stance so he's standing stick straight. "We live in the same house," he says. "It'd be nice if we got along."

The air of condescension in his tone is enough for me to decide I'm done with this conversation. "Evict me," I threaten, backing away. "You're counting down the days until I leave anyway."

I spend the rest of the tour modeling enthusiastic engagement in Giac's archeology lesson. This type of column is native to Rome. The obelisk was actually stolen from the Egyptians. The world's oldest shopping mall was right over here. Interesting. Excellent.

Giac knows elaborate details about the characters of the time, the politicians who stood in this very place thousands of years ago. If the United States ever succumbs to a similar fate, will a cute, young guide of the future tell a group of tourists about me? *"Here is where Isabella Rhodes stood when she was sworn in as California's youngest congresswoman." "And here is where she walked away from her dream forever, tail between her legs and head hung low, when she lost her first re-election."*

In all likelihood, I wouldn't be worth bringing up at all.

How many ancient Romans were lost due to already overcrowded history books? Maybe someone predicted the fall of Rome and tried to do something about it. Why do we instead celebrate the ones who successfully silenced him? Why do we praise the ones who contributed to its destruction? Are we not among ruins when we could be standing in the middle of a still-thriving empire?

Giac has to leave after we tour the Colosseum, so Benito and I share a quiet dinner at a restaurant Lucia picked for us in the Spanish quarter. We eat quickly while I dream of checking into my room, turning on syndicated television, and falling asleep to an episode of *Friends* dubbed in Italian.

At the hotel, Benito chats with the receptionist in quick Italian. I listen in for key words but barely understand anything. When Benito's tone grows harsh and his forehead creases, I know something is wrong. "What's going on?" I ask.

Benito turns to me. "They've gotten the reservation wrong. There's only one room available and the hotel is completely booked."

I swallow hard. I'm so tired from walking all day, all I want is to be off my feet and unconscious. I take out my phone and open up my browser. "Maybe I can find another room nearby," I say.

"No," Benito says. "That's what this man was just telling me, that all the hotels in the area are completely booked because of the *Natale a Roma*."

I have no idea what that is but I'm too tired and now stressed out to care. "Oh, well, I guess we can take the train back to La Musa and skip our plans for tomorrow."

Benito looks at his watch. "The last train would have left by now."

Shit. What are we going to do? Flip for the room and the other will sleep in the street?

"We'll just have to share," Benito says, and I almost choke on air. "Relax," Benito says in response to my sudden coughing fit. "It's two twin beds. We'll be fine."

The receptionist hands us our keys and soon I am outside room 12 on the third floor with Benito. He uses the key to unlock then enters. I follow him, and gasp when I see there is only one double bed in the center of the small, dimly lit room. "I thought we had twins?"

Benito rolls his eyes. “Chill, it’s usually two beds pushed together. We can pull them apart.” He walks over to the far side of the bed. “Help me.”

I grasp the side closest to me. We both start pulling but the bed doesn’t budge. “Maybe if we pull from the middle?” I offer.

Benito inspects the bed, feeling up the top side of it, his forearms flexing. “That won’t work.”

“And why not?” I ask, fixated on his protruding muscles as he yanks down the comforter, exposing the white sheets underneath.

“Because it’s only one bed,” he says.

My heart kicks up a beat. I stare at him blankly. “I’ll go sleep in the Pantheon.”

Benito exhales loudly. “Can you go two seconds without panicking? I’m sure the hotel will fix this for us.”

I look around to the generic wallpaper and a dull painting of a teapot hanging on the wall. It’s a nice place but hardly the type to provide luxury customer service. “This isn’t exactly a five-star resort. It doesn’t come with a butler and a penthouse suite or whatever else you’re used to.”

“With enough cash, you can make anyone your butler,” he swipes back. He looks up at me and smiles softly. I catch myself starting to smile back but quickly put a stop to it. He doesn’t deserve to banter with me. He sighs. “I’ll call down to the front desk. Do what you need to do.”

“You mean leave you alone while you work your rich-boy magic?” I ask.

"No, I mean, you know, bedtime stuff." He looks up at me. "Skincare, pajamas, brush your teeth, whatever girls do."

"You don't brush your teeth?" I ask. He sighs again. I relent. "Ok, ok. I need to shower anyway. And when I come out, there better be another bed in here." He gives me a thumbs-up and I make a mental note to google later if in Italy that gesture is the same as in the U.S. or more akin to the middle finger.

The shower is a spicket in the wall that pours water onto the bathroom floor with a well-placed drain capturing the overflow before it floods. It's not luxurious, but the heat feels good on my body, tired from the day, and I do my best not to think about Benito's forearms as I rub soap up and down mine. Instead, I fixate on the rollaway that Benito will bribe the hotel to send up, crawling into it, and falling fast asleep.

I take my time in the shower, and then more still as I apply my serums and moisturizers, skipping the heavier creams so I look glistening-no-makeup-chic and not shellacked-barefaced-monster. Once my teeth are brushed and flossed, my hair is taken out of my shower bun, and my matching shorts and shirt pajama set is on, I re-emerge into our dinky hotel room.

Unfortunately, there is still only one bed, and unfortunately Benito is lying on it, the TV blaring in Italian.

"Please tell me they're fixing this," I say, hopeful.

Benito looks up at me and his eyebrows shoot up. He says nothing.

"Well?" I ask.

"Oh, um—" He struggles to find his words but appears to snap himself out of whatever daze he's in. "Yeah, no such luck."

"You found the one man in the world who can't be butler-ized?" I ask.

"The correct term is butler-fied," he fires back. "And it was less a cash flow issue and more a lack of resources."

My eyes fall to him on the bed and the small space left for me next to him. Benito jumps up. "You can have the bed, of course. I'll sleep on the floor." He takes a pillow off the bed and throws it on the ground. He does the same to the runner at the end of the bed, even though it's barely long enough to cover him.

The last thing I want is to sleep next to Benito, but I also know he'd hold it over me forever if I let him sleep on the floor. God forbid he tweak his back and I have to hear him complain about it all day tomorrow. "Don't be ridiculous," I say. "We can share a bed for one night." I look at the clock. "It's only for like, what, seven hours anyway."

He glances at the clock as it turns from 11:01 to 11:02. "Six hours and 59 minutes."

A laugh involuntarily erupts out of me. He looks back at me and I swallow it.

"I can sleep on the floor. It's fine," he repeats, softer.

"No, I'm not going to let you sleep on the floor and then spend a day touring Rome."

"Especially since your preferred tour guide has left us," he grumbles.

"Excuse me?" I ask, flames shooting up my face. "Are you mad I brought Giac?" Is that why he's been so pissed off all day? Because I turned our reluctant duo into a slightly less reluctant trio?

He runs his hand through his hair. "No, it's fine. I just only came on this stupid trip because you needed an escort and then you invited someone else."

He crosses his arms over his chest. I soften a little. Oh. "I didn't think about it like that. Sorry. I should've told you not to come once Giac offered."

Benito rolls his eyes. Not placated. "No, that's not—" He stares at the teapot painting like it's the most fascinating work of art in the world and not just an excuse to not look at me. "That's not what I'm saying."

"I ran into Giac this morning and he said he loved Rome, and since you don't know anything about it either I thought he'd make the trip better," I say. "I thought you'd be happy you didn't have to spend all day with me alone."

Benito lets out a half laugh then sucks in a breath like he's embarrassed. He self-consciously glances at me before fixing his gaze onto the floor, rocking back and forth on his feet. "It's ok. I'm sorry if I was rude."

It's quiet for a moment, the only sound the hum of the wind beating against the open window. "You can sleep in the bed, Benito," I say.

Benito doesn't respond, so I walk over to him, pick up his pillow, and put it back on the bed. He watches me carefully. When I don't suddenly change my mind and throw everything back on the floor, he nods. "If you're sure."

I sit on the bed and look at the TV. An episode of *Real Housewives of Orange County* is on, the women screaming at each other in dubbed Italian. I know it well. "You like *Housewives*?" I ask.

"No," Benito says quickly. I raise my eyes at him and he nods sheepishly. "In boarding school, there was this girl who was obsessed. I… had a crush." He sits at the very edge of the bed, as far away from me as possible. "Everyone else was listening to football on the radio or getting drunk or trying to sneak into the girls' dorm, but I'd illegally download episodes of *Real Housewives* on my desktop so I'd have something to talk about with her."

I suppress a laugh. "Did it work?"

Benito shakes his head. "Considering she was my literature teacher, no." The laugh pops out of me and Benito rubs his arm nervously. "Didn't stop me from trying all through year 12, though." I laugh again. Benito relaxes a bit. "Now I can't help it. I find it comforting."

I do my best to move the conversation along fast enough to not be endeared by the image of a young Benito desperately bringing up the latest antics of Vicki Gunvalson to his boarding school teacher. "When I was in Congress, I used to watch it before bed every night. It's the perfect show to unwind and de-stress."

Benito looks up at me, surprised. "Exactly."

We watch silently together until the commercial break. As the show fades out, he turns to me. "I can check again if there's another hotel nearby. Really, it's not a big deal."

I tilt my head back, exasperated. "Oh my god, by the time you'd do that, it'd be morning." I lean back on the bed and point toward the bathroom. "Go do your skincare, your jammies, your nightly affirmations and I'll probably be asleep by the time you're back anyway." A yawn comes out of me as if it's a helpful sidekick.

Convinced, Benito nods, reaches for his bag, and goes into the bathroom.

I turn off the TV and bedside lamp, pull down the comforter on my side of the bed, and lie down. It feels even smaller once I'm inside, and I realize how close Benito's body will be to mine. Mean Benito who thinks I'm unserious. Dorky Benito who utilized his lack of supervision in boarding school to watch *Housewives*. Hot Benito who is hot.

I just need to fall asleep quickly. That shouldn't be too hard. I've been finding sleep easily lately and haven't taken a sleeping pill in over a week. I've slept better than I have in years in the last week. Without the pressures of pursuing my dream, the chaos of getting my dream, and the depression of losing my dream, reaching that coveted REM cycle is easier than ever. I don't even dream at night anymore. It's always pure darkness.

All I need to do now is drift off before Benito gets back. I've shared beds with many people platonically before. This would be no different than that family vacation in San Diego when I shared a bed with my cousin, Michelle. We talked for hours every night before we fell asleep—well, it would be a *little* different than that, but the point stands. This won't be Benito sleeping inches from me. It's Michelle.

I hear the shower turn off and I'm still not asleep. The sink runs for a toothbrush and I am wide awake. A few more minutes pass and the door to the bathroom opens. Benito shuffles around, putting items in his overnight bag before coming back to bed. I keep my eyes shut and pretend to be asleep.

It's just Michelle. It's just Michelle. It's just Michelle.

I feel the warmth of his body as he settles in next to me. We're so close that the edges of his clothes are probably touching mine. What does Benito wear to bed? Is he a long pants and soft button-up kind of guy or is he right here next to me in his boxers and a worn-out T-shirt?

And what is that smell? Pine and lemon. Why does he smell so good?

I have the sudden urge to reach out and touch him. It's probably just the fact that I haven't been this close to someone in a long time. Yes, that's it. It's merely a biological reaction to having a good-looking, good-smelling man in the same bed as me. Of course my animalistic instincts are taking over. Of course there's a sudden swelling of something in my gut. It's natural.

He rolls over and sighs. He must be facing me now, because I feel his cool breath on my neck. My stomach swirls. This is not an ideal time for my latent but ever-present horniness to make an appearance.

"Ugh, you're way too close to me," I say, trying to put a stop to the thoughts. I yank the sheets off of me, throw them over the top of Benito, and roll over on my back. "It's so hot in here. Why doesn't this place have AC?"

He sleepily moves the sheets off of him and they form a barrier of sorts between us. "You have way more room than I do. I'm basically falling off." He turns to his other side, away from me. "I thought you'd appreciate the lack of air-conditioning, since you love embracing Italy's traditions so much."

He kind of has me there. "You're right. I love this. I'm sweaty like Caesar right now. Dying of heat stroke but in a timeless, historical way." I turn my head and notice the outline of his strong shoulders, my face flushes and a bead of sweat drips from my forehead. "Nope. This sucks. I'm miserable. No wonder everyone was so stabby back then."

I think I hear him laugh, but his pillow muffles the noise. "Please don't stab me."

"Don't be so dramatic," I say, sitting up. "Given the limited resources, I'd obviously smother you."

Benito clicks on the bedside lamp and turns to me, and I finally get to size up his bedtime appearance: a worn-out Cambridge T-shirt and soft gray pants, his hair askew from the pillow. He doesn't say anything for a moment, stiffening like he's bracing for impact. Like whatever he's about to say will cause him physical pain. "I don't think you're going to leave because I want you to leave."

I relax. "I'm not actually going to murder you. I saw what happened to Amanda Knox, and she wasn't even guilty. It's the last thing my reputation needs."

He frowns and looks at me seriously. "I'm just being realistic."

I turn so I'm facing him. "But that's just it… you think me leaving is inevitable," I say. "I thought I was starting over, not taking a vacation."

He uses his arm to prop himself up. His forearm flexes and I have to actively force myself to look away. He continues, "Can you really blame me for thinking someone like you wouldn't want to stick around a nothing town like La Musa?"

"Someone like me?" I ask. I put on a valley girl accent, "A dumb, like, American."

Benito shakes his head. "No."

His eyes lock into mine. My heart picks up its rhythm. I try to find my bearings before the stirring can start again. "If you hate La Musa so much, why did you come back?"

He looks down at his hands. "It's—"

"Complicated?" I ask, finishing his sentence. "I know complicated. I also know that you don't walk away from your dream unless you have no other choice."

Benito flits his eyes back at me in recognition. "My father…" he starts. "He was the mayor here for many years. Decades, really. For longer than I can remember." Benito fiddles with the edge of the sheet. "The mayor's home has always been my family's home, and when he left, my mother was going to have to move out. She loves that house. She's too proud to admit it, but to leave would've crushed her even more than she already—"

He trails off but takes a deep breath, regaining his composure. "There was only one solution. I move back and run for mayor. I knew I'd win because I analyzed the data and ran the polls. Now I'm the mayor and she gets to keep living in her house."

My head goes fuzzy and my vision blurs, like my body's trying to rationalize the tremendous sacrifice with the curmudgeonly man I've known the past two weeks. "Benito… that's…"

"Pathetic. A grown man gives up everything he's worked for, his whole life, so his mommy doesn't have to move."

"No. It's… a beautiful and loving thing to do." It turns out Benito and I are alike. We both ended up back in La Musa because it's the only place we can be. "I'm sure your mother would understand if your heart is really in London."

"I don't know that it is," he says, almost laughing. "I don't know where my heart is, where I'm supposed to be or what I'm supposed to do." He rubs his hands against his knees. "And what about you? Where's your heart?"

My mind flashes to the Capitol building, the house in Beachwood, the La Musa clock tower. "I guess I don't know either. Maybe it's still searching for where it feels most at home."

He nods, fixating his gaze on me. We sit there silently, but it's comfortable. Maybe we understand each other. Maybe the friction we felt between us was because I resented Benito for wanting to change La Musa when I am so desperate to return to it exactly as I knew it, and he resents me for having the ability to go anywhere in the world and choosing the place where he feels imprisoned.

Or maybe the friction is caused by something else entirely, and I didn't notice it until our bodies were almost touching. I look down at his hand; it wouldn't take more than a few inches of movement for my fingertips to graze the tops of his. Maybe he's thinking the same thing, because his hand shifts slightly, narrowing the distance between us.

A loud knock startles me.

We both look at the door, but neither of us moves. There's another knock, this time more aggressive. "Maybe your butler's come around?" I ask.

"It's probably the wrong room. Ignore it," he says. Was that an invitation? I try to grasp the bearings of my various limbs. Where are they and where would they be better suited?

The knock returns. I'm closest to the door, so I fling the sheets off me and get up. A hotel worker is standing on the other side, holding a bottle of prosecco. "We want to apologize for the mix-up," she says.

I take the bottle from her. "Thanks."

I'm about to close the door when she stops me. "Wait," she says. "Are you… are you that congresswoman from California?" My blood goes cold. "Congresswoman Rhodes!" she shouts. I nod, barely able to move my head among the sudden ringing in my ears. "I thought so! I study political science at the university. I've watched videos of you."

I nod again. She leans in. "Keep fighting the good fight, ok?"

I nod again, desperate to get back into bed as soon as possible. "I will."

When I close the door, Benito is standing next to the bed. That's not really where I want him to be. Why isn't he waiting in bed for me to resume whatever tension was brewing between us? But then, like a lightning crack in the sky, I remember: London, girlfriend, Sutton.

Sutton.

It was easy to forget about the girlfriend when his skin was so close to mine, but whatever I felt toward Benito moments ago was clearly one-sided. The prickling of my fingertips like a current of electricity running through his body and into mine wasn't real. He has a girlfriend. He's not into me. It wasn't real.

Why are my feelings always so wrong?

"Do you want a glass?" I ask him, shaking off the shame of my delusion and hoping he didn't catch on to my brief but powerful yearning.

Benito smiles smugly. "Interesting how you agreed to keep fighting the good fight."

I start twisting the cork out of the bottle. The faster I can get this popped, the faster we can have a glass and I can forget the humiliation. "Is it?" The cork doesn't budge. "I've never been good at this. Damn it." I twist it with more force.

Benito walks over to me. "It's just interesting how that was your gut reaction when pressed. That you'll keep going, keep fighting." The cork pops and flies out of the bottle, hitting the ceiling then flying across the room. I start toward the empty glasses, but Benito holds on to the bottle, stopping me. "It's almost like you know deep down that you'll be going back."

I stare at him for a moment. Is he so for real right now? I put the bottle down and smash my head into my palms half out of frustration, half for allowing myself to forget why I disliked him so much in the first place. "Oh my god. You're relentless. What else am I supposed to say? No, I won't, actually, nice Italian college student, because I don't care anymore?"

Benito's still smug and I want to crack the bottle over his head. "I'm just saying, it's interesting."

I let my face accurately reflect the rage I feel inside. As a woman, especially a woman in politics, I so often have had to hide how I really feel, but I won't be doing that now. "You have to drop this. I'm not going back to DC. I am going to live in La Musa and work at a flower shop or something and just be happy and fulfilled forever. I'm not going back to my old life. Ever."

My expression must be effectively stormy, because Benito looks like he's about to take cover. He struggles to find his words for a moment, then very evenly starts speaking. "I said the same thing even one year ago, but—"

"I'm not you. I'm not going back." I take the pillow from his side of the bed and toss it on the floor. I do the same with the pathetically thin runner.

Benito shakes his head, admitting defeat, and lies down on the floor. I get back into bed and turn off the bedside lamp. This time, the darkness finds me quickly.

Chapter Seven

Where in the World Is Isabella Rhodes?
By Meredith Pope

After her devastating loss to the newly anointed congressional dreamboat, Levi Cross, no one would blame the former Congresswoman Isabella Rhodes for retreating back to her Los Angeles haven with her tail between her legs, hiding from the public to lick her wounds—especially since she was publicly rejected by said dreamboat. But now enough time has passed that we're starting to worry. There was a time when it seemed like you couldn't change the channel or scroll on TikTok without seeing the face of our horniest member of Congress (although, let's be real, there are probably way grosser members in the male faction, but they have the good sense to keep it offline, or at least distribute airtight NDAs).

Which begs the question, where is Izzy Rhodes? Rumor has it she's no longer staying at her parents' home in the Beachwood Canyon neighborhood of Los Angeles—the very home *Architectural Digest* toured that made the first-term congresswoman appear winningly humble. No, Izzy Rhodes hasn't been spotted at any of her usual local haunts, and her Georgetown studio was vacated just days after her term ended. A request to speak to Congressman Cross was declined, though his PR team told us Mr. Cross has not spoken to Ms. Rhodes. Her last social media post was on January 2nd, the last day of her term. It was a simple photo of Ms. Rhodes outside the Capitol with the caption *"It has been an honor"* and there's been nothing since.

Perhaps she's lying low in the wake of her humiliating sex scandal, or maybe she's waiting to regroup before returning triumphantly to the national stage—but we're hearing all media requests made to her team have gone unreturned. For all intents and purposes, Isabella Rhodes is completely out of the game.

If you, like us, are curious as to her whereabouts, don't worry. We'll be here with the scoop the absolute second she resurfaces.

THE DOOR TO MY BEDROOM CREAKS EVEN AS I TAKE EXTRA care to open it slowly. I've been doing my best to avoid Benito in the two weeks since Rome, but it's really hard when our bedrooms share a wall. He's everywhere all of the time. When I need to brush my teeth, he's in the bathroom. When I'm hungry, he's sitting at the kitchen island on a stool, drinking a cup of coffee. When I want to sit outside and enjoy the view and the spring weather, he's taking a call, pacing from one side of the yard to the other. I've resorted to staying in my room, which isn't hard when all I do lately is watch TV and read the first three chapters of every book I've been meaning to read my entire life, abandoning them when I inevitably lose interest because if I really wanted to know what happens to Bella Swan, I would have read the books years ago.

Which is why I was ecstatic when I ran into Giac at the farmers market yesterday and he invited me to breakfast this morning. It's not the sexiest time of day, but I'm grateful for the excuse to leave the house. I put on a floral midi dress that cinches enough in the middle to outline my waist and with a deep V-neck that gives me way more cleavage than I'm used to or frankly comfortable with having. In my career, my boobs were usually hidden underneath stiff button-ups and a blazer. I've forgotten that it's ok to remind people I have them, especially when meeting up with someone I intend to bone.

I carefully close my bedroom door behind me, waiting to hear the click to know it's shut, and then slowly finagling the rusted iron key into the lock. Just as I think I'm in the clear, Benito's bedroom door flings open. His face goes white when he sees me standing in the hallway. "Jesus," he says. "I didn't hear you out here."

"Then you should get your ears checked, old man," I say, though I still don't know how old Benito is, but I'd guess in the ballpark of my age.

He sizes me up. "Where are you going?"

"To breakfast," I say. I start to walk forward but he's blocking my path. "Can you move?"

His eyes fall to my dress, to my waist, to my cleavage. "Breakfast? By yourself?"

"No," I say, walking around him. The hallway's narrow enough that my arm lightly grazes his as I pass. "I have friends."

He narrows his eyes at me and then laughs. "No, you don't."

"I do. Vincenzo is my friend. *Non mi rompere la scatole,*" I say. "He taught me that." Benito stares at me quizzically. "It means you're annoying me," I clarify.

Benito shakes his head. "I know what it means." He sizes me up again. "So, you're going to breakfast with Vincenzo?"

"Do I need the permission of the lord of the house to leave or something?"

Benito's cheeks flush. "No, of course not." He backs up toward his room. "Have fun."

As we order cappuccinos at Caffè del Duomo, Giac is deep into a lively conversation with Giuseppe, who I didn't know had the ability. I pick up a few words here and there like "Sunday," "customers," and "cost" but am otherwise lost.

Once we get our drinks and *cornetti,* we find a spot on the patio. The morning light hits Giac in such a way that he glows like the cherubs that populate the frescos on La Musa's *duomo*. It's quiet across the piazza, but there's a palpable energy in the air with the warmer weather that's blown in over the past few days. A mother walks with her two daughters in their Sunday bests, both of them skipping and carrying flowers. Just beyond the *duomo,* the slope of the red-tiled rooftops gleams in the sunlight. I snap a picture of Giac because his aesthetically pleasing presence contributes to the overall ambience—and also because Marisol couldn't find him online and she's adamant about getting a visual.

"I'll send it to you," I say. "It's one to post for sure."

He waves it off. "I don't really do social media."

"Really?" I know Giac is only a few years younger than me, but the way he holds his cappuccino with both hands makes him look like an infant nursing a bottle, and I'm suddenly self-conscious about the depleting collagen in my face. "What's it like to be off the grid? I could use some help adjusting to it myself."

Giac laughs. "Not so bad. It helps keep a firm boundary between my students and my personal life. They're all so online all of the time and always asking if they can follow me."

"Smart," I say. "But if you change your mind, you could make a killing in brand deals. TikTok goes crazy for hot teachers." I freeze when I realize I've just called him hot out loud.

I'm not alone in this revelation, because Giac leans in, raising a single eyebrow. "So you like what you see?"

I search for the words, but it's like Giuseppe spiked my espresso with brandy and I feel jumbled.

"Well—" I stop mid-sentence because I notice Anita and Lucia walking toward us. They're beaming.

"Izzy! I thought that was you." Lucia bounces up to us and air-kisses me on both cheeks. Anita follows suit.

"Isabella," says Anita, "I've barely seen you."

She's being generous, because in actively avoiding Benito, I have been de facto avoiding her. "*Mi dispiace,* I um, haven't been feeling well." I hope the attempt at a fractured Italian apology will be enough to win me back her favor.

It must've worked, because Anita is smiling. "Not to worry. We shall catch up over Sunday lunch today."

All the blood rushes to my heart. I'd forgotten it's Sunday. The idea of spending an afternoon with Benito makes me want to flee the country. "Oh, that's so kind, but unfortunately I can't make it today." I look to Giac. "I wouldn't want to rush the plans I've made with Giac here." I gesture to him. "Have you met Giacomo DeLuca? He teaches at the secondary school."

"Giac DeLuca, of course. I've known your aunt for years, God help me. You must come to lunch too," Anita says. "I'm embarrassed you haven't received an invitation before. My son is the mayor now, and he should've invited you already." She mutters under her breath, "Rude boy."

Lucia interjects, "You must come. We'd love to have you."

Giac grins like a child on Christmas morning. I shoot him a look, but he doesn't pick up on my hesitancy. "I'd love to come," he says.

I swallow in hopes of keeping the rage fire in my chest that burns only for Benito from reigniting. "I guess we'll see you there."

I greet Giac at the door and lead us to the backyard. There are more people milling about than the last two weeks when it was just me, Anita, and a Benito who ate quickly and left early. I see Anita, Lucia, a handsome olive-skinned man corralling two young children who I presume to be Lucia's husband and kids, Vincenzo, Valeria, two bored-looking tweens, and of course, Benito.

I swallow my pride and walk over to him. He's chatting with Vincenzo.

"*Ciao,* Izzy!" Vincenzo enthusiastically embraces me in a hug and double air-kiss. "How wonderful to see you outside of the workweek! Sunday suits you, my dear." He looks off toward the tweens. "Beatrice, Antonia, come meet Izzy from California."

The tweens don't look up and stay engaged in their private, sullen conversation. Valeria, as wispy and elegant as ever, saunters over. "Ah, Izzy, so good to see you again." She air-kisses me and looks to Giac. "And Giac! You two are here together?" Valeria raises her eyebrows suggestively. Benito's eyes dart over to us, shifting back and forth between the two of us.

"We were getting breakfast together," I say, loud enough that Benito can hear. "And Anita generously invited Giac to come for lunch."

"Well, I am delighted you are both here." She turns to Vincenzo. "Speaking of invitations, why have you not yet invited Izzy over for dinner?"

"My love, she is a young woman without children, she does not want to dine with us."

Valeria fires back at Vincenzo in rapid Italian and he matches her vigor.

After their bickering subsides, I chime in, "I'd love to have dinner with all of you."

"Izzy is from Hollywood, you know," says Vincenzo. "Maybe we can even get our daughters to engage with a guest."

Valeria huffs then looks over at her children. "Antonia, Beatrice." After another ceremonious eye roll, they finally walk over. "Say hi to Signor DeLuca and meet Izzy. She came all the way here from California."

"*Buongiorno*, Beatrice," Giac says. The taller girl, with thick black hair like Valeria's and six layers of eyeliner, smiles shyly.

"Hollywood," says Vincenzo. "Neighbor to the stars."

"Well, Beachwood Canyon if we're being precise," I correct him. "But my parents live down the street from Charlie Chaplin's old house." By the looks on their faces, this is not an impressive anecdote to two Italian tweens.

"Do you know Tom Holland?" the littler one, Antonia, asks.

"Um… no. I don't."

Antonia rolls her eyes and the two walk away.

"Horrible girls," Valeria mutters.

"Giac," Benito bellows, his first utterance in the time we've been out here. "So nice of you to join us today."

"I had a late dinner, so I stayed the night," Giac says, looking to me. "Plus, it was a good excuse to make more time with Izzy this morning."

Benito's brow furrows and he looks from Giac to me and back again. "A late dinner and you couldn't take the early train back?"

Giac nods. "Well, I had breakfast plans, so I figured I should stay." He smiles at me, not sensing Benito has channeled Sherlock Holmes in his line of questioning.

"And after this late dinner you slept…?" Benito's talking to Giac, presumably, but he's looking at me.

I performatively roll my eyes. Giac looks between me and Benito, picking up on the weirdness. "I slept on my *zia* Paola's couch."

"Oy, poor boy," Valeria says.

Vincenzo does the sign of the cross. "Next time, my boy, you stay with us."

Valeria grins. "Or even with Izzy!"

Benito glares at her.

"Is it time for lunch?" I ask, desperate for a respite from the conversation at hand.

As if on cue, Anita clinks her fork to a wine glass. "Lunch is served, assuming my children help me bring it all out." Benito grunts and dutifully follows his mother into the kitchen. Lucia, with one of her children on her hip, motions for her husband to join him.

We sit, and Anita brings platters of food as per usual. She sets a vat of *pasta al pomodoro* right in front of me. "For our vegetarian," she says with a wink. I dive in, ignoring any semblance of mealtime decorum, and once again get swept away by the perfect balance of flavors in Anita's cooking.

"Izzy, Vincenzo, Valeria, you must tell me," Lucia starts, "how is my brother as a mayor?"

"*Dio Mio,* Lucia. They are not here to discuss something so boring." Benito rolls his eyes and pours himself a glass of wine.

"I do not mean to have a full performance review, I just want to know how he's adjusting to life back in Italy." Her littlest kid, who can't be more than two, starts fussing, and Lucia effortlessly pulls him into her lap. "I worry about him being so far from his beloved London."

"He does quite well. *Non preoccuparti.*" Vincenzo tucks his napkin into his shirt collar as he piles pasta onto his plate. "He's a tough but fair ruler." Vincenzo starts laughing. "No, no, I kid! But he is doing a fine job. And it helps that he has this one to, how you say, keep him in line at home." He points at me.

"Who? Me?" I say. "I don't think that's true."

Lucia's eyes widen in delight. "Ah, he has a woman to keep him on his toes. He'll do just fine, then."

Benito rolls his eyes again.

"My son has always loved women. Always appreciated a strong woman," Anita starts. Benito turns bright red and I stifle a laugh. I have yet to feel appreciated, but maybe it's because Benito does not see me as strong. Anita continues, "Ever since he was a little boy—women at the *mercato,* little girls on the playground, he had to copy exactly what they were doing."

"*Mamma*—"

"Oh, is that right?" I ask, knowing this is killing Benito. "And are you sure it was out of appreciation and not fear?"

Benito turns to me with a glum expression that almost takes the joy out of the moment.

"My, my Isabella, I am sure it is both," Anita says with a hearty laugh.

"Oh, don't make that face, *Benitino,*" Lucia says, waving her hand. "We tease because we love. Besides, all this has made you in shape to be a perfect man for Sutton."

I feel a chill of guilt trickle down my spine, then embarrassment. Sutton. I hate the reminder that the rush I felt when I was in bed with Benito in Rome, my skin mere centimeters from his, was one-sided, solo longing.

I look up to see Benito staring right at me. Does he know?

"Speaking of," Lucia continues, "when will this mysterious British goddess be gracing us with her presence? Six months is a long time to go with no visit."

"You haven't seen your *fidanzata* in six months?" Valeria asks.

Vincenzo nearly does a spit-take. "I have not spent more than a few hours away from Valeria since the day we met." He shoots Valeria a loving glance.

"*Papà,* don't tell people that." A horrified Beatrice hides her face in her hands.

Vincenzo ignores her. "My boy, this is not acceptable."

"He went to see her a few months ago, but she does not come here," Lucia says with a hefty amount of side-eye.

"The one girl in all the world who hates Italy," Anita mutters.

Benito drains his wine glass and pours himself another. "It is hard for her to leave work. I have told you this."

Anita leans back in her chair. "And we are supposed to love her when she cares more about work than my son."

"Benito," Vicenzo starts, "you must insist. We all need to meet her and make sure she's good enough for our lionhearted mayor." He turns to me. "Lionhearted… did I use that right?"

"Yes, although I'm not sure I agree with the sentiment—"

"Yes, bring her here," Giac adds. "Maybe we can go on a double date." He looks at me and smiles. I didn't realize we were anywhere near the "planning future dates" phase of this mild flirtation, but I sense he's merely contributing to the spirited teasing.

Lucia lights up. "Yes! Oh my god, just picture the four of you together: the perfect picture of the future of La Musa."

Benito slams his glass onto the table, and it makes a considerable thud. Wine splashes out and everyone grows quiet. Realizing the drama of what he's just displayed, Benito sighs and starts to blot the wine with his napkin. Thankfully it's *pinot bianco* and won't stain. "Sorry," he grunts.

He gets up from the table. "Sorry," he says again before walking inside the house.

"He has a hot head," Lucia says, waving it off like it's nothing. "He does not like to be teased about Sutton. He just needs to cool down."

"Ah, like that Tom Holland," says Vincenzo. Everyone looks at him, confused. "Beatrice, Antonia, you always talk about how hot his head is." I wonder if he's confused on the translation, but the sparkle in his eyes as both his daughters shoot him a horrified expression confirms otherwise.

"*Papà*," they yell in unison.

The conversation returns to its normal flow, and everyone continues eating. I clear my plate and Benito does not return. I pour myself a second glass of wine, no Benito. Anita brings out dessert. Still he's not back. There's a pit in my stomach that I realize is concern. Halfway through my *tiramisù*, I excuse myself to use the restroom.

I hear the voices outside switch to Italian as I enter the house, and I feel a pang of guilt to know they were only speaking English on my account.

The first-floor bathroom is down the hall toward the front of the house, but I duck my head into each room I pass, looking for Benito. He's not in the formal living room, the study, the parlor—or at least I think that's what that's called—the other living room, his father's office, or the kitchen. I peek my head out the front windows to make sure there's no one brooding on the stoop.

The grand marble staircase seems to be beckoning

me upstairs, luring me in with its dancing light and smiling family photos. I take a quick look around to make sure that no one else has followed me inside and ascend to the second floor.

I've done my best to keep to my end of the hallway, and it would be invasive for me to open every single one of the solid wood doors that line the hallway—what if there's something I don't want to see? Maybe Benito has Sutton locked up in a room, chained to her bed like a scene fresh out of a modern-day *Jane Eyre*.

I see that the door on the other side of Benito's room is open. I always assumed the rest of the hall was filled with more bedrooms, quarters for guests and maids from back when the house was built. I walk toward it.

I see him before I even reach the room. He's hunched over a writing desk, scribbling in a leather-bound journal. I wonder if I should turn around and leave him alone. After all, Lucia said he needed time to cool off, but did he really need more than 10 minutes to recover from mild to moderate mocking?

The old wood floor creaks and Benito looks up, understandably surprised to see me walking toward him. "What are you doing here?"

I freeze. It's a good question. What exactly *am* I doing here? I entered the house clear on my intent to find him, but I hadn't settled on a mission statement. "I don't know," is all I can say.

"If my sister sent you—"

"She didn't." I survey the rest of the room. It's large with vertical windows lining the south-facing wall, but empty. Other than the writing desk, a tiny bookshelf next to it, and an armchair, there's no other furniture in the room. The walls are blank. "What is this room?"

"My office."

"It's empty."

"Sorry, I wasn't expecting any guests." His eyes narrow. "Why are you in here?"

I collapse into the armchair. It's old-looking with an outdated green paisley-patterned fabric and its cushion's thinned to the point where I can feel the frame of the chair underneath. "This is not comfortable."

"Izzy…" He turns in his chair to face me, and I have to confront the true reason why I followed him up here.

"You were upset. I wanted to make sure you were ok." The words leave my lips before I have a chance to double-check that they're true. The way my stomach settles when his face relaxes into a smile confirms to me that they are.

"I'm fine. I just needed a break," he says.

"You don't like to be teased?" I let the corners of my mouth turn upward in his presence for the first time in days.

"No, I like to think I can handle myself in such situations." The corners turn even more upward. "It's not that." He looks down and twiddles with his fingers.

"What is it, then?" I ask, with a sinking feeling it might be something like *I miss my girlfriend terribly and the mere mention of her, the love of my life, makes me fall into a deep depression as I only have eyes for her.* Not that it would matter to me.

"Things with Sutton are complicated," he says.

Complicated because her beauty is beyond that of human comprehension or *complicated in that she has had an unfortunate breakdown and rather than get her the help she so needs I have locked her in the attic?* "Complicated?"

"We broke up."

His eyes flit up and lock with mine. I take a sharp inhale to keep myself from reacting outwardly. He smiles, resigned, which releases a flurry of butterflies in my stomach. "What?" is all I can muster.

"When I left London, we said we'd take a break, and I went back three months ago to call it off officially." He leans back in his chair and rolls up the sleeves of his button-down to his elbows. There's a flutter somewhere south of my waist at the sight of his forearms, but I try to block it out. The air feels thick suddenly, and I struggle to heave in a breath.

"Why is it a secret?" I ask once I can speak again, my voice coming out as barely a whisper.

He sighs, reaching his hand out toward the door and pushing it closed. Though everyone's outside, it feels as though we're truly alone for the first time since Rome. He scoots his chair closer to me, the edges of his knees brushing against mine. "If my mother knew I broke up with her to move here, she'd blame herself." He lowers his voice as though the solid oak door and the 3,000 square feet between us and his family is not enough of a barrier. "So I pretend I'm still dating her."

I'm not a fan of this trend where I find out I misjudged Benito and he's actually a selfless angel who deserves to be sainted and not a pompous curmudgeon. Or at least, I try to convince myself I don't like it, when really any evidence that he's a compassionate, loving human being makes me want to reach out and touch him.

To my own appalment, I place a hand on his knee. Benito looks at my hand and then quickly back to me, his eyebrows arched high. I pull away. "That's incredibly kind. But it's been half a year, I'm sure she'd understand."

Benito leans forward so I get a whiff of that pine and lemon scent, which upon further investigation in our shared bathroom, I've learned is his body wash. "She'd never say it in front of company, but she feels terrible that I came back. She thinks I did it for her, not because I wanted to, and it kills her." He rubs his left forearm with his right hand, and it takes every ounce of mental strength to focus on his words. "I just have to make enough of a life for myself here for her to believe me and then I'll tell her."

"Can't you tell Lucia?" I ask. "It's not fair that you have to keep up appearances with your entire family." I *want* him to tell her, I realize. I want someone else to know that Benito is not in love with Sutton. It's become as important to me as making sure Benito was ok after he stormed out of lunch, though I don't know why.

Benito smirks. "I'm sure she would be thrilled, but Lucia cannot keep a secret for more than one glass of wine."

Benito is not with Sutton. Benito is single. The confounding attraction I felt for him that night in Rome may not have been one-sided after all. I let my eyes fall into his and I wonder if he can see the realization as it dawns over me. The longer we hold eye contact, the more his face softens. I flash a quick smile at him, my guilt for what transpired in Rome assuaged. Benito's chest heaves and I'm sure if I were to touch a finger to his wrist, I'd feel his quickened pulse, beat-for-beat with mine. A door shuts downstairs, startling us both, but we still remain sitting there, eyes locked. "I'm sure you want to get back to your guest," Benito says, his voice small.

I look to him, confused.

"Giac," he clarifies.

My face falls. Giac. "Oh, yes. Of course." I stand up and he gestures for me to lead the way back downstairs.

Before I exit the room, he grabs my hand to stop me. It's the smallest of touches and yet my entire body stirs in response.

"Izzy," he says, not letting go of my hand. "Thank you."

Chapter Eight

"I CANNOT HAVE SEX WITH BENITO," I INSIST TO MARISOL on FaceTime later that night after explaining the events of the day. It's 9 p.m. and I'm exhausted, but I'm restlessly doing laundry in the small room tucked into the bottom corner of the villa in a desperate attempt to take my mind off Benito.

She's not buying it, giving me her signature look that roughly translates to *you and I both know you're being stupid*. Despite the fact that she's currently on a treadmill at the gym, no doubt with her phone propped up by her work laptop or a hundred-page bill, I can see her crystal clear. "You absolutely can."

"I have to think about the long-term." I pace around the tiny space. "I live with him, and this is a small town. If things get weird, it'll make everything weird. Or worse, the humiliation will drive me out of town and prove he was right to think I'll leave."

Marisol hops off the treadmill and moves to the elliptical. I see her pumping arms duck in and out of the screen. "You're being too puritanical about it. You're in Italy. I'm sure Benito has slept with thousands of girls."

The thought of that makes me queasy. "Don't you think that's a little reductive, Mari?"

Her arms stop suddenly, and she looks to the camera in shock. "Wait, was that racist?" She shakes her head. "I've been hanging out with too many congressmen."

"I don't want to be just another notch in Benito's bedpost."

"Oh my god, Izzy. You're over 30. Use a man for sex. Who gives a fuck?" I let out a guffaw, but she continues, "You want to tear his clothes off, right? So do it. Consensually, of course. You're used to being overly cautious and private when it comes to the people you want to have sex with, but you don't have to do that anymore. Stop thinking and let your horny self take over."

I let her words wash over me. Following my horny self has never led me anywhere good before, but it's becoming harder and harder to fall asleep at night knowing Benito and his forearms are just a wall away. I shudder. These are the exact thoughts that got me in trouble with Levi. I may never lust again.

"Are you thinking about Levi right now?" Marisol asks, her arms on the move again.

"No," I lie.

Marisol glares at me through the screen. "I hate that he made an entire nation slut-shame you, but this is not the same."

"I don't know," I say. "With Giac the stakes seem lower, but with Benito it feels too sticky to try and throw romance into the mix."

"It's not romance, Izzy. It's sex. You can have one without the other. You're hot, he's hot, why not bang it out? You hate each other, right? It's bound to be good."

My stomach churns because I don't know what I feel for Benito, but I know I wouldn't describe it as hate. Regardless, Marisol might have a point. Random hookups were a no-go when I was in Congress, but the same rules don't apply here. The problem is, Benito isn't random. Whether I like it or not, he's in my life indefinitely.

"It doesn't matter. It's not like I can just knock on his bedroom door in a trench coat with nothing underneath."

"You absolutely can."

"His mom is here!"

Marisol gives me the look again. She opens her mouth to speak but gets distracted. "Ugh, the speaker is calling me. Can I call you back later? Or better yet, call Benito."

I shake my head. "Call me. I'm sure I'll be up."

The washer beeps and I gather the next load of clothes from my room. Maybe Marisol is right, or maybe I want her to be right. What was the point in coming here in the first place if I live my life in the exact same way I always have? It's not like I have a reputation to protect anymore, and while the mayor with the new American lady might become town gossip, it's not like it'd be a national scandal.

Then again, it's worthwhile to consider the social ramifications of sleeping with your peer and roommate. No, it's too much to risk. My original intent was to come here and live an easy life free from complications. I can't sabotage my standing in a country because of my lofty personal goals again.

I reach my hand into the washer and yelp when I feel a shock. I check to make sure the washer's cycle has fully completed and try again: another zap. I jump backward in fear. My hand tingles from the electricity.

The washer is different than what I'm used to back home, but I thought I followed the directions Anita gave me exactly. I google instructions and make sure the dials are lined up exactly as it shows in the diagram I find online. The words are smushed so closely together it's hard to be certain. I almost reach again a third time but think better of it, conjuring up a foreshadowed image of me lying unconscious on the floor.

Unclear on what I do next, I stare at the open washer and my wet clothes that are prisoners inside. I guess I'll have to tell Vincenzo in the morning, unless—

I mean, I could go find Benito. It would make sense for me to go tell Benito. This is, after all, his house. Technically, he's my logical first call in case of emergency. It's not like I know the number of a mechanic. I could wait until tomorrow.

I mean, I *could* wait until tomorrow.

But by then my yellow sundress would be wrinkled beyond recognition. And I'm down to my last pair of clean underwear.

I walk back upstairs and dart into my room to change my clothes. I'm in pajamas, and despite the fact that we spent an entire night together, I feel self-conscious. I parse through the scant options for clean clothes and pull out a sweatshirt that says *Hollywood* across the chest. It's one of those kitschy drugstore souvenirs that my dad bought me as a joke when I left for DC but it's surprisingly comfortable and covers the fact that all my bras are currently inside the washer.

I knock on his bedroom door. There's no sound of movement inside. Maybe he's out. He said he broke up with Sutton, but he could have a new lover that's more geographically convenient. I knock again and after a few moments, the door swings open.

"Izzy? Are you alright?" Benito is bleary-eyed. He's wearing that old Cambridge shirt again and a pair of blue checkered pajama pants. Was he asleep?

"Yeah." I look at the time; it sounds like I've woken him up but it's only 9:30. "Sorry. Um, it's not an emergency, but the washing machine shocked me, and I guess I got a little spooked and wanted to see if you could come fix it, which I realize is ridiculous because you're not a mechanic—"

"I can help you."

"It's ok, I think I overreacted."

"You were shocked?" he asks.

"Yeah. Twice."

Benito walks out of his room and down the stairs. I follow him as he pulls a red toolbox out of a hall closet and six different Damsel in Distress fantasies flash through my head like an R-rated View-Master.

We make it back to the laundry room and he examines the dials. "So, what happened exactly?"

"I reached inside to pull out my clothes and it shocked me. Twice."

Benito finicks with the dials for less than a minute. "It wasn't all the way off."

"What?"

He turns both dials all the way to the left. The machine whirs off and the lights on the top of it go dark. "It's an old machine, and it's finicky. It has to turn all the way off before you retrieve your laundry." He reaches into the open door of the washer and pulls out my yellow sundress. He reaches in again but thinks better of it. "I'll let you do the rest."

"Thanks. Wouldn't want you to come face-to-face with my unmentionables." I think I see him blush a little and I cringe at myself. I reach into the washer but hesitate, my body still traumatized from the earlier shocks.

Benito watches me as I try and fail again. "It really got you, huh?"

"Not too bad, but I had a vision of me going all Ben Franklin's kite with the key, so I'm a little hesitant."

"Ben Franklin's kite?" Benito asks.

"You know… when he discovered electricity."

He sighs. "Did he really? Or is that another myth of American exceptionalism that you were told as a kid?"

"Oh shit, is it?"

Benito takes his hand and waves it in and out of the front of the washer. "You'll be fine, I promise."

I finally muster up the courage and pull out a pair of jeans at the top of the pile. I do a little curtsey after I escape shock free. "Success."

"You did it." Benito walks over to his unused toolbox and picks it up. "Happy to be of service."

Panic rips through me as he starts heading to the door. I need to act on the horniness now if I'm ever going to. "Leaving so soon?" I blurt out. Benito turns back to me, his expression twisted into a question mark. I quickly think up an excuse. "It's just… I feel bad, I woke you up for nothing."

"Sunday lunches are exhausting, and I tend to nod off early. It's ok."

"Do you want a glass of wine or something?" I ask. Benito studies me as if he's waiting for me to rescind the offer any second. "I know it's late, but…"

Benito nods. "I suppose one glass couldn't hurt."

He awkwardly stands in the middle of the kitchen while I struggle to open a bottle I was chilling in the fridge from Valeria's wine shop, my hands shaky from the nerves. "Sorry again for waking you up for nothing," I say, handing him a glass. I take a sip of the glass I poured for myself before gesturing for us both to sit at the kitchen table.

Benito sits in the chair next to me. "It's ok. I've been learning light maintenance for my tenants, so it's good practice."

I turn to him. "Tenants?"

"You know the blue building with the white shutters next to the *panetteria*?" he asks. I nod. "I own it."

"Wow," I say. "You own a building?"

He blushes a little, looking down. "I do."

"Cool," I say, trying to parse out why he seems so embarrassed to own a 600-year-old building. "What's wrong?"

"Nothing." He shakes his head. "It's just... my father gifted it to me. I always intended to sell. There were interested entities, but I never pulled the trigger."

"Your dad bought you a building?" I ask.

"I wanted a Bop It! but that wasn't really his style."

I gasp. "Oh my god, I forgot about Bop It! It was kind of sad to play as an only child. When it said 'pass it' and I would keep playing by myself, I felt like I was cheating." He glances at me rambling with mild amusement. I scoot my chair a little bit closer to him, the squeak of the wooden leg on the tile floor making the moment way less nonchalant than I was hoping. "Sorry. Your dad."

"My dad. His family is in the real estate business, so I think it was his way of trying to give me a taste for it. I would help him with maintenance calls whenever I was home as a kid, so I've grown to be somewhat handy, but there's still a lot for me to learn."

The Damsel in Distress fantasies re-emerge but I quickly shove them down. "When you said your father was mayor of La Musa for so many years, I assumed he gave up the family business."

He shakes his head. "He tried to have it both ways, surely to impress his own father."

"He was the mayor of the town and also trying to buy up the town."

"Exactly." Benito drains his wine glass. "In the past decade he had big plans to modernize but he was too focused on… other things for it to come to fruition."

"Is that why he left?" I ask.

Benito rolls the stem of his empty wine glass between his thumb and index finger. "The other things? Yes."

He stiffens and I get the sense he doesn't want to share. I may not know much about the art of seduction, but I'm pretty sure you're not supposed to interrogate your target about their father. "You don't have to tell me—"

"He had a woman. In Milan." He turns to me with a surrendered smile. "Well, *has* a woman in Milan, I should say. He's been with her for the past six months. Since he left my *mamma*."

I feel my face drop and my heart follows. "Benito, that's awful. That must've been really hard."

"For 20 years." The breath leaves my lungs. I try to put myself in his shoes. What would I do if I found out one of my parents… no, the thought is too dark to follow. It would destroy me. He shrugs, setting his glass down on the coffee table. "It confirmed what I always knew in the back of my mind. That he's not a good man."

"And your mom—"

The muscles on Benito's face tighten. "She pretends it's not happening. We're all pretending he doesn't exist for her sake."

"You shouldn't have to pretend your father doesn't exist." I instinctively rest a consoling hand on his shoulder.

He shakes it off. "I can't imagine a world where I'll ever speak to him again, so I don't see what difference it makes."

"Of course. I just mean, it must be hard for you too."

His eyes grow dark, and I find myself instantly missing their usual luster. "I wasn't here. I barely spent time with him. It's my mother who suffers. I don't get to—" He pauses, taking a breath. "It's not for me to feel anything but for her."

We're quiet for a moment. I'm at a loss for how to get this conversation to go in the direction I want. How does one be sexy amidst personal crises? "Well, you'll live here and be mayor and watch La Musa thrive again without any modernization whatsoever."

Benito laughs.

"I'm serious," I say.

"Look at this place," he says, pointing around. "Would it really be so bad to replace it with something newer?"

I look at the old stucco walls and the shutters, worn from years of keeping out the sun. It's not new, sure, but it has character. "My apartment in LA was one of those so-called luxury buildings with gray laminate fake-wood floors, eggshell walls, and brand-new appliances, but it was stagnant there. It had no energy, no character. It never felt warm or homey. My parents live in an old house in the hills above Hollywood that was built in the 1920s and it exudes history and story."

I lean back in my chair. "This place is like that, but its story is hundreds of years longer. The same is true with everywhere else in town. You can't tear that down. You can't—" I think of the anti-capitalist anthems that were part of the soundtrack of my childhood. The classic '70s vinyl my dad used to play for me, recorded just roads away from where I grew up. The protests they'd take me to in the hot sun that energized me as a kid. The moments that first inspired my life's path. I shift in my seat, taking a sip of wine. "I sound like my dad."

Benito laughs. "I'm familiar with the feeling."

I let out a huff, rubbing my temples with my fingertips. "Oh god. Is it unavoidable? Are we turning into our parents?"

I put my head on the table dramatically, which makes Benito laugh again. "I'm one mistress away, I think," he says, waving his hand in front of him.

I laugh, looking up at him. "Fortunately for me, I broke the cycle, because I don't think either of my parents ever had a sex scandal."

He laughs harder; it's loud and boisterous, echoing off the vaulted ceiling. I don't think I've ever seen so much joy on his face. Interesting, considering the source is me. Maybe I'm the one who brings this side out of him. I take a deep breath, pushing out that dangerous thought.

Benito's smile fades. "My father wanted to upgrade several buildings in town; he was in talks with several franchise businesses to convince them to move to La Musa. He was certain this place could thrive again if he made the tough but right calls. I'm starting to wonder if I'll have to do the same."

"Are things that bad financially?"

"Worse," Benito says. "In small towns like this, tourism is everything. We don't produce enough of anything else to make it boom economically." Benito stands and takes his wine glass, putting it next to the sink.

"I see." I follow him and do the same, because I can't quickly think of a reason to convince him to sit back down with me. He reaches for the toolbox off the kitchen counter. "Are you calling it a night?" I ask.

His eyebrows shoot up his face and he turns to me. "It's late. I figured—"

"You don't have to," I say. He continues to stare at me blankly with his hand still halfway toward the handle of the box. "I mean, if you don't want to."

"Should I not?" he almost whispers. I take in a sharp breath and take a step toward him. Benito stands up straight, the fight with whether or not to pick up his tools and leave apparently surrendered.

My eyes meet his and I try to read his expression. Is it nervous anticipation that matches mine or fear that his adversary is about to cross a line?

As if he's heard the question himself, he puts a

hand on my shoulder and runs it down my arm until he's grasping my hand in his. There's a dizzying feeling in my head that threatens to knock me down, but I feel safe knowing I'd fall directly into his arms. Every inch of me feels warm from the heat of his presence.

"Don't you hate me or something?" he asks, his voice small.

"I can overlook that," I say. He studies me for a moment, then squeezes my hand. My insides melt knowing there's a possibility of so much more contact to come. Benito opens his mouth to say something.

My phone rings.

My phone rings.

"Should you get that?" he asks.

"No, it's probably my friend Marisol. We were talking earlier, and she said she'd call back, but it's fine." It stops ringing for a moment only to start back up again immediately. "I'll silence it," I say, reaching for it. I almost drop it face-first on the ground when I see the name flashing on my screen.

Levi.

"Oh my god."

Levi. Why is Levi calling me?

"Is something wrong?" Benito asks.

"No," I say. "It's no one." I silence my phone and slide it into my pocket, but the energy of the moment is gone. I feel tears start to gather in the corners of my eyes and I want to scream. I'm so angry that the mere idea of Levi contacting me can elicit such a reaction.

The stirring in my body picks up at the thought of him leaving me here alone. "Benito."

His eyes land on me and I study them. There's some kind of puzzle he's working out. Some riddle he can't quite find the answer for, and I have a sinking feeling it's me. "No, I should go to bed." He points to the phone. "You should talk to your friend."

His back is to me and he's out of the room by the time I have my phone in my hand. I hear his footsteps start up the stairs as I stare at my phone screen. There's a text from Levi now, like he knows it'd be harder to ignore than a phone call, and he's never been one for leaving a voicemail. I debate deleting it without reading but my curiosity gets the best of me.

Levi: Isabella—can we chat? Need your thoughts on something.

It's fairly innocuous in the grand scheme of things. He was always asking for my thoughts throughout our decade-long friendship whether it was on the best way to organize a clothing drive after a wildfire or whether or not Father John Misty's latest album was as good as his last. But we are not friends anymore. And I am not going to let Levi Cross pretend otherwise.

I delete the message and block his number.

Chapter Nine

HOT. I NEED TO LOOK HOT AS HELL, I TYPE INTO MY translator app. The helpful sales manager has patiently waited while I stumble through the language barrier. Most people in La Musa speak at least some English, but she seems to know zero. Which is fine. I'm the one who's a foreigner, but it's been over a month in and so far, my Italian language skills consist solely of the phrases my language learning app teaches me and random idioms from Vincenzo. And I haven't yet gotten to the level where I learn how to ask the shopkeeper where she keeps the sluttiest lingerie.

Benito's been avoiding me since our late-night rendezvous a week ago. He leaves for work early in the morning before I wake up and returns well after dinner. While I've been enjoying being Anita's de facto child in his absence, I'm annoyed too. The idea that he regrets our almost… whatever moment, makes me regret it too. My original instincts to avoid anything more than cordiality with Benito were right. I need to focus on being unattached and unemotional.

I point at a skimpy nightie with lace trim. "More?" I ask the shopkeeper. When I was last in La Musa, me and the other girls used to come into this shop just to admire the pretty intimates, but when you're 19 you don't really need lingerie to seduce a guy. I guess you never really *need* it, but if I'm going to get the confidence to finally go for it with Giac, I'm going to have to know I look good under my clothes.

We find an understanding between my shoddy Italian and her exaggerated pantomiming, and I go into the fitting room to try on several pieces. First, an all-black lace bodysuit with cutouts on the boobs and between my legs. It looked elegant on the hanger, but on my short torso, I look like a kid wearing a worn-out swimsuit. Next, a red matching lace bra and thong. The bra looks good, but the thong is made of so little fabric, there'd be nothing to suck in my love handles underneath my dress. A bright blue teddy looks like the sorority girl version of a Violet Beauregarde costume. A silky green negligee makes me look like I'm one of Santa's helpers. And a pink corset makes it seem like I'm trying to seduce a viscount.

I put my regular clothes back on and exit the fitting room. In the main store area, I see Valeria chatting with the salesclerk. I try to quickly put my items back before she notices me but I'm not fast enough. "Izzy!" she says, waving.

I shove everything onto one hook as she walks over to me. "Valeria, hi."

She speaks in Italian to the other woman, and I hear my name. The woman smiles at me. "Izzy," Valeria says, "this is Francesca."

I wave at her shyly. "*Piacere.*"

"We were just discussing the town news, have you heard?" she asks. I shake my head. Valeria continues, "Apparently there's a big project in the works to completely change La Musa." She shakes her head disapprovingly. My heart sinks. Benito must be going through with his father's ideas. "If it happens, several of our existing businesses will have to close."

"Wait, really?" I ask.

Valeria nods. "Well, our leases would end, as the company doing the work owns the buildings. Some of these leases are 50 years old or more." Valeria sighs. "We could move, but where would we move to? It's not like there's other space available."

I say a quick prayer of thanksgiving that I did not sleep with Benito the other night. If what Valeria is saying is true, my original assessment of him is correct and he super sucks. It doesn't matter that I've seen his softer side—I've been blinded by horniness before. "The wine shop would have to close?"

Valeria sighs again. "It seems like it, yes. And the worst part is, whether intentional or not, the development affects mostly the women-owned businesses in town."

My gut boils. Sexist. Benito is also sexist. "That's completely unfair," I say.

"Completely," Valeria agrees.

"Is there anything we can do?" I ask.

"That's what Francesca and I were just discussing," Valeria says. "Us two and the other women affected are gathering at Bar Musa later this week to figure out a game plan."

My brain sparks. It's a familiar feeling, like when I learned the girls' soccer team at Fairfax High had to practice on the baseball fields, which don't even get watered in the off-season. It's like I hear an injustice happening, and my body's natural response is to spring into action. I take a deep breath. I need to stay out of this. It doesn't involve me. "Maybe I can help," my mouth spits out despite my brain's insistence on staying neutral.

Valeria perks up. "Oh, Izzy, you're too kind. I will let you know if there's something you can do."

"No, seriously," I say. My larynx and pharynx and vocal cords are apparently on a separate mission from my consciousness. "I have… experience in community organizing, and I could really help."

Valeria lights up. "We could use someone with experience. Definitely come, then," she says.

She gives me the details and we say our goodbyes. I pull the matching red set off the rack and pay for it. Giac will just have to deal with my love handles.

I take the initiative and invite Giac to dinner when I see him at the *caffetteria* the next morning. He excitedly says yes, and suggests we meet up that night at Ristorante Claudio. When I walk in wearing a loose but low-cut black maxi dress, my red set underneath, I remember it's one of the few truly upscale places in La Musa. White tablecloths, dim lighting, and live, inoffensive jazz greet us as we walk in. It's also uncharacteristically packed, and Giac must have an in with the staff, because we're quickly ushered to the last free table in the center of the restaurant.

A bottle of wine and an order of *arancine* quickly arrive at the table. "They like you here, Giac," I say.

Giac shrugs it off. "I've been here a lot over the years. Best carbonara in all of Italy right here if you can believe it."

"I'm a vegetarian, so that's a no for me. What else is good?" I ask, trying to discern from the menu what is and is not meat free.

Giac feigns shock. "Izzy, you cannot be a vegetarian in Umbria. What with all the wild boar, the..." He snaps his fingers. "Guanciale and ooo the prosciutto! The pancetta." Giac closes his eyes like he's in a trance.

"You know what else is here?" I start. "Mozzarella, parmigiana, ricotta, marscarpone..." My stomach growls. "I'm good."

Our waiter comes and we quickly put in our orders. I settle on the *umbricelli,* the thick, spaghetti-like pasta shape native to the region, *al pecorino* with plans to add a mountain of Parmesan on top.

"Izzy," Giac starts, "we've seen much of each other, but I feel like I know nothing about you. Tell me everything."

I freeze mid-sip of wine. This was supposed to be dinner, a bottle of wine, and sex—I hadn't prepared for the conversation part of the evening. "What do you want to know?" I ask.

Giac furrows his brow. "Everything. Where you're from? Why you came to Italy? All of it." He takes a sip of wine. "Benito mentioned something on the train about being a politician."

I nearly choke on the piece of bread I've been stress-eating while I figure out how best to answer as coolly as possibly. "Yeah, I dabbled."

"What was your job back in California?" he asks.

"Oh, I did a little bit of this, a little bit of that," I answer noncommittally.

"All I know about Los Angeles is from American television. Let me guess," he starts. "You were on one of those reality shows where people think they'll find love. You were the last woman standing, of course, but you decided you were better off without the *noioso* male lead and went off on your own instead."

"Noioso?" I ask.

"Boring," Giac says. "Tell me, I'm right, aren't I?" His toothy grin is visible through his wine glass as he takes in a long drink.

"No, I wish. I worked for Congress," I say, praying he doesn't care much about the ins and outs of United States government and is willing to quickly move on to the next topic.

Giac fixes his gaze on me then snaps his fingers together. "That's where I know you from!"

I squeeze my eyes together. Maybe if I focus hard enough, I can teleport to somewhere else. "No, no. I'm sure you don't know me. I wasn't famous," I say.

"Women eat!" Giac exclaims. I cringe. "Women Eat" became a rallying cry of sorts after one of my colleagues on the other side posted an unflattering photo of me going to town on some French fries at the LA County Fair. He'd said it was undignified and disgusting, and my lone retort was to tweet back, *Breaking News: Women Eat.* I didn't intend for it to become a whole thing, but hashtags went viral, shirts were made.

"You recognized me?" I ask. I want to die. I want to leave. I want to jump into a vat of tomato sauce and let it boil me like an *aragosta* meeting its end.

Giac nods enthusiastically. "My sister, she's 17, she asked for one of your shirts because that angry little brunette singer had one, so I googled what it meant... wow. I cannot believe it's been you this whole time."

My palms are slick, and I feel a bead of sweat drip down my back, landing somewhere in my thong. "Don't hold it against me," I say.

"What is there to hold against?" Giac asks, his eyes still wild with excitement over this revelation. "You should be proud."

The waiter comes by, delivering our food. I immediately start twirling a noodle with my fork. "I lost," I say, my head down. "And it was all so..." I can't bring myself to tell Giac the whole of it. To admit I feel anything other than wine-buzzed would open up the emotional floodgates. I don't want to do that again. I don't want to share like I did with Benito. I don't want the embarrassment, the humiliation, the pain, to exist here in Italy. "I'm starting over," I say. "That's why I'm here."

Giac raises his glass toward me. "Well then, Izzy. Let's drink to that."

Giac offers to walk me home and I don't protest. My plan is to sneak him up to my room, hoping the solid walls of the villa will be enough of a sound barrier to keep our tryst secret. I'm not exactly in the mood after our dinner conversation, but I can muster up the energy. Nothing makes me less horny than talking about my old life, but I can rally.

He walks me to the front door and before I open it, I turn to him. "Thanks for joining me tonight," I say. "It was fun." I twiddle with my set of house keys, stalling.

"It was," Giac says. He claps his hands together, rubbing them like he's nervous. "Izzy," he says. He licks his lips. "May I—" My stomach swells. This is the moment. Giac cocks his head. "May I use the restroom inside?"

"Oh!" I say, opening the door. "Of course."

I show Giac the first-floor powder room and walk to the kitchen to pour myself a glass of water. I can still salvage the evening. Giac is fun. Giac is cute. I'm fun and cute under the right circumstances.

When he gets out of the bathroom, we'll share a nightcap and see where it goes. I'm wearing a red lacy bra, goddammit.

"You're up late," a voice booms out. I nearly drop the glass into the sink, shattering it into a million pieces, but catch myself.

I turn and see Benito walking into the kitchen.

His hair a stress-mess as per usual but he's in a well-tailored suit and shiny dress shoes. "Jeez," I say. "Stalk me much?"

"Sorry," he says, suppressing a smile. "Did I scare you?"

"Yes, I thought you were one of the ghosts that haunt this place."

Benito stares at me quizzically. "This house has no ghosts."

"It absolutely does," I say.

Benito loosens his tie and walks over to the cupboard for a glass, filling it from the tap next to me.

"What's with the suit, 007?" I ask.

The right side of Benito's mouth twitches upward. "You think I look like James Bond?"

My cheeks flush. "No," I say quickly. "He's just a guy who wears suits. Often in Europe."

Benito smiles. "I was at a dinner. Official mayoral duties."

"Ah," I say. I haven't seen Benito since Valeria's revelation the other day. Meaning I haven't had time to give him shit about Valeria's revelation the other day. "Working hard on ousting all the women-owned businesses in town."

Benito's eyes flit up to me. "What?"

"Valeria told me," I say. "In your little development deal, the businesses that will have to close are mostly women-owned. I think it's interesting that the people who stand to lose the most in this so-called revitalization of La Musa are the women who've been keeping it afloat in its downturn."

Benito looks at me severely. “I’m doing everything I can to make sure that doesn’t happen, Izzy. Believe me.”

I look into his eyes, which I instantly regret, because there’s something about the way he’s looking at me that convinces me he’s being truthful. Like with me, he’ll always be truthful. My mind flashes to lying next to him in that bed in Rome, the heat of his body warming my cold, dead heart. It wouldn’t take much to kiss him, a thought intrudes. I could just lean in and put my mouth on his.

“Izzy, thank you.” I hear Giac’s voice, but my eyes are still fixed on Benito’s. I watch as his pupils grow to the size of a pinpoint. I turn to see Giac standing in the open doorway to the kitchen.

“Giac,” Benito says, but he’s still looking at me. “How nice to see you.”

“You recognize him by his voice?” I ask.

Benito’s nostrils flare. He’s in no mood for me. “There aren’t many other young men in La Musa who are old enough to drive but too young for laugh lines,” he says softly.

“Giac and I just had dinner,” I say, feeling like I owe him an excuse, though I’m not sure why.

Benito nods. He takes his glass of water and starts toward the kitchen exit. “I’ll leave you two to it, then,” he says. “Good night.”

He walks past Giac, looking back at me one more time before he leaves.

“Good night,” Giac says, grinning affably as ever. “I should be going.”

"Unless you want a nightcap?" I ask. I walk over to my cupboard and pull out a bottle of grappa.

Giac agrees and I pour. We take our glasses outside, since the night is comfortably breezy and not too cold. I sit on a love seat on the patio and Giac sits next to me. It's *dark*, dark outside. My city person sensibilities are still caught off guard by the sheer number of stars visible in the sky, the whole universe reflected back at me. It's easy to feel insignificant but also easy to understand that one tiny movement won't rock the entire galaxy off its axis.

I lean into Giac, my shoulder flush with his. I cross my legs so my top leg is resting over his thigh. I lean in ever so slightly, waiting for his lips to meet mine. After a moment where he doesn't take the hint, I lean in another centimeter forward, then another, slowly moving toward him until my lips are only a breath away from his. Giac pulls away.

Giac *pulls away.*

"Oh god," I say. "Sorry."

"Izzy—"

I stand up, draining the rest of my drink. "Sorry. I'm sorry."

"No! No. Don't be sorry," Giac says. He waves his hands fervently.

"I'm a freaking perv, the internet was right." I move toward the door, but Giac follows.

"Izzy, Izzy." Giac catches my arm. "You are beautiful and I love our time together. I'm sorry if you thought I was trying to be anything but a friend to you."

My cheeks get hot. I can't look at him. "Yeah. Ok, cool—"

"Izzy. I'm gay." Giac puts a hand on my shoulder, and I am finally still. He smiles as he takes a sip of his drink. "I thought you knew that."

My face burns. Gay? I have misread all of this. I quickly flip through my memories of the two of us and see it all in a new light: Giac was being friendly. He wasn't flirting with me all those times, he was *complimenting* me. He was being nice. I've been out of the game so long that I've forgotten how to play it. I've forgotten how to know if I'm playing it at all. "Gay?" I ask.

"Yes," Giac says. "Uh… I am attracted to men."

"I know what gay means," I say. "But… Valeria, she was basically planning our wedding."

He shrugs. "Like I said, I keep my personal life and my work life separate. She probably did not realize."

"There was the thing with Lucia at lunch… about double dating."

He grimaces. "I thought we were all joking around."

I turn to Giac. "Are you like, out?" I ask, my voice low. "Do people know?"

Giac laughs. "I've been out since I was 15. Yes, everyone I know well knows I'm gay, and that now includes you." He fishes his phone out of his pocket and shows me his background. It's Giac and a group of friends, smiling and wearing rainbow clothing. "This is from Perugia Pride last year."

I start pacing. "I can't believe I didn't know. I represented West Hollywood, for Christ's sake. I was in two pride parades last year, I've been on *Las Culturistas*, I was a guest judge on *Drag Race*." I run my hands through my hair. "I'm for the gays, Giac."

Giac lightly laughs, unsure of how exactly to proceed. "I don't doubt that."

"I can't believe I tried to kiss you. I'm so sorry. This is humiliating." I sigh heavily, leaning my head back, the stupid stars and their endless shimmer mocking me.

Giac swallows his laugh, shakes his head, and grabs my right hand. "I'll admit this is not the first time this has happened. Do not be embarrassed."

"No, you don't understand," I say. "I'm so lonely and desperate that I convinced myself a gay man wanted me. Everything they said about me is true. I live in a fantasy world where I'm the hottest person on earth and everyone wants me, but it's not true. I mean, clearly. First Levi, now you. I am pathetic."

"No, no. You're not." Giac strokes my hand like I'm a mewing cat and it honestly does help a little. "And for what it's worth, if I were going to have sex with a woman, I'd choose you."

I bury my face in my free hand. "That does not make me feel better. I'm sorry. I'm so sorry I hit on you. I'm a predator."

"You're not!" He jiggles my hand so that I will look back up at him. "I always thought we were on the same page. I always thought we were on our way to becoming good friends."

A smile forces its way out of me, despite the fact that deep down I am praying for death to find me quickly. "Well, I'd be glad to know I have you as a friend." It's hard to look at him, but when I finally do, I see that he is completely unoffended.

"Me too," he says. "It's hard to find new friends in La Musa. You know what they always say, hold on, let me translate—if you're old enough to drive a car—"

"Or too young to have laugh lines, you don't belong in La Musa." I join him in laughter and the shame begins to subside with excitement filling its place. I have a friend in La Musa. That brings the grand total to one, but it's one more than I started with.

I say good night to Giac and walk upstairs to my bedroom. I'm exhausted. I have a thin strip of fabric up my ass and the underwires from the bra are cutting into my skin. I want to take a shower and watch *Housewives* and go to sleep. I can't believe I shaved everywhere for this night.

The door to Benito's room is open and the light is on, no doubt because he wanted to make sure I came upstairs alone. I try to speed walk past his door but since I've yet to possess the powers of the Flash, he catches me.

"Izzy," he says. I stop and turn to face him. I've never seen the inside of his room, and it startles me how much it looks like a child's room, with bright yellow wallpaper and a tufted indigo duvet on his bed that looks like it's from the '90s. He's reclining on his bed, his back propped up by pillows with a frilly trim.

He's on his laptop but he closes it and puts it down next to him. He's changed out of his suit and is now in the same sleepwear as the other night.

"What?" I ask. Whatever this is, I know I don't have the energy for it.

"How was your date?" he asks. His face is still but it looks tense, like he's flexing every muscle above his neck to prevent any expression.

"It wasn't a date," I say, because now I know that it wasn't. "Why do you care?"

Benito shrugs, his face still unmoving. "I was just asking."

I take a couple of steps into the room. There are cherubs on the wallpaper. Chubby baby angels on the walls of Benito's bedroom. I point at it. "Did you pick this out?"

Benito rolls his eyes. "It's been there since I was a baby."

"Cute," I say. I step farther into the room. There are mid-century-style travel posters of London, Paris, and Barcelona on the wall above his bed. Above the dresser there's an intricate map of what I at first think is Great Britain but upon further inspection I realize is Westeros. "Nerd," I say.

Benito sighs and stands up, walking over to me. "I read *Game of Thrones* in high school and my mother bought this for me. I was barely here as a teenager, so I think she wanted me to feel as at home as possible when I was." He watches as I scan the rest of his room, though there's not much else to see: a small wooden dresser, a handcrafted rocking chair, a framed photo of him and the silhouette of a woman on a beach, the setting sun blasting behind them.

I pick it up and examine it. "Sutton?" I ask.

Benito nods. "My mother set that out too," he says. "Feels rude to throw it out."

Though I can't see him clearly, it's easy to tell that the Benito in the photo is smiling, happy, in love. "Do you miss her?" I ask, immediately regretting it. "Sorry. That's none of my business." I put the photo down, but it falls, the glass of the frame shattering. "Oh shit."

Benito walks over to me. "It's ok. Stand back." He walks out of the room briefly and returns with a broom and dustpan, quickly sweeping up the glass from the floor. "Well, now I have a reason not to display it."

"I'm sorry. Really," I say. "I'll buy you a new one."

"Izzy, it's ok." Benito looks up at me, his eyes wide. He stands, setting the glass-filled dustpan on his dresser. "And to answer your earlier question, no, I don't miss her."

I swallow hard, relaxing the tension I didn't realize I was holding in my neck.

He sits on the bed and runs his hand through his hair. "It was a relationship of convenience. Moving back here isn't what I wanted, but it did give me an excuse to end things." He laughs softly at himself. "That sounds bad, doesn't it?"

"I get it, I think," I say, sitting next to him. "Though I'm no relationship expert, as you and hundreds of millions of others know."

Benito turns to look at me. His face looks less rigid than normal. The lines on his forehead are softer and his eyebrows perfectly frame his bright eyes. "Do you mean with the guy who—?"

"Leaked my horny texts, yeah," I say. I look up at the ceiling and lean back on the bed. "I don't make a habit of sexting people I'm not even dating, for the record." I follow the outline of the stucco on the ceiling with my fingertip. "I thought we were waiting for each other, but he was waiting to pounce. I thought I loved him. I thought he loved me. But nothing about that sounds like love, does it?"

I mean it as a rhetorical statement, but Benito considers. "I don't know. I think it's brave to love someone when you don't know if they love you back."

He turns his body so he's sitting cross-legged on the bed next to me, his knee barely touching the top of his duvet next to mine. "Yeah," I say. "Maybe."

His eyes dance into mine and my whole chest swells in response. It's how I used to feel when Levi looked at me, like our hearts were having a conversation through our eyes. It's sickening, really, how much I romanticized every look. I thought it meant something, but it was just the chemical reaction in my brain triggering a full-body nervous system response. It wasn't love; it was neuroscience.

"Do you miss it?" Benito asks.

"You mean Levi?" I ask. I haven't really let myself think about the answer to that question. It feels dangerous to think of Levi in terms of anything other than the man who destroyed me.

"No," Benito says. "Congress. Politics. All of it."

I sigh. I haven't allowed myself to think about that either. I've been scared of what the answer is. "I don't know," I say. "Do you remember two presidential elections ago? When Eveline Reed lost to that… that fucking buffoon."

"I think the whole world remembers that," Benito says with a laugh.

"The most qualified person to run in decades losing to someone with no international policy experience just because she was a woman, a woman of color." I shake my head. "I remember watching her during her concession speech. How full of grace she was. How optimistic she was that despite her loss, she could still lead her supporters to create the change she promised." I take in a deep breath. "I signed up for a leadership summit right after that. I always knew I wanted to run for Congress someday, but the way she picked herself up after that loss was what inspired me to finally jump in and do it." I feel a lump starting to form in my throat. "But then…" I trail off.

"Izzy," Benito says. He lies back, so his head is next to mine. "You can't compare yourself to Eveline Reed. She is like *the* feminist political icon of this century. She's had a lot more experience with loss and disappointment. She's had the chance to build up that resilience."

"I know," I say, my voice cracking. "But I couldn't muster up even an ounce of that courage after my much-lower-stakes loss. Maybe that means I was never suited for the job in the first place." I squeeze my eyes to keep the tears from coming. I've already shed so many from this loss, I don't need Benito to see me like this.

"Maybe it means this loss will make you stronger when the next one comes along," Benito says.

We lie in silence for a moment, both of us staring at the ceiling. I wish I could believe that, but I know the truth: I couldn't actually hack it as a career politician. One loss and I fled to Italy, forever giving up, not on what I believe in, but on my ability to do anything about it. It doesn't matter if he thinks I want to go back or not, I don't deserve another chance.

I sit up. "I should go to bed. I'm exhausted," I say.

Benito nods slowly. "Yeah, me too."

I stand, fixing my messed-up hair as I do. "Sorry about breaking your picture," I say.

Benito's expression warms. "I'm not."

I skip the shower and slink into my pajamas, flipping open my laptop to find that I have to log into the streaming service where I watch *Housewives*. I click *forgot password* and open my email. There, at the top of my inbox I see his name again. Levi Cross. In fact, many Levi Crosses. I scroll to the bottom.

> **Hi IB** (the way he shortens my name because he'd rather die than call me Izzy apparently)**, been trying to reach you on your cell. I have an idea I want to run by you—you've been in my shoes before ;)**

Delete. The next one is from Congressman Levi Cross.

Realizing you might have my personal email blocked (you'll have to show me how to do that one day haha). IB, could really use your expertise—deciding a vote on a bill that was first intro'd last sesh and I want to know if you were leaning yes or no. Call me when you can.

Delete. Next from The Office of Representative Levi Cross (CA-35).

Hi Ms. Rhodes,
Congressman Cross has requested a meeting with you. Please respond with your availability at your earliest convenience.

Delete.
The most recent one from his personal email again.

Isabella, remember that hot August weekend we spent registering USC students to vote? It was one million degrees with 1000% humidity and you still showed up in a freaking suit. You looked so cute, energetically trying to engage the privileged freshmen in your khaki suit with sweat stains down your back. You said it was important to project authority, that people would take you more seriously if you dressed the part. Well, I took your note and now I never go anywhere not in a suit. Not even the gym. Seriously, Isabella, I'm running three miles on

the tread every morning in a suit. Don't ever let them see you flinch. I miss you. Please call me. There's so much I want to ask you.

Delete. I wish I did know how to block email addresses, because I'd block his. I consider researching but I don't have the energy. I reset my password and queue up the housewives.

Chapter Ten

The Nightly Show with Jason Rockweiler Season 46 Episode 92; Congressman Levi Cross, Kiernan Shipka, Vampire Weekend

20:01:58

Jason Rockweiler: Congressman, I hate to embarrass you, but—

[Mr. Rockweiler holds up tweet that reads *Sexiest Man Alive???* with a picture of Mr. Cross on a beach]

AUDIENCE: [Cheers and applause]

Jason Rockweiler: People are saying you're the hottest congressman alive.

Levi Cross: Hey, I'm there for the work, not the fame.

Jason Rockweiler: Now, I have to ask because everyone's been wondering, have you talked to your former adversary, your friend, your, shall we say… pen pal Izzy Rhodes since the election?

Levi Cross: I haven't.

Jason Rockweiler: Really? Because people are asking where she's been. She apparently hasn't been seen in public in months. Are you sure she's not hiding in your closet?

AUDIENCE: [Laughs]

Levi Cross: I'm not sure. Maybe I should check.

AUDIENCE: [Laughs]

Levi Cross: No, no. Look, Izzy is a friend. She's a good friend. She's a good human. I hope wherever she is, she's happy.

"WHAT ABOUT FLYERS? WE COULD PLASTER FLYERS ALL OVER town, build awareness," Mia, the owner of the butcher shop in town, pitches what is now becoming a laundry list of asinine ideas the women business owners have come up with so far. We're sitting outside at Bar Musa. It's a beautiful evening. It's golden hour and the piazza is dripping in sunlight, a reflection of the *duomo* casting itself into the top of my glass of white wine, but I want to bludgeon my eyes out. I'm trying hard to let them lead. I'm only here to consult, but if I have to listen to another terrible idea, I am going to scream.

"Too much paper," says Bettina of the titular Osteria Bettina. "We do not want to waste trees."

The other women hum in agreement. I tap my finger against the table. I promised myself I wouldn't get involved unless I'm directly asked, but no one is asking me anything. "Have you tried social media? Getting press involved?" I blurt out, the latent strategist in me tired of being banished to my subconscious. "If La Musa's development happens, it's bound to spread to nearby towns. You should get other communities involved. You need more voices to add to the resistance. We need to put pressure on the mayor to not go through with this."

The women look at each other. Valeria quickly translates for Francesca and two other women I haven't met who don't speak English. "It's a good idea, Izzy," Valeria says, "But there's not much social media activity in La Musa. We tend to do things the old-fashioned way and actually talk to each other." The women laugh at that.

"Isn't the whole point to resist modernization?" Bettina asks. Everyone at the table nods in agreement. "I think we should do a bake sale." The women excitedly nod in agreement.

"I love the idea of a bake sale!" Mia says.

"No," I say, or maybe it's more of a yell. "If your goal is to stop the development, you need to make people aware of what they're fighting for. You need to make La Musa noteworthy enough to save." I take out my phone and open Instagram, ignoring the hundreds of messages and notifications I've been avoiding for months. I navigate to Marisol's profile and scroll to the bottom of her page. "Look, when an… acquaintance of mine first decided to run for Congress in the U.S., no one knew who she was, but she let them get to know her through social media so she became someone they could get behind. We need to do the same for La Musa. We need everyone to know what it is and why it's special. We need to make sure that if anyone were to change it, there'd be an army of people willing to stand in front of the bulldozers."

No one says anything at first and I assume it's because they're floored by my brilliance, but when Valeria's done translating and they're still quiet, I realize they're just being polite, and they think I'm insane. "Or a bake sale," I say. "Bake sales are good too."

After another round of drinks, and another round of terrible ideas, we're no closer to stopping the development. While it's possible to bring the measure to the town, the best bet is still to convince the mayor to stop the development from going through, which means convincing Benito. Which is why I wait for him outside the La Musa city hall the next day during lunch.

It's balmy outside despite the fact it's only mid-May. It reminds me of those late summer days in DC when I'd take a break from a long committee session only to walk outside to 90 degrees with 100% humidity. I see Benito walk outside. He's furiously typing on his phone, his eyebrows furrowed over the top of his sunglasses, the salt of his salt-and-pepper hair a little more evident in the bright sun.

Still, he's striking. He really is handsome. Like, ridiculously handsome. Khaki trousers cuffed at the bottom, leather loafers, blue button-down as per usual, and with his face pointed down, his perfect cheekbones pop.

"Heading to lunch?" I ask, interrupting his phone gazing and my him-gazing.

He looks up at me, startled. "I was planning on it, yes."

"Want some company?" I brush my hair, wiry from the humidity, out of my face. "I don't want to bug you, but—"

"You're not bugging me," Benito says quickly. He puts his phone in his pocket and pushes his shirtsleeves up to his elbows. "I mean, if you're asking me to join you, I suppose I could manage it."

My eyes land on his forearms involuntarily but I quickly divert them before he can notice. "Ok then."

We go to a quiet pizzeria on the other side of town. It's tiny inside with all-white walls, three tables squished into the space, and a stressed-out server pacing the few feet from one side of the store to the other.

He seems pleased to have guests and offers us cold Cokes when we sit—a refreshing reprieve from the heat. I order a Margherita pizza with *mozzarella di bufala* and Benito chooses one with spicy sausage and burrata.

"So, what's on the agenda for today?" Benito asks, cutting a slice of pizza with his knife and fork.

"For lunch? Eating, drinking, being merry," I say.

Benito stares at me. "Don't try to fool me. You're looking at me like I'm prey."

My cheeks flush. How am I looking at him? Did I give myself away that easily? "No, I'm not."

"You are," he says. "You want something."

"No, I don't," I blurt out. Even though the purpose of this lunch date/stalking is because I do want something. Benito raises his eyebrows and takes a sip of Coke. "Ok, I do want something," I say.

Benito claps his hands together. "I knew it."

"It's the women," I say, and his face drops. "I'm helping them organize, but while they are all intelligent and competent businesswomen, much better than I could ever be, they suck at the political part." I adjust in my chair so I'm sitting up straight. "If the development goes forward, they have the most to lose, and I'm not ok with it. So I'm coming to you directly, hoping we can strike a deal."

Benito eyes me for a moment. His irises as stormy as the weather brewing outside. He takes another bite of pizza and shrugs. "Alright."

I study him as if I'm waiting for him to say *"psych."* "What do you mean?" I ask.

"I think you're right," he says, words I never thought I'd hear come out of his mouth. "It is unfair that it would primarily affect women-owned businesses. I don't want that."

He says it so easily, like this was always his opinion and I'm crazy for ever thinking this would be an uphill battle. "Why are you all of the sudden against the development?" I ask.

"I wouldn't say that I am against it, but I'm willing to explore other options if this particular situation would screw over the hard-working women of La Musa. I don't want to screw anyone," he says, and a little sizzle strikes down from my chest to my pelvis. Benito blushes a little. "You know what I mean."

"I was expecting more of a fight," I say. I'm not used to getting my way on the first try. Usually it takes negotiation, compromise. "Why the sudden change in heart?"

"It's not that I've changed my mind, it's more that I—" Benito pauses, taking another swig of Coke. The bottle chugs as he drinks. He sets it down on the table. "I trust you. I trust your opinion."

I look at him sideways. "No, you don't."

"I do," he says. He reaches across the table, placing his palm on the linoleum in front of me. "I'm sorry I was intent on pushing you away, convinced that you were going to leave at any moment. I see now that that was unfair. I was projecting my stuff onto you. Clearly you care about the people in town, and you care about La Musa."

"I'm staying," I say. "I told you that over and over."

"I know. I convinced myself you were here to bask in the Italian sunshine for a couple of weeks then bolt," he says. "I'm wrong, though, right?"

I agree that he's wrong, but I'm stunned that he's willing to say it out loud. I'd always assumed Benito was the kind of person who couldn't admit he was wrong, like so many people I worked with before—like me. "Why did you think that?" I ask.

"I mean, I know I'm not fully settled yet, but I've only been here two months. I'm still figuring it out. Do you think I'm lying? Do I come across as flighty?"

He shakes his head. "I guess it was a last-ditch effort at self-preservation on my part."

A breeze cuts through the restaurant and the stressed server holds down the paper tablecloths on the two empty tables to keep them from blowing away. "Because you're set on pursuing a changed La Musa?"

Benito picks at the crust on his pizza. "No, because I didn't want to get too… attached to the way things are now."

His eyes flit up and he casts his gaze into mine. My heart flutters. I do my best not to parse his words for some hidden meaning. A buried but detectable declaration that I'm not the only one confused as to what our dynamic truly is. "It must've been really hard to lose Sutton, London, and your father at the same time," I say.

Another breeze blows through. Benito runs his hand through his hair. "I think I knew it wasn't right. I knew somewhere deep down that I'd always come back. I thought maybe that's how you feel too. Maybe this is a temporary stopover, a chance to get over what you've lost before you return home." His words are directed at me, but it feels more like he's trying to rationalize my actions to himself.

"This is a new life, not a vacation. It frustrated me that you treated me like I was a flight risk when I have no intention to ever go back."

He opens his mouth to speak but this time I cut him off.

"I know you think I'll change my mind, but I won't. I know you think our situations are similar, and they are in a way, but you deciding to come back here for your mom is not the same as me going back home for my career. You don't understand what I'd be going back to. You don't know how bad it was. How humiliating. You don't know how much people hated me. I mean, sure, some people thought I was inspiring, but the people that hate me really, really hate me." Thunder rumbles in the distance, justifying the electricity in the air even though I'm quite certain its cause is somewhere between me and Benito. "I wish I could flip a switch and shut it all out, but I can't. I can't go back to that."

Benito clasps his hands together. "But the ones that loved you… that has to count for something. When you were first elected, they treated you like a revelation. You were on red carpets, magazine covers."

I shake my head. "The thing about being a woman, a suddenly very famous woman, is that it's great in the beginning: all the love, all the attention… you really feel like you matter and what you're doing is important, but then people start getting tired of hearing about you all the time, so a small group of contrarians emerge, and the sentiment grows, and before long, they'll find a big enough reason to hate you that it spreads even more. You can only be on top for so long before people remember that you're merely human and imperfect. And unless you're straight and white and male, it's not enough to be anything less."

I take a deep breath and a bite of pizza, summoning the magical healing powers of complex carbohydrates to calm the stinging feeling of rejection my confession stirs up.

There's another clap of thunder and the server bellows out, "*Mamma Mia,*" which is not something I knew actual Italians said.

Benito looks at his watch. "I should head back to work."

We pay and leave. The walk back toward the office starts off silently. *He didn't want to get too attached.* I want to ask if he still feels that way, but the old wound I've allowed myself to open up is too raw. He's right. I know what it feels like to get something you really, really want, and worse, when what you really, really want gets taken away.

No, it's better to keep whatever attraction I feel toward him locked up. Minimal risk might mean minimal reward, but it's the static I've been craving.

Thunder cracks again and the sound is close enough to startle us both. A trickle of raindrops follows a few moments later.

"Did you bring an umbrella?" I ask.

Benito shakes his head. "Didn't you?"

"I'm from Southern California. We prepare for rain by staying home when it's in the forecast."

Another clap of thunder allows the sky to completely open and dump buckets onto us. Benito scrunches his face up. "I've been living in the U.K. for years and the relentless rain was the one thing I was happy to have behind me."

The rain pours and Benito's button-up is instantly see-through. An outline of his pectoral muscles visible. "We need to get out of here," I say as Benito, right in sync, pulls us under an awning outside a gelato shop.

It's short lived, though, as a worker inside yells at us in Italian and shoos us away from blocking the entrance to his shop.

Benito grabs my hand and pulls me away. He starts to run, and I move my legs as quickly as I'm able to keep up. He turns down a narrow alleyway and we run still as the cobblestone pathway fills with water. I throw my bag over my head but it's useless—I'm already drenched.

There are signs for a garden ahead and we follow them, hopeful there's a communal overhang for us to duck under for the duration of the downpour, but there's nothing but open air and greenery. It'd be beautiful in clear weather, but in this circumstance, it's basically a swamp.

Benito stops running and turns to me. We both laugh.

And laugh.

And laugh.

He points at my overall wet-dog appearance. "There's no use. The rain hasn't spared any part of you."

He smiles wider than I've ever seen before, his grin nearly stretching ear to ear. I walk over to him and wring out his wet shirt collar. We watch the water drip down. "You should talk."

When I let go of his shirt, I realize how close we are. The rain can barely find its way between us. I wipe my wet face. "Do I look like a drowned rat?"

Benito stops grinning and looks at me seriously. "No. You look…" He strokes my wet hair out of my face and tucks it behind my ear. "Perfect."

I'm sure the heat radiating off my body will be enough to evaporate the raindrops back up into the sky. The water cycle perpetuated by my blushing cheeks.

"What do you think?" he asks, and I know that he needs me to confirm that I want his hands in more places on my body than just the side of my face, though they feel right at home where they are.

I press a palm to his chest, and it makes a little splash from the soaked material of his shirt. I grab his shirt collar again and pull him toward me, pausing when his face is mere centimeters from mine. "Don't you hate me or something?" I ask.

Benito freezes. He's so close I can see his pupils dilate, the irises of his hazel eyes burning bright gray, reflecting the stormy skies. "I could never hate you." He uses the hand on the side of my face to lock his fingers into my hair and lead my lips to his.

We finally connect and it takes a moment for the sensation to hit me, but once it does, I feel his kiss all over. Even through the unrelenting rain, his lips firmly collide into mine like they're confident this is where they should've been all along. It's been a long time since I've kissed someone, but I feel at home with Benito's mouth on mine.

We stand there for a moment, locked together, neither of us moving lest one of us gets spooked and runs away. Then he glides his tongue into my mouth and our lips move together. His hand slides down to my waist and he latches his free hand on to the other side and pulls me in, closing whatever gap was left, our bodies completely pressed together.

Thunder claps again and he pulls away, his hands still on my hips. He stares at me with an intensity, like he's trying to decide if he should take me right here and now in the middle of this public garden. I'm not sure I'd object if he did.

He drops his arms. "I need to get back to work."

I take my hand off him and am suddenly embarrassed. "Oh. Yeah, of course."

We leave the garden, and the rain starts to let up. My cheeks are flushed, and I wonder if I can blame it on the sudden change in weather.

I feel his hand in mine. He stops walking and leans back against a wall, pulling me in so I'm almost falling on top of him. He kisses me again. Short, but sweet. "I really have to get back," he says.

"Yeah."

"But… Izzy." He cocks his head at me as if to get one final read of my thoughts before he says what he really wants to. "Just to be clear, I'm really glad you're here."

Chapter Eleven

I WAIT FOR BENITO TO RETURN FROM WORK LIKE HE'S BEEN at sea. I peep through the window in my bedroom every time I hear a sudden movement, pacing across my room lest I miss his entrance. When I finally hear the creak of the front gate at promptly 5:15 p.m., I rush to the bathroom to run a brush through my hair. I've spent all afternoon preparing. I took a shower, I put on dry clothes, I changed the sheets on my bed—just in case. Vincenzo's gone home for the day and Anita has her knitting circle on Fridays; we'll be all alone.

I try to play it cool as I make my way down the stairs to greet him, but I'm basically skipping. When he walks inside, his head is buried in his phone, so he doesn't see me waiting on the stairwell landing. I clear my throat and he looks up. He immediately puts his phone in his pocket and smiles at me. "Hey." There's an awkwardness, and I wonder if he needs me to confirm it again, to be the one to break the proverbial ice.

"Listen," Benito starts, but we're interrupted when the closed door to the study opens and Lucia steps out, her usual breeziness hidden behind a pained expression. Worry lines appear where I thought there was only flawlessly smooth skin. I didn't even realize anyone else was here.

"Benito." She walks over and hugs him, hanging on for a long time. I look to Benito, hoping he'll make eye contact with me, but he doesn't. "We're all in the study. Come." She takes him by the hand and pulls him away. Benito looks up at me with an indiscernible expression and my heartbeat kicks up again but in a fearful way, not in a soon-I'll-be-making-out-with-Benito-again way.

Between the screen time and Lucia's demeanor, I know something is up, but it's probably nothing serious. If something serious happened, they would have told me. I'm sure whatever's gone on now, it'll resolve itself and we can pick up this conversation later. Tomorrow maybe, over a romantic candlelit dinner.

It rains all night, and I can't sleep, replaying the kiss over and over again in my mind, certain that Benito will knock on my door any minute. My eagerness to relive it keeps me from dozing off for more than an hour or two, the memory of Benito's lips on mine far preferable to a dreamless state of unconsciousness. I listen all night for the stairs to creak with Benito's steps but hear nothing. And yet when the early-morning light drips through the blinds in my bedroom, I feel energized.

There's probably a reasonable explanation. Maybe Lucia was merely stressed from the drive here. Maybe there was a mayoral crisis or an issue with one of his tenants, which is why he was so consumed by his phone, and he left to deal with that. Maybe Lucia needed help with her business and Benito couldn't sneak up to my room to explain, since she thinks he's still dating Sutton.

Yes, that makes the most sense. Benito's final look back at me should be interpreted as just that: He had to go with Lucia to avoid blowing his cover. He was spending time with his family last night, but he'll catch me up today.

I tiptoe downstairs and it's completely quiet. I clang around the kitchen as much as possible while making a pot of coffee and a slice of toast. Still, the house is empty. I press my ear against the study door and think I hear muffled whispers, but it could just be the wind, or the ghosts. I send him a quick text.

Me: just want to make sure everything's ok?

By nighttime, I still haven't heard from him. Either the entire family is still behind that oak door (maybe even trapped), or they all left and didn't bother to tell me. I do a lap around town at sunset, convincing myself it's to pick up dinner but knowing that I'm doing a little light surveillance in case the Farentinos are all happily enjoying an extra-long brunch and all my worrying was for nothing, but I don't see them.

I'm exhausted and I pass out early watching *Housewives*, my phone still devoid of texts from Benito.

By the next morning, I've still heard nothing from Benito and now I'm worried. There are only a few possibilities left for his silence. He either regrets the kiss and is hiding from me or something is seriously wrong. Or his phone is dead, and he lost his charger. Or he's dead in a ditch.

It's Sunday, and as Anita told me, Sunday lunch happens come hell or high water, so they should all be out back by noon. I will wait for him there. That way, if he does regret it, he can tell me today and I can move on with my life.

I shower and get dressed, hoping the way my yellow sundress clings to me in all the right places will alleviate any doubt he's accumulated about continuing what we started. The air outside is sticky, and the leftover humidity from the rain adds a layer of moisture to my look, in case my rain-drenched appearance the other day was part of the appeal.

I smell garlic and onion when I open my bedroom door and a wave of relief washes over me. Anita is cooking. All is well. A knot tightens in my stomach because if Benito's *not* dead, he is definitely avoiding me. I make my way downstairs and walk into the kitchen. I'm surprised to find Lucia standing over the stove, sautéing. "Good morning," I say.

Her eyes widen in surprise as she registers that I am standing in the kitchen. "Izzy? What are you doing here?" she asks, a stark contrast to the usual warmness with which she greets me.

"I mean, I live here," I say. "I was hoping to find Benito—"

"Did he invite you to Sunday lunch?" She rolls her eyes and gestures outside. "They're all out back." Despite her tone, I'm relieved to hear he's at least alive, though also even more confused because something is definitely up.

Lucia escorts me to the backyard; I can already tell it's not the usual vibe of Sunday lunch. I spot Benito, Anita, a tall gentleman about her age I've never seen before, Lucia's husband and kids, and a beautiful, tall brunette woman I've also never seen before.

"Benito," Lucia bellows in a scolding tone, "you invited Izzy to Sunday lunch?"

Benito looks over at us and his eyes widen in surprise. The rest of the party silences as well to glare at their new guest. I give a halfhearted wave.

"Did I?" Benito asks.

"No," I clarify. "I mean, I live here, so it's not that weird that I'm here." Everyone stares at me like that is the most absurd thing they've ever heard. "I wanted to talk to Benito about something, but, um, it can wait."

Anita walks over to me, beaming. "Nonsense. You'll stay. You're exactly right, Izzy. This is your home too, and for today at least, you are family." Her joyfulness stands out among the overall somber tone, her giddy grin unsettling in contrast to Lucia's frown. She grabs my hand and leads me back toward the older gentleman and Benito. "Lucia," she says, "get our guest a glass of wine." Lucia sighs and obliges. Anita gestures toward the man I don't know while I try to wordlessly communicate to Benito that I simply want to speak with him and perhaps make out a little. "Isabella, this is my husband, Raffaello."

I freeze. Benito's dad who's gone but not dead? The one who left his family for the woman he has in Milan? Anita is smiling and referring to him as her husband and I am the only outsider present to witness, so it can't simply be an act.

Raffaello turns to me and smiles affably. I can see the resemblance to Benito in his eyes. They have the same sharp cheekbones, the same salt-and-pepper quality to their hair. If I didn't already hate him based purely on secondhand information, I would find him handsome in a Hugh Grant kind of way. "Isabella, *piacere*," he says, his voice deep and gravelly. "I apologize that it's taken so long for us to meet. I've been away on business." *Funny business*, I think.

He sticks out his hand, so I decide to be pleasant enough and shake it. I turn to Benito. "I really just wanted to talk to you." I raise my eyebrows to emphasize, and Benito seems to get the hint.

"Of course, shall we go inside?" he asks.

Anita swats him on the arm. "Nonsense. Isabella hasn't yet been introduced to Sutton."

My eyes dart over to the beautiful brunette woman. Sutton? Sutton as in Benito's not-girlfriend. She's here. The panic that Benito might not have been truthful when he told me they'd broken up sets in. Is this Levi all over again? Thank god I only sent him the one text.

Perhaps sensing my anxiety, Benito walks over and places a sturdy hand on my shoulder. "*Mamma*, Izzy doesn't want to subject herself to our familial antics, let's not make her stay."

Anita swats his arm again. "She's already agreed, don't be rude." Anita waves at Sutton. "Sutton, my darling, come meet our tenant, Izzy."

Even though I know why Anita's not clued in on Benito's current relationship status, it stings to be referred to as merely a *tenant*. Benito lets his arm fall off my shoulder. He uses his pinky to stroke the side of my hand, which sends a chill down my spine but reassures me about a pinky's worth.

"I'd love to meet Benito's girlfriend," I quip. Benito's eyes fall on me, and he lightly shakes his head. It's not enough of a confirmation that I haven't been purposely misled.

Sutton saunters over, her long hair in perfect waves, in a black jumpsuit without a wrinkle; she towers over everyone at the party—a good two inches over Benito's respectable 70. "Hi there," she says, her accent more Kate Middleton than *Love Island*, unfortunately. "It's a pleasure to meet you—Izzy, was it?"

She sticks out her bony hand and I shake it. "Nice to meet you. I've heard so much about Benito's lovely *girlfriend*." I'm sure my tone is sharp, but Sutton appears not to notice, instead accepting my words as a genuine compliment.

I think I feel a bead of sweat drip from Benito's brow onto my skin. "We're running low on wine," he says. "Izzy, want to help me replenish?"

"Yep."

I follow him inside. As soon as we're out of earshot, he sighs heavily. "This is a nightmare. I wanted to come find you, but it's been pure insanity. Never in my life has there been a more chaotic 48 hours."

He runs his fingers through his hair and paces. Despite my confusion about the scene outside, I have the urge to wrap my arms around him again, relieving the tension from carrying the weight of his familial drama on his shoulders.

I remember that Sutton didn't flinch when Anita introduced her as his girlfriend. "Why is Sutton here?"

He sighs again and walks over to the collection of wine bottles on the kitchen counter, committing to our original purpose. "I assume my father brought her as some sort of peace offering. Or he meant to distract me with her so he could swoop in and manipulate my mother into taking him back."

He picks out a white and works to open it with a corkscrew. "He messaged me two days ago 'looking forward to seeing you, son' with absolutely no other context. He sent Lucia something similar, so we knew something was up—shit!" He drives the corkscrew too deep, straight through the cork. He works to readjust it.

"And then my mother wasn't responding to my messages all day, so Lucia decided to come down here herself because we both had a bad feeling, and when she made it back to the house, she found our suspicions were right: He was sitting in the kitchen with my mother like nothing had ever happened."

He finally gets the cork out of the bottle and pours a glass of wine. He hands it to me before pouring one for himself. I take a sip, digesting his words. "So he's back for good?"

"Who knows what lies he's told. I tried to talk some sense into *Mamma* but all she said was *fatti i cazzi tuoi*." He takes in the glass of wine like a shot.

"What does that mean?"

Benito laughs lightly. "It means mind your own fucking business."

"Huh. Vincenzo hasn't taught me that one." I watch as Benito starts opening another bottle of wine. I lean casually against the counter. "And what about Sutton?"

He gets the cork out of the second bottle more easily. "She was in Milan on business and my father convinced her to come with him. He told her it was a business trip, and by the time she realized what he was up to, it was too late."

I try to add it all up in my head. "But she answers to 'Benito's girlfriend.'"

"Yes, because we're still pretending to be together." He pours himself a fresh glass of wine as he waits for me to catch up.

"I know, but how did she know to commit to the ruse?"

Benito's eyebrows narrow. "Because I told her. How could there be a ruse if she didn't know?"

"Oh," I say, bridging the gap of information. "She knows you're lying to your family about the two of you still being together?"

"Of course. She works for my father, so if I hadn't, the whole plan would fall apart."

I nearly do a spit-take. "She works for your father?"

"Yes, for his family's firm in London; that's how we met." He gestures toward the backyard. "We should get these out there." He hands me one of the bottles of wine. "Did you not know that?"

I take the wine and follow him toward the outside door. "Um, no."

The conversation is cut off by our return to the party. By now, everyone is seated at the dining table. We set the bottles in the center. There are two open seats next to Sutton. Benito sits next to her and I'm on the other side of him, with Anita and Raffaello at the heads of the table and Lucia and her husband across from us.

Anita brings out a tray of *crostini*, and even the heavenly first bite of her cooking isn't enough to break the tension.

"Isabella," Raffaello's voice booms across the table, "I'm afraid to say your reputation precedes you."

I cringe and brace for whatever interrogation is next. "Is that right?"

Benito stares his father down sternly. "*Papà,* don't."

Raffaello's mouth widens into something that resembles a smile. "Relax. I only mean to say that Anita's done nothing but rave about you."

I do relax a little. "Oh. Yes. Well, she's been a lovely hostess. Both her and Benito have."

He nods approvingly. "I am sorry the town is in such a state for your stay."

I take a long drink of wine, the coolness of the condensation on the glass a good reprieve from the heat of the day and the tension at the table. "What do you mean?"

Raffaello leans back in his chair and crosses his legs. "You know, I have a vision of a better La Musa. A thriving city instead of a sleepy hollow."

I send a look in Benito's direction. "I don't think we need La Musa to change at all," I say.

"*Papà*," Benito says, "Izzy's actually been working with the women business owners in town to find more ethical solutions." I look up at him, surprised.

Raffaello waves his arm. "And that's all well and good, but it is not sustainable. You know this."

"We have the opportunity to find a solution that benefits our history and our future." Benito looks in my direction. My chest warms.

Raffaello laughs. "We shall see about that. Do not think my temporary absence from this place means I've abandoned my plans for it."

Benito's eyes flit to him like daggers. "I did not think your absence was temporary."

Anita slams her hand on the table and glares at Benito. Lucia gently shakes her head while Sutton and Lucia's husband look down. Raffaello, for his part, seems unfazed, instead letting another reptilian grin stretch across his face. "Even you have the capacity to be wrong, my son."

Benito breathes in, ready to fire back, but it's Sutton who interjects. "I think Ben's only surprised by your sudden return, Raffaello." *Ben.* "We did spring onto him a rather sudden visit, and he's never been one for surprises." She taps her hand on top of Benito's. Whether out of habit or commitment to the lie, it seems to assuage him.

"Pardon the interruption, Isabella—" Raffaello continues.

"You can call me Izzy."

"Isabella, you'll have to come back to relish the new La Musa once it's complete. If all goes well, we should have a five-star resort that I'm sure someone of your stature will find suitable."

I struggle to find the words to respond, but to my relief, Benito steps in. "*Papà,* she's not visiting, she's moved here."

Raffaello waves him off dismissively again. "American women have been taking a break from their lives in Italy for centuries. It's no secret that they all go home eventually. Our provincial life here can never be enough."

It's unsettling to know Benito inherited that particular point of view. "Actually, it's been refreshing. I've been hustling my whole life," I say.

"Yes." Benito's eyebrows furrow as he looks at his father pointedly. "Not everyone has to look elsewhere when they don't get everything they need here."

Anita sets her wine glass down with a clank. "*Basta.*" She gets up from the table and walks inside.

A pang of guilt flashes across Benito's face. Raffaello shakes his head. "Now you've upset your mother. Are you proud of yourself?"

Benito pushes his chair back. "I cannot sit here and pretend that everything is alright after everything you've done. If she won't acknowledge it, I will." He stands so he towers over Raffaello, who's still remarkably unmoved. "What you've done to this family is unforgivable, and I do not accept you as part of it any longer." Benito storms off into the house, slamming the door behind him.

Raffaello lets out an amused chuckle and finishes off his glass of wine. "Lucia, my darling, how goes business in Siena?" Lucia looks at him, her wide eyes filling with tears. She gently shakes her head and gets up from the table, following Benito inside. Her husband quietly follows a moment later.

It's me, Sutton, and Raffaello left, and my insides feel like a slithering army of worms. Sutton and Raffaello exchange a look I can't quite discern, but it causes Raffaello to let out a huff before walking inside himself.

"Should we stay here?" I ask, though I can't quite imagine leaving without any resolution.

Sutton laughs. "They'll calm down after a few minutes and the meal will continue. It always does." As if to hammer in the sentiment, she leans back in her chair and takes a luxurious sip of wine.

"This happens a lot?" I ask.

"Nearly every family meal, especially when the two Farentino men are at odds. Which is quite frequently." Sutton may have been more integrated into the family than I thought. She takes another sip of wine. "You're no stranger to debate. You must feel right at home." She looks at me knowingly.

I swirl the wine in my glass. "It's something I thought I left behind."

Sutton laughs again. "Is that really something you can leave behind, though? Isn't it a part of who you are? Personally, I find La Musa to be dreadfully boring, but with moments like today I'm certain you can get your fill of drama." She twirls a lock of her annoyingly shiny hair.

I look back at the house, hoping a member of the Farentino family will return, but no one comes. Sutton and Raffaello have made it clear they know who I am. Might as well address the elephant in the room. "I didn't get into politics for the dramatics, if that's what you're implying. I wanted to change the world." It sounds silly in retrospect, a childish dream even, but it's the crux of what drove me all those years. I wanted to make people's lives better.

Sutton adjusts, sitting up in her chair like what I've said energized her. "Well then, maybe you should settle for changing La Musa."

"I do not want to change La Musa."

She holds up her hand. "I appreciate what you see in it; it has its charms, no doubt, to some, but this place has been going downhill for years—decades, really. Think about it. You could have a hand in saving it. If you convince the women business owners to get on board, the revitalized La Musa could be your legacy."

If I knew I held such a powerful bargaining chip, I would have laid out their resistance more strategically. "For someone who's only here to keep up appearances, you have a lot of opinions."

She laughs. "God, you're right. It's my brain. I can't turn it off for more than a glass of wine." She leans back in her chair again. "Am I a spinster workaholic or am I doggedly ambitious? The line is so thin for a woman, is it not?"

I know what she means, but I don't trust her enough to let her bond with me. "Well, no one here thinks you're a spinster, do they?"

She laughs breezily. "True. It must be so odd to you that I agreed to Ben's little lie, but I did it for him. He's a good person. He's been good to me, and I know how important it is to him to keep his mother happy. If my being here helps, then I'll be here, pretending all is well."

I take a sharp breath in. What is with everyone and their surprise altruistic intentions around here? Still, there's an uneasiness in my gut. "But eventually, your breakup will become public, no? Aren't you worried his family, his father, will be angry with you for lying?"

Sutton smiles softly and the politician in me can't help but wonder if there's a scheme cooking beneath her effervescent surface. "No, I am not worried about that."

The doors fling open and Benito returns. He wordlessly sits and takes a long drink from his wine glass. Sutton passes him the bottle and he refills his glass. "Do you have it all settled, then?" she asks.

Benito tosses back another sip of wine. "Nothing is settled."

Sutton leans forward so her arm is resting on the table, her hand dangerously close to grazing Benito's. "Don't you think you're being a tad stubborn? I know you and your father have a complicated relationship, but he swore to me he's only returning because he intends to make things right."

Benito rolls his eyes. "Is that why he brought you? To be the messenger because he knew I wouldn't talk to him?"

"No," Sutton says with a bit of an edge to her voice. "I came here because you asked me not to tell Raffaello what's going on with us, and it would've raised red flags had I declined his offer."

"I'm sure it has nothing to do with winning favor with the boss," Benito says, his voice dripping with sarcasm. They're bickering, and I feel like I've suddenly become an innocent bystander in the middle of a lovers' spat.

"I should go to my room," I say, pushing my chair out. "There's clearly a lot you all need to work out, and I wasn't supposed to be here in the first place, so…" I stand up. "Nice to meet you, Sutton."

"Izzy, wait." Benito stands too. He glances at Sutton and back at me. "Didn't you have a… matter to discuss?" He looks at me pointedly.

It's an invitation. I could be alone with him. It's an enticing idea, but Sutton is here, his father is here. I don't know that there's a point. "Uh… yeah," I say. "But it can wait."

Benito takes a step closer to me and lowers his voice. "Are you sure? We can talk. If you want."

I look back at Sutton, who is watching us closely. "No. It's ok. I'll see you later."

Benito takes another step closer to me and places his hand on my arm. I look at it and he quickly pulls his hand back. Sutton's eyes widen, her interest piqued. "Good to meet you, Izzy. I have a feeling we'll be seeing a lot of each other."

I go up to my bedroom and collapse on my bed. My phone dings and I glance over at it, the screen full of notifications. I open the News app and nearly drop my phone on my face. There's a headline screaming at me in bold typeface.

Former Congresswoman Isabella Rhodes Trades Washington for the Italian Countryside.

Chapter Twelve

Ousted Congresswoman Isabella Rhodes Trades Washington for Italy—*The New York Times*

Under the Umbrian Sun? Isabella Rhodes is doing her best Diane Lane in rural Italy—*The Cut*

CAUGHT?! Isabella Rhodes Ran Away to Italy —*TMZ*

Traitor Rhodes loses her election so she moves to Italy? Pathetic!, an online comment from a former colleague of mine.

We're proud of Izzy for following her heart to Italy to start her next chapter of greatness, my dad's Facebook status.

THE NEWS IS EVERYWHERE. THERE ARE MEMES, THERE ARE think pieces, there is discourse. This is a nightmare. A cheap gossip rag published it first—a blurry photo of me in my bright yellow sundress, carrying a loaf of bread and a bouquet of fresh flowers down the cobblestone streets of La Musa. I look chic and European, honestly, but the invasion of privacy still makes me squirm.

Someone in La Musa is watching me. Or at the very least, someone recognized me, snapped a picture, and leaked it to the highest bidder. Everyone back home knows where I am, and suddenly the transatlantic flight and two-hour train ride doesn't feel far enough away.

My phone erupts with a FaceTime call. I click the green button and both my parents appear onscreen. They're huddled next to each other at the old wooden kitchen table my father built when I was little. Something about the image of the two of them there, in the room I've known since I was born, makes me long for home. The first twinge of homesickness after weeks of relishing my escape. Suddenly I'm longing for the big bay window that looks out into the backyard and the jacaranda tree that blooms bright purple in the spring.

"Ah, our daughter does still have time for us." My mother purses her lips and shakes her head.

I strain my eyes trying not to roll them. "Sorry, it's been crazy here. I'm sure you saw the news—"

"I'm proud of you, Iz." My dad grins. "You're not hiding anymore."

"Don't sugarcoat, Dash. I'm worried. What if one of *those people* follows you to Italy." My mother rubs her temples with her fingertips. "You don't have security like you did in Washington."

"The threats stopped once I left office. I really don't think anyone would do anything worse than pointing and laughing." A shiver runs down my spine. "Not that I wouldn't find that devastating."

"You know, CNN was speculating on why you chose this particular area of Italy, and they pointed to the conservation efforts in your area." My dad takes out his phone and shows me his screen, but I can't read it. "It's not a bad idea to bulk up your experience in the international arena—"

My mother shakes her head. "Dash—"

"What? Just in case."

"In case I want to run again? Yeah, no, not doing that." I never did get around to drinking that glass of wine Benito poured for me, and now I wish I was mentally lubricated for this conversation.

"And we support you in that decision." He looks to my mother. "We discussed it, and we do. But you should keep your options open. You're so young. There's so much time left." He scratches his head. "Well, for you, maybe, not the planet or democracy or—"

"You did end up taking that self-defense class, right?" My mother's lips stretch into a thin, worried line. "You know I don't condone violence, but maybe you should keep a weapon on you. Not a gun, obviously. But a taser perhaps? Maybe even something medieval—"

My father leans back. "If you're that worried, we can pay for security. I'll call Richard and see if he knows anyone internationally."

Richard was the head of my security team while I was in Congress. I sigh. "Please do not bother Richard.

I'm sure he's busy. I heard he works for Harry and Meghan now."

My mom gasps. "Montecito is lovely. Good for Richard."

"Also, I didn't leak my location," I say. My parents share a look. "I didn't want anyone to know that I'm here, and I really hope this all blows over, because I do not want anyone to care about what I'm doing. I'd prefer to be out of the news with all my failure behind me forever." They share another look. "What?"

"It's just." My mother leans in as if she's about to drop a secret she doesn't want the trees to hear. "We thought maybe you were getting bored, so you leaked your location to soft launch yourself back into the American political sphere."

I stare at them blankly. "I don't even know how to respond to that." I hear a knock on my door and my heart skips a beat. "Look, Mom, Dad, I have to go. I'll call you later."

"Iz—" I hang up.

"Come in," I say, sitting up straighter and running my fingers through the ends of my hair. The door opens and Benito's on the other side. He looks behind him before he walks inside and shuts the door, like he's making sure he's not being followed. He gingerly walks over to me, stopping when he reaches the edge of my bed.

"Hi," he says.

"Hi."

He takes a deep breath and runs his hand through his hair; the veins and knuckles on the top of his hands protrude and I'm suddenly lightheaded. "I'm sorry for everything that happened after—" He stops himself and gestures to the edge of the bed. "May I?" I nod and he sits so he's barely perched on the corner across from me. "That's not how I imagined things going. But for the record, I don't regret anything." He cocks his head at me, smiling. It seems like he's testing the waters, but I'm in no mood.

I show him my phone, cued up to the latest headline about my new locale. His smile fades. "Is this—?"

"Everywhere," I say. "So much for anonymity."

Benito's silent for a moment, staring at my phone and struggling to find his words. "I know this is not what you wanted," he says. "But maybe it's good. Maybe it's a weight off your shoulders?"

My stomach twists. "No. It's not *good*," I say. "Don't you see? Someone is watching me. Someone is reporting my every move. Someone is waiting for me to fuck up again so they can tell the world." I take my phone back and start pacing, my brain spinning with all the possible scenarios if someone had caught me and Benito kissing the other day. I'd be ridiculed again. Izzy Rhodes ran off to Italy to make out with her new flavor of the week the minute she was done with Congress. This is who she is. She's the girl who puts love first. She's the girl who's willing to sacrifice everything else for a boy. "This," I say, pointing between us, "cannot happen again."

Benito's eyes narrow. He shakes his head. "I was going to tell my *mamma* about Sutton tonight. It absolutely can happen again." He stands and meets me mid-pace, placing a steadying hand on my shoulder. "This has to happen again."

"What about your father?" I ask, dodging out of his grasp so my logical train of thought is no longer influenced by his touch. "You said you need Sutton to help in your war against him. What happens when he finds out you cheated on her?"

"I did not cheat on her."

"In the narrative you've been spinning with your family, you technically did!" I shout. Benito's eyes quickly move to the door and back and I lower my voice. "Oh god." I put a palm to my forehead. "This is just what I need. Someone takes a photo of us, Sutton goes public, and now I'm a homewrecking whore." My breathing quickens and I try to box breathe. It's how I kept myself from having a panic attack every time an unreasonable colleague made my blood pressure go over the normal limit. In one, two, three, four… hold two, three, four… out two, three, four…

"Izzy." Benito reaches for me, but I hold up my hands in protest.

"Don't touch me!"

Benito relents. "Ok, it's ok." He waits while I take another deep breath. "I'll keep up appearances with Sutton until I can get my father off my back and you and I will just have to… wait." I take another breath as Benito watches. Waiting. I'm familiar with the concept. "That's what we're doing, right?" he asks.

I put my hand on my heart, willing it to beat slower. "What?"

"We're waiting until the time is right. You're not… you're not saying no forever. Right?" He steps closer, his fingertips just inches from the edges of my hips.

I think back to that cold morning after with Levi. How he'd held me and kissed my head, telling me now wasn't the right time, but the right time would come. I know now not to hold my breath when someone makes such a promise.

"Ok," he repeats. His calmness is making me calm. Annoying, because I find spiraling energizing and I could stand to finish another chapter of *Anna Karenina*—well, *a* chapter of *Anna Karenina*. "What are we doing, then?" he asks.

I study his expression. His eyes are soft and the creases in his forehead are relaxed. He looks so harmless, it's disarming. "I don't know," I say. "I mean, the other day—I wasn't expecting that, and I wasn't thinking about what comes next." Besides more kissing.

Benito laughs. "Me neither. The other day, I wasn't thinking logically. When it comes to you, I'm never thinking logically."

My heart squeezes. Goddammit. This is the last thing I need. Another crush that unravels my entire life. Even if the vicious news cycle surrounding my reappearance slows, I still don't know if I can let myself fall as much as I want to. I was supposed to find a no-strings-attached Italian stallion, not a man who talks about waiting for me and is looking at me like… well, how Levi used to look at me. Like I'm important, like I matter, and like everything I want in this life is possible. Couldn't he have come in here with two glasses of *vino* and lured me into bed like a normal person? Why isn't anyone ever trying to use me? Other girls get late-night *u up* texts and all I ever get is to freaking yearn.

"So, Sutton," I say. "Is she sleeping in your bed with you?" The thought crossed my mind the second I saw her at lunch, but I was too scared to ask. If the answer is yes, I might hurl.

"No," Benito says. "Oh god, no. She told my mother she needs very specific conditions in order to fall asleep and took a guest room on the first floor. Not a lie, by the way." A shiver runs down my spine to remember that even if they're not sleeping together tonight, they did regularly sleep together at one point not that long ago.

"Good," I say. "I mean, I guess it's technically none of my business what you do." I look down at my floor. "The last time a guy said he was waiting for me, he ended up stealing my job, so… I guess it's a good thing I don't have a job."

Benito's eyes flit up to me. "I would never do that to you." He latches his fingertips into mine. "Maybe waiting is the wrong word. We're just… on pause." I smirk at the *Housewives* universe reference to when one of the titular wives is let go from her duties for at least a season or two. I wonder if he watched with Sutton. I will bring up Teresa Giudice to her and see if she reacts.

"We're on pause," I repeat.

Benito squeezes my hand. "I'll be right next door if you change your mind."

Benito leaves and I check my phone, which has now blown up with countless messages. I go to flip it onto Do Not Disturb but a phone call from Kate, my former campaign manager, comes in before I have the chance. She'd never call if it weren't truly important and if she hadn't exhausted every other option, so I answer.

"Hey, kiddo." Kate's voice is like an instant balm on my soul. She's in her late 40s but she was like a second mother to me throughout both campaigns and my time in Congress, always grounding and taking care of me, shoving food into my mouth or texting me at 2 a.m. to tell me to go to bed. "Sorry to bug you, but I'm getting inundated with requests for comment. I guess since your chief of staff and press secretary work for Cross now." Traitors. "I'm the last line of communication and I'd ignore it, but I'm genuinely worried they'd ship a news crew to Umbria."

"It's ok," I say, though my palms are slick with sweat at the idea of commenting publicly about anything. "What do we do?"

"We can say nothing if you'd prefer, deny any requests for comment, but I think you should keep it simple. Confirm that you're in Italy but reiterate that you're a private citizen now with an emphasis on private."

I sit back on my bed and fiddle with the edge of my comforter. No matter what I do, it doesn't change the fact that people know where I am now. It'll probably die down with the next international crisis, but either way, I'm in the news for the next 24 hours—and so is La Musa. "Actually," I say. "I have a different idea."

Chapter Thirteen

Where Is La Musa, Isabella Rhodes's new home?—*Washington Post*

Why You Should Add La Musa to Your Italian Summer Itinerary—*Traveler*

This Quiet Clifftop Hamlet Is the Forgotten Gem of Umbria—*NYT Magazine*

How the Internet Sold Out This Small-Town Italian Inn for an Entire Summer in 24 Hours
—*Teen Vogue*

I TOSS AND TURN ALL NIGHT THINKING ABOUT EVERYTHING: Benito, Sutton, Raffaello, Raffaello's horrible development idea, the loss of my anonymity, the fact that La Musa is now on track to become the hottest summer travel destination thanks to me. There's still a way to salvage this. More tourists in town aren't necessarily a bad thing for me. I'll wear hoods and sunglasses and take my meals to go and eventually, with enough positive buzz about La Musa, my presence here will be less relevant than its sprawling views and locally sourced restaurants.

It's nearly noon when I make my way downstairs in the morning. I hear Benito and his father in the kitchen. They're raising their voices at each other in Italian, but they stop when they see me enter. "Uh, *buongiorno,*" I say, with a halfhearted wave.

Raffaello relaxes and greets me with a double-cheek air-kiss. "*Buongiorno,* Isabella. Apologies for the loud start to the morning. My son and I have a business deal to make."

"There is no such deal," Benito grunts.

"My son fails to recognize that I own several buildings in La Musa, and it is my right to do with them as I please."

Benito shakes his head. "You cannot decide, out of the blue, to bulldoze centuries-old buildings to make a buck, *Papà*."

"Izzy." Raffaello smirks in my direction, including me in an argument I have no wish to be a part of. "If you suddenly had the opportunity to make your town not just a destination but a true modern city, would you not take it?"

I look back and forth between the two Farentino men. Up until now, Benito was advocating for a similar turn for La Musa. It's nice to find him on my side. "I don't know if you really want my opinion."

Unfortunately, or perhaps fortunately, the conversation halts when Vincenzo enters the room. "*Signore Farentino! Come sta?*" Vincenzo goes in for the hug, which knocks Raffaello off balance ever so slightly. Vincenzo beams. "Izzy, I know this man for *quanto?* Nearly my whole life. After school my wife and I tried big-city life in Roma—"

"Good to see you again, Vincenzo," Raffaello bellows, putting a stop to the friendly conversation. If Vincenzo is bothered by his harsh tone, he doesn't show it, happily bouncing over to the espresso machine to make himself a shot while Raffaello readjusts to be certain his presence looms over us at all times. While Benito emphasized that his parents relished small-town life, I'm getting the sense that part of the appeal for his father was feeling like a big fish in a small pond.

"Izzy, the rumors around town are that we have you to thank for an upcoming tourist boom." Vincenzo fiddles with the machine that whirs to life as it cranks out hot espresso. "Isn't that so fantastic?"

Raffaello claps his hands together. "Ah, yes, the tourists who will come here, see the state of things, turn around, leave, and never come back." He looks pointedly at me and I wonder how such a callous, horrible man created Benito and Lucia. Or how someone as warm and wonderful as Anita ever fell in love with him.

Benito sits up straighter. "Izzy has said from the beginning that all La Musa needs is more awareness, not to become something it is not. As someone who picked this town of all the towns in Italy to travel to, I think we should listen to her."

My heart squeezes. "It's true. I did say that."

This seems to appease Raffaello a little bit as he sits at a barstool. "You made the town, how do you put it, 'go viral,'" he says, contemplating. "You really think it can become the next trendy travel destination. The new Positano?"

I nod. "Yes. No tourists travel to Italy to see a modern, Westernized city."

Raffaello claps his hands together. "So you're who's put such ideas into my son's head." He turns to Benito and scolds him in Italian. I can't make out any of the words, but I think I hear *traditore*. Traitor.

"Izzy makes our town better." Vincenzo pauses, turning to me. "She's excellent company."

Raffaello ignores him. "Well, then who am I to stand in the way. It seems you have it all figured out." His tone teeters on the very edges of sarcasm. If I weren't so skilled at dissecting boomer male patronization, I might think he's telling the truth. I look over at Benito and he lets out the slightest of smiles.

"Then I suppose my visit was all for naught." Raffaello leans back on the counter and takes out his cell phone. "I heard my son was dragging his feet on the development deals I'd started, and now I know why."

Benito stares him down. "I thought you came back for *Mamma*."

Raffaello sighs heavily and stands up. "Visits can have more than one purpose." He walks over to Benito. "You must learn not to dissect everyone's words to find meaning that suits your narrative." He shakes his head and leaves the room.

Vincenzo and I wordlessly engage in a brief conversation of *"What the fuck was that?"* Benito fixes his gaze straight ahead but I can tell behind his stoic expression that he's reeling. "You ok?" I ask.

He abruptly looks up. "Fine." His phone rings and he steps outside to answer it.

"*Minestra riscaldata,* that's Benito and Raffaello." Vincenzo raises his eyebrows skeptically.

"What is that?"

"Another phrase for you. Reheated soup is never as good." He side-eyes toward the front of the house where Raffaello is and I'm stunned by the impressive display of shade from always-affable Vincenzo.

"You think there's no salvaging their relationship?"

Vincenzo shrugs. "I know I've never seen anyone in that family as happy as in the half year their patriarch's been gone."

If this is Benito happier, what was he like before? He doesn't exude joy as it is. The biggest I've ever seen him smile was, well, that day in the rain. Now, if Raffaello is back for good, I fear I'll never see him smile like that again.

"Izzy!" I hear my name when I exit Valeria's wine shop a week later and a chill travels down my spine. The increase in tourists hasn't happened overnight, but there definitely are tourists here, which is a change in itself, and it makes me nervous. I've yet to be recognized, thanks to my knowledge of La Musa's back alleys, and it's only a matter of time. I look up hesitantly and am relieved to see Giac walking toward me.

"Giac, *buona sera*," I say. He's wearing bright peach pants and a white linen shirt, his satchel bag slung over his shoulder as always. "I thought you'd be back in Perugia for the weekend?"

He shakes his head. "My *zia* is out of town so I'm using the opportunity for peace and quiet."

"Don't you have that at home?" I ask.

"No, I live with my family… four younger brothers and sisters running around." He shudders. "It's chaos." I make another mental note to thank my parents for never giving me a sibling. "Want to grab a drink?"

I hold up the bag of wine I just purchased. "You read my mind."

We walk back to the house, and as I open the gate to the front yard, I see the unmistakable sleek silhouette of Sutton walking toward us. She waves and grins when she spots me, and I have no choice but to be personable. "Sutton, hi."

"Izzy! I've been looking for you."

I do my best to smile and pretend I'm at all happy about the run-in, or that she's still here at all. She's been seemingly utilizing every square inch of the Farentino villa as her at-home office since she's been here, always on the phone or clacking on her laptop or both at the same time.

"I've convinced the family to do a Lake Como trip this weekend. We could all use the reprieve," she says.

"Lake Como?"

"Yes, the family home." She tosses her hair over her shoulder, and I try not to show my annoyance at her referring to it as *the* family home. "We're all heading up this evening, but you could join us tomorrow. It'll be the first time we've all been up there since..." She tapers off. I know the rest. Since Raffaello left. Since Benito and Sutton broke up. Since Isabella Rhodes was a congresswoman in the U.S. and not in Italy making out with Sutton's not-boyfriend.

"Well, that's very kind of you, but I couldn't possibly intrude." I've barely spoken to Benito all week, mostly because being around him makes me wish I never put us on pause. The last thing I want to do is watch another episode of the Sutton and Benito in Love show.

"Have you been to Lake Como?" Giac asks.

"No," I say.

"Then you must go. It is one of my favorite places in the world." Giac grins at Sutton.

Sutton lights up. "You could come too..."

"Giac." He sticks out his hand for her to shake it.

"Giac, you are more than welcome as long as you can convince Izzy here. It's a massive house, so don't worry about feeling like an intrusion."

My throat dries and I feel sweaty as I struggle to come up with an excuse. "I'm sure Anita doesn't need two extra people to entertain."

Sutton laughs. "Are we talking about the same woman? She loved the idea when I floated it past her, and I'll let her know that Giac will be joining us." Before I can say anything else she claps her hands together. "This will be great! I'll forward you all the details. What's your number?"

She takes out her phone and hands it to me to add my contact information. At this point it would be more uncomfortable to continue to decline her offer than it would be to go. Besides, I *have* always wanted to see Lake Como. I type my number. "I guess we're going to Lake Como."

Giac offers to drive us and picks me up at the crack of dawn the next morning. "Nice car," I say as I open the door to Giac's tiny Fiat, ducking to avoid hitting my head as I get in. I'm wearing a chambray romper and white sneakers, with my hair pulled back in a silk headband.

"It's actually my aunt's," he says, "but she isn't allowed to drive."

"Oh, has she lost her eyesight?" I ask.

"No," Giac says. "It was a town ordinance. Everyone voted and said, no more."

"Oh." I can tell from Giac's rigid shoulders that it's an uncomfortable subject. "Do you travel often?" I ask.

He glances over at me, which is slightly unnerving as we whip down the narrow cliffside road. "As much as school is on break. I spent a year traveling all over Europe, Asia, Africa. It was the best year of my life." He merges onto the *autostrada,* speeding up. "What about you? Your job must have taken you all over."

"Not really." I lean my head against the headrest. "I don't even remember the last time I traveled for fun."

"I need to see new places like I need to breathe," Giac says. "I don't like the idea that there are corners of the earth I'll never see. I want to know it all."

It's the exact type of comment that reminds me of our subtle but not insignificant age difference. The idea of seeing everything the world has to offer, while once maybe an intriguing idea, now makes me tired. "If you come to LA, you can skip the Walk of Fame in Hollywood. Now that it's not part of my district, I can be honest and say that it's a piss-covered money pit with a mediocre mall."

Giac shakes his head. "If you skip the less pleasant parts, you'll never appreciate the good." He points out the window. "See that?"

I look. There's perfectly pleasant countryside somewhere out there, but all I see is the wall that separates it from the highway and the thick early-morning fog. "Concrete? Yes."

"And it'll last forever. Hundreds of kilometers of nothing special."

I look back at the drab sight. "You're a great road trip buddy."

He continues, "But once we see Lake Como, after hours of nothing but road and concrete and dirt, it'll be even more magnificent in comparison." I remember when I had Giac's optimism, his zest for life. I remember the first time I stepped foot in the Capitol as an elected representative: There was never a more beautiful sight in the world. How quickly those two years went by, how quickly that building became a monument for my failure. I never want anywhere in Italy to feel like that. Even the concrete highway is a serene tropical paradise in comparison.

He offers me control of the music and I put on an old Joni Mitchell album. The folksy soundwaves that are distilled into the echoes of the twisty canyon roads I call home trigger a deep sense of longing that's been ebbing and flowing as of late, and I fold my knees into my chest. I never much liked being a kid; it felt stunting, and the impermanence of it all always made me anxious, but right now, I want to be seven again.

I want to be in the back seat of my dad's old Volvo, the windows rolled down on the way home from a long day at the beach, with salt and sand stuck to my skin. I want to pluck an aloe leaf from our blooming garden and rub it over my sunburn while my mother sways to the music, stirring a fresh pot of homemade jam on the stove, eventually getting so caught up in her movement that the bottom of the pan burns. I want to watch a sunset nestled between the two of them, a cool shiver reaching down my spine as the light disappears behind the mountains, signaling that it's time for bed, another perfect day done.

We arrive in Bellagio, a town located at the tip of a peninsula smack dab in the center of Lake Como, around lunchtime, and I'm nearly knocked down by the breathtaking views. The crystal-clear blue waters reflect the snowcapped Alpine mountains that surround it. It's quintessential Italy with multicolored villas lining the narrow streets. We stop at a viewpoint and stare at the lake ahead.

"Damn," is the only word that comes to mind.

Giac laughs, leaning back as he grips the guardrail standing between us and the water below. His arms flex. "Worth the long trip?"

I feel calm for the first time all day, the first time in… I don't even know how long. Giac makes me feel so at ease, like he's put my nerves on ice. "Definitely."

We decide to grab a bite to eat at one of the many small restaurants that line the crowded streets of Bellagio before we meet up with Sutton, who will escort us across the lake to the Farentinos' home. I lower my sunglasses onto my face as we find a quiet, inconspicuous table tucked into the corner of the outdoor deck. I order a Margherita pizza and, based on Giac's recommendation, a Campari Spritz. It's bitter and tart—but refreshing after the long drive. We sit in a comfortable silence as we eat. He's not freaked out by long pauses in conversation, and I like that about him.

We take a ferry across the lake to the small village of Tremezzo, then follow a path down the coast. Both Sutton and Benito described the Lake Como house as a home, but it's not a home, it's a palace. Giant, grand, a massive all-white estate sitting right at the lake's edge. While their La Musa house is fit for a nobleman, this is more suited for a king. Giac is in heaven.

"This looks to be in the style of Swiss architect Simone Cantoni," Giac says, admiring the elaborate painting on the foyer's domed ceiling.

Raffaello steps into the room to greet us, grinning smugly. "That's because it *is* Simone Cantoni." He gestures for us to follow him outside. Giac looks to me with his mouth agape and lets out a breathless squeal.

The backyard, which feels too basic a word for it, is even more grand: a giant terrace overlooking the water, what must be at least an acre of gardens, and a sparkling swimming pool. "Whoa," is all I can say.

"It's not bad." Raffaello winks at me. "We're having a dinner party tonight, and you'll both come, of course. Drinks are at five. Natalia will show you to your room."

"We do not need to bother Natalia." Benito steps out onto the terrace. He's wearing athletic shorts, which I don't think I've ever seen him in, and a T-shirt. It's weird to see him in this casual of a setting. If it weren't for the scowl on his face, I'd say he looks comfortable, relaxed. "I will show them to their rooms."

He leads us to the east wing of the giant property to a set of rooms across from one another. Giac yawns. "I am quite tired after the trip. I think I will take a nap if you don't mind."

"Not at all." I wave to him as he closes the door to his room behind him. I nod my head toward my room, motioning for Benito to follow me. I shut the door once we're inside. The room is all blue with white crown molding and a large king-sized bed in the center. He puts his hands in his pockets and waits for me to speak. "Sorry if me being here is weird. Sorry if coming here with Giac is weird. Sutton insisted and it all kind of spiraled out of control—"

Benito raises his hand and I stop talking. “Izzy, it’s fine. I’m glad you’re here.”

My chest warms. “You are?”

“Yes,” he says quickly, lifting his eyes to meet mine and flashing a quick smile. “I’m sure you and Giac will have a lovely weekend.” His eyes fall back to the floor.

I shift from one foot to another. “Giac and I are just friends. You know that, right?” It’s not my place to out Giac to Benito, but I shouldn’t need to.

He nods, but the expression on his face remains glum. “Natalia will bring fresh towels.” He walks toward the door. “I’ll see you tonight.”

Chapter Fourteen

I CHANGE OUT OF MY ROMPER AND INTO A MAXI DRESS that I threw into my small overnight bag last night. It's wrinkled from the long trip, but I do my best to smooth it out with my hands. I dot a little concealer under my eyes and over my sun-kissed nose and brush out my hair. If I had known just how fancy this house was, I would've come better prepared. I'm not new to galas and going toe to toe with the uber-wealthy, but I would feel better with a pair of pumps or a dress I didn't pick off the clearance rack three summers ago.

When I make my way outside, I'm greeted by Lucia handing me an Aperol Spritz. "Izzy!" She kisses me on both cheeks. "Benito told me you were here, and I was so glad." She holds my shoulders and raises her eyebrows. "And with Giac too…"

"We're friends. Just friends," I say. She raises one side of her mouth in response, not buying it. I spot Benito at the edge of the terrace, taking in the view of the late-afternoon sun on the lake. He's wearing a light, blue linen button-up and loose brown pants that are cuffed at the bottom—a more casual rendition of his standard uniform. I start to make my way toward him, but I'm intercepted by Sutton—looking perfect, of course, in a freshly pressed beige silk slip dress and fuchsia pumps that make her tower over me even more than usual.

"Izzy, glad you're here," she says, forcing me into a kind of rigid half hug. "There's loads of business associates here tonight that would be happy to meet you."

My throat suddenly thickens. "Meet *me?* As in, Izzy in Italy or—"

"The former Congresswoman Isabella Rhodes, of course," she says, as if it's as ordinary as any other job. "We've been trying to expand our business to the U.S., and we'd all love to pick your brain on policy." I cannot think of anything worse than foraging into the deep back pocket of my brain where such information is stored, but I'm trapped. I follow her.

"I don't know what Ben has told you about me," she says as we walk toward a small crowd of men. "But I don't bite."

"He honestly hasn't told me much, just that you're broken up." There's an edge in my voice and I can't tell if it's bitterness that she's talking to me about Benito or anxiety about whatever the next conversation has in store.

"He loved me once, if you can believe it," she says flippantly, and while I knew that on some level, it stings to hear it confirmed. "Despite how it may seem, he does listen to me. Your being here at all is evidence of that."

I stop walking and turn so I'm facing her. "I thought it was your idea to invite me to Lake Como."

Sutton throws her head back and laughs. "No, not here in Lake Como. Here in Italy." I don't follow; she loops her arm with mine and we continue walking. "He was so annoyed at his mother's insistence on taking in a boarder, but when he told me it was you, I convinced him to let you stay. That maybe we could use your expertise down the line."

I swivel my head back at Benito and then to Sutton again. The back of my skull prickles. I knew Benito was unhappy when I arrived and that he didn't exactly instantly warm to me, but this part is news to me. Before I can interrogate further, Sutton pulls me by the arm into the circle of men. "Gentlemen, this is the wonderful Isabella Rhodes, as promised."

It's like I'm a party favor, or the clown hired to entertain. I give a halfhearted wave. "Hey."

The men size me up and Sutton quickly runs through their names: Marco is a colleague of Raffaello and Sutton posted up in the Milan office; Don is a developer from New York; Alan is from London and works for a major hotel chain. They exchange pleasantries with me, and I learn their wives are on a tour of the estate with Anita.

"Congresswoman Rhodes," Don says, and I cringe, "I admit I was confused when I read that you moved here, but now that I've seen the place for myself, it makes more sense." He chuckles and the rest of the circle politely joins in. "That was a tough loss, kiddo," he adds, and I want to leave my body.

"Yeah, Italy's great," I say, failing to come up with a pithier retort. I'm sure Don is disappointed to find that legendary orator Congresswoman Rhodes is not in the room.

"I, for one, would never work in politics," Alan adds, for reasons unknown and incredibly unhelpful whatever they may be. "Too much feigned righteousness. And for what? A mere glint of power?"

Sutton nods, seemingly in agreement. "When Benito diverted from his predestined path to work in that godawful tiny old office in the House of Commons, I couldn't understand at all." The men engage in another round of polite, stilted laughter.

"Certainly a lovely lady like you could convince him to rejoin us, no?" Marco asks, the smoke from his lit cigarette wafting under my nose.

Sutton sighs dramatically and glances back at Benito. "I tried, but look where it got him: fucking *Umbria*." She reaches out her hand and Marco passes over his cigarette; she takes a puff. "When I told him he was meant for great things like his father, that is so not the direction I was hinting at." I want to punch her. How can she view Benito's sacrifice like that?

"I think it's noble," I blurt out.

Don lets out a mild guffaw. "Well, of course you do."

"No, I don't mean politics," I say, wielding a glare at Don because I have decided I do not like him and

I do not care if he likes me, "I mean sacrificing the benefits of your privilege because you refuse to see your mother's home become a—"

"Decrepit wasteland?" Sutton interjects, and much to my chagrin, the men laugh again. I hate all of them.

"Become a casualty of big-city commercialism and globalization," I complete my thought.

"Please," Sutton says. "All of us, including Benito, know commercialism and globalization is the only real way to save a town like La Musa. Why do you think we're all here?"

"The same reason I'm here," I say, not wanting to unpack the sinister nature of what she's just said. I look at her pointedly. "To get over a tough loss." I see Giac enter the party with a sleepy grin on his face. "Excuse me, my friend has just arrived."

I walk over to Giac without waiting for the reaction to what I said. It's becoming more and more obvious that Sutton's invitation was about more than a chance for me to see Lake Como. It's starting to feel like an ambush.

"I slept too good." Giac stretches his arms over his head and surveys the area when I meet up with him. Anita and the wives have returned from their tour and are cooing over a patch of fresh roses. "What an affair," he says.

I finish my drink. "No kidding. I thought my days of attending schmooze-fests like this were over." A server appears instantly with a fresh drink. "I didn't know the Farentinos had staff."

"In a huge house like this, you must," he says. "And what is a… what did you say, schmooze?"

"You know, like, a bunch of people being fake nice because they all want something from each other, but also being horribly passive-aggressive at all times?" I gesture toward Sutton and her cohorts. "I had to go to these kinds of events all of the time when I was running for office, and I hated it." Another server walks by with a plate of mini *arancine* and I take one off his tray and immediately stuff it into my mouth. The perfect blend of truffles and cheese erupts in my mouth the moment I take a bite. "Oh my god."

Giac tilts his head at me. "You do not seem to hate it."

I swallow. "The food's usually not this good at events like this."

The server passes us again and I take another. Giac nods toward the edge of the property. "Why is the mayor staring at us?"

I look over and Benito's still perched at the edge of the terrace. He turns away the moment I clock him, but I catch his fixed gaze. "It's a long story," I say, and then figure *screw it*. Giac is my friend and right now, I could use one. "We like, kissed once, but he's pretending to still be with Sutton for complicated reasons even though they broke up months ago, and the last thing I need is another public relationship scandal. I think he's a little jealous of us."

A quizzical look splashes across Giac's face as he tries to follow. "Jealous?"

"You know, because we've been spending time together but Benito and I, I don't know, like each other or whatever." I try to wave it off like it's no big deal, but the way my second drink seems to have instantly evaporated out of my glass gives me away.

Giac smirks. "You and the mayor, huh?" He grins again, teasingly. "He is cute. I get it."

I wave a finger. "Back off, I have dibs."

Giac scrunches up his face as he watches Benito join Sutton and her captive audience. "Do you, though?"

I gasp, feigning insult—well, *kind of* feigning. "I liked you better when I thought you were into me."

It's probably a breach of trust to share that Benito and I are anything considering his fake girlfriend is a few meters away, but it's a relief to debrief with someone who knows us both.

"So, what's the deal with the ex, then?" he asks. "Why is she here?"

I look over to Sutton, who's in the middle of a gesticulation-fueled story, skillfully holding on to the men's attention. "That… that I'm still trying to figure out, but it can't be good."

We sit for dinner, and I'm placed at the center of the table, with Giac all the way at the other end between Anita at the head and Lucia to his left. I am sandwiched between Don to the left and Alan to the right, with Sutton right across from me, and Benito next to her.

With their partners at hand, everyone's much more polite to begin with. I learn Don is in Italy for two weeks on business, but they're doing a week on a yacht next, sailing from Venice to Split. Alan and his wife have a summer home in the Italian Riviera, and he commutes to and from his office in London via private jet. Marco recently purchased a plush penthouse in Porta Nuova, Milan's bougiest neighborhood.

Sutton, for her part, is renovating her flat in posh Kensington. "I'm in dire need of a décor overhaul," she says, fiddling with the gold feather ring on her right pointer finger as she speaks. "It's 2014 twee-tragic in there right now."

Don slurps his wine before chiming in. "Make sure it's not too girly—I have a feeling Benito here will come crawling back sooner rather than later." He makes a jeering face at Benito as if he's in on the joke.

Sutton stretches her hand across the table to gently tap Don's arm. "From your lips to God's ears." Benito merely shakes his head.

I'm so tired of the elitist mood to the day. It's no wonder Benito's default state is "grumpy" if these are the types of people he's been surrounded by his whole life. It makes sense now that Anita and Lucia are much more upbeat, left out of Raffaello's reign of terror and free to live their unimpressive lives. "Maybe you'll end up in La Musa, Sutton," I say. "It's well on its way to becoming a bustling tourist destination."

Eyes shift among the business companions at the table and uneasiness seeps into my gut. Alan clears his throat. "Yes, well, with one of our properties in town, it's our goal to make La Musa the luxury standard in Umbria."

One of his properties? I've stayed in a hotel from the same chain before, and while the towels were soft and the bed cozy, it was well over $1,000 a night, not accessible to the everyday traveler. He must be joking. "Sure, add a SoulCycle and an Erewhon and we'll be well on our way," I say, and more shifty eyes erupt in response. The vibe is weird. I look to Benito, who's equally confused.

Raffaello gestures for a server to replenish his wine glass and sits back. "Izzy, Alan's company is interested in buying and renovating the old estate on the south end of town into a five-star resort."

My stomach drops. While the hotels are nice, it's the kind of luxury that exudes convenience: complimentary designer water, state-of-the-art fitness studios, Netflix on every 60-inch TV instead of syndicated sitcoms dubbed in Italian—none of that goes with La Musa's old-world charm. Benito interjects, "Villa Maria was built in the 15th century, you cannot tear it down. As mayor I will not allow it."

"Not tear down—" Alan waves his hands in front of him like he's presenting. "Renovate."

"Villa Maria is a private property, and if the owner wishes to sell"—Raffaello points to himself—"which he does, then he may do so. Just like he wishes to do with the dozen other properties he owns in town."

Don leans in. "And that's where we'd come in with a complete redesign of La Musa's main commercial district. Mixed-use spaces with modern amenities."

I look back and forth between Raffaello and Benito—what happened to our conversation the other day, when Raffaello acted amenable to the plan to emphasize La Musa's history? I could concede that one luxury resort in town wouldn't be so bad, but they are talking about destruction. They sound like, well, they sound like Benito when I first met him.

"And again"—Benito sits up straighter—"you cannot do any of this without the town's approval." I toss him a quick smile. I'm so glad he's changed his tune.

Raffaello blatantly rolls his eyes, making no attempt to disguise his disdain for his son in this moment. "The people in town know that revitalization is necessary to keep it from becoming a ghost town."

"Revitalization, yes," says Benito. "Not obliteration."

"No one wants La Musa to look like Silver Lake," I add.

"But they are interested in the town that was so special, Isabella Rhodes abandoned her old life to up and move here," says Don. A smarmy grin wipes across his face as if to charm me, but my blood starts to boil. He takes out his phone. "You laid the groundwork, Izzy, we plan to take this attention to the finish line."

I look to Benito, confused, but he shrugs back at me. Don searches for something on his phone and after a moment, flips it around to show me. It's my face. Or specifically, it's my face superimposed onto an ad that reads *La Musa, the perfect place to run away to.* I blink a few times to make sure I'm seeing it correct. "The fuck is this?" I ask.

"Our ad campaign, with you at its center, if you'll come aboard." Don grins at me like there's any possible world in which I say yes.

Sutton sighs. "Don, I wanted to present this to her in a more official capacity." She looks to me sympathetically. "I made a pitch deck." She sits back and crosses her arms. "It was very convincing."

My eyes dart around the table. Everyone is watching me, waiting. "You want me to be the face of the new La Musa?" I ask.

"You already are the face of La Musa," Don says. He scrolls through his phone and shows me another mock-up. It's my face, again, but this time it says: *La Musa, better than sexting.*

The rage I feel is too overwhelming for me to find words but too paralyzing to punch Don square in his piggish nose, so I sit and silently fume, counting the seconds as I breathe. This is even more insulting than having my texts leaked in the first place. This is using the most embarrassing moment of my entire life to bulldoze the town I love. This is making me the face of the development that would drive half the town out of business. "What makes you think I'd ever agree to this?" I ask, using every muscle in my body to keep my voice even and without any shake.

Don lets out an exhale that sounds like a laugh. "It's good PR for you, Izzy. You'd be paid famously, of course. Think about it. You own the scandal; it makes it look like you are above it."

Sutton, perhaps noticing the rage building inside of me, reaches her hand out in front of me. "Again, the deck goes more thoroughly into the cross-functional benefit analysis." She reaches for her phone. "What's your email? I'll send it to you."

"I don't want to see the deck!" I yell. "And I don't want to be the face of this PR scheme. It makes it look like I am proud of it. That it's what I want people to remember me by."

"Was this your idea?" I turn to see Benito staring down Sutton.

She shakes her head. "It was Don's idea, but I said I'd make the proposal to at least see if she'd say yes."

"You're unbelievable," Benito says, and Sutton's eyes widen in response.

"Son," Raffaello bellows, "you are the one responsible if La Musa fails. If I were you, I'd listen to Don. He knows what he is doing."

Benito turns to his father. "It is my responsibility. Not Izzy's. She should not be pulled into this." My heart warms hearing him defend me. If I weren't so pissed off, I'd reach across the table and grab his hand.

"She brought herself into this!" Don yells, obviously frustrated by the hostility. "You think it's a coincidence that her location is outed and all of a sudden every major U.S.-based publication is talking about La Musa?"

Benito turns to me. I take a deep breath. "My former campaign manager made a few calls," I say. "But I only did that to redirect the attention away from me and to La Musa. If this offensive ad campaign goes forward, my face will be associated with my failure forever."

Don huffs. "But at least we'd all be slightly richer."

Benito inhales sharply but I gesture for him to back off. I can handle this. "And that's the problem with people like you," I say. "You can't imagine doing anything if it's not in service of making yourselves richer. Well, unlike you, I didn't get into my field of work for the money. I did it for the people. I did it because I looked around my community and saw that members of it were suffering. I looked around the world and saw the inequality that prevails no matter how many times people in your class claim to be charitable.

"When I see struggle, my first thought is not how I can profit off of it. When my entire life went to shit, I didn't say yes to exclusive articles or book deals because I did not want the world to spend another ounce of energy on something so inconsequential. Unlike you, I am not a sellout. I am not an opportunist. I do not take advantage of the poor, or the weak, or the sick so I come out looking like Daddy Warbucks. There are good people in this world who fight for what's right, who fight for humanity, for the environment, for the world, who are truly selfless in their pursuit of a better society and while you might not be one of those people, I still have hope that I can be." I take a long sip of wine. The table is completely silent. I look across to Benito, who's smiling at me.

"Now, hang on—" Don starts.

"That's enough," Raffaello says calmly. "I think we can all agree that we've talked enough business tonight," he says. "Why don't we enjoy this lovely meal and excellent view for the remainder of dinner?"

"Hear! Hear!" Sutton says, raising her glass. The rest of the party follows suit. Benito points his glass toward me and gives me a slight nod. I wink back at him.

Conversation for the duration of dinner stays surface level. I excuse myself after dessert, when the men split off for cigars and the women retire to the parlor inside for *amaro* while the waitstaff cleans up outside—it's all becoming a little too *Downton Abbey* for me.

I retreat to my room and collapse onto the bed, exhausted from the day. My head is spinning but I'm content to lie like this all night even if it's a sleepless one. A knock on the door forces me up. My heart picks up a beat with the hope that I'll find Benito on the other side of it, but it's Lucia.

"Hi," she says, in a whisper that almost makes it seem like she shouldn't be talking to me. "I thought you might need an extra blanket. It gets chilly up here at night." She hands me a stack of soft, plush throws.

"*Grazie,*" I say. She smiles but it doesn't quite reach her tired eyes. I take a deep breath, "I'm sorry for making dinner contentious. Don was the invited guest, and I shouldn't have gone off like that."

"*Don* è *un coglione,*" Lucia says without skipping a beat. If I remember correctly, *coglione* is akin to calling someone an idiot, and I can't help but grin knowing Lucia sees him the same way I do. "You're our guest too, and he pushed you too far. *Papà* would never flinch in front of company, but even he is embarrassed."

"Really? I didn't know he was capable of shame," I say, and I immediately regret it when Lucia looks to me with surprise.

But then she laughs. "Benito has told you some things, no?" She sighs heavily. "It should tell you a lot that even our father feels bad."

She turns to leave but a pressing need to know her take on everything jumps out of me. "Hey, wait," I say. "Can I ask you a question?"

Lucia turns back to me quickly, almost like she was waiting for the opportunity to gossip. "Do I think my father still has his 'friend' in Milan? Yes, I do." She rolls her eyes and shakes her head.

I let out a short laugh. "No, although I wouldn't be surprised," I say. "But what do you think about Sutton?" She presses her lips together and looks up at the ceiling, like she's trying to decide if now is the right time to air out a long-held opinion. I try to help her along. "I mean, Benito and I have become friends, I guess, and I don't know… she seems a little…" Phony, harsh, vindictive, critical… there are endless ways to end that sentence, but I wait for Lucia to fill in the blanks.

"She's not what I pictured for him," she says. The diplomatic answer. "She's too much like my father, and honestly, Benito is so much like him too. He needs someone less intense, someone to ground him, someone to remind him there's more to life than work." *Someone who ditched all of her dreams for the specific purpose of doing nothing in Italy?* She continues, "Someone like—"

My heart flutters. I'd never expose Benito's secret breakup to his family, but it would be so nice to hear someone declare themselves as Team Benizzy.

Lucia waves her hands in front of her. "Someone like Giac, really."

I nearly drop the blankets she's so thoughtfully brought me. "Giac?"

She giggles and shakes her head, leaning forward to put a conspiratorial hand on my arm. "Not actually Giac, obviously, but someone like him. You and my brother are alike too, and I see how much Giac balances you out. You're always laughing when you're around him. Benito needs that." She gestures toward the moonlight dripping in through the window. "He needs more light."

I rack my brain for a response. She's not wrong—Giac is light. Giac is the human equivalent of an early-summer sun. Maybe Benito needs someone uncomplicated, not someone who sees an opportunity to verbally take down a family friend and takes it.

"Yeah, maybe that's what it is," I say.

"Don't get me wrong, I like Sutton." Lucia puts her hands up in surrender, but I don't know that I believe her. "She's beautiful, she's brilliant—"

"Sure, of course," I say through gritted teeth.

"Who knows what will happen? I've given up on trying to guess the next moves of my brother and father, as lately they've been totally unpredictable."

Lucia leaves me to ponder that as I change out of my dress and into the cream-colored silk shorts and tank top pajama set I brought. There's a soft cotton robe in the closet that I fling on as a breeze rolls off the lake, and I close the open window.

It's unsettling that the Benito I know is not the Benito Lucia is used to. For her, he's always been far from home: boarding school, Cambridge, his life in London. Raffaello's been the one who has been there. He was frequently away on business trips and "business" trips to Milan and God knows where else, but her whole life, up until six months ago, he was La Musa's Mayor Farentino.

Vincenzo said he hasn't ever seen Anita, Lucia, and Benito as happy as they've been lately, but that doesn't mean the new normal I found them in will last. Maybe Benito will return to London. Regardless of whether or not Sutton is in the picture, he's never wanted the small-town life. Maybe Raffaello is back for good, and maybe his family will continue to turn a blind eye to his more illicit extracurriculars. It'll be chaos, but there's a comfort in chaos if it's all you've ever known.

Maybe it's not possible to let go of who you used to be and escape old patterns. At least not forever.

Despite my exhaustion, I can barely lie still, let alone keep my eyes closed. Without the window open, the air in the room has gone stale. I desperately wish Simone Cantoni had installed a ceiling fan or that Italy had a penchant for central AC. I think of my bedroom in the Beachwood house with its slanted shiplap ceiling and the two big windows on the east and west side. My parents weren't the biggest fans of air-conditioning either, but when the cross-breeze cut through after the marine layer settled on summer nights, it wasn't necessary.

Knowing sleep won't find me anytime soon, I venture downstairs. The party has long since wrapped, and even the staff has gone home for the night. It's serenely quiet, and I can finally appreciate the view out back for its full worth. I perch myself against the terrace wall and breathe in the crisp air.

"Couldn't sleep?" I turn and see Benito walking toward me. He's in the same clothes from earlier, but his hair has been the victim of several stress comb-throughs.

"I think my room is haunted by the ghost of Marco Polo," I say.

He leans against the wall next to me, a slight, amused smile emerging across his lips. "Is that really the first Italian you could think of?"

"No, I was going to say Julius Caesar, but this just doesn't really feel like his vibe." I smile back at him.

His mouth tilts to one side as he looks at me. "That those are your top two proves troubling."

I turn so I'm facing him. "Since you're so elitist, who are your top two Americans?"

He thinks for a moment. "Joni Mitchell and Bethenny Frankel."

A laugh explodes from deep in my chest. "I mean, yeah. Our two finest."

He tries to keep a straight face, but a laugh breaks through. His mood is so much lighter than it's been all day, and a thrill runs through me to know I'm its cause.

The laughter settles into a silence, and it's not a comfortable one. My eyes drift back to the lake. The lights from the villas and the town across the water's speckled reflections look like stars on the dark water. "Today was a lot," I say.

Benito inhales sharply. “I shouldn’t have let you walk into that scene tonight. I knew who my father invited, but I had no idea what they were proposing.”

His eyes narrow as he joins me in gazing outward. There’s so much to unpack from the revelations of this evening, but right now I just want to be here, with him, in the now. “It’s a lot,” I say.

Benito, much to my chagrin, is ready to dive in. “I don’t think my father wants to be mayor again, but he’s always had an issue relinquishing control. A few small changes I could understand, or even encourage, but this is far beyond what I imagined. I won’t let what they envision happen to La Musa. And I won’t let them make you the face of it. I won’t.”

His shoulders start to shake, and I place a hand on him. He’s startled by the contact but relaxes. “I know,” I say. He turns to face me, and I lift my hand off him. “Sutton told me you decided to let me stay in the house because of who I am. Because I might be… helpful to you all.”

Benito sighs, running a hand through his hair. “Those were her words, not mine.” He faces the lake, staring out across the water for a moment. “You know we didn’t exactly click when we first met.”

I lean forward, trying to catch his eyes. “I know.”

“For what it’s worth, after that first lunch together—I knew I didn’t want you to leave.” He turns to me and the right side of his mouth quirks into a smile.

“It’s worth something,” I say.

He looks back toward the house; there’s only a spattering of lights visible through the windows, but he scans nervously for spectators. "I feel bad." Benito turns back toward the lake and drops his head in his hand. "You came here for a simpler life, and I've made it so complicated with my Shakespearean tragedy of a family."

I lean in so my eyes are level with his. "Are you kidding? Fake dating, trickery, secret schemes? This is a comedy." He smiles again and I feel victorious. I shift my weight so I'm closer to him, a mere inch between our bodies. "Don't feel bad," I say softly. "I want to be here."

His eyes meet mine and I feel a stir between my legs. It would take nothing more than the slightest of gravitational pulls for my lips to be on his. If only the world would turn a little bit faster.

"Are you ok after everything Don brought up?" Benito asks, failing to take this conversation the direction I want. To a conversation where no words are needed at all. "About your past. About what happened with—"

"I'm fine," I say, but there's enough edge in my voice that Benito doesn't let me off so easy.

"Izzy…"

An involuntary groan leaps out of my throat like it's been hiding there ever since the infuriating aforementioned altercation with Don the *coglione*. Benito watches me. He's waiting to see if there's more, but there's not. The five stages of grief for my dead dream have run through me and I now have no choice but to get comfortable with the fact that it's gone.

I take a deep breath. "All I ever wanted my whole life was to be in Congress. To be a person who can make the world better for the next generation. Every school election, every AP History test, every volunteer opportunity—it was all a chance to prove that my dream was what I was supposed to do." I crack the knuckles on my right hand as I continue, "But you can never really know for sure if it's right, you know? You can never really be sure if you're good at the thing you want to be good at. And there were little victories, little moments that validated that I was on the right path, but I was never certain I was good at it. I never felt worthy of any of the progress I ever made.

"And then I lost. I lost after my first term in a humiliating way, and it was like the other shoe finally dropped. It was like I was waiting for someone to say '*No, you're not good at the thing you've always wanted to do. You should stop.*' And then a whole district of people did. And I knew for sure it was true. So I stopped."

I look back to the lake and up at the night sky. I allow myself to feel dwarfed by the infinite wall of stars. My father used to let me look out his telescope while he pointed out the constellations. *"There are more planets out there than we can even fathom, Iz,"* he used to say. *"And yet you were picked for this one."* How insignificant destiny feels now.

Benito turns to me and brushes a hair out of my face, tucking it behind my ear. He keeps his hand on the side of my face and I lean into it. A light flickers inside the house and he pulls away. "But you did it. You had a dream and it came true. You made it true."

"Not the whole dream," I blurt. My skin prickles, my nerves on high alert—I haven't let myself think about this at all since I lost.

"No?" Benito scans my face. "What else?"

"I wanted—" I think back to the moment my initial election was called in my favor. I saw it all ahead of me: a decade or two in Congress, a run for Senate, and then finally, after years of proving myself, I'd set my sights on the White House. "President," I say, and the words sound so childish coming out of my mouth. Like something a third-grader says when asked what she wants to be when she grows up, not an actual career goal for an adult woman to actively pursue. "I wanted to be president. That was the dream. That was the whole dream."

I exhale as Benito takes it in. I can barely stand to meet his eyes. President. It all felt so possible not even a year ago, and now it sounds completely ridiculous. I steady myself on the fence's railing, still caught off-balance by how quickly life can change. "It sounds so stupid to say it out loud," I say.

Benito shakes his head. "No." He reassuringly pats his hand to my shoulder. "It doesn't. Not at all."

"It's ok," I say. "I know it's not happening. It's the one thing I was working toward my entire life, but now that life is over because I failed at the first real test. I'm a failure."

"No, Izzy," Benito starts. "You can't really think one setback defines you. You are so much more than a single failure."

"Am I, though?" I shake my head. "If you ask anyone to distill Isabella Rhodes into one sentence, what do you think they'll list? My accomplishments, or my loss and my scandal? That's why I came here. I had to come here because my name's become synonymous with weakness at home. I know now I'll never be president, and I can't be around the constant reminders of the version of myself who thought that was possible. I can't live like that. Even if it means I fade into nothingness. That has to be better."

Benito takes it in. He thought we were so alike in coming back to La Musa after a personal crisis, but while his reasons were saintlike, mine were selfish—a vengeful need to give up on the people I wanted to help because they gave up on me.

"That's not what I'd say," he finally says.

"What do you mean?"

"You said that's how anyone would distill Isabella Rhodes into one sentence, but that's not what I'd say." He shifts from one foot to another, glancing back at the house nervously.

I'm scared to know the answer if I ask the question, but I have to hear it. "What would you say, then?"

He takes a step closer to me, filling in all but the last few gasps of air between us. "Isabella Rhodes is… brilliant but not in a normal way. She's brilliant in a sharp, cunning, witty, kind of scary at times way that's able to make your whole world come into focus, that makes you wonder how you ever lived a second of your life anywhere but in her presence." He looks back at the house for a moment but seems to make a decision internally. He takes my hand and intertwines my fingers with his.

I cock my head at him. "Huh. I thought you were going to say 'Isabella Rhodes is very pretty.'"

He pulls me closer so there's no more gap. Our bodies pressed together like they need each other to breathe. "Oh, she has that covered too. Believe me."

A flurry of butterflies free themselves from my gut, taking over my entire body with a pleasant fluttering. Benito trades my hand for a strong grip on my waist. He waits for me to protest, and when I don't, he uses his free hand to gently tilt my chin upward, giving me one last look before leaning in. His lips meet mine with a gentle graze but soon the tempestuous tension that's been percolating between us gives way to a vigorous need to be one.

He slides his tongue into my mouth with ease and I exchange it for mine, taking my hands to either side of his head and running my left hand through his hair like he's done so many times. His hand makes the journey from my chin down my neck, my shoulders, my side, finally landing on a tender spot in the dip between my ribs and my hips. The thin satin of my pajamas is not too thick a barrier for me to let out the softest of moans.

As if the sound startled him, he pulls away, looking back to the house. "We shouldn't do this here," he says, and my heart falls.

"Right." I pull my robe across my chest. It's not an ideal setting what with Sutton roaming the halls, Raffaello looming, the aforementioned Natalia, and the yet-to-be-delivered fresh towels. Although based on how his eyes are fixed on my chest and the modicum of cleavage the robe allows for has me second-guessing how strong his resistance actually is.

His lips curl into a devilish grin. "I should show you back to your room, don't you think? Wouldn't want you to get lost in this big house."

My heartbeat quickens. "Yes, it's far. You should definitely accompany me. For safety."

Benito nods slowly. "In case Marco Polo's ghost shows up."

I smile. "Exactly."

The walk back to my room takes forever as we tiptoe through the house. It's dead quiet, and once we get to my door, I open it slowly, praying the creaking sound won't wake up Giac across the hall. Benito follows me without question, and I quickly close us in.

He doesn't wait another second before pulling me into his embrace, his lips back on mine like he's drowning and needs them for air. I pull away.

"What's wrong?" He bites the corner of his lip and smiles. "The walls are thick, don't worry."

I scrunch my face up because he really is so adorable, and I can't believe I'm about to ruin the mood with my overall anxiety around intimacy. "I don't really…" I rub my hands together. "It's um, it's been a while."

He cocks his head at me, trying to understand, but his smile returns as he gets it. "That's ok."

"No, I mean…" I struggle with whether or not to let the words escape from me, but ultimately honesty wins the battle. "That day in the rain… that was the first time I've even kissed anyone in years." It's so humiliating and yet I continue, "The last time was with…" I trail off.

"And you're feeling nervous?" he asks.

"No…" I take a deep breath. "I'm feeling rusty."

He laughs instinctively, then covers his mouth to stifle the sound.

I put my hands on my hips and he leans in, stroking both my upper arms. "How 'bout, just this once," he says, "you let someone else take the lead."

I look into his eyes, trying to decide if I can do this, but I don't really need any convincing. It's Benito. My body, my heart—they've already made the choice, and my head is outvoted no matter how hard it tries to overthink. He kisses me again and the butterflies do a series of flips in celebration, a victory lap for their host body finally getting the hint.

My fingers quickly find their way back to his hair, as if to put down an anchor and declare they're not letting go again. He pushes me against the wall, his hands gripping at my waist and then fiddling with the tie of my robe, eventually getting it loose and sliding it off my shoulders. He lays a trail of kisses down my neck and across my collarbone. "You're perfect, Izzy," he says breathlessly. "You're so perfect."

I pull at his shirt collar because as close as he is, I want him nearer. His body is like a blanket on top of mine and yet, I want to be warmer. I slip out from against the wall and lead him to the bed. Waiting for no invitation, he gently lowers me down onto it and crawls on top of me. His cheekbones are sharper from this angle, his eyes somehow brighter. "You are so beautiful," I say. My cheeks flush, but it's true. Handsome is not strong enough. Cute fails to capture it. He is stunning. He is beautiful.

He strokes my cheek. "Hey, that's supposed to be my line."

"I'm serious," I say as I start to undo the buttons on his shirt. "Since the moment I saw you and every moment since, I've been struck by you." The tops of his abs show through the opened center of his shirt, and I trace their outline with my fingertips. "You're beautiful. Inside and out."

His lips are quickly back on mine as his hands roam up my pajama top. He pauses briefly as he reaches the edge of my breast but then decides to dive in, moving his hands over me. He presses his pelvis against mine and I can feel I'm not alone with record-breaking levels of stirring between my legs.

I push at his shirt until he takes the hint and lets it fall to the floor. He lifts the edges of my tank top and I sit up to help it over my head, exposing my bare chest. Any shame that threatens to set in over my nakedness is thwarted when he lets out an exasperated sigh. Never have my B-cups elicited such a reaction. "I know I should talk about how I'm attracted to your brain, your beauty even, but damn it you're so sexy it drives me wild," he says, planting a luxurious kiss on the side of my neck.

I wrap my arms around his neck and pull him back on top of me. His hands find their way up my torso. I moan. More, I need more.

He takes the hint, lowering his head between my legs and pulling down my shorts. I take a quick moment of appreciation for having the foresight to put on my cute peach lace underwear this morning. He starts another trail of kisses up my inner right thigh, using his hands to lightly massage the flesh of my legs. He stops short of reaching for the top of my underwear and looks up at me for approval.

"Yes," I beg. "Please."

I help him pull my underwear down over my legs and he dives back in, parting my legs and letting his tongue find the right spot between them. Satisfaction washes over me as he moves in circles around me, like an itch that I've needed to scratch for weeks. A hand finds its way up my body and latches on to my left breast as he continues. Another long moan makes its way out of me from deep in my gut.

Taking the note, he continues, pressing his tongue even harder onto me, rhythmically moving up and down. The tingling that's threatened to take over every time I'm close to him erupts throughout my every vein, shooting euphoric pleasure to every corner of my body.

A groan leaps from my throat. "Oh my god," I say, breathlessly. "More," I hear myself say, though I'm pretty sure I'm floating three feet above my body. "I need more of you."

Benito lifts his head, climbing back on top of me, kissing the tender spot between my collarbone and the base of my neck. I fumble with the buttons on his pants; he takes the note and pushes them down his hips. I reach for him through his boxer briefs and he moans. He nods toward the nightstand. "Condoms. There should be condoms in there." He starts to reach for the top drawer but looks back at me. "Should I—?"

"Yes," I say, deciding I don't want to know why he knows where all the condoms are stashed in the house at this exact moment. "Obviously."

He grins. Once he's situated, he eases himself into me and I run my hands through his hair. I've fantasized about this moment so many times that I feel the need to take stock of my surroundings to convince myself it's really happening. The softness of his hair against my fingertips, the edges of his legs flush with mine, the heat of his body like a blanket over me, the squeezes of pleasure pulsating deep inside me. It's real. He's real.

Benito stops suddenly and locks eyes with me. "Is something wrong?" I ask.

He plants a delicate kiss on my lips. "No," he says, and it sounds like relief. "Nothing is wrong."

Chapter Fifteen

I WAKE UP THE NEXT MORNING TO SUNLIGHT POURING through the window and an empty bed. Benito snuck back to his room reluctantly hours ago, and I wish I was still tangled up in him. I open the curtains and inhale the view. With the morning fog lifting off the water like steam, it's an even more ethereal sight than the day before—if my body weren't still tingling after last night, I'd be worried this has all been a part of an elaborate, extended dream.

"Izzy? Are you up?" I hear Giac from the other side of the door. I snap back to reality and open the door. Giac's lips glide into a snide smile when he sees me. "Someone had a rough night."

I fling my hands to my head and walk into the bathroom. My hair is a mess, all askew with no discernible part, and my normally beachy waves have turned into a chaotic, tangled mess. I splash water on my face and try to work out the knots with my fingers. Giac finds my brush on the counter and hands it to me. "Bless you," I say, and run it through my hair until it no longer resembles a lion's mane after an aggressive hunt.

"There's breakfast on the terrace," he says.

"Of course there is." I head toward the door, but he is still staring at me with a foxlike grin on his face. "What?"

"Nothing." He shakes his head and laughs.

"Shut up." I playfully hit him on the shoulder. I throw my robe back on over my pajamas and we make our way downstairs.

"*Buongiorno,* Isabella." Raffaello greets me on the terrace with a double air-kiss and I cringe to notice he has an extra pep in his step this morning. The table from last night is adorned with pastries, bowls of berries, and freshly squeezed juices. When I sit, a server pours me a fresh cup of coffee.

"Isabella," Raffaello begins, "I hope you weren't too put off by my colleagues last night. They meant no offense, they're only excited about their work."

I stopped thinking about the events of last night somewhere between Benito's lips and his tongue, but now a pulse of nervous energy courses its way through me with the memory of it all. "Not at all," I say, because if we're going to rehash some portion of last night, I don't want it to be dinner. "I apologize if I made it contentious."

Raffaello claps his hands together. "Nothing wrong with a little spirited conversation. I'm sure you'll agree."

I nod. "It's kind of my love language."

The doors to the terrace swing open and Anita and Sutton walk out. Both their cheeks are rosy and sun kissed, and Sutton sets a loaf of bread down on the table. Anita flings her arms around Raffaello's shoulders and kisses him on the cheek. "We were able to acquire the honey you like, my love," she says, and I have to consciously stop myself from rolling my eyes. Anita and Raffaello have yet to make any sense to me as a couple, though stranger pairings have occurred.

"I love mornings in Como," Sutton says, stretching her arms to take in the sun. "Is Benito still not up? I was surprised he was snoring when I left, given that he's such an early bird."

"I'm sure he's exhausted after last night," Giac says with a knowing look toward me.

I nearly choke on my Nutella-filled cornetto. "We all are. What a great party. Thank you again, Raffaello and Anita, for having us." The words churn out of my mouth so quickly and chaotically that everyone is now staring at me with bemusement. "Giac, we should probably head back to La Musa soon, no?"

Giac shakes his head. He is enjoying watching me squirm way too much. "I am in no rush."

"Such an American sensibility to always be on the go," Raffaello says with a wave. "If you are going to live here in Italy, Isabella, you cannot always be thinking about what's next."

"Don't be condescending. She's adjusting." Anita waves her hand at Raffaello and I'm glad to know she doesn't allow herself to completely roll over and adhere to her husband's every wish in his presence.

Raffaello takes her hand and kisses it. I want to retch. "No, no. I mean no offense, Isabella." He's said this so many times the words have lost all meaning. "I want you to feel at home in our country. I do."

"I'm with you, Izzy," Sutton says, delicately stirring a sugar cube into her coffee. "The Italian way of life is perfect for a vacation, but I'm meant to live at a faster pace." She points her spoon at Raffaello. "And you're one to talk, Mr. Workaholic."

"There's a difference between working hard and never being able to slow down and enjoy life. I enjoy life's pleasures as much as I can."

I'll bet you do, I want to say.

The terrace doors open and Benito walks out to the patio. He's in those soft gray pants from the first night we spent together and a plain navy T-shirt. He rubs his eyes sleepily and my heart does a somersault when I notice his hair's still askew from where my fingers ran through it. "'*Giorno,*" he says, meeting my eyes first and smiling.

"Look who's finally up to greet the day," Sutton says. Benito averts his eyes from me and takes a seat next to Sutton. She rubs his back and once again I find my cornetto making its way back up my digestive tract. The logistics of the villa's sleeping arrangements under this ruse was not a question I thought to ask while Benito's tongue was in my mouth, but now my stomach turns sour at the thought of them sharing a room.

"Sleep well?" I ask.

Benito looks down as the server pours him a cup of coffee, but I see the ends of his mouth turn upward. "Not so much."

Giac leans in. "Why's that? You have a bad dream, *amico?*" I kick him under the table and muffle his wince by pouring myself a glass of grapefruit juice.

"On the contrary," Benito says. "I had a dream so good, I didn't want to fall back asleep and risk thinking about anything else." He eyes me again and the heat of his stare warms me more than the brightness of the blaring morning sun. I raise my eyebrows; he raises his back and I have half a mind to grab him by the hand and sprint back to my room.

Benito breaks eye contact and self-consciously glances around the room. "Sutton and I broke up," he blurts.

"What?" Anita gasps.

I lose track of what I'm doing, and my glass falls over, spilling juice everywhere, including in my lap. The server hops in right away to help me blot up the mess with napkins, but quite frankly I needed the cooldown. Giac hands me his napkin and I wipe what I can off my bare legs. I see Benito watching out of the corner of his eye as the napkin rounds the crease of my inner thigh. I stand up. "Shit. I should go clean up." I look around at everyone else at the table who's staring at me and to Sutton, who's glaring at Benito. "Sorry about your breakup."

I run into the house and walk swiftly to my room. Once I'm inside, I throw off my robe and root through my bag to find a suitable replacement. I slink out of my juice-stained pajamas and pull on a pair of white shorts. I pick out a green tank top and just as I'm done pulling it over my head, the door to my room swings open. Benito walks in and shuts the door behind him. I gasp. "You don't knock anymore? I could've been naked."

His eyebrows shoot up his forehead. "Is that supposed to deter me?"

I bite my lip to keep my pleased smile from giving me away. "Ok, perv."

He walks over to me and pulls me into a hug. He must've showered after last night, because he smells like an extra dose of himself this morning: pine and lemon with a hint of some kind of tangy-scent aftershave. "Good morning."

I let his hands run down my back, sliding onto my hips as he pulls back ever so slightly. "Why did you just tell everyone you and Sutton broke up?" I ask. "I thought you needed to keep your father appeased?"

"I know. I panicked." Benito kisses my forehead. "I saw you sitting there all dewy and angelic in the golden light and I couldn't do it anymore. I couldn't pretend to be in love with Sutton for another second when it's only you I want." He brushes my hair out of my face. "It's your fault. You distracted me with your beauty."

I take a deep breath. The ooey-gooey feelings are threatening to take over and I still need my wits about me. "What did they say after I left?" I ask.

Benito shrugs. "I don't know. I ran after you."

"Benito," I say. "They're going to know something's happening between us. You should go back there, explain everything."

"Or." Benito leans in and kisses me and I've officially lost the battle, my insides are mush. Every cell of me completely liquified by him, each nucleus sending the signal to surrender. I pull away.

"What are you going to do about your father?" I ask. "What are you going to do about La Musa?"

Benito sighs. "Jesus, Izzy, I'm trying to kiss you here." His face lightens, the lines around his mouth deepen with just how wide he's smiling. "My mother is downstairs, and I do not care if she walks in. That's how badly I want to kiss you, need to kiss you."

I take a step back farther, hoping more space will allow the friction between us to fall.

Law of gravity or whatever.

"We need to be rational about this," I say. "We need to have a rollout plan. A good spin." I dig through the covers on the bed for my phone. "I can call a fixer I know. She could help us crisis manage your family." I find my phone next to my pillow and start scrolling through my contacts. Benito's hand reaches over my shoulder and takes the phone away from me. "Hey!"

I turn and he's sitting on the edge of my bed and gestures for me to sit next to him. He reaches out his hand and I lace my fingers into his. "Let me handle my father," he says. "And my mother. And my sister. You don't need to worry about it. You just need to worry about us."

I jump to my feet. "So you do think I should be worried about us."

I'm still holding Benito's hand, so he jiggles it to get me to sit back down. "That's not what I meant." He takes a deep breath. "All of this drama with my father, with La Musa, it's not your problem. You shouldn't have to stress about it. Let me deal with it."

I nod. He's right. None of this is my problem. The fate of La Musa does not rest squarely on my shoulders. Just because I care doesn't mean I have to be in control. "What about Sutton?" I ask. "I'm sure she's not happy you outed your breakup."

Benito rolls his eyes. "If I know her at all, she's already using it to win brownie points with my father. Sutton will be fine. She'll go back to England, and we won't have to worry about her anymore."

"Are you sure about that?" I ask. From what I know about Sutton, although it's admittedly less, it's more likely she sees this as a temporary setback. "I think she had ulterior motives for participating in your little ruse."

Benito laughs. "Sutton always has ulterior motives, but again, don't worry about it."

"It's not my problem," I repeat. "Right."

Chapter Sixteen

GIAC AND I RETURN TO LA MUSA AROUND DUSK. HE PARKS his aunt's car at her apartment and walks me home. The streets are uncharacteristically full of tourists, and an unsettling feeling takes over as I notice most of them are American. We're nearly to my house when I see a man wearing a *Women Eat* T-shirt walking right toward us. A knot tightens in my throat. It's happening. I'm about to be recognized.

My stomach drops. This is the moment I have been dreading. My head is fogged from the memory of last night plus the exhaustion of the whirlwind trip, and I wasn't thinking clearly. I let my guard down and willfully walked down a street full of Americans without a disguise.

He lights up as he gets nearer; at least he's a fan. "Isabella Rhodes!" He's young—probably no more than 25 with bright blue eyes and dark hair underneath an LSU baseball hat. His socks are pulled up to his mid-calf and his pink shorts hit above the knee. If it weren't for the shirt, I'd think he was any other young, Gen-Z American tourist.

"Hi," I say, when he's mere inches from me—his big eyes glow as he takes me in and my nerves ease. I am safe. He likes me.

"So, you're really here, huh?" he asks, and I realize he's clutching his phone, maybe even filming this entire encounter. A smack of familiarity of my old life hits me and it's strangely comforting to slide back into this role. "I'm backpacking through Europe and rearranged my travels to come here after I saw the news about you."

I plaster on my best affable politician smile. "Well, it's gorgeous here, don't you think?"

He laughs louder than what seems natural, especially because I did not say anything remotely funny. "I figured if it's amazing enough that Isabella Rhodes freaking lives there, I should check it out."

I watch myself place a gentle hand on his forearm. "Well, I hope you enjoy La Musa," I say. "It was nice to meet you—"

"Charlie." He scoots closer to me. "Could I get a picture with you?"

I look to Giac, who graciously offers out his hand for Charlie's phone.

I slap on a smile and put my arm around Charlie. "Of course."

"You banged the mayor?" I see Marisol's eyes go wide. Congress is recessed, so she's back in Tucson, lying in an inner tube in her in-laws' pool to beat the desert late-May heat, no doubt multitasking in some other way I can't discern offscreen.

"Don't say that so loudly," I say. "I'll remind you I'm living at his very Catholic mother's house."

"And ya banged anyway." She tilts the phone down so I can see her fidget with her nose ring. "Jennings is going to freak when I tell him."

I feel a pang of guilt at the mention of Congressman Jennings. Nick was like a workplace big brother to me. He was among those to reach out when the news broke and among those I ignored. On my first trip back to DC after my loss, he didn't say anything, he just wordlessly handed me an everything bagel with lox from my favorite place on Fairfax when I boarded his jet. I grimace at Marisol. "You're keeping Congress briefed on my sex life?"

"He's fully convinced you've lost it, so I'm letting him know you're out there living your best life." I hear a splash and Marisol's out of the tube, wading over to the side of the pool. "I showed him a photo of Benito and he approves, FYI."

"How are you on the Select Committee of Intelligence when you can't keep a single secret?" I ask.

"It's because I'm keeping national security secrets that I must gossip about everything else to get it all out of my system," Marisol says. "You're keeping America safer by banging the mayor."

I sigh. "At least I'm still helping in some way." An unpleasant pang of FOMO strikes through me. It's unexpected. Why should I feel jealous of Marisol's congressional responsibilities when I'm banging the mayor? "There's a lot going on with the town, with his family, who knows if it'll even work out."

"Ugh." Marisol rolls her eyes again. "Can't one thing be fun, Izzy? Can't you not overthink on this particular matter?"

I consider. I wish it were that simple. "No."

"I hate you." She sets her phone down so I'm looking up at the bright, blue sky. I hear another splash and she returns to the screen with wet hair. "You would move to Italy under the guise of giving up your tumultuous career path only to latch on to the first man you find who just so happens to have messy drama."

It stings a little to hear it put like that, but then again, Marisol always has a way of succinctly giving the truth—and if it sounds cruel, that's on the truth of the matter, not her. "I guess I did trade one version of complicated for the other."

"You really did." She almost smiles. "At least this version has cunnilingus."

"Please do not use the word 'cunnilingus' when you recap this conversation during your next filibuster."

She ignores me. "I can see the headlines now: Rhodes Quits U.S. politics to Become Italian Politician's Wife."

I cringe. The last thing I want is for the media to catch wind of me and Benito. "I'm not going to be anyone's wife. And Benito's not a quote, unquote, 'politician.' He became the mayor of La Musa to help out his mom."

Marisol shakes her head to the side, seemingly to get water out of her ear. "Are you sure about that? He worked for a lord in the British House of Commons for years."

I rack my brain trying to remember the conversation where we discussed this. "Did I tell you that?"

She avoids answering and I decide I don't want to know the details. Reasonable doubt and all that. "You claim to have left it all behind and yet end up banging the one guy in your Podunk Umbrian town with similar aspirations to your old ones."

"It's not like that."

"How did you leave things?" Marisol asks, breezing past my denial. I don't know how to answer in a way that will satisfy her. We didn't leave things in any particular way. An alarm goes off on her phone and startles us both. "Shit, I have to go. I'm making *birria* for Jenny's parents."

"While you're in the pool?" I ask. Marisol shrugs and hangs up. I exhale relief that I don't have to explain where Benito and I stand. I don't even know. He and the rest of his family aren't returning to La Musa until later this week. It seems like there will be more of last night in our future, but how does that work, exactly, with the fissure in his family? Maybe Benito's right, and it's not for me to worry about. Until then, I'll count down the minutes until his body is on mine again.

*

I'm approached three more times by Wednesday. The first is an older couple from Vermont. They're doing a wine tour of Italy and stopped in La Musa to try the local *rosso*. They remind me of my parents: retired, laid back, inexplicably proud of me—they offer to buy me dinner, but I politely decline.

The next is a group of three women in their 20s from New York. They're renting a villa outside Florence and made a trip to La Musa for the day specifically because of me. I take a photo with them outside La Musa's *duomo*.

The third is while I'm having coffee with Valeria. She's thanking me for my help, as groups of tourists have already been stopping in the wine shop. She tells me she feels confident the turnaround will be enough to deter Raffaello, but the pit in my stomach tells me it's not.

A kid who can't be more than 13 runs up to our table at Caffè del Duomo. "Isabella Rhodes, you're my idol," she says, grinning with a mouthful of braces.

I sit up a little straighter. "You're so sweet."

"I want to be a politician just like you," she beams.

A prickle runs down my spine. "Well, I wouldn't say I'm a politician anymore, but thank you."

She shakes her head. "It doesn't matter. You're still my favorite—" She pauses and scrunches her nose, causing her glasses to push farther up her face. "What would you call yourself now?"

I take a moment. How do I define myself? Wine drinker? Pasta eater? The girl who's banging the mayor? "Nowadays I'm just Izzy."

She looks off up at the sky as she contemplates. "I lost my election to be student council president," she says. "So I guess I'm just Daisy."

My insides warm. She's adorable. "Being Daisy is the best thing you can be. Any label you put in front of your name is just an extra set of letters." Daisy beams but I feel a strike of guilt rush through me. If someone had told me that when I was Daisy's age, I would've thought they were insane. All my life, I never thought I'd settle for anything less than the ultimate dream.

Daisy poses for a photo with me and walks back to her parents. We finish up our coffee and I head home. It's hot today, and my room has been baking in the afternoon sun. I fling a window open to let in the evening breeze. The light drips through and it's that deep orangish yellow that only happens on the clearest of days, and the smell of blooming olive trees wafts through. It's peaceful here, even with the threat of recognition at every corner. It's beautiful.

I collapse onto my bed and thumb through my phone. I still have hundreds of unread texts and I've gotten so used to the little red number at the bottom of the screen that I don't even see it. There's a news alert about a bill that's just been passed in the House. I've avoided current events for months, but it piques my interest and I open it: *Congress Passes Tax Breaks for Top 1% of Earners*. I sigh. Damn it. This was a campaign promise the other side ran on and now it's headed to the Senate, where our party holds only a slim lead.

I can't help but think that I somehow could've put a stop to it. Levi, to his credit, was a "no" vote, but maybe if I'd won it would've set off a chain of events that didn't allow for this to happen. Or Marisol and I would team up and do a double press on our most amenable opponents. I was good at using words to get what I wanted, whether it was an impassioned speech on the floor or a Sunday morning talk show—the famous Rhodes Rhetoric won me a lot of favors.

When I was a kid, I could talk my way out of trouble or into anything I wanted. It was a skill so powerful my father eventually sat me down one day and explained how I should only use my mastery of language for good. There were two paths well suited for me career-wise, politician or scam artist, he told me. He said I could end up in jail or president, and the paths to either were narrowly split. An odd thing to tell a nine-year-old but still, I heeded his advice and doggedly pursued the White House, never once looking back until now.

How different life would be if he'd told me I'd make a good accountant.

I hear the creak of the front gate and run to my window. Benito's back. The anticipation energizes me. I snake out of my clothes and throw on the red lingerie set. By the time I tie my robe across my waist, there's a light knock on my door. I basically sprint to open it and grin when I see Benito on the other side, hands in his pockets, rocking back and forth on his heels.

"Hi, you," he says.

I bite the inside of my cheeks to keep my smile from taking over my entire face. "Hi."

It's only a moment or two more before we collide into each other, falling into bed and picking right back up where we left.

A frantic knock at my door frightens me out of a dreamy nap. It takes me a second to readjust to the waking world and realize my pillow is Benito's bare chest. I groan. "Who could that be?"

Benito strokes my hair. "It's probably my mother."

We both look at each other and then sit up straight. "Shit," I say, jumping out of bed and throwing my robe back on. "She knows." I pace around my room, looking for my underwear. "She's going to think I'm some kind of American tart."

"No, she won't," Benito says. "Because it's not 1956." This doesn't stop him from also getting up and pulling on his khakis.

We hear another knock. I look at him panickily. "What do I do?"

"I think you answer it?" he says.

"Ok, you hide." I point toward the corner of the room.

"Seriously?" he asks. "We don't need to hide from her, we are grown adults." I glare at him. He swallows, reconsidering. "We can tell her we were watching a movie."

I keep pointing until he finally obliges, his back up against the wall and out of view of the door as I open it. I have to hold in a gasp when I do not see Anita on the other side, but Sutton.

"Sutton," I say, trying to hide my stunned expression. "Hi."

She's in a pair of crisp white pants and a coordinating linen blazer with a pink scarf tied chicly around her neck. I feel self-conscious about the thinness of my robe and my sex hair. Isn't she supposed to be back in London? "Sorry to just drop in like this," she says. "I felt the need to apologize in person for throwing you to the wolves like I did the other night."

"*In bocca al lupo,*" I mutter. Sutton looks at me with a quizzical expression. "It means good luck in Italian, but it literally translates to *in the mouth of the wolf.*" I smooth my hair with my hands. "I'm just realizing how apt of an expression it is, that's all."

Sutton stares at me blankly for another moment then blinks. "Right, well, will you let me buy you a drink? I fear we've gotten off on the wrong foot and it doesn't sit well with me."

I study her face, which is so completely frozen by Botox, I wouldn't be able to tell if she had any emotions about her and Benito's breakup becoming officially official. "I thought you'd be on your way home by now," I say.

Sutton shakes her head. "Not quite. Please let me make it all up to you before I go."

She's up to something, that much is clear. But I'm kind of curious as to what her play is. "Sure. Why not."

She grins. "Good. I know I've sprung this on you, so why don't I give you time to freshen up"—she eyes my appearance—"and I'll meet you at Bar Musa in an hour?"

I close the door behind her and wait until I hear her footsteps fade down the hall. I turn to Benito, who sheepishly creeps out of his hiding space. "The fuck was that?" I ask.

"You don't have to go," Benito says. He walks over to the bed and sits, propping himself up with his right arm. The vein in his forearm pops, and I resist the urge to run my fingers up it. "She's like a bee: You ignore her, she goes away."

I sit next to him. "Or you let it sting you and it dies later, learning an important lesson about karma."

Benito raises his eyebrows at me. "Jesus."

I tap his hand with mine and stand up. "I need to see what she's up to. Maybe it'll help."

"Help?" Benito asks.

I run a brush through my hair. "With La Musa, with your father, with everything." I lean and plant a quick kiss on Benito's lips and shoo him out of my room.

I change into a pair of wide-legged jeans with a white bodysuit. Most of my clothes are thrifted or at least bought on sale, important during my campaign considering my politics, but now I wish I'd taken up the offer from the fancy Hollywood stylists who offered their services to me. I don't want to feel inferior to Sutton. I have no reason to.

When the clock tower chimes 6 p.m., I find Sutton already on the patio of Bar Musa, sipping on a spritz. She stretches her hand into the air and waves at me as I enter. "Izzy! Good. For a moment there, I wondered if you'd changed your mind. What's your drink?" She reaches her long arm back into the air and gets the attention of a server. He happily bounces over to us.

"I'll take a glass of the pinot grigio," I say.

Sutton shakes her head. "No, Izzy. Please, we're celebrating."

"We are?"

"It's on me," she says with a wink.

I rack my brain for a suitable replacement, but truthfully, I just wanted wine. "Glass of prosecco, then," I say.

Sutton nearly jumps up. "Brilliant idea. Make it a bottle," she says to the server. "*Due bicchieri.*"

"What are we celebrating?" I ask.

Sutton twirls her straw in her drink and finishes the last few sips. "Hm?"

"You said we're celebrating." The sun has not yet dipped below the buildings, but I take my sunglasses off so she can see my eyes.

"Ah, yes." She claps her hands together. "We are celebrating because I realized you and I have the same goal."

My eyebrows narrow. "We do?"

"Yes." The server returns and pops the bottle of prosecco, pouring us each a glass. "I was thinking about you all wrong, Izzy. I saw you as competition and I'm sure you can see why."

My mind flashes to Benito. "Because...?"

"Because you stood in the way of the development deal. You have Benito's ear, as well as the women business owners, and their reluctance is our biggest complication."

I wait for the rest. That sounds more or less exactly what the situation is. "Is that not it?"

Sutton throws her head back and laughs. "No, of course not. I thought it was to rebrand yourself, which is why I thought the ad campaign would work, but that's not it. Your goal, really, is to make a place for yourself in La Musa."

I take a long sip of prosecco, certain there's some other bomb she's going to drop any second. "I guess that's the truth, but how is that your problem?"

Sutton takes a tiny sip of her drink and smiles slightly over the top of her glass. "Because the answer to your goal is the same as the answer to mine." She sets her glass down and leans back in her chair. "I've got it all worked out."

"Have you?" I ask. I'm starting to get the sense that the apology she promised is never coming and I won't like the alternative.

"You should be the mayor." She takes another sip of her drink like it's as simple of a suggestion as *"I'll let you freshen up."*

I laugh. "What?"

"You should be mayor," she repeats. "Think about it. It gives you a place in La Musa. You have the experience. You'll have a hand in saving the place. It's perfect."

I wait for her to tell me she's kidding. That her grand plan is actually for me to buy out the local *panetteria* or be crowned princess or something else that makes more sense. "Benito is the mayor."

Sutton smirks. "That's where what I want comes in."

A bad feeling rises from my gut to my chest, the bubbles of the prosecco burning my esophagus as they travel back upward. "I thought you said what we want is the same."

"It is. I want you to be mayor." She taps her fingers on the table, her long nails making a clicking sound. "Because I want Benito back in London with me."

Chapter Seventeen

I FIX MY STARE INTO SUTTON'S DARK EYES. I KNEW HER reasons for being here were not as selfless as *"Benito's been good to me."* She wants him. She wants to use me to get him back. And the worst part is, she thinks she's doing me a favor. "I do not want to be mayor," I say.

The sun descends below the rooftops of the piazza that surrounds us and Sutton tops off her glass. "Don't let the way Benito goes about it fool you, it doesn't have to be so horribly stressful." She offers the bottle to me and sets it down when I don't take it. "Benito resigns, he and Raffaello endorse you to run in his place, you approve the development deal, you sit back, relax, enjoy your life knowing your Wikipedia page doesn't end with your last election."

My mind buzzes with questions. Primarily *how dare you.* "Is it even legal for me to be mayor? I'm not an Italian citizen."

Sutton waves it off. "We'd work it all out, don't worry about that."

I sit up straighter. It's not going to be easy to convince her I don't want this. "I'd be a puppet for Raffaello's business. And don't even get me started on that offensive ad campaign pitch. You're using me."

She leans back, exasperated. "Good god, Izzy. Must everything be so sinister?" She laughs, pushing the bottle back toward me again. I relent and refill my glass. "Support Raffaello or don't. The point is, it'd be your battle to fight. Not Benito's. He belongs back in London. He chased the wrong family legacy. He needs to return and fulfill his destiny."

My breath catches in my throat. She's preaching to the wrong choir. I know destiny is a mirage, a trick into letting life pass you by while you chase a shiny object through a sparse desert to no avail. A way to convince yourself you have a purpose instead of accepting that you are a sack of organs and bones meant only to breathe in and breathe out until you no longer can. "Sutton. I don't want to be mayor. And if you really cared about Benito, you'd know that he doesn't want to go back to London."

Completely unaffected by my words, she laughs. "Benito does not know what he wants." My stomach does a flip. She's right about that. He more or less said the exact same thing to me weeks ago.

I take another sip of prosecco. "Will you make a PowerPoint to convince him to go back?"

Sutton's lips stretch into a sly smile. "If it'll help."

I finish my drink and don't bother to fight Sutton

when she offers to pick up the check. I walk through town on my way home and my brain is buzzing, both from drinking two glasses of prosecco in quick succession and from what Sutton confessed. Benito is surrounded by so many people who don't have his best interests at heart. No wonder he was skeptical of my intentions.

I can't help but feel like I've meandered too far from my original mission. I was supposed to come to Italy, sleep, drink wine, eat pasta, and that was it. I wasn't supposed to care about anything else. I wasn't supposed to care about any*one* else.

Once again, I've failed.

I'm so deep in thought, it barely registers when someone shouts my name. It's a grating voice. Deep, low, with a sharpness that causes the hairs on the back of my neck to stand up straight. "Isabella Rhodes!" I hear again, and my instinct is to keep walking, but my legs freeze. I turn around.

I'm not surprised when the man approaches me. He's red faced, bearded, massive with bulging shoulders and a beer belly. "You!" he shouts again as he gets closer. I freeze.

"Isabella fucking Rhodes," he says, spitting all over me. "You have some nerve moving to another country. It wasn't enough to ruin ours?" A woman catches up to him; she's petite and wearing a backpack around her shoulders. She stands a few feet behind him with an equally disgusted look skewed in my direction.

I try not to cower or worse, verbally spar. What was Richard always saying? Stay calm. Try not to escalate the situation. I make my voice as still and even as possible. "I am living my life out of the public eye. I am not trying to ruin anything."

The man's eyes go black. He takes a few steps closer so there's barely any distance between us, a foot tops. "You existing at all ruins everything." An ominous chill trickles down my spine.

The man moves closer to me, a mere inch between his face and mine. "You're a waste of a human being. You don't deserve to enjoy the rest of your life. You tried to ruin all of ours. You tried to ruin America. All while you were trying to screw everyone in Washington."

I put my hands up in surrender. None of that is true, but he has a good foot of height on me, and without Richard or any of my other former bodyguards, I'm defenseless. This isn't the first time I've feared for my life during an altercation, but the lack of strong people who know how to disarm on my side makes the threat feel more real. "I don't want any trouble."

He moves closer and squats down so we're nearly nose-to-nose. I swallow hard. "If you know what's good for you, you'll disappear. You got it?"

An arm darts between us, a measly protective shield against this truly massive dude, but enough to keep him from getting closer. I quickly turn my head to my right and see Benito. "I need you to walk away before I call the police," Benito says.

The man laughs loudly, and my eardrum shakes from the booming noise. "What are the Italian police going to do? Huh? Arrest me with spaghetti handcuffs?"

I laugh because it's a funny image, but I'm terrified. Still, Benito doesn't budge. He holds his arm steady, walking closer until he wedges himself between us. The man's female companion lays a gentle hand on his arm. "Come on, Matt. Let's go. She's not worth it."

Matt stares me down for another minute as if he's deciding to finish me off right there. I have no doubt he could squash me with his bare hands and treat himself to gelato afterward with no remorse, but he backs off. He spits just to the right of me as if to show his dominance one last time, and leaves. We watch them walk away, the opposite direction from my house.

Benito grabs my hand, and we book it the last quarter of a mile to the house. The run does me good and helps to shake off the nerves. When we walk through the front door, I exhale, relieved. Benito follows me up to my room, locking the door behind us. "Are you ok?" he asks.

I fall onto the bed and fold my knees into my chest, getting into fetal position. "Yeah, yeah. I'm good. That hasn't happened in a while, but I knew it was a possibility after the news came out."

Benito sits next to me. "This has happened before?"

I nod. "I used to get accosted a lot in the early days of my term. I hired security and stopped going out in public without them and it got better, and after..." I lift my head and look at him, still woozy from the alcohol and the adrenaline. "After I lost, it got a lot better."

Benito's face contorts, and even from my lying-down position it's easy to recognize it as the same as my parents' when I first told them about such encounters: pity, sadness, fear. I don't want him to look at me like that. Not because it's humiliating to look like that in front of another person, although I don't love that either, but because it was never supposed to come to this. If I had just stuck to the plan—no attachments, no ties to my old life—none of this would have ever happened. I'd be watching the sunset, drinking a glass of wine, wondering how I ever cared about anything other than life's simplest pleasures.

"I'm sorry you went through that," he says. "I'm sorry you had to go through that again." I sit up so I'm level with him. He reaches his hand like he's about to rest it on my knee but places it in his pocket. "Do you think you need security here?"

I shake my head. "I don't know. Maybe. I guess it depends if it happens again or not."

Benito inhales sharply. "It's unsettling to think you're unsafe here."

I shrug. "It's the reality of my situation no matter where I go. I came to the most off-the-grid town I could think of, and I still ended up outing myself. Unless I want to live on my aunt's ranch in remote Northern Ontario, I don't think it really matters."

"I'm going to find out who outed your location and give them a formal condemnation." Benito runs his fingers through his hair. “A formal condemnation, Izzy.”

“You don’t need to do that,” I say.

“I should’ve done it a long time ago.” He starts pacing. “Let me get in touch with the police.” He takes out his phone and scrolls. “Or maybe we send this man’s photo to every business, and they can refuse him service. We’ll leak his name to the press. Matt.” He scoffs. “I hate that name. Matt.”

I stand up and put my hand over his phone. “Benito,” I say. I shake my head. “You don’t need to do anything.”

His eyebrows furrow. “Of course I do.”

I shake my head. “This is the reality of who I am. Or who I was.” I clasp my hands together. “We could freak out, that’s one option. Or”—I tilt my head at him—“we could forget it all.”

Benito’s face scrunches up even more and I miss its softness. I don’t like that I added to his ever-mounting stress. I resist the urge to run my fingers over the lines on his forehead. “Forget what?” he asks.

I sigh. “Your father trying to ruin the town, the fact that you didn’t like me at first, the fact that I didn’t like you at first, my sordid past, my dead dream, Levi, my PG-13 sex scandal, your ex-girlfriend trying to make me mayor so she can have you all to herself back in London. Really, it runs the gamut. Anything else you want to throw in there, we can forget. We can *Eternal Sunshine of the Spotless Mind* any and all unnecessary complications. We can do that.”

His face drops. "Wait, what? Sutton is trying to what?"

"That's what drinks was about. She floated the asinine idea by me. You resign, I become mayor, you return to London to fulfill your destiny or whatever." I wave it off. "Which probably includes getting back together with her."

Benito rubs his hands together, digesting. I wonder what I can do to speed up the process and cut to the part where he agrees to a more laissez-faire perspective. It's not too late for me to slip into a state of dormancy. Food, wine, sex with Benito—*that* could be my new purpose. Izzy Rhodes's next big move. "I can't believe she said that to you," he finally says.

"She thought she was doing me a favor. She thinks what everyone at home thinks too, that I need a big life with accolades and glory, but I don't. I really don't." I place my hand in his. This is taking too long.

"And you're sure of that?" he asks.

I tilt my head back, frustrated that he keeps asking questions instead of unbuttoning his shirt. "I can't have this argument with you again."

He turns his body so he's facing me, my hand falling off his knee in the process. "No, I know you want to be here. I understand why you left, I understand why you can't go back to the life you knew, but are you sure this will be enough?" He runs his fingers through his hair. I remember the feeling of when I copied that exact gesture and my breath catches. "Eating pasta, drinking wine, *Mamma's* lunches every Sunday, the closest city two hours by train. Can you honestly tell me you won't get bored once the novelty runs out?"

My eyebrows furrow. Why are we discussing the intricacies of the future when I've just sworn to focus on the present? "You're overthinking it," I say, knowing the irony of how often I've done the same about everything else in my life. "I came here with a resounding intention to be nothing but a woman in Italy. It's an added bonus that I've met you, I've met your family, Vincenzo, Valeria, Giac. Everything got so messy, everything's been a mess since I lost the election, but it doesn't have to be that way. It's not too late to flit through the rest of my life."

Benito's eyes widen. He looks at me like he's doing a scan, parsing through every part of my body looking for signs that I'm bullshitting him. If one hair's askew or one muscle of my face not fully relaxed, it'd be enough for him to retreat. "I don't want what happened today to ever happen again," he says. His last line of defense. If he's looking for reasons to push me away, it's not a bad one. Valiant, even, to sacrifice his own wants over the need for my safety.

"If it does, we'll handle it," I say. "The last remnant of the life I left behind. A scar on an otherwise completely clean slate."

He smirks. "You're sexy when you speak in metaphors."

I grin. I'm in. I move my hands to either side of his head and pull him to me. His lips meet mine and my stomach settles knowing the last time wasn't the last time, and this won't be the last time either. I'm getting what I wanted. I'm getting everything I came here for.

Benito lowers me onto the bed and crawls on top of me, delicately pushing the hair out of my face. He smiles at me before kissing me again. This is what I wanted.

Chapter Eighteen

I WAKE UP THE NEXT MORNING TO MY PHONE RINGING. The sun is peeking through the curtains, but Benito's still asleep next to me. He looks so peaceful, the worry lines on his face smoothed out without the stress of the waking world pestering him. I could get used to this. No plans, no stress, just lazy mornings with Benito after a long, good night.

Marisol is FaceTiming me, so I take my phone into the hallway and shut the door to the bedroom behind me. "Hey," I answer, keeping my voice quiet so I don't wake Benito.

Marisol raises her eyebrows when she sees me pop up onscreen. "What's with the whispering?" She leans in to get a closer look. "And why is your hair so messy?" I raise my eyebrows. Marisol grins. "Good for you, Izzy."

She spins in her chair, and I can tell from the turquoise tile detail on the wall that she's in her district congressional office in Tucson. My stomach drops, though I don't know why. Suddenly, my skin's itchy. "You're working late," I say, my voice breaking over the newly formed lump in my throat.

"Yeah, whatever. What else is new. I'm not done talking about your thing." She props her elbows on her desk and leans her head against her hand. "How's it going?"

I fixate on the degree hung up behind her. An honorary doctorate from the University of Arizona, where she attended undergrad, given to her last May when she was the commencement speaker. Mari won her re-election in a landslide, her opponent conceding a mere 15 minutes after polls closed. "It's going good," I say, leaning back against the wall because I'm a little lightheaded.

"Uh-oh," Marisol says, picking up on my trepidation. "Is his penis weird? Does he call himself 'daddy'?"

"He's asleep in the other room, Mari. It's not a good time for an info dump," I say, an edge to my voice.

Marisol surveys my expression like she's questioning if she should interrogate further. "Ok..."

I do my best to shake off the weird feeling that's crept over me. "It's good, though. I'm happy. I'm back on track to fade away into the Italian countryside. It's good."

"Only you would turn relaxation into a goal," she says, rolling her eyes.

"Shut up. You would too."

"No, I would never make that a goal." She flips through a multipage document on her desk.

"Relaxation is for the retired and people with office jobs who think they're burned out."

I try to read the text of the document as she scans through. I remember late nights like the one Marisol's currently having. Reading, marking up documents, late-night phone calls trying to make a deal. It was a rush. I loved mining the chaos of a hundred different possibilities to find the best path toward ratification. Marisol puts the document aside and puts her attention back on me. "As much as I love a good morning-after debrief, that's not why I called," she says.

"No?" I ask. "What's up?"

Marisol rubs her lips together. "Ok, don't like freak out, but I'm running for Senate."

A pit opens up in my stomach, like I've just been hurtled down the tallest peak of a roller coaster. "What?" I squeak out.

"I know," Marisol says. "I didn't expect it to happen this soon, but Franklin is retiring next year and he's announcing and endorsing me. He like, loves me for whatever reason and thinks I'd be a perfect person to bridge the deepening gap between the right and the left in Arizona." Marisol rolls her eyes. She's as progressive as they come, but her family's long history as beloved owners of a Tucson restaurant makes her pseudo-royalty in Southern Arizona, and it's reasonable to assume with Franklin's endorsement, she could easily win over the whole state with her staunchly pro-middle-class agenda. "I probably won't win," she says. "But I mean, I have to do it, right?"

Marisol and I bonded over many things, but our mutual goal of finally putting a woman in the White House was one of them. And Marisol is about to be one step closer to making sure that woman is her. I'm thrilled for her. This is great news. But I also have an overwhelming urge to throw my phone across the hallway.

The door creaks open and Benito comes out. He's pulled on his clothes from the day before and his blue button-down is uncharacteristically wrinkled, his hair as messy as mine. "Sorry, did I wake you?" I ask.

He shakes his head. "I heard voices and figured, considering what happened yesterday, I should make sure they were friendly ones."

"What happened yesterday?" Marisol asks from the other end of the phone. "And who am I speaking with?"

Benito sits down on the couch next to me and waves. "Benito. *Piacere*."

"This is Marisol," I say, racking my brain to remember if I've ever mentioned her to Benito before, but I don't think I have. I've avoided talking about my old life with him unless absolutely necessary. "She was my best friend in Congress."

"Nice to meet you and all that. What happened yesterday?" Her eyebrows perk up, knowing there's a story.

I take a deep breath. "Another successful run-in with one of my fans."

She lets out a one-syllable laugh. "Those are always fun. You're ok, though, I take it?"

I try to brush it off. "Fine."

Benito leans in so he can see Marisol clearly. "It's happened to you too?"

"Oh yeah," she says, leaning back in her chair, "Izzy got the worst of it, though. I'm a Latina lesbian, so they'd already written me off. Izzy is cute and straight and quote, unquote, 'radical' to them—mostly in that they know she'd never fuck them. That's what bothers them the most."

"I thought we decided it was more that I look like I should be their demure, obedient housewife but am anything but that?"

"Same diff."

Benito watches the conversation back and forth like we're playing a game of tennis where the ball is on fire. "That's horrible."

"You should've seen Izzy take one of those old geezers in Congress down, Benito. It was beautiful." Marisol does a chef's kiss gesture. "I'm able to pick up the slack now, of course, but it's not as fun."

"I've seen a preview of it, so I can only imagine," Benito says, smiling, but there's a glint of sadness in his eyes.

"Hashtag women eat," I say.

Marisol throws her fist in the air. "Women eat, Benito!"

We hang up and Benito pulls me close to him. A heavy sigh escapes out of me. "What's wrong?" Benito asks.

"Nothing," I say, though there's a growing sense of an unnamable feeling in my gut. It's a feeling like homesickness mixed with sadness mixed with loneliness mixed with guilt. It happens every once in a while, like I'm suddenly grieving the fact that I'm alive and this is it, this is who I am.

"That sigh was not nothing," Benito says. He kisses me on top of my head. "You can tell me."

I look up at him. His eyes are bright in the reflection of the morning sun cascading through the hall window. "Marisol is going to run for Senate."

"Wow," he says. "That's great, right?"

"Yeah," I say. I look down at the ground. I am happy for my friend. This is good for everyone. Marisol is amazing. She'll be great. She should be president someday, because she'd be a great one. Why can't I shake the gnawing feeling that it should be me instead? I stand up. "I should get dressed," I say. "I'm having coffee with the ladies."

Eventually I have to find a job and my own place, but Anita doesn't seem in any rush to kick me out. For now, this is my life. Benito, leisurely coffee dates, long lunches, cocktails, dinner, wine, a stroll at dusk, the wind in my hair—this can be my life.

"Hey." Benito grabs at my hand before I can walk back into my bedroom. "You sure you're ok?"

"Yeah," I say. "I'm great." Benito looks at me with worry in his eyes, but I don't have the energy to assuage him.

He smiles softly, a glint of gloss on his eyes. "Ok, then. Have fun."

"To Izzy!" Mia raises an Aperol Spritz and the other ladies and I cheers with matching bright orange cocktails. It's a perfect sunny day. The kind you see on the travel reels of a blond, hot influencer. We're on the patio at Osteria Bettina because coffee turned into lunch which turned into after-lunch drinks. We're toasting me, for not the first time, because my outing made La Musa trend, and I'm the one who convinced the mayor to turn against the development deal. Benito more or less came to that revelation on his own, but whatever, I'll take an accolade. Besides, Benito's meeting with Raffaello to firmly decline his company's renovation proposals today. By nightfall, all the drama will be in the past.

I glance at my phone and a headline about Senator Franklin catches my eye. The news is out and soon Marisol's candidacy, and his endorsement, will be too. Senate was always the most logical next step for me. California's senators are young, but maybe in 10 years or 20 I could make a run. And in another four or five years toss my hat in the ring for president. Maybe I wouldn't get the nomination on my first try, but I would the next time.

I made sure my reputation in Washington was the right mix of spitfire and squeaky clean. A fighter, a warrior for her constituents, for what would make the world a better place, but without even a speck of corruption or scandal. I had good relationships with my colleagues who fought for the same things I did and garnered just the right amount of animosity from those on the other side.

Hatred of me was galvanizing for voters, that's what Kate said whenever I was wary my verbal takedowns went too far. The more they talked about me on the news, the better for me overall. The attacks, the vitriol, were good as long as they were met equally with progress on my campaign promises. The abuse was worth it until it wasn't.

I don't miss the death threats, the security scares, the spamming from trolls, but I miss the high of doing something right. Those moments snapped everything into focus. It wasn't just about me, that's what I always said to voters, to the media, it was about the people. I was meant to be a representative of the people. The only thing I had that was solely for me was Levi, and he turned out to be my downfall.

Now my entire life is for me, and I'm not going to let how I used to see the world make me feel guilty for that. I tried. I really, really tried, and it didn't work. Why would I go back to a life of public service now that I've seen the other side? Now that I know the public turns on you the second you admit you're imperfect.

I'm significantly buzzed when I leave coffee/lunch/drinks at around 5 p.m. The sun is starting to set, leaving bright pink streaks through the sky. I walk past the *duomo,* the clock tower, the center of town with its various shops, bars, and restaurants, all bustling much more than they were three months ago. I try to capture a whiff of pride. This is because of me, right? I came to La Musa and now it is in better economic shape because of me. Why doesn't it feel like a victory?

I walk into the house to find Benito and Anita conversing in Italian in the kitchen. They stop when I walk in. "Izzy!" Anita says brightly. "You'll join us all for dinner tonight?" I don't know who *"us all"* includes, but I nod. *"Perfetto!"* Anita chimes.

Benito pours us each a glass of wine and Anita takes hers to the backyard. Once we're alone, I turn to him. "How'd it go with your father?" I ask.

Benito runs his finger along the stem of his glass. "We were able to reach an agreement."

I wait for him to face me and tell me the whole story, but he doesn't. "... And?"

Benito takes a long sip of wine and looks in my direction, not quite meeting my eyes. "He convinced me that converting the old estate into a hotel is the right move. We have more tourists than the inns in town can handle, and it's a beautiful property. It does no use to anyone sitting vacant."

It's a reasonable compromise. A small, luxury resort in a historic villa that would make La Musa more attractive to high-end tourists is not the end of the world. "Ok. That makes sense. What about the rest?"

He glances around the room as if he's making sure no one else is within earshot. "He agreed to kill the deal on developing the rest of town."

I grin, but Benito's still stoic. "That's great!" I nudge him with my elbow. "Why aren't you more excited?"

He takes a deep breath. "There are strings attached. With my father there always is."

"I'm not surprised." I laugh. "I knew Raffaello wouldn't walk away from a deal with nothing. What are the strings?"

Benito looks back down at his wine glass. "I'd have to go work for him."

My heart sinks. That's the last thing Benito would want. "In Milan?"

He shakes his head. "In London."

The bottom of my stomach hollows out and I worry I'm about to vomit up the three Aperol Spritzes in my system. "But you're not doing it, right?"

Benito's eyes finally meet mine. They're not as bright, not as sparkly as I know them to be. "I don't think I have a choice."

The edges of my limbs tingle and every nerve in my body shatters. I've felt this way once before. A mountain forms in my throat and when I open my mouth to speak, no words come out. Benito swallows hard, his Adam's apple bobbing up and down like an unanchored rowboat. He clasps his fingers around mine.

I try to process what this means. Benito agreed to move back to London, just like that. Sutton's getting what she wants, she warned me she always does. Only, I didn't think it'd be that easy. I didn't think Benito would leave me so easily. "I—"

We're interrupted when Anita walks back into the house. Benito gives me a pointed look and shakes his head. He hasn't told his mother yet, but I'm certain he'll spin it so she'll be thrilled. She knew Benito didn't want to come back here and now he's going back to London, where he always wanted to be. I was so worried about convincing him I wasn't a flight risk that I never stopped to consider that he might be the one to leave. My stomach churns. I should've eaten more today.

"Izzy, are you alright?" Anita asks. "You look ill."

I hold up a finger. "Fine," I choke out. "I just need some air." I put my wine glass down on the counter and flee out the front of the house. I inhale sharply when the fresh air greets me outside. The front door creaks open and I see that Benito's followed me. He wordlessly leans against the fence next to me. "What the hell?" I croak out.

Benito takes a deep breath and revels in a long blink. "I know how it must sound to you—"

"It sounds like you're going back to London," I say, the tears starting to work their way out from the inner corners of my eyes.

He takes a step toward me. "All he's wanted this whole time was for me to come back to the company and secure my destiny. It's been his plan. It's why he's done everything that he's done. Sutton said—"

A rage fire erupts in my chest. "Sutton? You talked to Sutton about this?"

Benito's eyes flash to mine and I see a glint of frustration. "Only to get her perspective on everything. She's the only one who knows my father like I do."

"Sutton wants you. Sutton wants you back in London. Of course she'd tell you to take it." I feel hoarse, like I've been scream-singing for hours at a concert. I try to make sense of where I am. Are my feet on the ground? Because it feels like my whole world has been flipped upside down. Again. "How do you know your father will keep his word?"

Benito exhales loudly. "I don't. He made a lot of promises, but I don't know that I trust him."

"This is the worst quid pro quo ever," I say. Benito smirks. I hate that I amused him when it's taking everything in me not to slap him across his perfect face. "You're leaving me. Just like that. After everything?"

I see him swallow hard again, like my words are unpalatable but he has no choice but to accept them. "I'm leaving. I'm not leaving you."

I roll my eyes. What difference does it make? "Don't sugarcoat this. Don't try to make this better. You're still leaving. You sacrificed yourself. You're the hero. The savior of La Musa. You traded your watch for gold combs for my hair, and I sold my hair for a chain for your watch. We're tragic. You'll always wonder about Izzy, the one who got away. And I'll be sitting on a porch when I'm 80, telling my grandchildren about my fleeting few months with the hot, young Italian mayor. Whatever. It doesn't change the facts. You're leaving me."

He takes another step closer and reaches out for

me, but I flinch back. "Izzy, I'm not leaving you. I'm getting out of your way."

My eyes roll so hard I think they might finally get stuck that way like my mother always warned. "That's a twisted way to look at it."

"What steps have you taken to actually make a life here, Izzy? You don't have your own housing—"

"Not yet," I say. "But I'll start looking."

Benito ignores me. "You've barely learned any Italian—"

"I haven't gotten around to it yet. I can start."

"You don't have a job—"

"I'll get one at a flower shop or something."

"There is no flower shop in La Musa!" Benito practically screams.

"Wait, really?" I realize he's right, and every time I've bought flowers in town is at the farmers market. So much for that idea. "That doesn't track."

"See, you've made no real plans, Izzy. None."

I look at him; there's a pleading in his eyes. If I weren't so annoyed with him, his pained expression would break my heart.

Benito sighs, his hand finding its way through his hair. "You say you want this to be your home and yet you've done nothing to make it your home. I am tired of pretending to go along with it all when I know you will not stay here. I can't be a part of this delusion that you can have a quiet, complication-free life."

I try to burn a hole through his face with the rage behind my eyes. Not 12 hours ago he very happily took part in that delusion. "Yes, I can."

"No, you can't. That's not how life works, and more importantly, that's not how you work. Look at how that plan's worked out so far. You fought against the town's development since day one, you took on my father, his business associates, Sutton. It is not in your nature to be an inactive participant in the world. Soon you will realize that, but I suspect you already do. Sutton said—"

I cut him off. That's enough. "Sutton doesn't know a thing about me. She wanted me to be mayor."

"You should be the mayor!" Benito yells, though he's not angry. It's like he's pleading with me. An impassioned lawyer making his case. "Or the CEO of something, or a businessowner, or…" He takes a step toward me. "Or president." I glare at him; how dare he throw that in my face. The dream I now recognize as childish and naïve, the one I know will never come true. "The point is, Izzy. You could never be nothing."

I absorb his words. After every argument we've had, I thought he finally understood my mission. Better yet, I thought he wanted to be a part of it. "If you don't want me, there are easier ways to break it off," I say.

Benito runs both his hands through his hair again and shakes his head. "It's not that. Please know that. If it were as simple as being with you or not, I'd choose you." He takes a step closer. "I see you. I always have. I see how amazing you are. I see how smart you are. I see how one-of-a-kind you are. I want to be around you all the time. I know if I stayed, I wouldn't be able to stay away from you, but I can't be part of letting you throw that all away. I want you to want more for yourself. You should want more for yourself."

A chill runs down my spine. I don't know how many ways I can say that I'm not that person before he will finally believe it. "I told you. I don't want to be the person I was anymore."

Benito is silent for a few moments then shakes his head again. "That's just it, Izzy. You can never stop being who you are." He looks off in the distance, like he's staring at a future that is certain to everyone except for me. "Soon you'll see that."

"Fuck that," I say breathlessly. I'm out of fight. I'm out of energy. If even Benito can't see that I'm really, truly done, how will anyone else? What corner of the earth do I have to move to to finally convince everyone that I am done caring? That I am done trying? "Have a nice life in London. With Sutton."

Benito stares at me. I try to discern what exact emotion is behind his gaze but he's impossible to read. "I wish things worked out differently," he says.

I cannot possibly utter another word without erupting into a full-blown sob, so I say nothing. Benito watches me for a moment before turning and walking back inside. As soon as he's gone, I sink to my heels. I let the tears loose and fear I'll never be able to contain them again. I run upstairs to my bedroom and slam the door shut.

Chapter Nineteen

ONCE THE INITIAL STING OF WHAT BENITO DID WEARS off, I start to spiral. What am I supposed to do now? Benito's leaving. I can't really achieve the chic, wispy 2000s movie heroine aesthetic I crave when I'm brokenhearted. Once again, my life is ruined by my feelings for a man. Except it's worse this time, because I knew better. What is the point in even staying in La Musa? It's become another monument to my failure. Maybe I should join a convent. I don't think I believe in God, but at least I wouldn't have to worry about men.

I FaceTime my parents. It's midday in Los Angeles, and they're at the natural foods store in Los Feliz, down the road from our house. It's an ordinary Friday for them. They're no doubt prepping for a weekend of pickling, gardening, and jam-making. "Mommy," I say when I see her appear onscreen. I haven't called them Mommy and Daddy since I was in third grade, but now, I need to. "I want to come home."

My mother's brows furrow. "Izzy, what's wrong?"

I see my dad pop onscreen. "Iz, check out this strawberry." He shows me a massive berry but his face contorts into the same look of concern as my mother's when he sees me crying. "What's wrong?"

"I just..." I can barely croak out a phrase through the sobs. "I need to come home. Can I come home?"

They look at each other before looking back at me. "Of course," my mother says. "Come home. As soon as you can."

"Use our credit card," my father says.

"Ok," I say. "Thank you." I hang up and search for flights on my computer. There are only two direct flights from Rome to Los Angeles, and there's an open middle coach seat on the 3:10 p.m. tomorrow. It's over two thousand dollars, but I book a one-way ticket.

Tomorrow. I'm leaving tomorrow.

I take my suitcase out of the closet and stuff my clothes into it. It takes less than an hour to pack up my entire life in La Musa, and in 24 hours' time, I'll be somewhere over the Atlantic, like it never happened at all. It stings. It doesn't feel right to leave, but how can I possibly stay?

Sleep doesn't find me all night as I toss and turn, periodically jumping out of bed convinced I forgot to pack my passport or my phone charger or my yellow sundress. As soon as the sun is up, I'm out the door, quietly creeping out of the house and lugging my suitcase down the same path I took up the cliff barely three months ago. The first train leaves La Musa at 8:45, and I am on it as it barrels toward Rome.

Half a day later, I land in Los Angeles, and I float to baggage claim. My parents are standing there, waiting for me. Everyone knows you only pick someone up at LAX if you truly, truly love them, and the sight of them makes me cry again. They rush over and hug me tight, just like they did the first time I returned from Italy, more than 10 years ago. I wish I was still her. Not a kid but not really an adult. A human still forming. A person who believed everyone when they said she could do anything she set her mind to.

They help me load my suitcase into their old SUV. Los Angeles unfolds before me as we make our way home. It feels like a lifetime since I've been here. Could you always see the Hollywood sign from this far away on the 10? Did the sky always reflect so brilliantly against the skyscrapers that dot downtown? Is it always so clear that you can see the snowcapped mountains that border the city? I've lived here most of my life, but now I feel like a foreigner.

More tears fall as I walk inside my parents' home. It's just as it's always been with the afternoon sun cascading through the big bay window, the old wood floor creaking as I walk across it, the stairwell banister dented from where I took a LEGO to it in 1995. I want to disintegrate into it. I want to become as stationary as the teak furniture that's always been here. I want to exist, but as nothing more than a monument of where other people lived. The rocking chair in the corner that no one ever sits on, but no one would ever dare give away.

My childhood bedroom is stripped of the décor of my adolescence but remains otherwise untouched. I draw the thick beige curtains and collapse onto the lumpy mattress of my old full-sized bed. I crawl under the covers and pull the quilt my mother made for me when I was a baby up to my chin. How hard would it be for me to stay here forever?

I shut my eyes and wait for the darkness to find me. It quickly does.

I wake with the sun the next morning. I slept 15 hours, longer than I've ever slept. I'm in the same clothes I wore on the plane, and I feel grimy, so I run a scalding-hot shower for myself and change into an old pair of shorts and a T-shirt that I find in my dresser. When I go downstairs, my father is making buckwheat blueberry pancakes.

"Morning, Iz!" he says, with a cheery grin. "Hope you're hungry."

My stomach growls in response. I haven't eaten since the measly in-flight breakfast service yesterday. "Starving, actually," I say, taking a seat at the table in the nook that overlooks the backyard. My mother is outside in the garden, pulling weeds. She waves when she sees me looking at her.

"What did Italy do to make you want to get out of there so quick?" my father asks. I freeze. How exactly do I explain all of this to him? And where do I begin? Even though I'm over 30, my father and I don't have the kind of relationship where I can say, *"Well, there was this boy and he didn't like me as much as I like him, which seems to be the theme of my life..."*

"It was a mistake," I say.

Unfortunately, my dad is not one to let sleeping dogs lie. He glances at me between flipping pancakes. "Which part?"

I sigh. "I don't know. All of it, I guess."

My mother enters with the brightness of the morning sun splashed across her face. "Smells good, Dash," she says. My father's name is Frank, but she's always called him Dash. I've never asked why. "Izzy, are you feeling better after that long rest?"

"No," I say.

She sighs. "What happened over there? And don't say nothing. I know you wouldn't flee so quickly if it was nothing."

My father takes the pancakes off the griddle and piles them onto a plate. "She said it was a mistake, Coll. That's all I know."

"Which part?" she asks, echoing my father's exact question.

"Can I have some of those?" I ask as my dad divides the stack into three servings. He brings me a plate and they sit on opposite sides of the table, watching as I pour syrup on top and start eating. "Can the interrogation wait until after breakfast? I've been in Europe for months and my body misses processed food."

My father winks at my mother. "Well, at least we know the real Izzy's in there somewhere."

"We're just worried, honey," my mother says. "It's been so hard for you since… since November, and it seemed like you were finally finding some version of happiness again."

I glance back and forth between the two of them. "Are you serious? You were against this move from the start."

They share another look. "I'll admit we didn't get it at first, but we were coming around," my mom says.

My dad nods, concurring. "We've been so worried, Iz. We just want to see you figure out what's next."

I drop my fork to my plate. "I don't know how many times I have to say this: Nothing is next. I am not meant to change the world. That burden should not be on me." Thinking of Benito's words stings. Thinking of Benito stings. I am thousands of miles away but it's like he's in the room with me.

My mother hands me a napkin and I realize in my dramatics I have splattered syrup all around me. "No one's saying you have to change the world, but you can't sit around and do nothing for the rest of your life."

My dad laughs. "You don't have to do anything great, but you will. It's in your nature. You've been nothing but driven since you were a little girl, and even if you can't see it now, you will figure out a way back."

I push my chair out and stand up abruptly, the friction of the chair's legs on the creaky floor causing a loud screech. "And why do you think I was so driven? It's because you always told me I had no choice but to do great things. You drove into me that

I was predisposed for greatness, and then when I finally worked hard enough, when I finally earned the opportunity to do that, I crashed and burned. I failed. I lost. What was the point of all of that drive? What good did any of it do?" I take another bite of pancake because I'm working up to a storm-off, but I really am so hungry. "Why do I have to do great things? Why isn't it good enough that I simply exist?"

I'm asking them, but I know that I'm really asking me. That's what this has all been about, hasn't it? The person I most disappointed with my failure was myself. I went to Italy hoping to find *il dolce far niente* and an existence that relied on stasis, but I wound up caught in Benito's drama and saving a town from the brink of financial collapse. I told myself I was doing it to preserve my anonymity, but there was at least a small part of me that wanted to feel important again.

It's not that I *have* to do great things, it's that I want to. I want to make the world better, and make other people's lives better, but I've been lying to myself if I thought that was a selfless crusade. I wanted credit. I want my name to mean something other than "*flamed-out, sex-crazed congresswoman.*" I want to matter.

"Sorry," I say as my parents both stare at me wide-eyed. "Excuse me."

I run up the stairs back to my room. I know my dad's right; I have to figure out what's next. But right now, all I want is sleep.

Chapter Twenty

I WAKE A FEW HOURS LATER TO MY MOTHER LIGHTLY shaking me. "Izzy," she says. "Get up. There's someone here to see you." My mind flashes to Benito. Did he follow me here? I get up and brush my hair, changing out of my casual clothes and into a floral dress that's hanging in my closet and is one of the few articles of clothing I own not hastily balled up in my suitcase. I anxiously head down the stairs, stopping when I see a male figure through the screen door. I look to my mother, who's pretending to read on the couch in the living room. I take a deep breath and open the door.

He's smiling at me, which is annoying because he does not deserve to feel any semblance of happiness in my presence. And it's not really a kind smile but more of a supportive grin you give someone who you know is in crisis and you don't want to add to their grief. I do my best to keep my face from showing any emotion, least of all shock that he's standing on my parents' doorstep.

"Hello, Levi," I say. I open the screen door and he reaches out to hug me, but I pull the door back in, blocking him. "What are you doing here?"

He nods toward the front porch, but I don't move. "I need to talk to you, Isabella, and you haven't responded to any of my emails, my texts, my calls," he says. "It's important."

"Unless it's a matter of national security, I don't think it is," I say. "And if I recall, even then you'd be the one more equipped to handle it." I'm surprised how quickly I'm able to summon my anger toward him, considering I was sleeping not five minutes ago.

Levi laughs lightly and tilts his head back. "I deserve that. But I'm serious. I really do need to talk to you."

I look back to my mom, who's fully watching us now, and she shrugs. I walk outside and lead him around to the side of the house. It's where I used to take calls with Priya in high school about our crushes and all the drama, out of earshot of my parents, which also came in handy during congressional recess. "How did you know that I'm back?" I ask, proud that I've barely noticed how good he looks in tailored, expensive blue jeans and a gray shacket, his blue eyes popping out against the dreary backdrop of the June Gloom morning.

Levi rubs his hands together. "LA's a big city but it's a small town," he says, adding an Old Hollywood transatlantic inflection which he does when he thinks he's being cute. Like he can win me over by summoning the spirit of Jimmy Stewart. I debate telling him now that I always found it cringe but was willing to overlook it. "Someone spotted you at LAX," he admits. "It was on Deuxmoi."

"Great, so everyone knows I'm back," I say, but I'm surprised to find it doesn't really upset me. Maybe after everything I've been through, I'm finally realizing that if other people know I'm struggling, it doesn't matter. I get to feel what I feel, and they'll just have to deal.

"Isabella, I've made a huge mistake," he says, taking a step closer to me. I instinctively take a step backward, my back flush with the exterior wall of the house. "I never should've turned away from you," he says.

"That's an interesting way to frame it," I say.

Levi reaches out toward me, and with nowhere else to go, I let his hand land on my shoulder. "Now that I stand where you stood, I get it," he says. "I get how lonely the job is, how hard it is to go through it without anyone who gets it." He lightly caresses my arm and I feel absolutely nothing.

I glare at him. "That's not why I was texting you, dumbass," I say. "I wasn't lonely. I had friends. I was on top of the freaking world. I was texting you because I thought I was in love with you."

Levi's eyes widen like this is some kind of surprise. "Whatever the reason," he says. "It was wrong of me to suggest that they sent any kind of negative message about where your priorities were."

"I know that," I fire back. "I know you never actually believed any of that. It was all a strategy to win the election." Does he think I'm that dense? I believed he loved me too, so maybe I am.

"Anyway." Levi puts his other hand on my shoulder so he's bracing me like I'm about to sub onto the field with five minutes left in the second half. "We can finally let all of that be in the past and look toward the future." His expression goes blank and his gaze shifts to my lips.

I raise my eyebrows. Is this motherfucker about to kiss me? He leans in, but I put my hand up, his nose crashing into my palm. "No way," I say. "Definitely not."

Levi takes a step back, putting his hands up. "Not the vibe, got it." He crosses his arms and stands up straight. "That wasn't what I came here to do," he says.

Now I'm officially confused. "Then what did you come here to do?"

"I need you, Isabella," he says.

I consider hitting the side of his head, not as an act of violence but because he sounds like a computer that's glitching. "Do not try to kiss me again," I say.

"Not like that," Levi says. He looks around like he called for backup but when no one comes, he turns back to me. "I need you to come work for me."

My jaw unhinges and my mouth drops open so quickly, I wonder if it's broken. "What?"

"Come work with me, Isabella," he says, putting his hands into his jeans pockets and shrugging his shoulders as if to make himself smaller. "I think we'd be great together—professionally."

I force myself to close my mouth and take a long breath inward. "You… what?"

Levi rubs his right temple. “My approval numbers haven’t gotten anywhere near your first-year high,” he says, and the hairs on my arms stand up. “I don’t get it. I made all the right PR moves. Went on the late-night shows, started dating an actress, I thought we followed your plan perfectly.”

“My… plan?” I ask, because he’s yet to mention anything about policy.

“You did the whole fame thing,” Levi says. “And it worked brilliantly. You were everywhere. How did you do that without looking like a slimeball?”

“Well, for starters, I wasn’t a slimeball,” I toss back. Levi drops his head down. “Levi, there was no strategy. The virality, the fame, that all happened organically, and then it was about capitalizing, about using it to maximize my effectiveness in Congress. To get good bills passed and bad bills struck down. At the end of the day, it was about always putting the job first.” My breath catches in my lungs. Even though I always knew that to be true, the world tried to convince me I had my priorities elsewhere. It feels good to say it out loud. Maybe I liked the attention, maybe I even loved it, but it wasn’t why I did what I did. It was part of the ultimate job I wanted.

The thing about dreaming of being a public figure is that you have to be able to handle it when your entire life is public—and know how to deal with it when the most shameful parts of your life are exposed.

“Well, whatever,” Levi says, any facade of professionalism that he came into this conversation with starting to crack. “I still think it’s a good idea.”

He walks back up to me and grabs on to my hand with such a death grip, I don't bother whipping it away. "We were good together, Isabella. Back when we were just two kids trying to make LA better. Those were the good days. We can have that again. On the national stage. Picture it."

I think about what life was like before Congress, when I was working for a nonprofit by day and meeting with community members in church basements at night. Levi and I would knock on doors during the weekends and ask for signatures on petitions outside grocery stores. I wouldn't say those were the good days, necessarily—they were grittier, harder, all sweat and protein bars and dealing with angry rich people who just want you out of their way—but there is a certain rose-colored sheen over those memories. Things were simpler then, and every personal win felt like an affirmation that I was on the right path. That all of it would be worth it when I was being sworn in on the Capitol steps.

It's tempting, in a way, to work with Levi again. Despite how it ended, for years I loved it. For years, I loved him. I could be back. Not everyone gets to be president. Famously, very few do. My dream doesn't have to stay the exact same forever. It can change, it can grow.

"Well," Levi says. "What do you think?"

I look into his eyes—they're deep, ocean blue. It would be easy to forget La Musa ever happened. A blip on an otherwise straightforward path. I could dive back in and never look back. I could work for

Levi. I could set my pride aside and do it for the good of the people.

But there's no fucking way I'm doing that.

"I think, Levi," I say, "that you should go to hell."

His face twists at my rejection. "Isabella, come on. I need you. America—America needs you."

I roll my eyes. "Even my ego isn't that big, Levi."

"You ran away to that dinky little Italian town, and it was cute for a minute, but you had to come back. I needed you to come back," he says.

"Wait a second," I say, my brain putting the pieces together. Everything he's said today has been a manipulation. He tried to kiss me because he thought I still loved him, and it'd be easier to persuade me to come work for him. He needed me to come back, to be on his side so his approval numbers would rise, and he knew breaking my anonymity would be a good way to do it. "It was you. You leaked my location."

Levi doesn't deny it. He doesn't say anything.

"Oh my god. How?" I ask.

Levi shrugs. "Hired a PI."

"Are you serious?" I ask. I should be mad, but it's actually a huge relief to know it was him and not some random in La Musa who was secretly watching my every move. It was just some creep Levi hired to watch my every move.

"I didn't know where you were. I didn't know if you had gone to regroup somewhere, ready to enact revenge for the texts leaking."

"Oh, so you admit that was you," I say.

Levi raises his hands. "I knew that you thought it was me. I had to know where you were, and when I found out you were just… doing your best Meryl Streep character, fleeing to Europe in the midst of a personal crisis, I knew leaking your location would wake you up and you couldn't hide anymore."

I want to punch him, but instead I laugh. I laugh really, really hard.

"Isabella?" Levi asks.

"Levi," I say. "Please leave. And don't ever come here again."

Chapter Twenty One

I SPEND THE WEEK SHADOWING MY PARENTS, MAKING UP for taking out all my anger on them when I first came home. They forgive me, because of course they do.

I'm basically a retired person for seven days. A sunrise hike to the Hollywood Reservoir or Griffith Park, gardening after, coffee on the deck, pickling, jam-making, and an abundance of downtime. Even though I spent months after my last day in Congress doing nothing, I never really took the opportunity to unwind. Now, I've allowed myself the chance to rest, and as each day goes by, my muscles are more relaxed and the frayed ends of my nerves more even.

The farmers market down the street is the first time I venture out into my former constituency. I cling to my mother's side like a shy toddler, never allowing her more than a few inches out of my sight. I see a few people look at me with a glint of recognition as we sift through chard in a vegetable booth, and I'm thankful for the people of LA's preference to stare and judge rather than confront or say hello.

My mother has been a longtime customer of Judy, who I always called The Honey Lady. She smiles as we approach her. "Good to see you, Izzy. You look well."

"You too. Do you have any Orange Blossom left?" I ask. Judy hands me a bottle and we pay her. It's a refreshingly mundane exchange. A similar chain of events occurs when my mother runs into a friend from her pickleball group. And again when I see a neighbor from my old apartment off Crescent Heights.

I come to the crushingly embarrassingly realization that not everyone thinks about me as much as I do. And not everyone is as obsessed with my failure as I am. Maybe there will always be negative connotations associated with my name when it comes up in the online discourse or in the political zeitgeist, but outside in the actual world, I could be free. There will always be red-faced Matts to deal with, but the world is mostly filled with Honey Ladies.

My phone dings somewhere between the homemade hummus booth and the artisan bread.

Marisol: you're gonna want to read this

The text has a link to an article. I click it and it takes me to the front page of *New York Magazine. We All Owe Isabella Rhodes an Apology.* I freeze. My mother is ahead surveying the sourdough. I duck to the other side of the tents and FaceTime Marisol.

"Is it bad?" I ask when she answers.

"You didn't read it?" Marisol pushes her hair out of her face. Wherever she is, it's windy.

"No, I didn't read it. I don't read anything about me anymore." I hear a seagull and can't tell if it's coming from my end or hers. "Where are you?"

Marisol groans. "Chesapeake Bay. Disgustingly charming here. Jenny's visiting and wanted us to do something, in her words, not boring."

"You can call me back later," I say.

Marisol shakes her head and shifts so I can see the water behind her. "There. Now we're both enjoying the beach. You should read it."

The thought is nauseating. I really don't want to know what anyone else has to say about me. I don't need to rehash the past year again. "I am trying this new thing where I don't radically spiral every time someone brings up my past."

"Even more reason to read it. Trust me." A boat loudly honks its horn behind her. "Jesus!"

"Does it mention Italy? Does it mention—" I can barely bring myself to say his name. "The B-word."

Marisol rolls her eyes. "No, the besotted mayor makes no appearance."

"Ok. Good." I look around to make sure no one else is within earshot. "How did you find this article?"

Someone hands Marisol an ice cream cone offscreen and she takes a lick. "It's about Isabella Rhodes. It's trending, babe."

"Wait, what?" My heart drops. I see Jenny join Marisol onscreen and wave.

"Hi, Izzy. So nice to see you, but I need my wife

to stay off her phone for more than two minutes at a time. Say bye, Mari." Jenny waves.

I could spiral about the fact that I'm trending, but what if I didn't? What if I let my friend and her wife have a nice day at the beach? "Bye you two. Have fun!"

"I won't, but thank you!" Marisol yells before the screen goes black.

I peek back out at the market and see my mom is still distracted by the bread choices. I sit on the curb and open the article. I start reading.

In late October, the latest in a long line of congressional sex scandals made the news when text messages between Congresswoman Isabella Rhodes and then-opponent Levi Cross leaked to the public. The predictable barrage of vitriol toward Rhodes exploded on the internet, eventually tanking both her reputation and her re-election chances. The difference between this and the dick pic chronicles of the sex scandals of yore was that Rhodes didn't actually have an affair, she just wanted one. And since when is being a human being who craves sexual contact with another human being, when you are not married and that person is not your employee, a crime? Or even a fireable offense?

"Izzy?" My mom pokes her head through the back of a tent. "What are you doing back here? Let's go." I exit out of the article. I don't need to know the rest. Despite what Marisol thinks, I don't need to harp on what someone else wrote about my personal life, but the sentiment came through.

I follow her to our car and scroll social media as soon as I'm buckled.

This is so true, there was a witch hunt for Izzy Rhodes and for what? one person says.

A prominent columnist from *The New York Times* writes, *Congresswoman Rhodes deserved better.*

Since when is being horny a crime frfr, another internet stranger writes.

Not everything is 100% positive, but it proves what I could never see: The hatred directed at me after my texts leaked won't last forever.

I take a deep breath and scroll to the bottom of my hundreds of unread text messages and start reading. They're overwhelmingly positive. Former colleagues in the House, journalists, college friends, acquaintances—they're all wishing me well, hoping I'm loving Italy and are happy to hear I'm choosing to move on with my life.

One of my former staff members sent over the name of a restaurant I have to try if I'm ever in Arezzo. Priya said she'll be in Rome later this summer if we want to meet up. Congressman Jennings merely texted *Italy? Noice.* Everyone that reached out was surprised but thrilled for me. I'd convinced myself that all of the people in my life looked at me with disappointment or, worse, pity since the Levi incident, but their messages tell a different story. They're supportive. The idea that I didn't deserve any respect after I lost was one no one else shared. At least no one else that counts.

I scroll through my emails and it's more of the same. Well-wishes, congratulations, travel suggestions.

My heart skips a beat when I see a familiar name in the barrage of unread messages: Eveline Reed. I click on it.

Izzy—welcome to the club of unpopular successful women. Keep up the good work. Take it from someone who's been in your shoes before: Every loss is an opportunity to come back even stronger. Don't let this asshole be the one to end your story. We need you. Please reach out if you need support.
Eveline

I re-read it three more times and double-check to make sure the message is coming from her official gubernatorial campaign email. Eveline Reed believes in me. Eveline Reed knows who I am, and not just because of Levi. Eveline Reed thinks the world needs me. It shouldn't matter what one person thinks of me, but it matters that Eveline Reed thinks about me at all. By quitting, I'm letting what Levi did to me define me. And I can't let that happen.

When we get home, I open my laptop and do something I haven't done since shortly after taking office and search my own name on the internet. I used to have a Google alert set up for "Isabella Rhodes," but once the coverage on me got to be too overwhelming, my team would weed out the garbage and only show me pull quotes from legitimate sources. While I spent months dwelling on what I didn't do right in my time in Congress and my re-election, I never stopped to take a moment to be proud of myself for what I did accomplish.

Since I was a kid, it was my dream to be a United States congressperson. And I was.

My search brings up the highlights first: the *Women eat* tweet, clap backs to my colleagues who tried to degrade me, the historic first time California elected a woman my age. Then I scroll further: the climate bill I co-sponsored which ultimately didn't have the votes to clear the House, the Sunday morning news show blitz I did with Marisol to garner support for gun control, my refusal to vote "yes" on an infrastructure bill my own party put forth because I didn't feel like it went far enough to protect workers.

Even if I didn't achieve everything I set out to do when I was elected, I sure as hell tried. That has to count for something. That has to matter. At least to me. I thought running away would free me, but maybe the best way forward is to do something bigger, something better.

But first, I have to clean up the mess I left in La Musa.

Benito wanted me to stay out of his family's drama, but screw that. I tell my parents I'm going back and book a flight for the next morning. It all feels parallel to when I made the split-second decision to go to La Musa all those months ago, only this time my purpose seems clearer. And I'm packing much lighter.

I work on my pitch the entire flight over, finessing every detail until it is absolutely perfect. I only have one shot to get this right—and I'm going to get it right.

My heartbeat kicks up as I board the train to La

Musa. It's hot and humid. The weather's warmed significantly in the two weeks I've been gone, and I'm drenched in sweat as the train pulls into the La Musa station. I doubt Anita's rented out my room to someone else already, but I still keep my expectations low as I go to the house, opting to knock on the front door instead of using my key. I could use a shower and a meal, but I need to do this before I lose the gumption.

"Izzy!" Vincenzo nearly knocks me over with a bear hug as soon as he opens the door to greet me. "You're back!"

"I'm back," I say. "Is Raffaello home?"

"Indeed," Vincenzo says, taking my rolling suitcase from me. "Signor is in the kitchen with Signora Sutton."

Sutton. Of course she's still here. A butterfly flutters in my stomach to realize that probably means Benito's still here too.

He leads me to the kitchen where Raffaello and Sutton are camped out at the kitchen counter, both heads down in their laptops. "Hi," I say.

They look up. They don't really seem surprised to see me, just annoyed.

"Just the two people I wanted to see," I say. Sutton's eyes narrow and Raffaello scoffs. They're not buying it. "I have a proposal for you." I open my bag and pull out two stacks of paper, placing one in front of each of them.

Sutton crosses her arms. "Let me guess, you aren't happy with Benito's resignation."

"I'm not," I say, sure to keep my voice even and calm. "But it's not about that." I readjust to make myself as tall as possible. "Let the development deal go through under the condition that all the locally owned business in town get to keep their leases at the current rates when construction completes."

"Do you have the authority to offer that?" Raffaello asks.

"Benito's resigning, that means it's your call."

Raffaello perks up. He looks to Sutton. She nods. "And in return?" he asks.

"I'm prepared to offer something of value to you, but there's another condition."

Sutton sighs. "And what's that?"

I take a deep breath. "You will free Benito from his promise to work for you in London."

Raffaello and Sutton share another look. I can't quite discern their energy, and my stomach is in knots while they wordlessly deliberate. Finally, Sutton turns to me. "Ok. And this mysterious offer of what we'd get in return?"

I adjust so I'm standing tall, confident. "I will be the face of the town's tourism ad campaign." Sutton raises her eyebrows and Raffaello leans in, interested. "Using my image to attract tourists to La Musa will work," I say. "We have evidence of it, and I will allow Don and your other colleagues to use the mock-ups they showed me. For one year." I point at the contracts. "It's all laid out in there."

Sutton's eyes narrow. "You know, this is no guarantee that Benito won't return to London anyway." She stares at me pointedly. I don't know if she always knew what was percolating between me and Benito, but she's certainly clued in now.

"I know," I say. "It doesn't matter. The point stands. Your development plan can go through and I will be the face of it as long as Benito is free to do what he wishes and the businesses already in town will be protected."

They're silent for a moment, considering. "Benito has never known what's good for him," Raffaello says finally, his voice gruff.

"Raffaello." Sutton nudges him with her elbow. "I'll work on persuading him sans blackmail, but I think it's a win-win. The monetary value of what Izzy's offering… we'd be daft to turn it down."

"Is that a yes?" I ask.

Sutton nods, ceding her approval, and gestures for Raffaello to make the final call. He looks down at his hands in his lap for a moment, but when he lifts his head, I know he's made a decision. "Fine. Deal."

I can't hide my grin. "Great." I temper my excitement to a professional level. I fish a pen out of my bag and hand it to them. "These contracts affirm what we've agreed upon today, guaranteeing neither of us go back on our word. I'm happy to wait while you read through the conditions."

The door to the backyard creaks open, and when I turn, I see Benito walk through it. He stops when he sees me, frozen in the room like he's just been hit by a stun gun. "What are you doing here?" he asks after an awkward moment.

"I'll let you fill him in," Raffaello says, taking the contract and gesturing for Sutton to follow him outside.

Benito continues to stare at me like I'm an illusion, like if he blinks, I'll disappear. "You're back?" he asks, his body stiff and statuesque, not giving me any indication on how he might feel about the fact that the answer is yes.

"I'm back," I say. "And I have good news."

Benito holds up his hand. "You should know, I had no choice when it came to resigning. I tried to compromise with my father on the development deal, ensuring the safety of the women-owned businesses, of all the locally owned businesses, but—"

"It's ok. I know," I say, cutting him off. "I took care of it."

Benito lifts his eyebrows. Fair, considering as far as he knows, I'm still set on prioritizing an easy breezy life over everything else. "You said you have good news?" he asks.

I clap my hands together as if to zap away the tense energy in the room. "Yes. You don't have to go to London." Benito's eyes widen. "I did what I do best, and I made a deal," I say.

It's so quiet, I can hear Vincenzo's hearty laugh from across the house. Benito shifts from one foot to the other before eventually taking a step closer to me. "What?"

I fill him in on the details of the arrangement I made with Raffaello, all while Benito stares at the ground, thinking. "You were right," I say. He looks up at me. "Not about me being mayor, but that I can't do nothing. I do need a purpose. It's who I am. You helped me realize that."

The slightest of smiles emerges from Benito's lips but he remains otherwise glum. "I'm surprised you'd enter into any such deal with my father, knowing how quickly he revokes his word."

I cock my head at him and smile. "I said I'm taking care of it."

Benito runs his hand through his hair. "So that's it, then? I'm not going back to London?"

"Not if you don't want to," I say. I take a step closer and place my hand on his shoulder. "You deserve a chance to figure out where your heart truly lies."

Benito casts his eyes into mine. They glow. My heart pumps warmth through my chest, my stomach, my head. "And what about you?" he asks. "Don't you deserve the same?"

I think about the Beachwood house, DC, the coffee shop on Santa Monica, the cozy Italian place in Foggy Bottom, lunches at Anita's, Benito, La Musa. "I'm working on that too."

My stomach stirs as Benito maintains his eye contact. After the long journey, I feel disgusting. I'm hungry, I'm tired, but the way he looks at me makes me feel like he doesn't see all of that, like he'll always look at me with the same mix of understanding and awe. He runs his hand through his hair again and his forearms flex. I resist the urge to reach out and grab his arm. He's here now, but it wasn't all that long ago that he was content to skip off to London and leave me forever.

"Your room's still yours," Benito says, his voice quiet. "Assuming you want it."

"I do," I say. "For now. Thank you." There's so much I want to say to him and yet, no words come to mind. Do I owe him an apology? Does he owe me one? Does it matter? "What will you do now that you don't have to go to London?" I ask.

Benito takes a deep breath. "Well, considering I've only known that for a few minutes, I don't have an answer yet."

I performatively roll my eyes. "You mean you don't make all your major life decisions on a whim like I have lately?"

I hear the scribble of pen against the countertop. Sutton gathers up the signed contracts and walks over to me. She grazes her fingertips over Benito's shoulders, and I feel a twinge of jealousy. "Ben, did you tell Izzy about the big *fiesta* this Friday? The party?"

"*Festa*," Benito corrects her. "And I didn't have the chance yet."

Sutton turns to me. "You'll come, obviously. Practically the whole town is. It gives Benito the chance to formally announce his resignation and endorse Raffaello as his mayoral replacement, and now we can announce the development deal as well." Benito's eyes flash to me.

"I never say no to a party," I say. Sutton smiles ever so slightly but follows up with no details. "Um… just tell me when and where."

Raffaello clears his throat. "Here. Tomorrow. 5 p.m."

"I'll be there," I say. I look to Benito but his eye contact has expired. There's an awkwardness and I feel like it's because I'm still standing here.

I start to walk out and rest a hand on Benito's shoulder. "See you around?" I ask. He nods. Or at least I think he does. I walk out of the house to find food because I'm starving and I don't want to spend another minute in the kitchen with Sutton and Raffaello. I put on my sunglasses and hope no one recognizes me as I trek out into the center of town. But then again, let them see me. Let them see Izzy Rhodes looking tired, disheveled, sweaty, and hangry. It's the truth. It's who I am right now in this moment. I don't need to hide.

Chapter Twenty Two

I TAKE CARE AS I GET READY THE NEXT EVENING. I blow-dry my hair with the hope that when the humidity inevitably kicks in, I'll be left with only a few bouncing waves. I pick out a light blue linen dress and a pair of flat strappy sandals. Functional enough to help with setup as I promised Anita yesterday, but presentable enough to make a good impression on the people of La Musa.

Also, cute enough to spend the whole day with a guy I've hooked up with a couple of times.

When I walk downstairs, dozens of people in white shirts and black slacks are shuffling in and out. Staff are busy readying the house, carrying long buffet tables through to the back and setting up a welcome bar in the foyer. I walk through the house to the kitchen, where Anita is directing a full crew. It takes several moments of standing among the chaos before I even have a chance to let her know I'm here. "Anita, hi," I say, when there's finally a pause in the clanging of pots and rapid instructions.

She looks up at me, still holding a knife as she shows a chef how to chop. "Good. You're here."

"Yes, although it looks like you have everything under control." Another crew of workers files through, carrying large buffet-style trays.

"Hardly," she says, waving away the chef and getting to work on mincing garlic. "I'm behind. Would you mind setting the tables outside? Everything you need is out there, and make sure the centerpieces are evenly spaced."

I glance outside warily. The fearful look in all the hired help's eyes make me question if I'm up to the task, but there's also no world in which I refuse. "Of course."

I head out back where it's refreshingly less crowded. In addition to their already ridiculously long dining table, a few others have been set up as well as a spattering of smaller high-tops. I pick up a stack of napkins and start folding them.

"Izzy?"

I lift up my head and see Benito walking toward me, carrying several bouquets of flowers. "Hey," I say. The door to his bedroom has remained tightly shut since I've been back.

He sets the flowers down on the main table. "You're a bit early."

"Your mom asked me to help."

Benito glances around at the copious amount of hired help. "I can see why."

I smirk. "Maybe this was all an elaborate setup by your mom. She's using forced proximity to get us to make peace."

Benito shifts uncomfortably. He reaches for a vase on the table and starts working on the floral arrangements.

"Benito, I was kidding," I say. I walk over so I'm standing on the opposite side of the table from him. He wordlessly hands me an empty vase and I copy how he methodically pulls one stem out from each bouquet to add to the vase, cutting off the ends. "Unless I'm not?"

He sighs. "I was upset the morning after you left. I knew you left because of me, but the sight of your empty bedroom… it was a lot. She asked me what was wrong, so I told her about you, about us. I told her everything."

I lose track of what I'm doing and nick my finger on a rose thorn. "Ow. Everything?"

"Everything." He looks up at me.

"So your mom knows about that night in Lake Como? Great." I smash my palm to my head.

Benito looks at my hand in horror. "Jesus, Izzy. You're bleeding." I pull my hand off my forehead and look—sure enough, there's a stream of blood coming from where the rose pricked me. Benito picks up a napkin from my freshly folded stack and walks over to me. He takes my hand and wraps the napkin around my bleeding finger. "I told her an abridged, mother-friendly version of everything."

He holds the napkin tight against my finger, creating pressure. He takes my other hand and gently guides it to take his hand's place. When he lets go, I feel a twinge of loss. He starts to walk toward the house. "You're just going to leave me here to bleed out?"

"Relax. I'm getting the first aid kit."

I look back at the rose culprit, now bloodstained on its stem. How appropriate that the world's most romantic flower stabbed me. A sign, perhaps, that I should be done with all of it for good.

Benito returns to finish fixing me up. He removes the napkin and opens up the Band-Aid, wrapping it around my finger so clinically, it's almost like he, too, was startled by the warmth of our earlier contact and is trying to keep things between us sterile.

"Thanks," I say, when he's done. Benito quickly goes back to working on the floral arrangements. "Hey," I say. He doesn't look up. "I'm sorry. I'm sorry I left without saying anything. I'm sorry we fought. I'm sorry I didn't hear what you were saying. I get it now. I really do. You were right. I can't be nothing. I can't do nothing. It's not who I am."

Benito stops what he's doing and nods. "Thanks." He goes back to his work, and I wonder if that's where we'll leave it, but after a moment, he looks up. "I'm sorry too. It wasn't up to me to tell you how you should live your life. Especially when mine's a mess. Izzy, please know, you don't need to do something big with your life to be important. You being you is enough. It's more than enough."

My eyes lock into his and I feel immediately at ease, like the past few weeks never happened and we're rain-soaked in the middle of the gardens again. I snap myself out of the fantasy. "And what about you? I mean, what will you do now that you can do anything you want?"

Benito looks down again and then lets out a laugh. "I have no idea."

We finish our work wordlessly, and when we're done, Benito excuses himself upstairs to get ready. I find Anita directing traffic as the staff puts the last touches on the setup. As always, the house looks stunning. "I didn't realize how elaborate an affair this is," I say.

Anita shrugs. "It's not every day your son resigns as mayor and your husband announces a major development deal that will completely change the town you've lived in your whole life."

She fidgets with the champagne flutes on top of the welcome bar. I can't get a read on her. Her passive attitude toward Raffaello's actions has always been at odds with her personality, but a woman like Anita has to have a limit. "They built this town on top of a hill to defend it from invaders. A thousand years later it's finally falling," I say.

Anita rests a hand on my shoulder. "Don't be too sure about that."

As the guests start to file in, I take my place outside with a cool glass of wine. Everyone I know is here: Lucia made the trip from Siena with her husband; Vincenzo and Valeria; Giac; an older woman with him I presume to be his dreaded aunt—even Giuseppe put on a fresh T-shirt for the occasion.

"It's hard to picture a changed La Musa," Vincenzo says, raising his glass to meet mine.

I take in the view of the countryside against the light of the dipping sun. "I know. It doesn't seem right."

Vincenzo smiles. "You know Paola," he says, pointing to Giac's aunt. "It is rumored that she was cursed when she was a baby, and ever since, every party she enters is doomed."

I look to him in horror. "Jesus. Really?"

He does a sign of the cross. "Yes. That's why I invited her."

He winks at me. Benito walks over to us, interrupting. He looks distressed. He looks great, sharp, in a pale green button-down and beige linen pants, but the top buttons of his shirt are undone, and he massages his chest with his hand. "Have you seen my *mamma*?"

I do another cursory look around the yard. "No, I haven't. Why? Are you ok?"

"No." Benito shakes his head. "I made a mistake. I said something I shouldn't have. She walked away in a huff and now I can't find her anywhere. The announcement is soon."

"I'm sure she's around here somewhere." I nod to Vincenzo and follow Benito inside the house. "What did you say?"

"It was a slip of the tongue. I didn't mean to upset her. I didn't mean to say it at all." He opens the door to the study but quickly closes it again when Anita is not inside.

"What did you say?" I try again.

Benito runs his hand through his hair. "She was saying even when my father takes over as mayor, he'll still travel back and forth to Milan for business, and I said *'not only for business.'*"

He looks at me sheepishly. I let out a little laugh. "Oh, yeah, she's disowning you for sure." Benito sighs heavily and I instinctively grab his hand. It catches us both off guard, but I commit to it. "Don't worry. She probably is upset, but maybe she just went somewhere to cool off."

Benito relaxes a little. I stroke my thumb against his hand. He looks up at me and smiles slightly. "How do you do that? You bring me back to earth so quickly."

It's a dizzying statement because I suddenly feel like I'm floating 10 feet above the ground. "I've been told I'm good at humbling people," I say, letting go of Benito's hand because the contact is starting to feel too good.

Benito laughs. "You are. It's funny, La Musa is my hometown, but before I met you, I never cared what happened to it. And now—" His face falls, presumably with the reminder that soon it will be a shell of its former self. "A part of me wonders if I should stay here if only to fight my father on every change he wants to make until the bitter end."

My stomach twists at the unknown of where Benito will end up. "Is that what you want? To stay?"

Before he can answer, Anita emerges from one of the other doors in the long hallway, carrying a manila folder. She doesn't seem upset. In fact, she's grinning. "Come, come, you two, the big announcement is about to begin."

We follow Anita outside. I take the last empty seat at the long table and Sutton pulls Benito over to where Raffaello and Anita stand facing the party. Raffaello clinks a fork to his wine glass to get everyone's attention. "*Buona sera, amici,*" he begins. "As you all know, I have lived in La Musa for many decades, and I am grateful to be back after business took me out of town for several months."

I hold in a groan. Raffaello continues, "My son did an excellent job filling in as mayor while I took my leave, but I'm back now and, well, Benito?"

Raffaello gestures toward Benito, who clears his throat. "Yes, I will now resign as mayor of La Musa, as many of you already know. But now it is official. I am resigning." He takes a step backward to signal he's done speaking. There's a brief spattering of applause as the crowd reacts to the news that's already been gossip fuel in La Musa for weeks.

Raffaello laughs in the vein of a supervillain as he places a sturdy grip on Benito's shoulder and beckons him forward. "And do you have any suggestions for a replacement, son?"

There are a few sparse giggles from the crowd. Anita interrupts before Benito can say anything. "Raffaello, why don't you share your other happy news first?"

Raffaello claps his hands together. "I'm also very excited to share that my family company is spearheading a project to revitalize La Musa." He gestures to Sutton, who produces a large poster board with a rendering of the completed project. From the picture, it looks nothing like the town I know. The *duomo* remains untouched, and the clock tower still stands watch, but the "revitalized" buildings are sleek, modern, and designed to look exactly the same.

It's worse than I thought. My breath catches in my chest. I notice a few guests whisper to each other. Raffaello points at the picture. "I know it's a big change, but this is the best way to make La Musa a thriving commerce center, and to put us on the map as a major player in Umbria. I have lived in this town a long time, and I promise I have its best interests at heart."

Anita lets out a cackle so loud, it casts a ripple through the entire party, seemingly echoing out into the countryside below. Raffaello points at her, unfazed. "My wife here can hardly contain her excitement."

Anita laughs again. "No, no. I'm sorry. No." She waves her hand in front of her mouth in an effort to pull herself together. "It's just… hearing you say you have the town's best interests at heart is quite funny, considering the only interests you care about are your own." My eyes dart up to catch Benito's. His jaw drops and he quickly covers his mouth with his hand. There's a grumble from the crowd of guests as we wait for what's next.

Anita turns back to the table behind her and picks up the folder she was holding earlier. She walks toward Raffaello. “You could never be the business success your father wanted you to be, so instead you tried to make La Musa your kingdom. You bought up as many properties as you could, waiting for the day you could sell them all and turn a giant profit not just for you but for your family’s company. It would’ve worked, honestly, if not for your wandering eye.”

She hands Raffaello a photograph. From where I’m sitting, I can only see the back, but I guess its contents based on how quickly Raffaello’s face grows pale. “You will not ruin La Musa like you’ve ruined me.” Anita pulls a multipage document out of the same folder. “I told you a month ago if you did not return home, I would file for divorce.” She throws a look toward the crowd, grinning. “So, you came back. I ask you all, was it because he loves his family and wanted to make it right?”

The crowd remains silent. Lucia quietly gets up from her seat and joins her family. She puts an arm around Benito, and they stand behind Anita, showing their support. Anita continues, “No, he did it because he knew if I divorced him, half of all this would become mine, and I’d never agree to such a heinous deal.” She pushes the papers into Raffaello’s chest, forcing him to take them. “That copy’s yours.”

Anita takes the rendering of the development from Sutton and shows it to the crowd. “Tell me, do any of you want La Musa to turn into this?”

Sutton raises her hand dutifully but lowers it quickly when Anita shoots her a glare. No one else in attendance shows even a morsel of support. “That’s what I thought," Anita says. She turns back to Raffaello. "I am divorcing you. Half of this will be mine. I will not agree to sell or to make any such changes. You can try to fight me if you want, but if you care about your reputation at all, I wouldn't." She points toward the picture Raffaello's still holding. "There's more where that came from."

It's dead quiet. I feel like we should applaud, but that doesn't seem appropriate. I thought I was in the driver's seat here, but I got it all wrong. Anita was ready to take Raffaello down on her own, and she did it spectacularly. Raffaello is bright red. Sutton looks like a dog with its tail between its legs. I know they're both calculating their next move, but I can't imagine there's a good one to make other than fleeing.

Benito breaks the tension by stepping forward. "Earlier, my father asked if I want to endorse anyone for mayor, and I do." Raffaello looks to him, perhaps clinging to the glimmer of hope that his son might throw him a bone. Benito grins. "The next mayor of La Musa should be my mother, Anita Farentino."

Now, the party erupts in applause. The guests stand one by one, cheering for Anita as she hugs Benito. Lucia joins them in their group hug while Raffaello remains on the outside of the family, perhaps permanently.

Vincenzo stands and raises his glass. "To Anita! I, for one, cannot wait to call you my new mayor."

Valeria stands and clinks glasses with her husband. "*Salute!*" Raffaello watches in petrified horror as the party guests walk over to Anita to congratulate her.

She waves them off. "Nonsense, nothing will change. The food is ready. *Mangia! Mangia!*" She redirects people toward the kitchen and the long buffet tables full of food. I see Raffaello sneak out through the side yard, no doubt off to somewhere or someone to lick his wounds.

I turn to Vincenzo, still impressed by Anita's show of force. "That is not how I saw that going," I say.

Vincenzo smiles and pats me on the shoulder. "*C'è un nuovo sole tutti i giorni,* Izzy." He gestures around at the overall cheeriness of the festivities. "There is a new sun every day."

I walk over to Anita. "That was badass," I say.

She shrugs. "I did what I should have done long ago. And when Benito told me he came back here only for me, I knew I could not let him sacrifice everything again." She looks over at Benito and smiles. "Someone else beat me to the punch in freeing him from his father, but it was still worth it. We've all sacrificed too much for Raffaello." She winks at me and heads inside.

When Benito said he told Anita everything, he really did tell her everything. It makes sense that this was the last straw. Anita's love for her children overpowers everything else, as it should. She loves Benito way too much to let him become a pawn in Raffaello's game—I guess we're alike in that way.

I look around the party for Benito, but I don't see him anywhere. He's not in the backyard, or in line for food, or even refilling his prosecco glass at the foyer bar. I check upstairs and see the door to his office is open. When I enter, Sutton is zipping up a suitcase, an air mattress deflating next to her while Raffaello pleads with her in rapid Italian. He touches her lower back. My heart sinks. Is *Sutton* Raffaello's secret mistress?

Raffaello leans in close, his mouth close to her ear, but Sutton quickly shimmies out of his grasp, pushing him away. "Raffaello, no. You are drunk, you are sad, you are embarrassed, but I am not interested, and I am your colleague. I suggest you walk away now and never try this again if you want to keep it that way."

My eyes widen. Good for Sutton. My women's intuition kicks in and I walk into the room, not wanting her to be alone with him for another second. Sutton might not be my favorite person, but no one deserves that. "Hey, Sutton, I have that thing you asked me for," I say. She stares at me quizzically and I widen my eyes, cocking my head ever so slightly.

After an awkward moment, Sutton nods, understanding. "Right, good, thanks," she says.

"Can you give us a sec, Raffaello?" I ask. He glares at me and doesn't budge. "It's, um, woman stuff."

Raffaello backs up out of the room with his hands in the air.

When he leaves, Sutton looks at me, annoyed. "I can handle him myself," she says, but her voice is quiet.

I shrug. "I know."

Her expression softens. "Thanks."

"Are you ok?" I ask.

"I'm good." She takes in a sharp breath. "Raffaello is the worst."

A half groan, half laugh escapes out of me. "I thought you two were like, besties."

She rolls her eyes and throws her hands up in the air. "All part of the game."

I smile at her. Pretending to be buddy-buddy with terrible men is a game I know well. "Have you seen Benito?" I ask.

Sutton lets out a little huff, the girl power moment apparently passed. "You just missed him. He told me to go back to London, so I am." She laughs, but it sounds manic. "Thank god. I hate it here. I'm glad I won't have a reason to come here again." She's trying to act casual, but her shoulders are scrunched up nearly to her ears.

"Benito's definitely not going back with you, then?" I ask.

Sutton stands and sets her suitcase upright, pulling the handle out. "No. He's not."

I suppress a smile but I'm glad to know that at the very least, Benito's not returning to London. "Well, it was… nice to meet you," I say.

"I'll be in touch," she says with a nod, brushing past me to roll her suitcase out of the room.

"You will?"

Sutton turns back around, her shoulders falling. "Right, with Anita as mayor, I suppose there will be no development deal and no need to use your face for an ad campaign." She uses the elastic around her wrist to tie her hair back into a ponytail. "Perfect."

"Sorry," I say, though I'm not sure I mean it. "It's just, it wasn't really something I wanted to do, but I was willing to make the trade for the sake of—"

She puts her hand up to cut me off. "It's fine. I get it. I'd do the exact same thing."

I feel another twinge of empathy for Sutton. She's ambitious, smart, a go-getter. I may not agree with her ethics, but I appreciate her drive. "For what it's worth, I don't think you need me to be successful. I wouldn't be surprised if you're running Raffaello's company someday."

Sutton's face softens for a moment, but she puts her hand back on her suitcase handle and starts to roll her way out. "Then I guess we finally agree on something."

She leaves and I'm back to square one on my hunt for Benito. I leave the Farentinos' house and look for him outside on the street.

He's nowhere.

I follow the street down toward the center of town. Despite the fact that a sizeable amount of La Musa's population is at the party I just left, there's still a lot of people out enjoying the warm summer night. I check the patio at Bar Musa in case he decided he needed a stronger drink than the wine his mother was serving, but he's not there.

I head toward the town's center and spot a man sitting on the steps of the *duomo*. He's rolling up the sleeves of his shirt—it's Benito.

I walk over to him, though now that I've found him, I can't remember why it was so urgent. "Hey," I say.

He looks up at me. He smiles. "Hey."

"Can I…?" I gesture toward the spot next to him on the steps.

"Please."

The sunset's only just forming, but it looks to be spectacular with orange and purple rays casting across the sky, reflecting the brilliance of the town. "I love it here," I say.

Benito laughs. "Good, considering all you've been through."

"When I got here, I didn't think it was possible to feel anything other than anger and grief for what I thought my life should be like. Now, I'm excited for the future again, but I'm also so happy to live in the present. It's changed my perspective on how to live my life." I roll my head back, embarrassed. "Oh my god. I sound like one of those women in all those movies about Italy."

"Is that such a bad thing?" he asks.

I look at him. He's so stunning, especially now with the light illuminating him. "It's not. It's very much not."

We sit silently for a moment. Two little kids skip across the piazza, gelato dripping down from their cones to their elbows while their parents run after them. A group of friends toast at the Bar Musa patio, their wine glasses clinking.

I turn to Benito. He rests his hand on top of mine. "You're going back, aren't you?"

Tears well in my eyes. I wasn't expecting to feel so emotional about this. "I am," I say. "I have to finish what I started." I can't work for Levi, obviously, but the texts and my loss can't be the end of it for me. I have to try again, even if I fail. Even if I fail so horribly, I have to relive the same embarrassment over again. Making my mark on the world doesn't have to be a smooth path.

A single tear falls down my cheek and Benito wipes it away, his own eyes starting to well. "Good," he says. "I can't wait to see what you do."

I take his hand with both of mine. "I so badly wanted to be the person that stayed here with you. You have to know that. But I'm just not."

"I know," he says, his voice breaking at the ends of his words.

He wraps me into a hug, and I latch on to his sturdy shoulders, burying my face into his chest. I try to memorize the feeling of him against me, the smell of his cologne, his breath on the back of my neck.

We unwind ourselves and he brushes the remaining tears off my face. "Let me know where you end up?" I ask. He nods. "Maybe we'll run into each other again someday."

"Yeah," Benito says. "That would be nice."

"*In bocca al lupo,*" I say, forcing a smile out despite the tears.

He does the same. "*In bocca al lupo,* Izzy."

I'm at peace as I make my way to the train station the next morning, the light barely risen above the horizon. Despite the early hour, it's a beautiful midsummer morning. I'm sad to leave, even though

I know it's right. I'm sad to leave Benito, even though I know I can't stay here. Maybe that's the price of wanting what I want. Maybe I'm not meant to have a happy love life and professional success. And maybe that's ok.

When I make it down the hillside to the station, the clock tower dings at the top of the hour. I still have a few minutes before the train is due. The countryside on the other side of the tracks is aglow with the early-dawn light, and I soak in these last precious moments of Umbria, taking one last deep breath of fresh Italian air.

I open Instagram on my phone. There's a barrage of messages and notifications but I ignore them, instead clicking *Go Live*.

My face pops up on the screen in front of me, perfectly lit and shining.

"Hi, everyone," I say, watching as the viewership count slowly ticks upward. Fifty viewers, then 100, then quickly climbing into the thousands. "It's been a minute, I know."

I pan the camera around me. "I wanted to show you all this beautiful place I've been calling home for the past few months. As I'm sure you've heard, this is La Musa. It's been the perfect place for me to regroup and reset."

A flurry of red hearts lights up the corner of the screen. "I've completely fallen in love here." My heart skips a little. I meant the place, but in saying the words aloud I realize that's not really what I meant. "I know, I know. You're probably sick of hearing about my love life, or lack thereof, but it's true. I've fallen in love with an… amazing person." Me two months ago would be mortified to know I'm saying this all publicly, and that I am willingly allowing my personal life to be part of the cultural conversation again, but fuck it. I love Benito. I am in love with Benito.

"After… everything that happened with my leaked texts, with the scandal that came from it, I felt so embarrassed to be in love, especially with someone who clearly didn't love me back. I thought the exposure of those texts made me look weak. That they made me look like a kid with a crush, like I didn't care about my work as much as I cared about getting a text back from the boy I liked. But that's bullshit."

The wind whips my hair into my face, and I brush it back behind my ears. "Someone really wise recently said to me 'It's brave to love someone when you don't know if they love you back.'" I smile at the memory. Benito and his bright eyes. "Love makes me strong. Loving someone when I don't know if they love me back requires strength; it requires resilience. I know that because that's how I feel about all of you.

"I fought for my constituents, for Los Angeles, for California, for the world, because I love it. Even when I didn't know if you all loved me back, I still fought for you because I love you. I love my city, I love my community, I love my fellow people, and that didn't go away just because the world decided not to love me anymore."

I stand up a little straighter. "And that's why I'm coming back. I'm not done yet. You have not heard the last from Izzy Rhodes. I don't know what's next for me, but I know I want to continue to work for the people and the place that I love so much. Because that's what you do when you love someone. You fight for them."

This entire video will definitely be headline news by the time the morning shows air, but good. It should. Let them know that I'm back and this time, I'm not going anywhere.

"Izzy!" I hear a commotion from the other side of the platform, followed by heavy steps running toward me. I turn to see a man in a blue button-down, linen pants, and a sleepy grin now a few feet away from me on the platform.

Benito.

His presence catches me off guard. I thought we left things on a perfect albeit bittersweet note. I rest my phone on top of my suitcase, failing to turn the video off, and watch as he jogs to close the distance between us. "What are you doing here?" I ask.

He's out of breath but wide-eyed, a look of determination on his face. "You said I deserve a chance to figure out where my heart truly lies." I nod. He runs his hand through his hair, which makes my heart twist. "What if it's right here?"

"In La Musa?" I ask. Benito spending the rest of his life here—I can picture it. Turning old and gray amidst the unchanging view. I feel a strong pulse of longing that I won't be here with him to witness it.

"No." He shakes his head. He takes a step closer to me, winding his hands into my hair and pressing his forehead to mine. "Right here."

It feels good, too good to be near him again. My body already aches knowing it won't last. "I can't stay here," I say, my heart tearing apart. If he begged me to stay, I'd be tempted, but I can't. I know I can't.

"I know," he says. "But I can go anywhere. I want to be wherever you are, because I love you, Izzy." I try to feel the earth under my feet, digging my thumbnail into my finger to make sure I'm not dreaming. He sweeps my hair out of my face. "I am so in love with you. And I can't even begin to think of coming up with my own dreams without being there to bear witness to yours." Not bothering to wait for my response, he closes the last gasps of air between us, pressing his lips to mine. His kiss is soft and light and I'm only moderately aware that I'm still broadcasting all of this live.

I pull away, but only enough to whisper back, "I love you too."

He grins. "I need time to sort out the mess with my family, to figure out a job, how to move to be with you, how to—"

"Build a life in Los Angeles with me?" I ask.

There are logistics, there will be a media storm to contend with once I get home, but whatever. Benito loves me, and he wants to be part of my dream. If people want to judge me for that, then so be it.

His grin widens. "Maybe I'll work at a flower shop or something."

Epilogue

SIX MONTHS LATER

I BITE MY NAILS, TEARING OFF A BIG CHUNK OF WHAT HAS already basically been chewed down to the stubs. It's a much smaller gathering than a year ago, but the wine is flowing and I've already had to refill the charcuterie board twice. Marisol is here, talking my father's ear off about solar panels and lightly scolding him for not installing them on the roof of the house sooner. I've been consulting on her campaign for the past few months and will likely take on an even bigger role in the new year. Kate is her campaign manager and also currently dipping a carrot into hummus—while my campaign was a much lower-key affair this time around, she lent me her expertise when she had the chance.

I moved out of my parents' house and into my own apartment off Melrose Place. It has arched doorways, ancient appliances, the original carpets, and tons of charm. I start my day with coffee on my balcony that looks out to the Hollywood hills. I miss La Musa every day. I miss Benito every day, but he'll be here as soon as his visa is sorted out, and I've never been so happy to be home.

My newly re-energized Instagram following can't wait either—ever since I unintentionally broadcasted Benito's love confession to the entire world, every post is full of *We need #Benizzy! We demand more #Benizzy* comments.

I refresh the browser on my laptop and squeal. Kate motions for the party to quiet down. I hold my breath as the results load.

Mid-City West Neighborhood Council Election Results

Council Board Members: Lucas Leung [Incumbent], Surabhi Veenapani [Incumbent], Julian Cabrera, Emily Smith, and Izzy Rhodes.

The room erupts into cheers and applause. Marisol hugs me and my mom kisses my head. It's not Congress or the Senate, but I'm back in public office. After this I could run for City Council, State Assembly, Senate, governor, eventually president. The future is wide open. Maybe I'll crash and burn in pursuit of my dream again, maybe I'll never get past this step, but I have to keep going, I have to keep trying. Maybe the dream isn't the destination, it's the journey—or whatever the wooden sign my mom bought at HomeGoods said.

The buzzer in my apartment rings and interrupts the celebration. It's a late straggler to the party, but the booze is free-flowing, so the more the merrier. "Come on up!" I say in the intercom and buzz them in, opening the door to greet whoever is headed up the exterior stairs.

My breath catches in my lungs when I see the

familiar gait, the tousled hair, and the shirtsleeves rolled up to the elbows. I quickly shut the door behind me, quieting the party inside.

"Hi," he says as he approaches.

I'm still too stunned to form words. "Benito?" I choke out. We FaceTime every day and last I checked, he was in London, moving the last of his stuff out of Sutton's apartment.

He forms a meek smile that doesn't meet his eyes. "Sorry to just drop in on you like this."

"Are you kidding?" I barely choke out before Benito separates the distance between us, and with one swift step his lips are on mine. I wind my hands into his hair and pull his body closer to mine. Finally, finally, everything feels right. I thought getting elected to Congress was the best night of my life, but this is so much better—and there are so many better days ahead.

I hear a celebratory whoop from behind the door and we break apart. "Oh, yeah," I say. "I won."

Benito's smile widens. "Of course you did."

We've talked a lot over the past half year about what our lives here will look like. As much as I would love if his only passion was me, I know he needs a purpose too. He's been consulting for Kate alongside me for a few months—and there's a real possibility that he'll become a campaign strategist, but I told him to take his time and make sure he enjoys it and it's what he really wants. No matter what he decides, I'll be here, cheering him along. And I know he'll always do the same for me.

He nods toward the party. "Ready to go back in?"

I cock my head at him. God, he's so beautiful. My phone screen did not do him justice. "Mmm, not yet." I basically jump him, running my hands through his hair and bringing his lips back to mine, but I hesitate before we connect. "Wait, what about immigration?" I blurt out, because my practical side is such a mood killer.

"I took care of it," Benito says. "I'm dating someone who knows a guy."

The End.

Exclusive Bonus Content

SUTTON

ANOTHER SIX MONTHS LATER

AT LEAST I'M NOT IN BLOODY ITALY.

That's the thought that keeps me afloat as I walk through the lobby of the Beverly Grand Hotel. I'm on my first real holiday in… I don't even know how long. It's not so much a vacation as an exile. A *leave,* as Human Resources Susan put it. *"We just want to be sure you're alright, Sutton,"* she'd said, her smile not quite matching the strain in her eyes as she waited for me to yell, to scream, to throw her hideous Tower Bridge paperweight against the wall. That's all anyone's been doing at work lately—walking on eggshells around me, praying they won't be the one to set one of my little episodes into motion. *Tirades* as Susan so elegantly put it. *Brash berating sessions* as stated in the official complaint from my direct report.

But it's not my fault. It's not my fault that everyone in my life simultaneously decided to go off script. It's not my fault that as a result, my meticulously crafted five-year plan went up in flames. It's not my fault that now even the tiniest disturbance sets off a bomb in my chest, making it hard to breathe, to think, to speak. *"Sutton, do you know anything about panic attacks?"* Susan had so condescendingly asked several months ago after a conference call with Raffaello and our other Italian partners ended in me storming out of the room and hyperventilating into a brown paper sack in my office.

I know about panic attacks. The outburst was a result of my body's repulsion to incompetence, not a panic attack, I told her, ignoring the sensation of the walls closing in on me, my nerves recoiling and urging me to flee even though I knew rationally that Susan and her tiny ceramic kitten collection on her desk were no real threat.

I swore then to keep myself in check. It'd never been difficult before that day in La Musa. Every other day of my adult life had been the same: up at 5 a.m., coffee, Pilates, two-mile run, shower, work, one to two and three-quarters hours of recreational activities, in bed by 11 p.m., repeat.

Keeping my emotions in check was easy until Raffaello yelled at me in the middle of the Florence airport, insinuating his son's wayward actions were my fault. It was like everything inside me unraveled, and I could no longer control my limbs. My head was light and my pulse quick, like all forces that held me upright were gone and the slightest movement would tip me to the ground. I couldn't bring myself to dispute his claims no matter how quickly my brain churned. I just sat speechless until he finally left me alone at my gate. I got on the plane, balled myself up in my business class seat, tucked my long legs underneath me and cradled my head in my hands, shaking all the way back to London.

Pathetic. That's what this past year has made of me—a pathetic mess.

But it was like the more stringent I tried to be with myself, the more I lost my grip on mental stability. I was plagued with recurring dreams of the day Benito told me he was moving to Italy. The way he promised it wasn't forever, just until his mother got back on her feet, and then he'd be back.

I clung to those words for three months, certain it was a temporary setback in an otherwise flawless execution of living life. Benito would return. Since he'd quit that horrible House of Commons job, he'd finally agree to work for his father, we'd get engaged, then married at my family's Cotswold home, have between one and two and three-quarters children, and accumulate wealth until we died. Our life was all laid out there like a freshly pressed three-piece suit, all Benito had to do was step into it.

No part of me expected him to permanently end it when he returned three months later, but still I was certain a few more months in that decrepit hamlet he calls a hometown and he'd be begging me to take him back. What is old-world charm in comparison to two six-figure salaries and a 1,000-square-foot flat? I'd even compromised and picked a unit on the west side of the building instead of the east because *he* wanted to be able to watch the sunset from the terrace.

I tried to explain this all to Susan, but according

to her, *"That is not a reasonable excuse to yell at your employees and threaten to fire them if they so much as chew too loudly."*

I was asked—no, forced—to take a leave of absence. Ordered to do absolutely zero work until the mandated month was up. If I was caught even checking my email, I'd lose my job forever. And the prospect of that was much worse than any accusation Susan could wield at me.

The problem is, every other "holiday" I've taken in my life has been for work. I don't trust myself to board a yacht in Mallorca and not try to network, to raise a glass of rosé in Provence without scouting potential development locales, to lie on a beach in the Maldives without my phone tied to my fingertips. The concept of rest and relaxation is not necessarily lost on me, but I believe in the power of multitasking, and it feels like a waste of time if not leveraged for additional profit potential.

I was halfway to spending my month away learning Photoshop to fake a vacation when I got the call from my mother. "You're going to Parker Lane's wedding," she said as soon as I picked up. It was 4:45 on a Tuesday, which meant she was midway through her first pre-dinner gin and tonic.

"What?" I asked. "Parker is getting married?" Parker was an unofficial cousin to me. Our mothers were best friends, we were like family growing up, but I haven't seen her or her sister in a decade. We used to swap summer visits—alternating between spending weeks in their small, coastal California town and at my family's country estate.

When I was somewhere around age 16, Mum complained about the long flight, and we stopped making the trip. They'd come here once a year, then every other year, then eventually not at all. Now, Parker's been mostly offline in the past few years, but we keep up via texts on birthdays and holidays like all distant friends who don't have any particular reason not to like each other anymore. I tried to remember the last time I reached out. Apparently long enough for her to get engaged.

"She's getting married. Your father and I were invited, but you know I can't make the long flight, of course," my mother said. I heard the familiar clink of ice against glass from the other line. "But now I've thought about it, and it's rude not to send someone from our family. Willa's my oldest friend. Why wouldn't one of us go?"

She's changed the subject whenever I've brought it up, but I didn't think she and Willa had spoken in years, and the fact that it's explicitly forbidden discourse in our home made me certain they'd had a massive falling-out. "You talked to Willa?" I asked.

"She's one of my oldest friends, darling, I don't need to talk to her to know she'd want one of us there."

So that was a *no*. "Mum, wedding invitations are not like opera tickets. I cannot just go in your stead. If Parker wanted me there, she would have invited me."

She scoffed. "You *were* invited. I received invitations for the whole family." I heard another clink of the ice. "What do you think of me, Sutton? That I don't know basic wedding etiquette? I was at Will and Kate's."

I rolled my eyes and was grateful she could not see me and scold me for it. "Everyone was at Will and Kate's."

"And you'll be at Parker's too," she said. "You need somewhere to go that's far away from work, right?" So she had been listening when I told her about the forced leave during our obligatory weekly family dinner on Monday. "People do not work in California. It's perfect. The wedding's the 26th at five."

It's over a month away, but after a quick call to Parker, I not only confirm that I am in fact invited to the wedding but also to stay at their house with them for the four weeks leading up to it. *"It'll be just like old times!"* Parker squealed. It's not ideal, but my mother's right—the last place anyone would expect to find me is California.

I land in Los Angeles and will take the train to finish the short journey up the coast—but there's something else I have to do first.

I'm regretting my choice to come here just a bit when I do a scan of the clientele as I walk up to the hotel bar and order a classic martini. The multiple pairs of shorts that surround me and the fact that I have to specify I want my drink made with gin and not vodka, a twist and not an olive, a stark reminder why I rarely cross the Atlantic. I finish my drink quickly and signal to the bartender for another. I need to be appropriately lubricated for seeing my ex.

Not that I feel negatively about it at all. It would be irrational to still not be over Benito—it's been over a year since we broke up. It would be inane to hate-scroll through Izzy's Instagram where there's a nauseating picture of them on the beach at sunset with the caption *Happy doesn't even begin to cover it* when my brain is spiraling late at night. It would be inappropriate to feel any type of way about seeing Benito again.

"Sutton," he'd said that night in Lake Como, after sneaking back to his room in the wee hours of the morning, curling up to sleep in the armchair when some deranged part of me hoped he might settle into bed next to me. *"I think I love her."* My heart sank. Since when was love something we cared about? I thought we were aligned in that a partnership was more about mutually assured stability and success and not feelings. Feelings are fleeting and impermanent. Property, career, security—those are things we can guarantee we take with us from day to day.

The whole situation is all so horribly trite.

"What are you drinking?" I hear a man's voice ask. I turn as he leans against the bar, his forearms poking out of his hooded sweatshirt and revealing the tackiest koi fish tattoo I have ever seen. His hair is shellacked with gel and pushed up in the middle, his face greasy with sweat from being a few drinks in already, but he's handsome—in a way.

"Can you not tell by looking at it?" I ask.

He laughs. "You know what, hell yeah, I love this energy. That was a lame as fuck way of hitting on you, and you should call me out on it." He sits on the barstool next to me. I do a quick scan of him and notice he is, at least, wearing full pants and shoes that cover his toes. "What I meant to say was," he starts again, leaning in so I can smell the whiskey on his breath, "I'd like to buy your next one."

"No, thank you," I say. "I have to go meet up with my ex and his new girlfriend."

He laughs again. "Shit. That is the 'my dog ate my homework' of rejections."

"Sadly, I'm serious," I say, finishing off my martini.

He stares at me again, like he's waiting for me to crack a smile. I don't. "You are serious." I nod. He shakes his head. "Don't go to that. Have a drink with me instead." He cocks his head, locking his eyes into mine as if relying solely on the seductive power of their bright blue color.

I get up and slide my handbag off the bar and over my shoulder. "I really can't." I get the bartender's attention and point to the man. "He'll be taking care of my tab."

The ride share app sends me one of those driverless vehicles. *"Hello, Sutton,"* an all-too-realistic voice greets me as I slide into the back seat. The steering wheel whirs like it's haunted as the car veers through LA traffic. A nauseating 20 minutes later, it pulls up outside a blue-and-white building on a tree-lined street. I'd gotten the address from Lucia, only after I told her the whole purpose of my mission and swore my motives were pure.

I buzz into the building and knock on the door of apartment 102. After a brief moment, the door swings open and Benito stands on the other side of it, his eyes wide as he takes me in. "I thought you were sushi," he says.

A pit in my stomach opens up, seeing him again. The last time was six months ago, when I came home to find Benito in my apartment, rifling through a box of his things I hadn't gotten around to sending him in some last-ditch hope that he'd come back for them and realize he'd made a huge mistake. He had an agitated look on his face and his hair was, of course, a mess, annoying to me because I was always telling him to leave it alone.

"Did you break into my apartment?" I asked.

"Sutton, hi," he said. "You weren't answering your phone and I still had a key." He took said key out of his pocket and tossed it to me, then went back to digging in the box.

"I see you found your things," I said, scared to make too much noise like he was a wild animal who'd gotten loose at the zoo. "I meant to send them to you, but I didn't know where you're living these days." If I really wanted to know that information, I could've found out, but he was too distracted to care.

He looked up at me. "I've been everywhere, really." He stood up. "There's a box. A small box. It must be here. It's nowhere else." He started rifling through the drawers of my end table.

"Um, excuse me," I said. "You don't live here anymore."

Benito ran his fingers through his hair. "Then help

me." He locked his eyes with mine and stared me down with a pleading glance. "Please."

I scoffed then walked over to the kitchen. "A box. A small box. Any other descriptors?" I opened a drawer and made a big show about searching through it even though I know exactly where everything is in my apartment, and I knew there was no small box that belonged to him.

"I don't know," he said, now checking under the couch cushions for some reason. "It's a box, a small box, Sutton. I think it's red… velvet."

I stopped what I was doing and all the blood in my body rushed to my chest. "Like a ring box?" I asked.

Benito dug his hand into the edge of the armchair. "Yes. A ring box."

I closed the kitchen drawer. I knew what he was looking for. I'd found it years ago, when I was unpacking his things after he first moved in, stuffed among his socks. He was looking for a ring. An antique, marquise-cut diamond engagement ring. Not my taste, but workable. "It's not here, Benito," I said. "Why would it be here?"

He let out a frustrated sigh. "You're right. It must be somewhere in my mother's house, but I couldn't find it and I also could not tell her I don't know where it was, especially since she was so hesitant to hand it over when I was dating—" He stopped himself and looked up at me, embarrassed. "Anyway, I'll get out of your hair." He took the rest of his belongings and left.

*

"You ordered sushi for takeaway?" I ask, examining what I can see of Benito and Izzy's LA apartment from the doorway. It's disgustingly homey. Photos of the two of them stand in for actual artwork and tchotchkes line every free inch of shelf space. I half expect a *Live, Laugh, Love* sign to hang over the mantle. "Do you want a foodborne illness?"

"It's perfectly safe," Benito says, still dumbstruck by my presence, understandably. "What are you doing here?"

"Benito? Who's at the door?" Izzy rounds the corner and smiles when she sees me like she's happy with the surprise. A true politician. "Sutton?"

"He thought I was your sushi delivery," I say.

"That's why I buzzed her in," Benito clarifies, eyeing me cautiously like he's waiting for me to snap.

Izzy nudges him. "I told you it was coming by robot." She shows him her phone. "It's been stuck up the street where there's that divot in the sidewalk for like five minutes. You might have to go rescue it."

"Why is everything in this city done by robots? Are the humans really that incompetent?" I ask. They both turn back to me. I take a step into the doorway. "Could I come in?"

Benito shows me to an armchair in the living room while Izzy fetches me a can of sparkling water. When she returns, she and Benito settle into the couch opposite me. "How have you been, Sutton?" Benito asks.

I wonder if he knows. Last I heard, he and Raffaello still were not speaking, but it's possible he's heard about my difficulties at work through other gossip channels. "I've been great. I'm here on holiday. Headed up the coast tomorrow."

"Amazing!" says Izzy.

"*You* are taking a vacation?" Benito asks. His eyebrows narrow. "Here?"

Izzy playfully swats at him. "You're going to love it. It's so beautiful, serene, peaceful up there." She inhales deeply, as though she's breathing in the fresh ocean air. "It's all sweeping views, crisp linens, leisurely wine tastings. You know, it's actually called the California Riviera because of its resemblance to the Mediterranean."

I try to suppress my disgust at this but it's twofold. For one, nowhere in America could ever compare to Europe, and secondly, everything about that sounds terrible. "Wonderful," I choke out. "And how have the two of you been?" I ask, mainly to get the focus off me.

Izzy and Benito look at each other and beam. My stomach churns, threatening to expel its two martinis. "We're great," Benito says. "Or at least, I'll speak for myself. I'm great." He places a hand on Izzy's knee, and she laces her fingertips into his.

"We're great."

"Amazing." I take a sip of the off-brand sparkling water and almost gag at its acidity, sparking a coughing fit.

"Are you alright?" Benito asks.

"Mm-hmm."

Izzy's phone dings. "Food's here. I'll go get it."

"I can do it," Benito offers all too quickly.

"No, no," Izzy says. "I'll go. You two catch up."

She leaves and Benito and I are quiet for a moment. "I'm glad to have a moment alone with you," I say.

"Oh?" Benito asks, once again eyeing me with a hefty amount of suspicion.

"Don't be nervous," I say. "I have only good intentions."

Benito continues to stare.

"I have something for you," I say. I reach into my purse and pull out a box. A small, velvet box. I hand it to him.

He looks to it and back to me. "Is this—"

"Your ring," I say.

He opens it slowly, like he's worried it's a trick and snakes are about to jump out at him. When the sparkly ring finally shows itself, his eyes get big and he smiles. He looks back at me. "You said you did not have it."

I take a deep breath in. "I lied." I'd taken it out of the sock drawer when I'd found it all those years ago. We weren't getting engaged anytime soon, I knew that then, but such a piece needed to be stored properly. I'd locked it in the safe in the back of my closet, planning to sneak it back into his sock drawer when the time was right. I didn't think he'd notice it was missing until he needed it, and I guess I was right. "I wasn't ready to part with it then," I say. "I wasn't ready to part with… all of it."

His eyes flash back at me, but his expression is soft. "Your unwillingness to give up is one of your best qualities, but I fear it may one day be your downfall," he says, and my heartbeat increases a little bit, even though I know he doesn't mean it maliciously. "Thank you for giving it back."

"Thank you for not reporting it stolen," I say.

The door opens and Izzy returns holding a white plastic bag. "I feel so bad that we can't tip the robots. This one was named Sheldon. Sheldon!" Her eyes glance back and forth between me and Benito, picking up on the vibe. She spots the box right as Benito quickly snaps it shut. "What's that?"

Benito stares at his lap and then looks back up. "Izzy," he says. A forewarning sense of fear envelops me, like when you see a car swerve away from another and you know it's about to run straight into you. He stands up and takes her hands. "Isabella Catherine Rhodes."

"Benito—" I say, hoping to at the very least remind him I am here as he cannot possibly be about to propose with me still in the room.

He doesn't seem to hear me, though. Izzy smiles as Benito drops to one knee. "I had no idea what it felt like to be truly known and understood until I met you." Ok, rude. He continues, "I don't know what the rest of our lives look like. I don't know what other obstacles life will throw at us, but I know you will do great things no matter what. And I know I already did the greatest thing I will ever do in my life when I fell in love with you." He opens the box. Izzy's eyes start to well as she sees the ring. Of course *she* likes it. "I am in love with you beyond anything I've ever dreamed of, and I cannot believe how lucky I am that I get to be by your side for the rest of my life. Will you marry me?"

Izzy gasps, as though the question is a total surprise even when he is on bended knee holding a diamond ring. "Benito." She self-consciously looks over at me and I'm relieved to know I have not suddenly turned invisible.

"By all means continue," I say, waving my hand. "I've borne witness to most of your relationship thus far. Why shouldn't I be here for this?"

Izzy's cheeks blush and she turns back to Benito. "You showed me who I was when I had completely lost track of it. I promise to always do the same for you. I am so beyond in love with you, it transcends what I ever thought was possible. You make my wildest dreams feel real because you are real." A single tear cinematically falls from the corner of her eye. "Yes, I will marry you. Obviously."

Benito slides the ring onto her finger—it's a perfect fit. He stands and they kiss passionately. I clap my hands together. "Congrats." They break apart and look at me. "I think I'll get out of your way, then," I say. I slide my purse over my shoulder and walk toward the door. Before I leave, I look back at them one more time. They really do radiate happiness. I have to admit that, at least internally. Benito mouths the words *"thank you"* at me before returning his lips to Izzy's.

My breathing becomes more labored in the robocar ride home. I roll down a window for fresh air and place a warm hand on my chest. Benito is engaged to another person. I knew I had lost him, but the last thread of hope that he might suddenly change his mind and come back to the life I had planned for us is finally severed. I don't have my job, I don't have Benito, and now, I don't even have a grip on my own emotional reaction to it all.

Back at the hotel, I make my way to the bar. The man from earlier is still there, nursing a whiskey neat. He spots me and grins. "Come back to let me buy you another drink?" he asks.

"Actually," I say. "Why don't you come back to my room instead?"

Acknowledgements

First and foremost, I want to thank everyone involved with the Arizona in Italy program in Orvieto, Italy, in Summer 2011. Those weeks in the Umbrian countryside not only informed the setting of this book but were a formative experience for this author when she was 19 years old.

Thank you to my amazing agent, Jillian Davis, who is the true definition of a rockstar. Thank you for believing in me and this book and for helping me shape it into the version it is today. And sorry for all the panic texts. Thank you to the whole team at Kaplan Stahler for your support on this journey.

To the entire Arndell team, I am so beyond grateful you took a chance on me, a first-time author, and have loved this book as much as I do. Christine, Alina, Meagan, Abbey, Keeley, Kellie, Fiona, Jodie, Rachael—you are, in my opinion, the best in the business, and I'm so happy to be debuting with this amazing team. Thank you also to Lindsey and Imogen for your editorial guidance.

Thank you to everyone who read this book in various stages of its development: Michelle, Sarah, Fortesa, Jenna, Saige, Lena, Nick—your feedback was pivotal in those anxiety-inducing early drafts.

To Michelle Wangsgard again, because I wouldn't have even thought I could write a novel without your encouragement. You are my favorite writer always.

To all my friends, who are my biggest cheerleaders and who never fail to celebrate every single one of my wins. I truly believe I have the best friends in the world, and I am so grateful. A special shoutout to The Fab 5, Sandra OMG, Graveyard Girlies, Twisted Sisters—I don't know what I'd do without my emotional support group chats.

To Caitlin Covert and Alexsa Oglesby, you have been there for me through every single one of my creative endeavors since we were 10 years old with nothing but unwavering support and love. Every choir concert, every play, every short story—I share this with you both. You are family to me, and I love you.

To my parents, thank you for always keeping me tethered to the ground despite my sky-high dreams. I have always believed I could do anything I set my mind to because of the way you raised me. Thank you for all the love and support over the years, because I've needed it.

To my sister, Emily, thank you for your friendship and love since the literal first day of my life. Sorry I wrote a book about how the dog is my favorite sister when I was six, because you're the only one who deserves that title.

To Riley and Beau, it'll be a while before you read this, but everything I do is to make sure I'm your favorite aunt.

And lastly, to you, the reader. Thank you for picking up this book and diving into this world with these characters and this story that I love so dearly. Whatever led you here, I'm so grateful you chose to spend your time reading my words.

Author Biography

Caitlin Alice Gilbert is an author and screenwriter based in Los Angeles. Born in Michigan, she grew up between the Midwest and Fountain Hills, Arizona, home of the third-tallest year-round fountain. She is a graduate of the University of Arizona where she studied Film and Television and Creative Writing. She has spent over ten years working in the streaming industry at companies such as Netflix, HBO Max, Disney, and the now defunct Watchable and Quibi, the downfalls of which were not her fault. When she's not writing, Caitlin is taking in theatre or live music, playing tennis, cheering for Angel City Football Club, going on a long walk, or watching way too much TV.

Connect with Caitlin:

Facebook: Caitlin Alice Gilbert - Author
Instagram: @caitlingilbs
Substack: I Don't Know How to Feel
TikTok: @caitlinalicegilbs
Website: caitlinalicegilbert.com

Connect with Arndell

Love this book? Discover your next romance book obsession and stay up to date with the latest releases, exclusive content, and behind-the-scenes news!

Explore More Books

Visit our homepage: keeperton.com/arndell

Follow Us on Social Media

Instagram: @arndellbooks
Facebook: Arndell
TikTok: @arndellbooks

Stay in the Loop

Join our newsletter: keeperton.com/subscribe

Join the Conversation

Use **#Arndell** or **#ArndellBooks** to share your thoughts and connect with fellow romance readers!

Thank you for being part of our book-loving community. We can't wait to share more unforgettable stories with you!